OTHER BOOKS
by Lisa Rayne

THE COUNSELORS

Counselor Undone

KANSAS CITY GRIFFINS

Quarterback Casanova

INTERNATIONAL LOVE GAMES

Runaway Heart

THE SHADOW LAIRDS

Never Cross a Highlander

UNTAMED

~ A Lawmen of Lawless Novel ~

LISA RAYNE

FIRE SIGN
PRESS

Kansas City | Los Angeles

UNTAMED
Lawmen of Lawless Series (Book 1)

Cover design by Mayhem Cover Creations
Interior design by Lisa Rayne
Edited by Jennifer Graybeal
Proofread by Kaitlin Slowik

Fire Sign Press
a division of Fire Sign Media, LLC
PO Box 9150
Kansas City, MO 64168

ISBN: 979-8-9914841-0-7 (Trade Paperback)

First Edition: August 2024

Print edition manufactured in the United States of America

For Mama Dee Dee,

Whose fanatic love of westerns and the American cowboy
lives on in this granddaughter and who taught me
the meaning of unconditional love.
I miss you greatly.

UNTAMED

CHAPTER 1

Kansas Plains, 1888

HE'D SWORN OFF KILLING people, but some men were just too stupid to let live.

"Dammit all!" Blaaze Lassiter scrambled to his feet as the sound of retreating horse hooves awoke him from a sound sleep.

Dunst Huntley was making a run for it. Again.

Blaaze thought he'd put the fear of Satan into the outlaw after yesterday's getaway attempt, but apparently he was losing his touch. He hopped toward his mount, one boot under his arm while he fought to pull on the other. He cursed again when his foot seated in the second boot only to feel a piercing stab to its sole.

"Ouch!" He yanked off the well-worn leather and turned it upside down. Three large stones toppled one by one to the ground.

Huntley, the menace, he thought with a grumble.

Yeah, that decision to stop bringing 'em in dead instead of alive was about to go by the wayside. Huntley had been a fool to tempt fate—and *him*—to keep that shabbiest of promises that hung by the merest of threads. Blaaze should have known better than to stick his foot in an unchecked boot on the trail. Yet and still, any scoundrel who tampered with another man's footwear deserved whatever retribution befell him.

After thrusting his foot into the now-empty boot, Blaaze reached for his saddle.

But it wasn't there.

He turned in a quick circle, eyes darting efficiently across the campsite, then whipped the other direction for a second look. His saddle was gone. He squinted at the spot where he'd left it and saw the rope that should have been around Huntley's waist and wrists.

Blaaze picked up the sliced strands Huntley had managed to saw through, most likely using the jagged rock discarded nearby. He really was losing his touch. How the hell had he slept through a bound man freeing himself, disposing of a saddle, and managing to gear up another horse to escape into the night?

He was getting too old for this crap. Time had been when the pass of a butterfly overhead would wake him from a sound slumber. He slept—or used to sleep—light as a mama bear listening for her cub's cry and could awaken from that soft cloud of quick napping clear-eyed, sharp-witted, and quick-handed. Apparently, those days were coming up fast on gone.

With a grimace, he pressed a hand to the chambray shirt covering a blood-tinted bandage wrapped around his abdomen. The tied-off strips of cotton covered a bullet wound from several days past. He'd lost a lot of blood, but at least the bullet was gone thanks to a brief sojourn with a friend on the edge of Indian Territory. The last thing he needed was lead festering in his gut while he tried to wrangle this hombre all the way to town.

Heavy exhaustion rippled through Blaaze's recently fevered body, but that was no excuse for shoddy work. Maybe he should have hauled Huntley down to Fort Smith directly. The journey would have taken longer than his current destination, so he'd dismissed the notion. Right now, he reckoned getting the outlaw that much sooner to federal court and sentenced to death might have been worth the extra days on the trail.

Frustrated, he threw down the ruined rope and grabbed a fistful of his longtime steed's mane. With a grimace, he swung up on the big, chestnut bay stallion. Surely, Huntley didn't think not having a saddle handy or the four-day-old gunshot wound in Blaaze's side would stop Blaaze from chasing after him. And once Blaaze caught up to the scoundrel, his bullets were gonna fly a whole lot faster than that mare's giddy-up. The man had better hope his mood had swung back toward bringing him in alive when that time came.

Blaaze urged Scout into a gallop, not giving the stallion his full head due to the nearly moonless sky. The steady pace would be enough to catch Huntley whose horsemanship wasn't exactly stellar and whose mare—though beautiful and stout—couldn't outrun Scout on her best day.

It took two miles of riding before Blaaze heard the clop of the mare's hooves ahead. Huntley had slowed his pace. No doubt feeling safe and cocky, thinking he'd left Blaaze in a fix that would take hours to undo.

Yeah, the man was an idiot.

Blaaze hadn't become known as the best manhunter in four states and three territories by letting minor setbacks throw him off track. He kicked Scout into a renewed charge and rode down the mare and rider. The sparse moonlight hit Huntley's face when he turned to look behind him, and his look of surprised terror made a fierce satisfaction rise in Blaaze.

Maybe the man wasn't so dumb after all. He knew the wrath of hell was about to flare down on him. Apparently, he'd simply been feeling lucky. Too bad his luck was about to run out.

Blaaze swiped the gun from his holster and pointed it toward the back of the outlaw's shoulder. "Huntley, if you don't want a bullet in you, I suggest you pull up this instant."

A shriek and a jerk of the mare to the left was Huntley's only reply.

With a squeeze of his knees, Blaaze urged Scout to follow.

Huntley yanked his reins the opposite direction. He began swerving left and right. Blaaze took more care with Scout. Such maneuvers were dangerous in this rough terrain and low light. At this rate, the man was going to kill himself and save Blaaze the trouble.

No sooner had that thought crossed Blaaze's mind than the mare lost her footing. She stumbled, couldn't recover, and went down with Dunst flying ass over tin cups into the nearest brush. Her equine squeal shattered the night, and Scout replied with a long, deep nicker and hard head shake.

Blaaze pulled up. "Easy, boy," he crooned then whipped off the stallion and rushed to the mare. He kept inside the string of expletives he wanted to let fly so as not to scare the mare more than she already was.

The anxious horse's eyes flicked his direction, and she jerked against the ground, floundering to try to get up. Blaaze placed a hand on her neck to coax her to stay still and sought to calm her with soothing caresses and soft words. He needed to check her before he let her try to stand.

Scout pawed at the ground with tensed ears and an earnest whinny. The mare's anxiety was getting to the stallion. Blaaze looked up when an angry snort from Scout signaled additional trouble.

A patch of bushes wiggled, and Huntley crawled from beneath the tangle of branches. Scout reared on his hind legs and kicked menacingly in Huntley's direction. Seemed the stallion and Blaaze were of the same mind. Watching the mare's distress made them both want to pulverize the man.

Instead, Blaaze ran a gentle palm down the mare's front left leg and did curse this time when she balked loudly at his touch. After further inspection, he found no broken bones. She'd likely only bruised a muscle or tendon. He breathed a sigh of relief and dropped his head, chin momentarily finding his chest.

Had either of her legs been broken, he would have had no choice but to put her down. He hated that part. A horseman all his life, he understood it would have been the humane thing to do, but he'd have rather shot Huntley. Or broken his legs. Both of them. In multiple places.

Blaaze looked into the mare's eyes. Her unease stared back at him. Reassured it was more from fear than injury, he rubbed his hand over her neck.

"It's okay, girl. You're good to go." He moved back and allowed the horse to stand.

A rasp of dirt signaled Huntley's attempt to ease away while Blaaze's attention was diverted to the mare. Without looking around, Blaaze aimed the gun still in his other hand directly at the spot from whence the sound of shifting gravel had come. He cocked the hammer of his Colt. The satisfying snick transitioned him from caretaker to life-threatener.

His gaze slowly met Huntley's. "You move another muscle, and I'll take care of you the way you almost forced me to take care of this mare."

There was no mistaking what Blaaze meant. The remedy for the mare's near plight would have been a fatal shot, and Blaaze was pissed enough about Huntley's carelessness with the horse to take out Huntley solely on principle. The man dropped onto the nearest boulder. In his haste, he almost missed the stone seat and landed on the ground. Whatever he'd read on Blaaze's face must have finally convinced him he'd pushed Blaaze a might too far.

Good. Blaaze hadn't thought he could get any madder tonight, but he'd been wrong. Dead wrong.

He whipped his hat off his head and slapped it twice against his leg. He gave a deep sigh. This whole disturbance had cost him energy and more time. Energy Blaaze didn't have to spare, and more time he'd have to spend with Huntley. Which meant more time during which he'd likely get another urge to kill the outlaw.

That wouldn't do. He needed to get this over with.

He grabbed the rope off Huntley's saddle, stalked toward Huntley, and tied the man's hands good and tight with an old fisherman's knot his father had taught him. He'd tried to be considerate earlier by not binding the man too snugly before letting him bed down for the night. His mistake.

His oath as a marshal was making him soft. He'd apparently left Huntley sufficient slack that he'd managed to maneuver well enough to find that jagged rock and ruin Blaaze's best cowhide lasso. Wouldn't happen again.

This man was a means to an end for Blaaze: a ticket to Blaaze's personal freedom. A little over four years ago, Blaaze had let a buddy talk him into becoming a deputy US marshal to assist with the capture of a wayward gang of thieves and train robbers. Blaaze had been a bounty hunter at the time, a content bounty hunter who minded his own business and captured vermin like Huntley for a price. He'd done it his way, which didn't always fit within nice and tidy rules, but it had gotten the job done.

Blast if his record for capturing scumbags hadn't backfired on him. A reputation for a fast gun, a ruthless streak, and a don't-quit-till-the-job-is-done attitude had made US Deputy Marshal Bridger Malone seek Blaaze out with a proposal. Blaaze had said no to the proposal without hesitation or waffling, but Malone, the bastard, was the only man Blaaze knew with a stubborn streak as long as his own. Plus, this particular manhunt held personal significance for the marshal.

Malone intended to see every one of these particular outlaws hunted down to justice even if the lawman had to follow them into the depths of hell and drag them back. So the man had followed and hounded Blaaze across three states until Blaaze had finally agreed to the gig. Blaaze had succumbed to the government oath and put on the silver star that identified him as a deputy marshal. Then he went off chasing bad guys with a passel of rules shackling his hands and cramping his style. He was certainly glad that straitlaced tomfoolery was almost over.

Blaaze's disposition wasn't suited for rules and regulations and such. He liked it better when they didn't care if you brought them in dead or alive. This bringing them in alive caused a whole lot more work. Work he didn't much feel like doing then, and he certainly no longer felt like doing now.

The rest of this capture was going to be done his way.

He'd always felt the best way to nab outlaws was to act like one. The next foul move Huntley made, he was going to find out why Blaaze had the ornery cuss reputation he had. He'd earned it, shoot-out by shoot-out and close call by close call. The stories that floated around about him didn't even come close to some of his most harrowing escapades. So when it came to Huntley and his shenanigans, Blaaze was more than done playing nice.

He swung up on Scout and forced the outlaw to walk back to camp. He had no intention of risking further injury to the mare by forcing her to carry the man's weight. Since the scoundrel didn't know how to properly treat a horse, he could walk from here on. Blaaze couldn't wait to turn over the walking headache to the sheriff in the upcoming town so he could be done with it all.

This would be Blaaze's last capture. He was at his limit. What he wanted was a bath, a bottle of whiskey, and a woman—in that order. Actually, he'd rather have the woman first, but with the five days' worth of trail clinging to his skin and clothes, even the cheapest sportin' woman on the plains wouldn't give him the three seconds it would take to get his soldier out of his britches. Not that he'd ever pay for the enjoyment of a woman's time. And, of course, there was the little matter of the gunshot wound in his side.

With another grimace, Blaaze tugged at the days-old bandage staunching the blasted wound. The unhealed hole hurt like the dickens and probably wouldn't allow the bedroom performance he had in mind anyway, so it'd likely be a few more days before he could thoroughly sample a woman. But he didn't intend to wait a day longer than necessary for that drink.

With a mind toward a full bottle of liquid amber, Blaaze

trussed up Huntley good and secure when they got back to the campground, and then tied him to a tree for good measure. Less than twenty-four hours separated Blaaze from peaceful, retired bliss, and he wanted to get to their destination by early afternoon the next day. Having to deal with townsfolk before he could officially retire required Blaaze get a good night's sleep. Peopling wasn't exactly his strong suit, so he needed to make sure his companion caused no more interruptions to the evening.

Blaaze propped his recovered saddle against a tree opposite the bedded-down Huntley and reclined on the curve of the seat. He tied the slack from the rope binding Huntley around the boot on his left foot, opting to leave his boots on this time. He wasn't taking any more chances. If Huntley so much as looked as if he was thinking about wriggling free, the man would greet the sheriff as a trussed-up corpse.

~

The sleeping arrangement worked out mighty fine. Blaaze awoke the next morning from a restful sleep good and ready to get his human delivery over and done. When they topped the rise overlooking their destination shortly after midday, Blaaze could feel the tension ease from his tightly wound soul.

With a pat to Scout's neck, he surveyed the layout below.

Lawless, Kansas.

Not exactly a bastion of high living. Or a bustling populace. Which was exactly why Blaaze had chosen it.

His eyes went unerringly to the local saloon he remembered, grateful it had survived the challenges of frontier business life. He wondered if its proprietor, the lovely Lady Lila, had managed to do the same. Blaaze had always liked Lila's spunk and determination, but what he remembered most about the lady was she ran a top establishment where a man could get a clean bed, a full belly, and a pure drink of whiskey rather than that watered-down crap he'd suffered in places like Abilene and Kansas City.

While a clean bed and a full belly weren't bad additions to his current wish list, man oh man, was he ever craving that whiskey.

A hard yank from the end of the rope anchored to the horn of his saddle distracted Blaaze from his blissful daydream of two fingers of neat, sweet mash aged in charred-oak barrels he could almost taste. He had nearly forgotten about the varmint trailing behind him on foot with wrists bound together. Nearly, but not quite.

He glanced over his shoulder at the wanted man. Blaaze had finally tracked him down outside of Westport, Missouri. The trading post had fallen on hard times after the war between the states, but outlaws still used the town as a starting point to outfit themselves before heading west to accomplish deeds unfathomable. Dunst Huntley was one such outlaw. He was the last of the men assigned to Blaaze from Marshal Malone's wanted gang of thieves and thus, the last man Blaaze needed to bring to justice before he could retire with a clear conscience.

The man had tried to make a run for it. Huntley had fled into Indian Territory with the hope that fear of the native nations forced to live within the confines of the Territory's boundaries would keep Blaaze from following. Hadn't worked out so well for the scoundrel, and now he found himself at the end of a rope. For now, the rope was around his wrists and not his neck, but everything in due time.

Huntley continued to tug and pull. Not with much effort,

though. He'd been walking behind Blaaze and his horse in the sun-bright morning for ten miles. He was about as ready to drop from fatigue as Blaaze was from the tedium of trail life, but Blaaze held no sympathy for the man. He and his gang had pulled off a bank robbery down Texas way that they'd ended with an impulsive killing spree of all the bank patrons, amongst whom had been Malone's young bride. Huntley then proceeded to rob and pillage his way across most of Kansas and Missouri. Once he got before a judge, he'd be sentenced to hang, so Blaaze could care less about his current discomfort.

Besides, all the struggle in the world wouldn't have done the cowboy much good. Blaaze had been roping horses and handling livestock since he was a young'un. When he tied a knot, it stayed tied—lest, of course, you sawed through it with a rock. He frowned at the thought of his destroyed lasso but pushed past the renewed irritation.

His mind strayed to the only thing he did better than tie a knot, which was shoot a gun. Well, there was at least one other thing he did better, but he wasn't going to think about that other something until he and his johnson could actually indulge. So he'd keep his mind on getting rid of this outlaw, who wasn't going anywhere until Blaaze was ready to let him go. And the only place Blaaze intended to let him go was straight to jail.

Blaaze gave a hard yank on the rope to silently admonish the prisoner for his annoying behavior. Disturbing a man's whiskey-filled daydreams was another crime in itself. Not prepared for the rope jerk, Dunst lost his balance and landed face-first in the rain-parched Kansas dirt. A cloud of dust exploded around his face, and he coughed on the earthy storm.

Content with the result, Blaaze rubbed a hand across his bristly jaw and contemplated the shave he needed to add to that bath he longed for. Figuring he'd waited long enough to feel human again, with a slow, languorous hand he adjusted his favorite hat, a dark brown Stetson courtesy of Uncle Sam's coin, then gathered Scout's reins. Reminded this capture fell under his obligation as a deputy marshal, with a sigh, he regretfully tossed a canteen toward Huntley. It wouldn't do to have the man drop dead this close to town after all the effort Blaaze had put in to keeping him alive till now.

Huntley pushed to his knees and gratefully scooped up the canteen.

Not waiting for the man to drink, Blaaze said, "If you don't want to be dragged into town, Huntley, I reckon you'd best get on up."

"Dammit, Lassiter!" Dunst struggled to stand, fumbling with the open canteen and fussing the whole time. "Let me go, you sumbitch. You got no right treating me such. I ain't done nothin'." He took a deep swig of water and coughed, nearly choking on his wayward gulp. "I done told you, you got the wrong man."

"Wrong man, my ass," Blaaze mumbled under his breath.

Not bothering to check whether the outlaw had managed to finish drinking or recap the canteen, Blaaze headed toward the very last town he would ever have to enter dragging a no-good scoundrel along to meet his justice. That Huntley had to make the long, last miles of the trek on foot served the man right after he'd endangered his beautiful sorrel mare by trying to escape in the dead of night. Lucky for Huntley, they'd not been too far outside of Lawless at the start of the day. The spring weather made the constant sunshine reasonably bearable, and the close proximity of a jail meant Blaaze might actually manage to keep his tenuous reprieve on ending the man's life.

A few miles past the bottom of the rise, a handwritten sign greeted the pair outside the east entrance to the town. In big black letters on the back of a weathered and cracked chunk of wooden board, someone had scrawled, **Don't start no shooting, won't be no shooting.**

Blaaze scoffed at the message.

Another sign, a few paces farther in, warned, **All visitors must check firearms with the sheriff.**

Well, that was new. Blaaze wondered in passing what had transpired in Lawless since his last visit to bring about the curious change. The thought didn't linger long. It was no matter. Undaunted, Blaaze rode leisurely past the sign, packing his favorite pearl-handled Colt holstered under his worn duster, a second one in his saddlebag, and a Derringer hidden in his right boot.

He didn't give over his guns for any reason to any man.

He had no intention of starting in Lawless.

He'd get his whiskey, take care of his legal business, then ride out to the land he'd purchased during his absence through a friend. If he was going to hang up his guns, he'd darn well do it at home. No one need be the wiser.

With a light touch, he directed Scout into town.

Chapter 2

Perfectly coiffed, fashionably dressed, and impeccably mannered as always, Mary Catherine Templeton stood staring out the window of Miss Eileen's Boarding House. The location, she'd quickly discerned upon her arrival two days ago in this listlessly blooming town, was the singularly appropriate establishment for an unmarried woman traveling alone to stay in Lawless.

What a godawful name for a town.

What had she gotten herself into?

Miss Eileen, the establishment's proprietor and a widow, had aged a decade longer than her deceased, beloved Herman and had made it a point to advise her new Colored tenant that, as a respectable widowed woman, she'd have no shenanigans in her place. Mary Catherine shook her head. She wondered if all the fine patrons of Miss Eileen's Boarding House got the same speech. As an unwed maiden, Mary Catherine adhered to the utmost standards of propriety. As if she'd even consider such behavior outside a proper relationship.

Not simply absurd, but downright unthinkable.

Pensive, she ran two slow fingers through the light film

of dust covering the windowsill and thought Miss Eileen needed to be as diligent with her cleaning as she was with her unnecessary exhortations in morality. Nevertheless, Mary Catherine appreciated the propriety of the place and was glad to know that the moral standards of the townsfolk were not as threadbare as the town itself.

The main street of the burgeoning community was no more than dirt lined on either side with raised wooden planks that stood in as sidewalks for the sprinkling of storefronts that faced off from opposite sides of the dusty thoroughfare. Earlier, she'd noted an armed, mounted man ride past leading a bedraggled character tethered to a rope. Notably, the man was being forced to walk despite the presence of a riderless, second horse.

The tied male was likely some criminal or unsavory character, or maybe they both were. Something about the way the rider sat with lazy arrogance on his horse, dark hat pulled low over his brow, imparted the unnerving impression of the gunfighters she'd read about when researching life out west. The thought sent an ominous prickle of foreboding racing down her spine.

She missed Cleveland already.

She was a city girl, born and raised. This frontier life was turning out to be more of an adventure than she had dared consider when she'd fled Ohio with the last of her savings tucked inside her purse. After the long train ride to stagecoach journey, she had arrived in Lawless tired and anxious to search out the bequest that had led her here. But she'd had to wait until today to get a meeting with the attorney-at-law handling the bequest. The full day's wait had given her time to explore the meager town and, unfortunately, to second-guess herself.

A glint of sunshine sparkled off the glass of the window

through which she perused Main Street. The glass was spotless despite the subpar status of its sill. The solar glimmer reminded Mary Catherine of the puckish glow off the huge, bald spot of the pompous bank executive back home with whom she'd had her last job interview.

The man had delivered the final rejection of her months-long search for bank employ. That decisive—and painful—rejection had ultimately resulted in her conceding defeat on the unorthodox but respectable life she had intended to lead as an independent professional woman. A life she considered befitting an educated woman with superior training in figures and finances.

Her father, God rest his studious, spectacle-wearing soul, had not left her much, but the importance of a college education and an arranged marriage to the eldest son of one of the most prestigious families of the Race in Cleveland had been a part of his legacy. Though she had not, and still did not, want the marriage arrangement, the education she had wanted fiercely.

She sighed as a familiar melancholy settled over her. She felt like a woman out of place for her time. She wanted to rail and scream against the injustice of being born a woman with a head for figures in a time when men ruled banking and financial services. No one back home had understood her fascination with figures and formulas.

Her parents, Dr. Jarod Templeton, Doctor of Philosophy, and his adoring wife, Mary Beth Templeton had raised their only child to appreciate the advantages of a higher education and had aspired to help her elevate her social status. Neither had lived to see her finally graduate with her degree, but they had left her a fine two-bedroom house paid in full. She'd eventually had to choose between maintaining that home paid in full and being able to support herself while finishing her studies. Ultimately, she'd chosen college.

The decision had been hard. She didn't take for granted the challenges members of the Race faced to own their own property despite the changes in federal law shortly after she was born. And as advanced as Cleveland might be in some ways, Ohio remained shrouded in a bevy of so-called "Black Laws" that heavily restricted daily life for Colored residents of the state. But a degree had always been her dream, and she believed her parents would have understood and supported her choice.

So with the help of her fiancé, she'd been able to secure a loan against her home to meet her needs. She'd thought she'd have time to get a job and pay off the loan before she ran out of money to support herself or been forced to actually tie herself to the man. Things hadn't worked out that way.

Her money had about run out and she had yet to marry.

Without a job, she'd faced a near-barren pantry and no way to continue the upkeep or note payments on the two-bedroom home. That is, without hastening the marriage she'd been strategically avoiding to the erstwhile dashing and rich Jeremiah Dixon Beauregard III she'd left behind in Ohio.

Dashing and rich had not been enough for her.

She had gone to that last bank interview already one payment behind on her loan, desperate, and needing to secure employment by the end of the week. If she became a wife, her dream of a professional life would die. Eastern men were as small-minded about the female gender as they were overly occupied with status through bloodlines and family wealth. Unless you were seeking domestic work, secretarial work, or a teaching position, as a woman, you were considered properly suited for nothing other than homemaking and childrearing.

Hogwash. She was made for more than that.

Not that there was anything wrong with homemaking or childrearing. When she was young, she'd actually thought she'd have a family one day and had paid attention to the instructions of her mother regarding the proper upkeep of a home. She knew her way around a kitchen. It was not that she found cooking or any of those other things beneath her. She simply found business and numbers so much more fascinating, and she'd learned the way of the world did not support a woman of her station having both.

Picking up her reticule from the square, knitted, tan doily atop the battered chest of drawers to her left, Mary Catherine fished inside for the folded letter she'd received six months ago through her parents' attorney-at-law. The man had helped settle her parents' estate, but this missive had not been about them. It related to the estate of another.

She brushed the letter but did not remove it. She had initially not seriously considered the option it held. It had required she give up too much, or so it had seemed.

It had initially felt like quitting, and she'd never been a quitter. Templetons did not quit. They persevered.

She'd not be the first Templeton to descend into destitution. That determination, plus the debt she owed her parents who had sacrificed much for her dreams, had finally spurred her to take action on the letter. Though it had originally seemed a distraction of a windfall, she now considered its news a divine intervention.

Out of employment options and down to her last dollars, she had replied a few weeks ago to the Kansas attorney responsible for managing the estate of a distant cousin she'd not heard from in over a decade and a half. She'd been fifteen the last time she'd seen—or heard from—this particular cousin. Now she was set to meet with the cousin's attorney to receive legal documents transferring a business enterprise fully to her and the books of account detailing the business's financial state.

A business. A business of her own on the Kansas Plains.

It was not a city position in banking, but it would have to do. At present, her life-altering quest could take her only one way. This would be the end of the line. It was succeed or . . .

She wouldn't think—couldn't think—about the *or else* portion left off that mental success ultimatum.

There was no way but forward. She'd come all the way from the civilized cities of Ohio to the untamed plains of Kansas for a second shot at financial stability and monetary independence. She'd had enough money to make it to Lawless, but not enough to pay for a round-trip ticket and still be able to feed and lodge herself until such time as she could take possession of her unexpected inheritance.

She'd been warned not to expect much, though the business was reportedly profitable, with revenue streams from food, beverage, and lodging accommodations, including a room Lila had used as living quarters. In view of that, not much sounded like a good start. She'd go with it.

Returning to the window, Mary Catherine glanced out again and rethought the forest-green day ensemble she wore with its long row of tiny pearl buttons over a finely stitched, pale pink, silk chemise. The women on the street sported casual day dresses or simple rustic smocks that looked more suitable for housework than a trip into town. Perhaps it was best to try to fit in as much as she could with the local dress customs on this first day of encounters.

Walking over to her open trunk, she surveyed what

wardrobe she'd managed to bring with her. She noted the full-length, lemon-yellow skirt she wore for Sunday walks and picnics and considered it maybe more appropriate for the business she had to do today. She selected a long-sleeved, white blouse to wear with it and thought, *When in Kansas . . .*

Quickly, she changed clothes and turned to the full-length, oak cheval looking glass that stood in the corner of the room. Her front view showed nothing out of place. A twist of the hips and a glance over her shoulder showed the substituted skirt laid appropriately smooth over her backside. So she jauntily placed on her head an asymmetrical, lemon-yellow hat with a smart white ostrich plume curved across the crown. Wrist-length, white gloves followed before she tucked her reticule into the bottom of her trunk and covered it with a stack of garments.

She checked herself in the looking glass one more time to ensure the fashionable hat sat properly positioned at a slant and confirm nothing else was out of place. She knew better than to sport inappropriate attire. Such behavior would not have been right or proper, and if there was anything a Templeton lady was raised to be, it was right and proper. Nothing was more important than a good first impression, and she was determined that the townsfolk's first impression of her be favorable.

Armored for her first true encounter with the locals, other than Miss Eileen of course, Mary Catherine picked up her matching parasol. Time to go introduce herself to her new employees and check out this business establishment she had inherited. She placed her hand on the tarnished brass doorknob of her room, paused, and took a deep, calming breath to gird herself for day one of her new life as a citizen of the wild frontier that was Lawless, Kansas.

Hopefully, her inheritance had more going for it than her first view of its town seemed to suggest. More importantly, she silently prayed she could avoid a run-in with any undesirables, like that villainous-looking ruffian she'd witnessed ride past her window. She stifled a shiver and turned the knob.

~

Blaaze pulled up Scout and the roped mare in front of a long, wooden hitching post across from the huge glass window of the town saloon. Still mounted, Blaaze listened to the din of light laughter and clinking glassware that trickled out through the propped-open double doors. The sounds evidenced a crowd enjoying their liquor and entertainment but not making so much of a commotion as to disturb the peace.

Good. Further evidence he'd chosen the right place to settle down.

The familiar noise of contained male debauchery coupled with the aroma of a well-seared steak made Blaaze long past ready to get his retirement started and join the imbibing crowd.

Scout dropped his head to drink from the tub-sized trough beside the hitching post, and Blaaze's right leg swung achingly over the back of his saddle. His foot gingerly sought the ground. Dismounted and realizing he remained slightly kinked at the waist whilst he clutched at his saddle horn, he slowly corrected the slouch in his posture that telegraphed his injured status.

He took a quick glance around. Satisfied no one had caught his invalid moment, he wrapped Scout's reins around the hitching post then took a slower, closer-up perusal of the structures lining each side of the main road.

Not much had changed since his last pass through, warning signs outside the town notwithstanding. A few more buildings extended Main Street by about an additional two blocks on both sides. The boom in storefronts stood testament to the growth happening in Lawless and other towns being populated by Coloreds migrating to Kansas and western territories

The States were just over a decade out from the Compromise of 1877. The political bargain had made clear the series of laws put into place to establish equity in the post-Rebellion South had failed. The failure had spurred many freedmen to seek the promise of self-determination offered by former abolitionist communities and open territories.

Unlike the town his father had fled to over forty years ago when his pa had escaped enslavement in the low country, people of the Race made up the majority of the population in Lawless and were actually able to own the land they settled on thanks to the passage of civil rights laws. Add to that the opportunities from the extension of the railroad network across the Great Plains, and the town's expansion was understandable. Despite its middling growth, Blaaze was happy to see things were still relatively quiet, slow-moving, and uneventful here.

Just the way he liked them.

"Come on, Huntley." Blaaze unwound the end of the prisoner's leash from Scout's saddle and grabbed the lead rope for the mare. "You've got a date with the sheriff."

He'd turn over the mare to the sheriff as well. As much as he'd like to keep the beauty, she wasn't worth starting off his residence in Lawless labeled as a horse thief. A deep sigh escaped him. He contemplated leaving Huntley outside the saloon, secured to the hitching post for safekeeping while he quenched his thirst first, but duty got the better of him. He guided the mare a few degrees north and walked toward the sheriff's office.

On their way to the jail, he took further stock of the new businesses perched along the stretch of dirt that dissected the middle of town and sighted the combined livery and blacksmith shop a short walk past the end of the boardwalk. He had business to handle there later, but the sheriff's office, unfortunately, needed to be his immediate priority.

The Lawless seat of the law was now buttressed by a larger mercantile on one side and on the other by a building that sported a brand spanking new sign advertising a Western Union telegraph service. Blaaze would have need of that too. He had to wire a certain US marshal to send someone to come get this captured bandit and the abominable hunk of silver weighing down the vest he'd donned this morning under his duster. He scratched at the illusory itch beneath the hidden weight on his chest then glanced at the still-struggling human package at the end of his rope . . . literally.

Four years, three months, and twenty-two days since he'd started his government-sanctioned bandit hunt. The gig was supposed to be temporary. Blaaze didn't find much temporary about four years, three months, and twenty-two days. But who was counting, right?

He'd made a promise. A man kept his word or died trying. At least, this man did. So here he was years later delivering on the last of that promise. He'd been looking forward to this day—the day he'd rid himself of his star-shaped burden—for every minute of those four long years, three hectic months, and twenty-two ever-lovin' days. He'd take care of his business at the jail and afterward send his follow-up telegram to Malone.

Then, he thought, *I've got a date with a peaceful corner table of the saloon and a brand-new bottle of whiskey.*

After four years, three months, and twenty-two days, nothing best stand in his way or he was going to be ornerier than a bull denied his mount on a prize heifer during mating season.

He finished quickly with his business at the sheriff's office and left unimpressed with the man wearing the badge. From his second stop, the telegraph office, he'd intended to head over and check out the new mayor, but the telegraph operator informed Blaaze the mayor was somewhere in Nebraska on business. Content to get to the saloon that much sooner, Blaaze stepped onto the boardwalk and turned that direction.

The heels of his boots echoed a solid clomp with each step. The closer he got to the saloon, the more eyes fixed on him. Many didn't bother to leave their presumed safety behind closed doors but peered conspicuously through paned glass windows.

Blaaze passed an audience of slack-jawed matrons, who looked at him like they expected him to rob them of their pearls, if they'd been wearing any. Several old men seated a few steps away from the ladies halted their bickering in front of the barbershop long enough to give him a curious eye. Though he'd agreed to temporarily leave his one Colt at the sheriff's office to avoid a lengthy confrontation that would delay his ultimate goal, he still wore his empty holster. He suspected many of the onlookers had seen him ride into town armed. Plus, his five-day-old scruff and bloodstained shirt likely added to their impression of him as potential trouble.

Choosing to ignore the suspicious glances, he gripped the front and back of his Stetson to give it a two-handed adjustment and nodded cordially at the matrons. The youngest, who must have been pushing seventy, gasped at his greeting and fell into her buddies clutching the front of her gown. Fanning her rapidly with her own bonnet, one of the friends gave him a ferocious frown. A quick glance around showed half the looks of curiosity he'd been getting had also morphed into frowns, while many of the others had simply gone wary. More townsfolk gathered at the fringes of the street to gawk at him.

Great. Just great.

Not wanting any trouble, he carefully surveyed the growing onlookers to evaluate whether any seemed primed to accost a newcomer. Satisfied his audience intended no trouble other than rude stares, Blaaze headed directly to the saloon. He sauntered into Lady Lila's Den of Spirits with the hefty weight of new silver dollars and a bank draft in his pocket thanks to the bounty on the now-jailed Huntley. The sheriff had assumed Blaaze had come to collect the price on the man's head, and Blaaze saw no reason to disabuse the lawman of that notion. Seeing as how Blaaze didn't want anyone in town to know he'd taken on a silver star, sliding into his old role as a bounty hunter suited him just fine.

He'd square things with Marshal Malone later if there was any issue with a federal man of the peace taking compensation for apprehending a suspect. He could always hand over the money with the star and leave it to Malone to figure out the legalities. Right now, all Blaaze cared about was finding a table and chair in a back corner and drinking himself into a better disposition.

He strolled to the long bar that stretched before most of the west wall and took a moment to remove his Stetson and run a hand over his straggly hair, which, like his face, was long past needing a barber's care. A tall, lanky fellow he'd never seen before stood shining glasses with a beige rag.

The man looked up. His hand stalled on the glass he currently polished, but he didn't speak. Though he covered it fairly well, that Blaaze made the man nervous was plain to see. His already pale visage blanched a few shades into ghostly white.

Aside from presently being a scruffy, dust-covered bum, Blaaze had a look about him that regularly made folks nervous. He'd never understood it. He was an easygoing fella.

Well, unless you decided to piss him off.

But if you didn't piss him off, there'd be no trouble from him. He could be nice and fairly accommodating. Now wasn't one of those nice and easy and accommodating times, though.

He was cranky, hungry, horny, and dirty. Whiskey couldn't fix the last three, but it'd do right fine for the first. He hoped this gentleman had no intention of playing any games with the speed of his service or the quality and proof of the whiskey he'd be handing over in exchange for some of the coins in Blaaze's pocket.

Sensing Blaaze's growing impatience, the barkeep swallowed loud enough for Blaaze to hear. The man hesitated before he set aside his rag and the glass, now quite shiny, and stepped up to the back edge of the scuffed-up bar. "What can I do you for, mister?"

CHAPTER 3

BLAAZE PERUSED THE BOTTLES of spirits shelved in neat rows across the mirrored wall behind the barkeep and nodded at an unopened bottle of whiskey. "Your best bottle of whiskey." He tossed a silver dollar onto the scuffed wood before him. "Start me a tab and add on a room for the next three weeks."

Blaaze's land didn't currently contain any shelter fit for human occupancy. He'd get to raising a roof for a house in the next few days.

"The top floor room in the back corner open?" Blaaze asked.

The man should have no problem understanding which room he meant. Lila's personal rooms took up the whole of the other end of the top floor. She usually kept the corner room of the upper hall open for special guests. He'd always been one of her favorites, and one of the few men she trusted so close to her own quarters. So he didn't anticipate a problem, but the man seemed to have to think things over before he could respond.

The barkeep looked around anxiously. Not finding

whatever he was looking for, he turned and grabbed a bottle of whiskey before he responded. "Actually, that room is currently occupied." His tone slid toward apologetic, but he had no gumption behind his start of a refusal. "We have—"

"Occupied by whom?" Blaaze's tone dropped to a menacing irritation. Unimpressed with the obvious timidity before him, Blaaze wasn't accepting a *no* from this beanpole.

Whoever occupied that space was going to have to vacate.

When the man's face flushed from ghostly to red, Blaaze guessed he was looking at the culprit. He gave a cursory glance at the bottle of whiskey the barkeep set down before him and noticed it had already been opened.

Blaaze shook his head and pointed at a bottle on the highest shelf with a noticeably darker color. "Get me a real bottle of whiskey, a glass, and then move your stuff out of my room." He threw down another silver dollar to cover the second bottle of whiskey he had every intention of coming back to get and part of the cost for the addition of the room.

Once again, the man looked around. This time, his eyes rested on two cowboys who had stepped through the doorway from outside and his tension ebbed. Blaaze didn't turn to look but took the men's measure by peering into the looking glass behind the shelves of the bar. He'd seen the two hombres earlier, before he'd turned over Huntley to the sheriff. The tallest one had given Blaaze the eye, and if Blaaze wasn't mistaken, the man was kin to an outlaw Blaaze had dropped off in Lawless a little over four years ago.

This couldn't be a good sign.

Blaaze wasn't sure what the barkeep and the criminal's brother had to do with each other. But he hoped whatever their plans, they waited until he'd gotten half this whiskey from the bottle into his gullet before they decided to make a move. He wrapped one hand around the neck of the whiskey bottle and slid two fingers of the other hand into the mouth of the shiny glass tumbler he'd been given.

He sauntered past a four-man poker game and Barbara Jean, who was refilling the coffee mug of one of the locals. A full-figured gal old enough to be his mother, Barbara Jean—known to her friends as Babs—had a rich brown complexion unblemished by frontier living. No doubt her sunny disposition and unlimited lust for life played a role in her deliciously aged beauty.

Being the notorious flirt that she was, she threw her free hand to one hip and crooned seductively at him, "Welcome back, cowboy. It's been a while."

He shot her a playful wink and kept moving.

Used to his man-of-few-words demeanor, Babs simply chuckled. "Now, don't be startin' nothing you don't intend to finish, Mr. Lassiter. It's just cruel to get a lady's hopes up that way."

Shaking his head at her antics, he continued toward the back corner that sheltered his favorite table. The three gentlemen already sitting there nearly knocked over the table in their haste to abandon the private spot. They managed to salvage the liquor they'd been imbibing by snatching their drinks off the table, but some of their chairs weren't so lucky. Two banged, one after the other, onto the wood floor, which was relatively clean, Blaaze noticed, despite the fair-sized early crowd.

Leaving the chairs where they'd sprawled, Blaaze approached the abandoned table. The gentlemen's haste passively amused him. He appreciated the deference. He would have asked nicely for the table . . . or as nicely as he could muster in his current condition, but it was nice he didn't have to.

He swung his leg over the nearest of the two remaining upright chairs. His duster flared with the movement, and he lowered his butt onto the armless, solid oak seat. Out of habit, he adjusted so his back angled into the corner. From this position, he could see every cranny of the saloon's main floor. No entrance, window, door, or stairway could escape his gaze.

The tumbler made a clunk when he set it on the table. He took in a deep breath, nirvana settling over him as he uncapped the whiskey bottle and let the scent waft to his nostrils. He poured two fingers into the glass and recapped the bottle. Unfortunately, the two cowboys weren't content to leave him be. They walked boldly to his table. Arrogance clung to each, much like their heavily rumpled shirts.

Without hesitation, the brother of his former captive reached down, dipped a dirty finger into Blaaze's whiskey, then sucked the nectar from that dingy digit. The man made a hum of appreciation before he snatched the tumbler from the table and drank the glass dry. A loud "ahh" followed. The soon-to-be dead man wiped his mouth with the back of his hand then, with a wide grin, returned the tumbler steadfastly to its former spot.

As far as throwing down a gauntlet went, that was as good a method as any.

Blaaze's jaw tightened. Guess he was going to have to wait for that drink of whiskey a beat longer.

Suffering this irksome interruption was enough to make a tired, alcohol-starved, sex-deprived man flip his lid, but Blaaze kept his cool. An uncool head left a man gutshot or dead. He'd already had close to a gut shot, and he wasn't looking to get dead. He stood slowly and whipped the sides of his duster off his hips. The two cretins glanced at each other then gave him a puzzled look.

Belatedly, Blaaze remembered his hip was devoid of his pearl-handled weapon. He still had his Derringer safe and snug in his boot, but he needn't reveal his small backup weapon to stymie this minimal nuisance. He checked the hips of each cretin to verify they weren't wearing guns either. This business of everyone walking around unarmed was going to cramp Blaaze's style, but he didn't mind so long as every man had a level playing field.

Actually, he did mind—at least a little.

It wasn't that he was opposed to throwing fists when the need arose. He simply wasn't currently in the mood to expend the energy or aggravate his healing wound. Retirement meant he got to take it easy. Throwing fists didn't amount to easy.

His glance trailed down to his empty glass, and thoughts of taking it easy were no longer currently top of his list. He was going to have to teach these boys a lesson, and he was going to have to do it the hard way.

Thinking to take advantage of Blaaze's preoccupation with his empty glass, the tallest of the two interlopers threw a quick punch. Blaaze feinted backward to avoid the flying fist, and with a one-two combination, retaliated hard enough to knock out the punch thrower. Before the unconscious body hit the floor, a bottle of warm liquid broke against the side of Blaaze's head.

Every muscle in his body went taut.

He turned his dripping head slowly.

Dread spread eerily through his chest, dread laced with a fleeting hope that his bottle of whiskey had not been used as the bludgeon. A squint at his bottle-less table confirmed his worst suspicion. The table stood empty save for the lone tumbler of the purloined two fingers of heaven. Broken glass and the precious amber liquid spread across the floor at his feet. Any chance he'd had of not descending into a full-bodied rage evaporated.

Anger rose so fast and hard Blaaze didn't have time to actually feel the emotion. The pure, instant rage drove him without thought to grab the whiskey murderer with both hands, make a half spin, and hurl the man sideways. The cretin went flying toward the huge window painted in bold letters on the opposite side with the name of the establishment.

Blaaze didn't see the lady in yellow until it was too late.

The airborne human crashed through the window and knocked into the prim lady in citified attire. Her tiny umbrella took flight, and she flipped bum over head across the hitching rail into the watering trough Scout had used earlier. She landed face down with a splash and quickly flopped over like a trout fighting a hook. She sputtered as her loosened hat slipped on doused curls down her face to cover her eyes. With a hysterical flurry of arms and legs, her small, booted feet poked out one side of the trough and her arms propped over the opposite side to hold her upper body above water.

She hesitantly released one arm to try for the hat across her face, but she began to slip back into the water and hastily put the arm back. It took her three tries before she managed to coordinate pushing the drooping hat out of her eyes without her head sinking deep beneath what water remained in the trough. Once successful at freeing her vision, she struggled to free herself from her public bath but couldn't manage the task, bent in half as she was in the narrow confinement.

Blaaze stepped through the broken window and hurried toward the woman who floundered in the drink up to her breasts on one side and her thighs on the other. He glanced into the trough right into splayed legs. The modest width of the trough kept the yellow-skirted lady bent in a pike position, legs nearly straight up and currently wide open. Her soaked bloomers stuck to her shapely, stockinged thighs. While the damp view revealed none of her most private parts, the promise of what lay between those thighs made his groin come to life.

He swore silently. If this half-drowned, messy-haired woman could tempt his libido, then clearly his enduring lack of womanly companionship had made him as randy as a pubescent teen—any willing female would do.

Needing to act quickly before she became any more indecent—or hysterical—Blaaze reached into the trough, spanned her waist with his hands, and lifted. A twinge tweaked near his side wound, but the feel of her in his hands and the drooping hat feather tickling his nose garnered most of his attention. She seemed to weigh little more than a couple of bags of feed, though she had decent height for a woman once he set her on her feet. The heeled, ankle-high dress boots housing those feet made a squishing sound upon hitting the ground, and water gushed over the tops like the flow of a full well after a hardy pump of the handle.

An elegant, gloved hand once again shoved the drooping hat, with its annoying wet feather, out of her face. "Look what you did to my clothes!"

She pulled at the layered pleats of her skirt to untangle the bunched, wet fabric and blocked his view of the spouting boots. He looked up the line of the drenched skirt, now molded awkwardly to curved hips. The pale-yellow color had gone nearly gossamer. The shape of her body stood on blatant display, though with the layers of undergarments she wore, nothing of the flesh beneath was revealed. A further glance up her torso showed the same was not true of her soaked white blouse.

"Oh, I'm looking all right," he drawled in a voice nearly inaudible and noticeably husky even to him.

The lady wore the requisite corset underneath, but her corset had slipped or gone askew, and the chemise underneath was white. Both were so wet they clung to her like the slinkiest nightgown. One of her budded nipples, a darkened tip on a perfect mound, peeked noticeably over the top of the failing waist-cincher. The sprouting bulge in his pants solidified. The redirection of blood flow made him a little slow on the uptake.

"Wait." His gaze shot to hers once her words sank in. "Me? Lady, I'm not the one who knocked you into the drink."

"Yes." Her regal nose lifted with haughty authority. "But you threw the man who did."

She had him there.

Apparently, the follower and not the leader in the little interlude that had started all this, the man in question had gotten up and scrambled away without being noticed.

"What appalling behavior. People must be allowed to walk the streets without fear of being accosted. Have you no manners?" Her dignified tone belied the unkempt state of her clothes.

Whoever the prim miss was, she had all the right womanly parts in all the right places, but unfortunately the tone of an educated woman. An *eastern* educated woman by her accent. Her proper eastern upbringing dripped all over her like the water that continued to leak from her clinging garments.

What the hell was a woman like her doing in Lawless anyway?

She had no business loitering outside a saloon. She would

be fair game for every drunkard and lowlife who patronized the place. Didn't she have any better sense than to even consider walking on this side of the street?

Slowly, so as not to draw attention to his movement, Blaaze adjusted the sides of his duster to cover the stiffness between his legs.

His attention drawn once more to the perfect mound she didn't seem to realize was on display, he retorted, "Don't you have any better sense than to stand outside a packed saloon?"

"Me!" she screeched. "You're blaming this on me? Surely, you jest."

Her hands slammed onto her hips, and she huffed. Her chest rose and fell with her exhalation. Blaaze watched, enthralled by the movement, and nearly groaned. His soldier now stood at full salute and his engorged state bordered on painful. His denims felt a size too small, but too fascinated by the first sight of a woman's body he'd had in months, he unwittingly tortured himself with his inability to look away from the tantalizing view beneath her water-thinned blouse.

"The least you can do is look at me when I speak to you," she said with a clipped tone that put him in mind of Mrs. Winters, the rotund schoolmarm who ruled the one-room schoolhouse of his youth.

"Um, what?" he said without adjusting his eyes from their current vision.

"What on earth are you looking—?" She screeched again upon glancing down. "Oh my word!"

Her arms flew up to cover her chest, breaking his view and his hypnosis.

"You cad! How could you stand there and look at my . . . look at me . . . let me just . . ." An embarrassed flush lit her face.

It was the most curious sight. Her walnut-brown skin failed to hide that the flush went all the way down her throat and disappeared into the neck of her blouse. He had never seen a woman blush across her entire upper body. The thought of where that heightened color might end caused a fresh stirring in his crotch.

His jaw set. This was not happening.

No way was he tempted by this buttoned-up, haughty, slip of a woman with her eastern accent. He liked his women lush and endowed. And silent.

Not that this woman's curves weren't nice enough.

And those breasts seemed near perfect . . .

But *silent*, she was not.

She continued to rave, trying—unsuccessfully—to discreetly tug up her slipped undergarment. Something about the window and property damage and outlaws starting barroom brawls. He was too busy watching her try to cover herself, while simultaneously trying to fix her attire without anyone noticing, to pay attention to what she was saying.

She stepped closer to the window and started to gesture toward it before she thought better of lifting her arm. "Look at that damage. Do you have money to pay for this?"

After a second, her nose crinkled. This time her face displayed aversion rather than eastern superiority. She completely lost her train of thought as she looked him over. Her expression made clear she'd decided *no* was the answer to her question. Her eyes widened in horror and what he read was . . . *disgust?*

He cringed inwardly, now regretting he hadn't taken the time for a bath. He'd been too focused on getting the drink he still hadn't managed to consume. The bloodstained clothing he continued to sport certainly didn't help her impression of him. He nearly gave in to the urge to sniff his pits to determine whether an offensive odor might carry the few feet between them, but he dared not draw more attention to his less than respectable state than their encounter had already caused.

Remembering he still needed a shave, he ran a subconscious hand over his mouth and jaw, then realized his scraggly hair was also on full display because somewhere in the scuffle he'd lost his hat. Despite his awareness of his subpar physical appearance, her obvious condescension bothered him. That he was bothered by her assessment of him as lacking bothered him even more.

Other people's opinions of him weren't high on his list of concerns. He went his own way and did his own thing, and anyone who didn't like it or him could go pound mud for all he cared. So how dare this uppity female, who had no business in a town like Lawless and certainly no business on the end of Main Street that housed the baser elements of the town, impose her disapproval on him. Renewed anger surfaced, this time directed at the eastern female and her attempt to look down her nose at him—although she actually had to look up.

His eyes narrowed. Whatever she saw on his face made her take a huge step back, and momentarily forget her need for blouse discretion. A small rush of breath escaped her lips. No one heard the sound but him, but the satisfaction he derived from the subtle indication of her transition from scolding to fearful wasn't lessened in the least by the lack of public witness.

Done with being lectured like a schoolboy who'd forgotten to write out his multiplication tables, Blaaze took one more irrepressible glance toward her arm-covered chest, then turned away from her.

"Miss Templeton. Miss Templeton!" an approaching male voice called behind him. "Good Lord! What on earth happened?"

Blaaze glanced over his shoulder to see a man in a baggy suit rush toward the cranky miss. The man's eyes widened comically before he yanked out of his jacket and draped it over her shoulders. With a look of utter gratitude, Miss Templeton quickly slid her arms into its sleeves and gripped the lapels tightly across her chest.

Something about the name Templeton seemed familiar to Blaaze, but the memory wouldn't fully take shape. He ignored the prickle in his brain and the gallant gentleman who had helped the soaking miss regain her propriety. He walked away from the couple toward the gaping hole where the saloon window used to be, stepped over the low sill, and pushed through the saloon crowd that had gathered inside to peer out at the happenings.

The crunch of glass at his back let him know the Templeton woman or the gallant arrival or both had made to follow him.

"Where do you think you're going?" her strained voice demanded in that polished eastern accent.

He ignored the accent, the tone, and the nagging woman they belonged to and walked faster.

"Wait just a minute, mister." Her scolding voice grew louder behind him. "We need to talk about how you're going to pay for my window!"

Chapter 4

Mary Catherine almost wanted to cry. Her window, her lovely window, had been destroyed. She'd stood admiring the huge pane and the decorative letters in which her cousin had chosen to display the name of the establishment. Her first thought had been maybe, just maybe, her start here in Lawless had potential.

Her dunk in the trough had disabused her of that notion.

She wiped a hand across the water dripping from her hair down her forehead. Exasperated, but mostly embarrassed, she followed the surly cowboy responsible for her condition through the window he'd broken and almost ran into him. He'd gone completely still when she'd mentioned his paying for her window.

He turned slowly. "*Your* window?" His brow puckered. "What do you mean your window? Where the hell is Lila?"

Mary Catherine stiffened at his use of profanity. He seemed to notice but didn't have the decency to look chagrined over the slip in manners. Of course, she couldn't be certain he had any.

"You knew Lila?" Mary Catherine asked with soft

surprise. She'd not seen or talked to her cousin in years. The thought of talking with someone who knew her was enticing, though this man probably wasn't Mary Catherine's best choice.

From the look of him, he was not only as untamed as this county but also lethal. Though, apparently, the man was not fond of hygiene. He looked as if he'd never learned to bathe.

Despite this failing characteristic, one could not overlook the natural power and masculine presence that emanated from him. He exuded a sense of danger that had made her shiver the moment he'd looked down at her in the watering trough with those intense, brown eyes that reminded her of the melted chocolate her mom would pour over fresh-baked rum cakes. He was a palette of darks except for his medium blue shirt—dark brown face, nearly black hair, deep brown opened vest above the darkest denim, all under a long, dust-covered coat.

"Of course, I knew Lila. Everyone in town knew Lila or at least knew of her."

His mouth quirked a bit at the edge when he said that last, making her wonder what exactly his relationship with Lila had been.

"So why the hel—" He cleared his throat, cutting off the profanity he'd been about to utter. "So why are you standing in her saloon making claims on her window?"

His voice was low and deathly calm but the demand behind his request for an answer was no less clear. Mary Catherine couldn't prevent herself from taking a small step back from him a second time. Her father had taught her at a young age to be aware of predators. And the human kind were the worst kind. She'd learned to confront such predators and bullies, but today her sense of self-preservation was stronger.

"Well, I . . ." She fumbled her words in the face of his stare, that intense stare that made her feel as if he was not just looking at her but through her.

The gentleman who had come to her clothing rescue stepped forward and offered his card to the outlaw-looking character. "Let me introduce myself . . . um . . . sir."

The ruffian refused to take the presented card. He stood stoically staring at the man who, of the same height as she, stood a whole head shorter than the imposing window-breaker.

The gentleman returned the unwanted card to the back slit of the small, leather satchel he carried and ran a nervous hand over his thinning hair. "Well, um, I'm Jeremy Blakely, attorney-at-law. I represent Lady Lila's estate, and this here is her cousin, Miss Mary Catherine Templeton from Cleveland, Ohio, who has inherited all of Miss Lila's earthly possessions, including this building and the saloon business it houses."

"Lila's estate?" The simple question came out languid and the attention of chocolaty brown eyes slid back Mary Catherine's way. His gaze gave her a once-over, as if he were taking her measure more closely this time.

She had the sense he was comparing her to what he remembered of Lila. She wondered if she'd come up lacking. She probably did if her cousin had changed little over the years. Lila had been an uncommonly beautiful girl whose figure had blossomed early. Mary Catherine had always felt plain and boring by comparison.

"So Lila's dead?" His eyes held a flat intensity, but his voice gave away true feelings of regret.

Mary Catherine simply nodded. She sensed a sadness in him that even in her miff over the broken window she didn't have the heart to minimize or disrespect.

He gave a curt nod and turned away. She made to follow him, but the attorney grabbed her arm and shook his head. Even he sensed the change in the gunslinger. Although she really needed to find out the man's name so she could quit calling him that in her head.

She watched as the ruffian stepped over two overturned chairs, a broken table, and a mess of glass and liquid all over the floor. He reached down and grabbed a brown hat from a less sullied area of the floor. He beat it against the side of his leg, reshaped the top and brim, then settled it almost lovingly atop his head.

He stepped to the bar and took a stool. A thin barman gazed warily at her. Mary Catherine had not noticed the man or the others filling the saloon—including several scantily clad women with painted faces—who had apparently been watching her and the gunslinger from various corners of the room.

"I'll have another bottle of whiskey," the now hatted cowboy said to the barman.

The thought of him leisurely drinking whiskey after what he'd done shook Mary Catherine from her stalled reverie. He was not going to order whiskey at her bar, in her saloon, when he'd caused all this damage. He needed to pay for this first.

She shook off the attorney, whose hand had remained on her arm, and followed the culprit to the bar. "Wait a minute. There'll be no whiskey," she said adamantly.

He turned his head leisurely toward her and glared. "Excuse me?" His tone was cold, and hard, and implacably serious.

A shimmer of cowardice threatened to make Mary Catherine back down, but Templetons didn't back down. They stood up for what they believed in. She'd stand up for herself. He had damaged her property, and he would have to pay for it, former acquaintance of Lila's or not.

With a deep breath, Mary Catherine summoned her courage and glared right back at him. "Take a look around, sir. Cleaning up this damage and replacing the broken furniture, not to mention the window, will take time and money. Money I expect you to pay. Until you do, you'll not be served here." Her hands started for her hips, but the borrowed jacket gaped open, and she remembered the see-through state of her blouse. Quickly, she grasped the sides of the jacket and slapped them closed by emphatically crossing her arms instead.

His eyes tracked her hand movements before his gaze returned to her face, and their stare-off continued. She met his added scowl with a defiant demeanor perfected over years of being a lone, and often disrespected, female in a male-dominated discipline. No one else in the room made a sound. It was as if they'd all collectively decided to hold their breaths until the ruffian decided what he'd do.

Without removing his eyes from hers, he reached for the whiskey bottle the barkeep had set down. He made no sound. One big hand simply wrapped around the base of the bottle and held. A glimmer flickered behind his irises. Something that looked an awful lot like a dare.

Not liking being dared in front of all these people, several of whom she suspected were now her employees, Mary Catherine responded without hesitation. She darted out a hand and wrapped her fingers around the neck of the bottle. One of his eyebrows rose in surprise and a bit of a taunt. He knew, as did she, if they were to fight over this bottle, his superior strength would win out.

She didn't care.

Stepping closer, she put her other hand on the neck of the bottle as well, momentarily forgetting to secure the lapels of the jacket that guarded her modesty. Even two hands to his one, she'd lose in a tug-o-war, but she didn't intend to let go. She'd make him fight her for this drink and hope the jacket stayed in place while she did.

His eyes narrowed to a contemplative squint, but nothing else changed in his manner or expression. The squint told her everything she needed to know. He'd made the same assessment as she. If he wanted this whiskey, he'd have to fight a woman for it, and he'd have to do it in a room full of spectators.

She bit her lower lip at his steady regard but held firm. Let's see how much of a ruffian the man really was.

~

Watching the eastern miss stand her ground with him, several men rose to their feet when they realized what might be about to go down. Although Blaaze didn't move his head to look at any of them, he knew exactly where each would-be Good Samaritan stood and exactly what threat, if any, each posed. He wasn't concerned. Even outnumbered, he'd not be the one to lose.

"Lassiter!" someone shouted at him. "You know better than to hassle a lady. We'll not stand by and let you cause her any hurt. Take your bounty hunter ways elsewhere."

Not one for much conversation, Blaaze didn't respond to the man.

"Lassiter?" The uncertain inquiry whispered from the lady's lips.

They'd not been officially introduced, so she'd heard his

name for the first time. Something about the sound of his surname in her proper, eastern tone sent an odd pulse of fire singeing through his veins. He'd finally gotten his inexplicable arousal under control, and here she went stirring things up again. He concentrated on the liquid fire she was preventing him from drinking to shut it down.

Deciding just because the lady was irritating the hell out of him there was no reason to totally forget his manners, he touched the brim of his hat with his free hand. "Blaaze Lassiter, at your service, ma'am," he said in his best aw-shucks, midwestern drawl.

She simply blinked at him, temporarily speechless. Having already classified him as a worthless bum, she'd likely not thought him capable of a mannerly introduction. Whatever the reason for her momentary lack of self-possession, she regrouped quickly and gave him a queenly nod in return.

Perhaps encouraged by his rare show of etiquette, she made a huge gambit that he had some gentleman's code beneath the layers of better days seen. In a voice laced with more confidence than the rapid pulse at her neck revealed she felt, she demanded, "Pay up or leave, Mr. Lassiter. Those are your choices." She tugged at the bottle . . . unsuccessfully.

He wasn't ready to let go.

When he wouldn't release the bottle, the pulse in her neck accelerated, but she continued her double-handed grip on the neck of the whiskey bottle. Despite the physical signs of her unease, the woman kept her aplomb. Seems the city lady was tougher than her prissy exterior suggested.

Slowly, he rose. Still holding the base of the bottle, he said loud enough for everyone to hear, "I'm going." Then he leaned in and whispered for her ears only, "But I'll be back."

An obvious shiver ran through her. Satisfied, he opened

his hand one finger at a time and released the bottle. This wasn't the time or place to settle the score with Miss Templeton. He'd leave that for a different day. With an unhurried saunter, he headed for the door and departed without looking back.

Once he cleared the saloon, Blaaze's rile came back full force. He stomped to the livery stable down the street and stormed into the blacksmith shop in the back. He fumed at the audacity of that citified miss who'd just kicked him out of *her* new saloon without his bought and paid-for bottle of whiskey. Or, more accurately due to the recent turn of events, her bottle of whiskey till she saw fit to honor the transaction. At least, hers for the time being.

What the hell? Just what he needed in the middle of an already crappy day. More crap.

Blaaze marched without speaking past the hulking blacksmith who held a curved and glowing, hot, red hunk of metal at the end of long, black iron clamps. When the tradesman was done shaping the hunk of metal, it would be a horseshoe. At the moment, it was simply a fire-hot U-shape and possibly a very painful weapon. The man holding it certainly looked as if he wanted to use it on Blaaze, but Blaaze ignored the irritated look on the man's face.

A giant of a man, Blacksmith Tobias Nathaniel Craig stood about three inches taller than Blaaze's over six-foot frame and about half again as wide. The man looked as if he could bend metal into horseshoes with his bare hands. Truth be told, he probably could. But Blaaze ignored the man's current irritation at Blaaze's gruff intrusion because Blaaze had a singular purpose, and Tobias was the only man Blaaze knew within a day's ride who could help him with that particular purpose.

Given the eastern missus had kicked Blaaze out of the saloon, Blaaze's best bet to quench the thirst he nursed, and ease his hankering to grab that certain missus around the neck and squeeze, was Tobias's bootleg alcohol. Assuming Blaaze could find it.

Tobias made the best moonshine within four states and three territories. Probably farther, but Blaaze had yet to test the theory.

Although the manufacture and sale of intoxicating liquors had been banned under the Kansas Constitution since January 1881, people still manufactured it, still sold it, and still drank it. If you did it right, you could avoid the fines and possible jail time written into state law. Saloons managed to have the protection of their towns since even the lawmen often drank there, and unsurprisingly, those towns with a justice of the peace sometimes had that office located inside their local saloon.

Breweries had slowly begun popping up across the state as well. Although quite a few independent bootleggers like Tobias existed, many proper townsfolk frowned upon them openly plying their wares. So the bootleggers did their selling on the sly through secret networks and private hideaways. Enterprising ones could make a fair living if they were good and smart. They simply had to be careful.

As one such good and smart moonshine peddler, Tobias kept his stash well hidden. But Blaaze knew it had to be here. Tobias would keep his stash where he spent the most time and could keep the best watch over it. Blaaze needed a drink bad enough he'd risk Tobias's wrath to find the right hidey hole.

Deep in his funk, Blaaze shoved some boxes to the side in a far corner full of hanging reins, bridles, and other horse and carriage implements. Pulling up a loose board fitted into the ground, Blaaze rooted around in the hole it covered. Not finding what he wanted, he frowned and turned to the blacksmith, who stood stoically glaring at him.

"Where's the stash?" Blaaze asked, his tone as impatient as his disposition.

"*The* stash? You mean *my* stash, don't ya?" Tobias dropped the red-hot metal to his worktable and gave it three hard whacks.

Clang. Clang. Clang.

"Seeing as how we're in business together, that'd be *our* stash, you obstinate cuss. So where's it at?" Blaaze crossed his arms and gave his friend a don't-mess-with-me look.

Tobias continued without concern or hurry to pound the horseshoe he was shaping. "I think you mean we're *going* into business together. And our deal was for the livery business. We said nothing about the other."

Two pounds rang out. *Clang. Clang.*

"Since you do 'the other' mostly inside the livery, the two are one and the same."

"Well, we'll see about that," Tobias said without looking up.

Clang. Clang. Clang.

"And all the same, I've yet to see your share of the investment you promised me." Tobias looked up this time. "Until such time as I do, this here is *my* livery and that there is *my* stash. And my stash only." His hard expression dared Blaaze to contradict him.

The look would have made any average man quake in his boots, but Blaaze was no average man. Tobias and he had been friends for nigh on a decade and a half. Blaaze understood what Tobias could do to a body who crossed him, but Blaaze wasn't in that category. He hoped.

Tobias was the only man in this town Blaaze wholeheartedly trusted. And that was saying a lot. Not many men earned Blaaze's trust, which was even harder to earn than his respect. He'd like to think Tobias felt the same about him.

Blaaze shoved a hand into the deep pocket on the left side of his duster and hauled out the bag of remaining silver coins he'd netted upon delivery of Dunst Huntley. He tossed it onto the lid of the closed barrel a few feet from where Tobias stood pounding and made a beeline for the shelf Tobias had unwittingly indicated with the movement of his eyes when he'd spoken about "his stash." Blaaze trusted the man to have his back in a fight or hold his secrets till death, but he was worthless in a card game. Tobias had more tells than women had gossip.

With determined steps, Blaaze strode toward the designated shelf and moved the medium crates positioned at the front. Tobias wouldn't be that obvious in the placement of the precious, sought-after elixir. With the shove aside of one last crate, Blaaze spotted what he needed.

He grabbed a mason jar from a crate all the way in the back. The crate contained about a dozen such jars. A quick twist of a lid and a long, deep drink of the white brew drew Blaaze's eyes closed while the taste of the sweetest liquor he'd ever drank slid restoratively down his throat. Not yet content, he chugged another swig and nearly sighed with the pleasure that hit his gut and the uplift that hit his spirit.

Tobias came up behind him and snatched the jar from his hand. "Take it easy, you crazy coot. I don't want to have to dig a hole and bury you out back. Uncle Nathan's recipe is nothing to fool around with."

Known as Nearest to most, Tobias Nathaniel's "Uncle"

Nathan had taught his namesake and best friend's son a charcoal method for making whiskey that Tobias had paired with a process for white lightning garnered from his Scots-Irish great grandfather. The nonconformist great grandfather had come into the family after he'd fallen for a beautiful escapee from enslavement he'd met while hawking his wares at a cathouse in Lexington, Kentucky. The result of the combo was moonshine that went down smooth as a spoonful of molasses but had enough kick to kill a bison if not distilled properly or imbibed with caution.

Screwing the top back on the mason jar, Tobias gave Blaaze the side eye. "I'd say welcome back, Lassiter, but you're as ticky as a stallion with a wasp at its hindquarters. You can't have been in town more than twenty-four hours or I'd have heard. So what the hell could have gotten you this riled up already?"

Chapter 5

BLAZE SNATCHED THE MASON jar back from Tobias and leaned against a stack of hay bales off to the side. After a more discreet chug, he offered, "Saloon's got a new owner. A woman from out east."

Tobias nodded. "I figured Lila's estate would be settled up soon. Didn't figure on another woman coming to claim the saloon, though."

"Not a woman, a buttoned-up harridan with a penchant for giving orders." Blaaze filled Tobias in on his full encounter with Mary Catherine Templeton from Cleveland, Ohio.

Tobias got a good laugh out of her arm-wrestle refusal to let Blaaze have his paid-for bottle of whiskey.

"I don't see anything funny. A woman should know better than to get between a thirsty cowboy and his whiskey. If she'd've been a man, we would have come to blows."

"Is she pretty?" Tobias asked between chuckles.

"What kind of a question is that? Did you not hear anything I said?" Blaaze stared at him in amazement.

"I heard all right." Tobias found his own perch against a barrel a few feet away and positioned himself to stare back at Blaaze. "Now answer the question. Is she pretty?"

Disgruntled, Blaaze scratched his temple with two fingers. "I didn't notice one way or the other."

"The hell you didn't," Tobias challenged while giving him a considering look. "And the fact that you won't answer the question gives me my answer."

Blaaze shot him an evil look. "Does not. You're speculating. And about whether or not some new shrew in town is good looking. I might as well send you over to the sewing circle to chitchat with the grandmas and town matrons."

The blacksmith waved off the insult and pushed off the barrel to pull the jar of moonshine from Blaaze's grip. He took a moderate swig before asking, "Why didn't you just pay for the damage? It's not like you don't have the money."

Tobias was one of the few people who knew Blaaze's undetectable financial status. He could buy that saloon several times over and still have a nest egg that would last him well past old age. He'd been good at bounty hunting. With no wife or kids and only himself to support, he'd spent very little of his gains over the years. He'd banked heap-loads in depository institutions across the country and hidden a stash or two of cash in places he frequented, in case he had an immediate need. He liked to be prepared. For anything.

Heck, dipping into his banked funds wouldn't even have been required to settle up with Miss Templeton. Blaaze could have given her on the spot some of the coins he'd tossed at Tobias and been done with the matter. But her nagging temperament had made Blaaze contrary. The snooty miss had assumed—*wrongly*—that he didn't have the money to cover some measly window and a few broken tables.

Pfft, he silently scoffed.

Because of her attitude, Blaaze figured Miss Templeton could hold her pretty little horses. And he didn't mean that "pretty" literally.

He'd pay up when he got good and ready and not a minute before.

"It's the principle of the thang," he finally replied.

"What principle? You mean the principle of you being difficult for the hell of it, as usual?" Tobias moved to hide the jar of moonshine.

Blaaze snatched it back before the big man could and scowled. What a total mischaracterization of his nature. He was not a difficult man. He'd simply gotten a bad reputation for a few misunderstandings is all. But he wasn't about to launch into a useless defense of himself. It wouldn't have done him much good with Tobias anyway. Once Tobias got his mind to something, it stayed got.

"You can scowl all you want." Tobias leaned against the barrel again and crossed his arms with a smug grin. "I've never known you to let a woman get under your skin this way. Guess I got the answer to what's ticking your hide. Well, other than whatever made you bleed onto your favorite shirt." Tobias pointed at the stained shirt peeking from beneath Blaaze's duster and vest. "This Mary Catherine Templeton must be quite a lady, shrew and all that she be, to put the mighty Blaaze Lassiter into a tiff."

Blaaze went to toss the jar of moonshine at his friend but thought better of wasting the precious brew.

Tobias's deep laughter was his reward.

"Makes me wonder," Tobias said. "Is the staunch loner about to find out that no man can remain detached forever no matter his obstinate determination? Seems beddin' 'em and leavin' 'em without a thought may be coming back to haunt you, ole drifter. Looks like you've found you a woman who's causing you all the thinking without the benefit of any of the beddin'." He paused dramatically. "Yet."

"Don't be ridiculous," Blaaze said in a clipped tone. He might be feening for some coupling, but he wasn't *that* desperate. He wasn't taking that woman anywhere near a bed. Where he planned to lead her was straight to a stagecoach out of town as soon as feasibly possible. She didn't belong in Lawless, and certainly not as owner of the one place in town a man could be a man without interruption to his drinking or whatever else he had in mind.

"A man only wants to do two things with a woman who makes him feel that way," Tobias surmised.

Blaaze was almost afraid to hear his friend's two suggestions. The man had an uncanny way of intuiting events before they happened.

Tobias stood. "Avoid her or screw her till neither one of them can think straight." He picked up his ball-peen hammer, returned the tool to its place, then looked back at Blaaze. "Which way you leanin'?"

An uneasy shiver ran down Blaaze's spine, but he pushed it aside. He wasn't interested in Tobias's prophesying and didn't bother answering the absurd question. Nothing was getting him tangled up with that woman. He couldn't avoid her at the moment, but bedding her definitely wasn't on his mind.

The thought of the scoldish Miss Mary Catherine Templeton put a full-on damper on his hard-won moonshine bliss. Though she apparently had family ties to Lady Lila, the woman he'd just met was the complete opposite of Lila, whom he now remembered had also been named Templeton. Lila had been from somewhere back east, and once upon a time, Templeton had been her family name. That was why the surname had sounded familiar. Lila had stopped using it shortly after arriving in Lawless. Not that anyone cared what her surname was. Everyone knew her as Lady Lila and that's what she preferred to be called.

If the recently arrived Miss Templeton stuck around as owner of the saloon, saloon life was about to get stale.

He gritted his teeth against the image of Mary Catherine's damp, white blouse molded to a perky, peekaboo breast. He knew he needed to slake his baser needs with a good romp in the sheets, but he still couldn't understand what it was about this woman that had gotten his blood so heated. He knew why she'd gotten him riled. He simply didn't understand why she'd gotten him woody.

She was pretty enough he guessed, in a contained, ladylike sort of way. In all honesty, he hadn't paid much attention to her overall womanly assets. He'd been too distracted by the endowments up top.

Well, and by those big brown eyes above high cheekbones.

Hmm. And that face of flawless walnut skin.

But then there was that mouth of hers that nagged and fussed.

Nagged and fussed with a pouty fullness, something irrepressible prompted from inside him. The lusciousness of those lips conjured illicit thoughts even in the remembering, and there went that wood rising again.

Ugh and dammit! he cursed to himself.

He gave a quick glance in Tobias's direction to make sure the man hadn't noticed his changing state. Last thing he needed to add to this day was giving Tobias Craig a chance to gloat. Best leave the mystery appeal of the new saloon owner for personal deliberation at a more private time.

Instead, he'd fortify himself with another douse or two of moonshine to take the edge off all the frustrations and emotions that had plagued a day that should have been the start of the sweet peacefulness of retirement. Then maybe a second round with Miss Mary Catherine Templeton, intractable saloon owner, might take on a certain appeal.

He did have a room to claim after all.

What would the eastern miss do, he wondered, when she found out he'd be sleeping in her precious saloon? The thought nearly made him smile. Nearly, but not quite.

Replacing the lid on the almost empty mason jar and setting it aside, Blaaze looked up at Tobias. Since most folks came through the livery to stable a horse, shoe a horse, or borrow a horse, Tobias's place sat on the pulse of local information. Blaaze decided to take advantage of his friend's access to key tidbits . . . and the chance to change the subject. He had two puzzles to solve: why nobody in town could wear a gun anymore, and what had happened to Lady Lila.

He figured he'd start with how a woman who'd been the perfect picture of health when he'd last seen her had ended up dead. "Tell me what happened to Lila."

"Wagon accident," Tobias said baldly before moving to handle some equipment.

That surprised Blaaze. "A wagon accident? Lila is . . . *was* an exceptional horsewoman and a more than competent wagon driver."

"Yeah, that's what I thought, too, when I first heard. We'd been having some trouble about town, and the accident occurred shortly after she'd begun having issues of her own with some new rabble-rousers in town. They'd come into town rowdy and boisterous and quick to shoot whomever annoyed them. In fact, their vicious killing sprees is what led to the sheriff calling a halt on wearing weapons in town. Nobody could ever prove they had anything to do with Lila's accident, but we've got our suspicions.

"Shortly after Lila's passing, I heard them boys took on with the brewery owner who settled outside of town about a year or so ago. Claimed he needed help staving off possible thieves intent on stealing from the brewery at night," Tobias added.

"Claimed?"

"*Claimed.*" A hard nod emphasized Tobias's confirmation. "I said what I said. Man keeps that brewery guarded like he's got gold stashed up in there. His men are all loaded for bear. Only idiots would try to steal from his brewery, and people around here just ain't that stupid."

"Hmm." Deep in thought, Blaaze hadn't realized he'd made the murmur aloud.

"Hmm, what?" Tobias asked, stopping his work untangling a mass of bridles.

Blaaze looked Tobias squarely in the eyes. "I would think a town's sheriff would be able to handle them boys without needing everyone else to stash their firearms." He rubbed spread fingers down his bristly chin. "Tell me more of what you know."

~

Mary Catherine occupied a table in a back room of the saloon and listened to Lila's attorney review the books of account.

Soaked and unkempt, she sat embarrassed before the man. All because of some ne'er-do-well who traipsed the streets with manners that behooved someone raised with wolves.

Proper attire and a well-groomed person went a long way toward presenting a formidable presence when confronting people who threatened your wellbeing or could impact the achievement of your dreams. Mary Catherine had faced teasing as a child from peers when her clothes hadn't been as fashionable as theirs. Since her father had taught at Cleveland High School, she'd been privileged to attend the city's first public high school when a lot of families only sent their sons. But the Templetons hadn't had the same money as many of the other families, at least not during the time she'd matriculated.

Thanks to that experience, she'd quickly figured out that having less-than could be disguised by not looking like you had less-than. And even after her parents' financial status had improved, and she had truly had the social acceptance she'd previously craved, she had never let herself be caught unkempt in public.

Until today.

Nothing about her appearance suggested a formidable presence. She currently lacked both proper attire and a well-groomed person. All her attention to detail to present herself to the people of Lawless and make a good first impression on her new employees had been for naught.

The cowboy had taken that away from her with his mal behavior. The man had likely-predator written over every inch of his person—unbathed as it had been—and she looked like something a cat had scrounged from an alley and dropped at its owner's feet. Without her usual impeccable, external armor, she had felt at a disadvantage before the man that her smaller size alone would never have caused.

The look he'd given her when she'd called him to task for the broken window and his role in the state of her clothes had made her fear the man might pull a gun on her at any moment. She still wasn't sure he wouldn't have absent the crowd, but she'd recovered quickly from the momentary lapse in aplomb. Any display of weakness before a man like that would lead to quick persecution or fast death. Neither boded well for her long-term plans for survival in this wild territory.

No matter. She hadn't let the man see her shaken confidence.

All the better, she had regrouped and not let the incident actually derail her confidence—at least not in full, and not in a way anyone could see. She'd kept up appearances as best she could under the circumstances. Still, the ruffian's words ricocheted through her brain like the ominous portents he'd meant them to be. *"But I'll be back."*

He'd seemed a man of his word. For their next go-round, she wasn't at all certain she'd be the one to come out the victor. Relief had flooded her as she'd watched him lazily saunter out of the saloon. Although she wanted—no, *needed*— his restitution money, she also needed to find a way to collect on the damages he'd caused without having to face the man again. Perhaps she could get the attorney to collect for her. She was going to have to learn quickly not only how to run a saloon but also how to handle bigger-than-life frontiersmen like Blaaze Lassiter.

The fire in those dessert-colored eyes, and everything else about the man, came into full memory: tall, hatted, clothed in that long duster, a languorous mosey of complete command, and a deep voice like gravel smothered in the most decadent patisserie cream. When he was around, everything else faded into oblivion. Her pulse thudded, and she almost shivered again. The man was dangerous—in more ways than one.

Was that the kind of clientele this saloon attracted?

If so, she wondered again what she possibly could have gotten herself into. She wanted the means to support herself independently through a business enterprise. She wanted the means to salvage her family's home and legacy of property ownership. But ruffians and gunmen and scantily clad, painted ladies? Those were out of her realm of experience.

She began to wonder if she could do this.

She took a deep breath. Of course, she could do this.

Couldn't she . . .?

Shoring up what remaining confidence she could muster after the events of the morning, she returned her attention to the attorney-at-law. He stared at her expectantly. She'd obviously missed a question or some grand revelation he awaited her to be impressed by.

"I beg your pardon, sir. What did you say?" she asked.

He smiled at her indulgently. That smile men often gave women they felt they had to humor because of the presumed mental inferiority of the female gender. "I understand that it can be a bit much for you to understand all at once but know that I'm available any time to help you. You can check with Charlie Wheaton, the bartender, about the day-to-day financial matters since your cousin's passing. He's been handling the bar purchases and payments over the last few months. I was only engaged to oversee the legal matters and manage the transfer of property rights. But I'd be happy to have my office manager keep the saloon's books of account for you so you can focus solely on running the business. No need to overwhelm yourself with all the details right at the start."

Mary Catherine smiled back with a faux, saccharine upturn of lips. "Why thank you, Mr. Blakely. I certainly appreciate the offer."

She reached for the ledgers in front of him. Actually, they weren't true ledgers, more like notebooks someone had filled with lists and columns of figures that were designed to hold the mysteries of saloon life and all its profits.

Nevertheless, she slid them to her side of the table. "I think I'll be fine. But if I need you, I will absolutely call on you."

His expression fell for the briefest of seconds before he managed to gather his aplomb and falsely return her smile. Her refusal of his assistance had not been expected.

Tight-lipped, he gave her a quick nod. "Why certainly."

One of the attorney's earlier statements made a delayed impression on Mary Catherine's dazed mental state. *"No need to overwhelm yourself with all the details right from the start."*

Overwhelm herself from the start? The cad.

Like every other man she'd encountered during her quest to use her degree in a professional capacity, he considered her to be incapable of managing a business or its financial matters. *As if* she would call on a man for services who assumed "from the start" that she was incapable.

Never in this lifetime.

She'd show Mr. Blakely and everyone else in this town. After all, it couldn't be half as hard as finishing a bachelor's degree in mathematics in the top percentage of your class at a well-known and respected college. Her alma mater had been co-founded by Underground Railroad facilitator Owen Brown, father of the rebel abolitionist John Brown. The latter was known for leading a raid on the federal armory at Harper's Ferry in 1859 in his quest to start a liberation movement for those enslaved.

Thanks to the advocacy of Owen Brown, who served as one of the college's first trustees, and others like him, Oberlin College was the first predominantly white institution in America to admit men of the Race. In 1837, it began admitting women to become the first co-educational college in the land. Men like the Browns had done much to make sure her people had access to the same education and liberties as whites in this country. She had no intention of squandering that education or opportunity. Even if she had to take advantage of such opportunities—still limited as they were— by running something as unexpected as a saloon.

Mentally refortified and staunchly determined, Mary Catherine stood to dismiss the man. She looked down at her blouse. It had dried some, but she was not close to proper. Completely wrinkled, the blouse also retained a dingy hue from the trough water. Nevertheless, she began to remove the jacket he had loaned her so she could return it.

He motioned her to keep it on. "No. No. You hold on to that for now, miss." His pale face turned a bright shade of red. "You have more need for it than I at the moment. I'll collect it from you another time."

Mary Catherine tried not to blush at the memory of why she had a need of it more than him. The barely shielded bosom the unmannerly Mr. Lassiter had stared at so boldly had been on display for Mr. Blakely as well. Though she'd managed to resituate her corset, that the man remembered what once could be seen beneath his suit coat was evident in his expression.

Mortified, she nonetheless managed to thank the man and offered him her hand to shake.

With gentlemanly indulgence, he shook her hand then

gathered his leather satchel. "I'll be sure to check on you by the end of the week," he said before he headed out the back door.

Mary Catherine dropped back into her seat, her back straight and butt perched such that she didn't lean all the way back into the chair. Even a touch overwhelmed, she automatically maintained the proper posture instilled in her from an early age. She placed a hand on the notebooks in front of her.

Mr. Blakely had explained that his audit of the business immediately after Lila's death had determined the saloon was doing okay. Supply purchases and employee wages were being covered by the saloon's revenue, and there was a little left over in the bank for her to live on, but not much. If she was going to make any kind of life for herself, she would need to increase profits substantially.

The attorney had gone over most of the more obvious debit and credit entries in the notebooks, but she'd noticed during his run-through that several accounts were dappled with codes and abbreviations. She'd have to decipher what they all meant and get access to the books of account containing the debit and credits incurred since the attorney's audit. Perhaps she'd discover a stash of cash suitable to replace the large, glass pane broken by the gruff cowboy.

Speaking of which, that broken window had a frame that still gaped wide open. She needed to address that immediately. She could not have patrons entering through a hole in the wall, and if she was to begin inhabiting Lila's old rooms upstairs, she'd need the safety of a sealed building.

Oddly comforted to have something concrete to focus on, Mary Catherine stood and gathered the notebooks against her chest. Window first, then employee introductions, then arrangements to get her belongings moved upstairs. Afterward, she'd settle in and decode the notations in the books she held.

Mr. Blakely had promised to check on her at the end of the week. What a long week it was going to be, especially if somewhere in the midst of all her tasks the tall, hatted, moseying Mr. Lassiter came back a-calling as he'd promised.

CHAPTER 6

BLAAZE SAT AT THE bar after returning to the saloon and turned toward the window he'd broken using a man-sized bludgeon. His mouth, momentarily forgetting it didn't like to smile, curved upward at one edge for half a second.

The markings on that window had been the source of much commotion when Lila had first taken over the saloon. *Lady Lila's* had arched in large, curly red letters across the entire top center of the pane, with *Den of Spirits* in smaller, block white letters in a straight line underneath.

He remembered the first time Lila had painted that window. The women of the town had been furious, and the men had been taken aback by the new name. A tough, world-wise woman, Lila had taken over the saloon when her beau—the recalcitrant, blond-haired prior owner—had pissed off the wrong drunk and taken a bullet he couldn't recover from. Lila had run the place after her man's death despite the towns-folk's protest over a woman taking charge of the preferred gentlemen's gathering place.

The harbinger of unwanted change, the window had promptly—and mysteriously—been smashed. Lila had swiftly replaced the glass, but the vandalism kept recurring. Each time her pane got broken, Lila had purchased a new one and had the letters on the window painted bigger and brighter with each replacement.

One of the few proprietors of color on Main Street, Lila had been determined to maintain the legacy left to her, and she wasn't going to let being a woman stop her. The two of them had become comrades over time, and he'd become a frequent visitor to the saloon. Not one to suffer bullies and appreciative of a curvaceous woman full of unrepentant sensuality and sass, Blaaze had occasionally had to lend his backup to Lila's stand when a certain rowdy element saw fit to damage more than windows.

Eventually, the sheriff had taken an interest in the place, and Lila had had all the protection she needed. That and the reasonable fear that Lady Lila might soon take to putting signs on the walkway out front or having rouged ladies sashay the streets with them, the window smashers had finally relented. The anonymous bullies had learned the hard way that when you poked at Lady Lila, the usually affable creature would unsheathe her claws.

With a slow glance around the establishment, Blaaze looked for the new proprietress. Mary Catherine Templeton was as unlike her cousin as any woman he'd ever met. The easterner would be chewed up and spit out by this rough community and unforgiving frontier. He didn't understand what could have possessed a lady like her to move to Lawless, Kansas, of all places. And take over a saloon, no less.

Not finding the lady of interest, Blaaze turned back to the nervous beanpole behind the bar who stood mutely in observance of him. "Where's the new lady of the house?"

The man looked at Blaaze as though he thought Blaaze was going to jump over the counter and beat him senseless. Blaaze nearly shook his head, finding it baffling why his simple question made the barkeep so nervous.

"Um, the lady hasn't returned from her business meeting as of yet, sir." He glanced over Blaaze doubtfully. "If you're looking for personal entertainment, I could see if Miss Charlotte would indulge you."

Charlotte? Blaaze looked around the place for said Charlotte but didn't see her. No doubt he'd likely find her upstairs engaged in some of that entertainment he'd just been offered. A tall, leggy blonde with a tough-as-nails disposition, Charlotte wasn't anywhere near his preferred brand of female indulgence. Despite his woeful musings on the trail, he wasn't of a mind to start paying for his companionship, particularly not with Charlotte. He'd seek his entertainment elsewhere.

Blaaze gave the bartender the same doubtful once over he'd just received. Was this dude currently the one who managed the upstairs amenities? Blaaze puzzled over the possibility. What he saw of the man did little to suggest he had the presence or backbone Lila would trust to handle her entertainment business even in an executor capacity.

Had so much changed after all in the time Blaaze been gone?

Four years, three months, and twenty-two days, he reminded himself. Guess some things *did* change.

Too tired to delve into the specifics, Blaaze perused the bottles of spirits shelved in neat rows across the wall behind the barkeep and nodded at another unopened bottle of whiskey. "Not currently interested in any entertainment 'ceptin your best bottle of whiskey." He tossed a silver dollar onto the scuffed wood before him, assuming he'd be paying for this second bottle despite not having had the opportunity to drink the first—due to no fault of his own. "Put the remainder on my tab."

As the twirling coin wound down to stillness, Blaaze heard a sharp, female intake of breath. One foot on the bar's footrest, the other planted on the ground, he made a slow swivel on his stool to see Mary Catherine Templeton emerge from the back room, a set of notebooks gripped firmly against her chest.

She went still upon laying eyes on him. Time stood still while she took in the sight of him, still unkempt—intentionally. He'd done it to spite her uppity assumptions about him earlier, but now he somewhat regretted still being the unbathed, trail-weary heathen he'd appeared when they'd first met.

Eventually, the lady found her voice. "What are you doing here?" The proper eastern accent and carefully enunciated words once again reminded him of the chastising voice of a schoolmarm.

Blaaze unhurriedly uncapped the bottle of whiskey beside him and reverently poured two fingers into the tumbler on the bar. Lifting the tumbler to his lips, he took a long, slow drink that drained the tumbler of its contents before he sat the glass gingerly back on the bar using only his thumb and index finger.

Without releasing the glass, he looked at her and said with a solemn intensity, "I had a drink to finish."

Glancing at the whiskey bottle beside him, the lady's eyes narrowed, and Blaaze could see the fume sparking beneath her composed exterior.

"I thought I made it clear you wouldn't be served here

until you paid for the damages you caused." She stood with her back straight and made her statement with an air of utmost authority despite still sporting a man's suit coat and looking two shades above a drowned cat.

She'd abandoned the droopy hat and its annoying feather somewhere. And while no longer in the neat style she'd probably left her quarters with this morning, her damp hair coiled loosely at the base of her neck. She'd tucked a pencil upright in the coil, and a few wispy, dark tendrils of her thick, partially tamed tresses flowed in loose waves around her oval face and perfect complexion.

Not that he noticed things like wispy tendrils or flawless complexions on women.

Usually.

Forcing himself not to notice those traits on her either, Blaaze internally puzzled over how the lady could look prim and proper in a damp blouse and wilty-looking skirt, but somehow the lady managed.

She approached the bar but made sure to stop a few steps from his seat.

He poured another finger of whiskey and took a dramatic, noisy sip, before he responded to her non-question. "You did."

She turned to glare at the bartender, clearly upset he'd deigned to ignore her earlier declaration. Looking back at Blaaze, she advised, "Well, you can just finish that drink and depart forthwith."

Forthwith? Blaaze contemplated the word. Fancy talk to go with the fancy miss. "Can't do that," he finally replied.

"What do you mean, you can't do that?"

"I can't do that because I'm boarding here tonight and for the next few weeks." He touched his hand lightly to the brim of his hat and nodded his head at her to salute the occasion.

Her mouth fell open, and she dropped the notebooks onto the bar. "No! Absolutely not."

He stood, towering at least a head above her. Since the early regulars had thinned and the evening crowd had not yet filled in, no one intervened on the lady's behalf this time. Not that anyone needed to intervene. He'd never hurt the woman, but he had no intention of letting her push him around.

"Yes. Absolutely. In fact, I'd already paid for my room before the minor altercation that caused that little gap in your wall." He motioned in the direction of the massive hole now being evaluated by two carpenters.

She followed his motion and noticed for the first time that men were measuring her wall. "What are they planning to do with those boards?"

"Board up the hole, of course." He shrugged. "Unless you'd like us to leave it open so's anyone can come remove the furniture hereabouts and any of those lovely spirits shelved in full view behind your bar."

Her mouth dropped opened again.

He leaned toward her and placed a bent finger under her chin to close her mouth. "You might want to stop leaving your mouth open, sugar. You're gonna start catching flies."

To his utter—hidden—amusement, she swatted his hand away almost daintily.

Ignoring his smart-ass comment, she insisted, "It's not boards you need to have installed, Mr. Lassiter. But a window."

"I understand that, ma'am," he said, sliding into his aw-shucks drawl. "But we can't get glass delivered this quickly. It'll take some time, so the boards are the best I can offer for the time being."

That wasn't exactly true, but she didn't know any better.

He propped a boot back onto the bar footrest, leaned on one elbow against the bar, and said with all seriousness, "That is, of course, assuming I get my room."

Her schoolmarm air of authority faltered, as did her expression. "Wh-what?"

~

Mary Catherine couldn't believe what she'd just heard. Surely, the man was not serious.

The cowboy straightened and gathered the bottle of whiskey from the counter. "If I'm being banished until glass is reinstalled, then the hole in your wall stays until you find someone else to fix it." He turned toward the carpenters. "Hold up there, Miguel. Seems the little miss has changed her mind about fixin' up that hole."

"*Perdón, jefe?*" One of the two men, both of whose complexions and attire revealed them to be of Mexican heritage, asked before giving her a look that suggested the man worried for her sanity.

Mary Catherine didn't speak much Spanish, but she knew enough to understand the two carpenters took their orders from the cowboy, and she was about to be left with a hole in the wall big enough for a wagon team to jump through until such time as she, herself, could figure out how to fix it. New to town and not having yet ferreted out the full services and amenities the town had to offer, she doubted it was a task she could pull off by bedtime.

"You can't do that!" She took an anxious step forward. "You owe me that window."

He shrugged at her again. What an annoying habit.

"And you owe me that room. It was a bargain fairly made, and paid for, before our little incident. For which, I might add, you improperly blamed me."

She started to speak, but he lifted one long, lone index finger to stop her.

"Uh-uh," he crooned with a wave of that elevated digit. "Let me finish," he said before he dropped the admonishing hand. "I was just defending myself. Doesn't seem fair to leave a man without sleeping quarters due to a simple misunderstanding and a rather unavoidable accident."

"I'd not go as fair as to say it was *unavoidable*, Mr. Lassiter. You need only have controlled your temper." She thrust her hands onto her hips in an effort to control her own temper. "And that's the equivalent of blackmail, you … you … *heathen*."

His brows shot upward in mock surprise at her insult.

A twinge of chagrin hit her over her lack of decorum. Her mother would be appalled, but this scoundrel was toying with her. His put-on disinterested manner, his sarcastic chiding, and even his false sense of outrage over her jibe evidenced his utter lack of consideration for her position in this establishment.

"Blackmail is such a *strong* word, Miss Templeton," he drawled. "I'd say it's more of a … heated negotiation. My offer stands as issued. Take it or leave it."

Mary Catherine glared openly at him. She'd been holding it together nicely, but he was determined to push her over the edge. Worse, he seemed to be getting a perverse pleasure from taunting her. His heavy-handed ploy to make her give in had finally shaken loose the fume she'd been trying to control from the moment she'd spotted him boldly sitting at her bar with a bottle of whiskey.

Squinty-eyed, he returned her look with the same flat expression he must use when he faced off with a man. He looked every bit the gunslinger she'd thought he was the first time she'd seen him out her boarding house window. Still, she didn't blink, and she didn't look away. She also didn't respond.

He gave her half a second more before he poked at the mad she was trying to get under control. "Well?" he asked, his knee bent slightly forward such that it lent a cocky tilt to his stance.

That aura of power he exuded pervaded the space. The stained shirt and travel grime he'd yet to shed didn't hide the innate virility that seeped from his pores. Clearly, he was a man used to getting what he wanted, and he wasn't above a little underhandedness to get it. How dare he try to blackmail her into giving him a room upstairs. Torn between anger, frustration, and annoyance, she was about to tell him so when a man entered the saloon through the propped open double doors.

"Greetings," he said, removing his hat in deference to her female presence before he glanced at the huge hole where the window used to be. "Well now, this looks to be a mighty fine problem." He shook his head and tsked under his breath. "Saloon management can be quite unpredictable."

The stranger tweaked the top points of his hat absently while he surveyed the place.

When he'd looked his fill, he stepped over to Mary Catherine. "Howdy. Name's Jake Clanton. You must be Miss Templeton. Miss Mary Catherine Templeton, that is." He offered her his hand and an ingratiating grin. "I'd heard said the new saloon owner was another woman. So I had to come see for myself."

Mary Catherine placed her hand in his.

Rather than shake it, he bent over it and lifted it toward his mouth. "They left out the part about what a beauty you were, however," he said, and then kissed the back of her hand.

Out of the corner of her eye, Mary Catherine saw Blaaze Lassiter lean on the bar and cock himself at an angle to watch her interaction with the newcomer. The blackguard made no effort to hide the rolling of his eyes.

In her present state of rumpledness, she was barely presentable, let alone a beauty. So she had no misconceptions about Mr. Clanton's genuineness. The man was laying on the charm—a bit thick and a bit obvious.

She accepted the compliment graciously, nonetheless. "Thank you, Mr. Clanton. It's a pleasure to make your acquaintance. Would you like some refreshment?"

Mr. Clanton glanced at one of the barmaids with a decidedly ungentlemanly look in his eyes, before he answered. "No, but thank you. I don't have time today to accept the benefits of your hospitality. I've come on a business matter." He reached inside his jacket and pulled out a business card. "I own the brewery just outside of town. I've been supplying the saloon with beer and spirits on credit until the new owner— that'd be you, apparently—could arrive and settle up accounts. I'm not one to kick a man . . . or, er, a woman, you see, when she's dealing with a loss in the family. So I let this matter slide as long as I could."

Without reply, Mary Catherine glanced at the information on his card.

"Now that you're here, and I assume the estate has been properly transferred to you, we need to square up our business." He took a quick look around with a greedy gleam in his eyes that expanded from the barmaid to the saloon as a whole.

An uncomfortable feeling invaded Mary Catherine. Something told her this man wanted to do more than simply square up accounts.

"Perhaps you and I could be of service to each other. You don't seem the type to run a house of spirits and such." Jake Clanton's eyes cut to the barmaid once more.

The inappropriately open lust in his eyes appalled Mary Catherine. Though the woman in question, as well of most of the other servers in the place, was more undressed than dressed—a situation Mary Catherine intended to remedy with appropriately modest attire—none of the women deserved to be openly leered at.

Mary Catherine cleared her throat indecorously to regain Mr. Clanton's attention.

He nonchalantly grinned off the misdeed and ran a hand down the front of his shirt. "My apologies for the distraction. As I was saying, you don't seem the type to run a house of spirits and such, so perhaps I can offer a solution to benefit us both." He motioned with his hat to the card in her hand. "On the back of my card is an offer to buy the place from you. Cash on the spot."

And there it was, she thought.

"We'll consider your tab paid in full, and you won't even have to cover the current damages to this place. We'll call it all even, and you can go set yourself up in a seamstress shop or some such or find a nice gentleman to marry. We've certainly got enough bachelors in the town environs." He smiled as if he'd given her the tip of a lifetime.

Mary Catherine narrowed her eyes at his mention of marriage. Bad enough he'd come to relieve her of her business. He had to add a little flimflam to the mix—flatter the poor, in-over-her-head woman then try to take her jewels. In a manner of speaking.

Just another man set to underestimate her. She'd had her share of those. Her fiancé who'd tried to get her to sell her parents' home and set a wedding date, the bank executives who'd doused her employment dreams, and now this man wanted to join the bunch.

She didn't know why she'd dared to hope men spirited enough to attempt to tame a frontier might be a little more forward-thinking where women were concerned.

Her mistake.

Noticing her aggrieved expression, Jake Clanton corrected himself, "Or do . . . whatever." He chuckled with a shrug and ran his hand down the front of his shirt again. "Let me take all this worry off your hands, miss. What do you say?"

Chapter 7

MARY CATHERINE STARED AT the back of the card she'd been given. Blaaze hadn't missed the indignation in her eyes when Clanton had suggested she marry. That didn't seem to be an option she found particularly appealing, and from the look on her face, Clanton's buyout offer held even less appeal.

"You want . . . to *buy* . . . my saloon?" She looked up at the brewery owner, speculation in her eyes.

While the drawn-out question might impress some as confusion, Blaaze had no misconceptions that this woman was in any manner confused. The intelligence lighting her eyes went part and parcel with that educated diction of hers. He wondered if Clanton had yet figured out he wasn't dealing with some fluff of a female but a woman with a brain sharp enough to cut a man. Something Blaaze had figured out the moment he'd pulled her soaking wet from the trough.

"Mr. Clanton, I only arrived in town yesterday evening, just squared away the legalities of inheriting my cousin's business this morning, and now you want me to simply hand it over to you?"

Yeah, Blaaze had been thinking the same thing.

"Now, Miss Templeton, you wouldn't be simply handing it over. That there is a fine and fair offer for the business, I assure you."

"Since I haven't had time to thoroughly review the books of account, I'll have to reserve my opinion of whether or not the offer is fair. Assuming I were interested in selling, of course. Which I'm not."

"Now don't be hasty with your decision, miss." Clanton twirled his hat in his hands absently. "I realize I may have caught you in the middle of a bit of a situation here. I'm willing to give you time to think things over. What say I come back tomorrow about this same time?"

"That won't be necessary." Mary Catherine crossed her arms over the borrowed suitcoat she still wore, Clanton's card sticking up from her right hand. "I won't have changed my mind by tomorrow."

Clanton started to say something else.

Anticipating where he was going, Mary Catherine cut him off. "Or any other day. My cousin's saloon—*my* saloon—is not for sale. But I thank you for your time." She offered him back his card.

At Mary Catherine's firm words, the false charm evaporated from Clanton's face. "I'm not a heartless man, Miss Templeton. I understand there may be some sentimentality wrapped up in this bequest. Nevertheless, I do have a business to run. If you're not interested in selling to me, then I need your brewery account squared away in full. And that's not an insubstantial sum. You can ask Charlie about the particulars," he said indicating the man standing behind the bar. "I'll give you two weeks."

"Two weeks!" Babs shouted from across the room.

"I thought you said the saloon owed a substantial sum?" a rancher named Mark Petersen asked in an affronted tone.

A low grumble spread throughout the meager crowd, and several frowning men stood up. "Yeah," they said in unison.

"You trying to take advantage of the lady, Clanton?" Mark asked.

"She just got here," Babs added, walking toward Clanton. "How do you expect her to get things in order in two weeks? You'd have never given Lila such terms."

A tight expression lit Jake Clanton's face at the onlookers' interference. He quickly suppressed his emotions and raised his hands in a placating gesture, his hat dangling from one of them. "Now, gentlemen"—he nodded toward Babs—"and ma'am, there's no need to get riled. Of course, I'm going to be fair."

Blaaze didn't consider two weeks very fair, but Mary Catherine had her champions. So he was staying out of it.

Glomming on to the opening Babs had given her, Mary Catherine chimed back in, "It would seem to me, Mr. Clanton, that fair would constitute at least thirty days to settle the saloon's accounts."

Clanton blinked at the lady, clearly surprised by the sharp—and reasonable—counteroffer. He gave her a more discerning once-over before glancing around the room of glaring men and one irate Babs who held a menacingly hot pot of coffee.

He cleared his throat thoughtfully. "Well, I don't see the harm in a couple more weeks. Thirty days it is, Miss Templeton." With a deferential bow, he placed his hat firmly back on his head and exited through the saloon doors.

Eyes on the back of Clanton as he headed across the

street, Mary Catherine walked slowly to the bar. She pulled a piece of paper from a pad under one of the ledgers she'd stacked there.

"Charlie?" She slid the paper toward him, then handed him the pencil she'd plucked from her hair. "Exactly what might this not so insubstantial sum be?"

Charlie wrote a number on the slip of paper she'd given him. When she looked at it, she blanched. A not so insubstantial feat for a brown-skinned woman. She stared stoically at the piece of paper containing the sum total of her brewery debt then at the business card in her other hand. Finally, she looked over at Blaaze.

Without breaking eye contact with Blaaze, she queried the barkeep again. "And Charlie? Exactly how much is Mr. Lassiter paying for this room he reserved?"

Charlie leaned over the bar and whispered the amount to her. Not that this particular amount was any big secret. Folks around here knew the going rates for Lila's upstairs rooms. All of them. Even the ones reserved for the saloon's more popular hospitality service other than boarding and drinking.

Mary Catherine's expression remained impassive. Blaaze considered the woman might make an excellent poker player. She certainly had better control of her features than Tobias.

"That one's a little more expensive because it's the biggest boarding room in the house, and Miss Lila always reserved it for special guests," Charlie added without being prompted.

Mary Catherine surveyed Blaaze from head to toe. Her impassivity slipped a might, and he could almost see her unspoken question. *Exactly how special of a guest were you to Lila?*

The—*imagined?*—look vanished quickly. Resurfaced disapproval of his appearance took its place. Once again, Blaaze lamented having skipped his trip to the barber and the bathhouse. Sometimes his streak of contrariness blew back on him. He needed to remedy both the lack of a shave and a bath mighty quick. The reception he was getting in his current state was beginning to mess with his pride.

"Okay, Mr. Lassiter," Mary Catherine said. "You want to board here? Then you can. So long as you pay double what Mr. Charlie quoted you."

Coming up behind Mary Catherine, Babs whistled. "Double? Woo, now."

Mary Catherine simply glanced over her shoulder and shrugged.

Blaaze cocked a brow at the Templeton woman when she looked back at him. Yeah, what Babs said. *Double?*

"That being my best—and biggest—room, I need to make sure I get top rates for it." She smiled for the first time since he'd met her. The smile came full on and suggested a little devilment in her current ploy. "As you witnessed, I have bills to pay. So I can't be irresponsible with my amenities." Her smile widened into a not-very-discreet challenge. "That's my best offer. Take it or leave it."

"Responsible?" he grumbled. "More like a fleecing." But Blaaze couldn't really blame her.

He'd put her up against a wall with her broken window. Clanton had put her up against a wall with his demand for full payment of her account. She'd decided to do what any animal does when backed into corner. Go on the offensive.

Good for her. The unbidden thought surprised him, but seems he'd been right about that sharp brain of hers. She was not only sharp but quick.

Dammit, he thought. While his pockets could handle the markup, it didn't mean he liked getting one-upped by a gal.

The lady didn't belong in Lawless, but he had to admire

her quick-wittedness and determination. Based upon what he'd learned about Clanton from Tobias, though, this naive gumption of hers was going to get her tangled up with a passel of snakes that were going to take her down with a few poisonous bites she'd likely not see coming. Blaaze needed to make sure he stuck around to protect her from herself until such time as he could get Miss Templeton to come to her senses and flee the premises . . . not just the saloon but the town altogether.

"All right, Miss Templeton, we'll do things your way," Blaaze said.

A slight flinch beneath her right eye was the only sign he'd surprised her with his agreement. No one else in the place likely caught the movement. But when your life depended on how fast a man could draw, you learned to notice every eye twitch and every finger flick.

Yeah, the woman would make one hell of a poker player.

With a wave of his hand, Blaaze grabbed the attention of the carpenters and motioned to the window. "Go ahead and get 'er done."

"*Sí, amigo*," Miguel replied and got to work with his partner.

As Blaaze looked back at Mary Catherine, he thought about the what-for she'd been about to give him before Clanton had walked in and the look she'd given Clanton when he'd suggested she find a nice man to marry. Miss Mary Catherine Templeton had a temper. She hid it beneath well-bred manners, but the lady had a rile underneath all that proper. He made a mental note of the information. The eastern miss would need more of that fire to survive unscathed in this town until such time as he could convince her to go back where she came from for her own good.

Clanton's offer might be the solution to sending Miss East packing. According to Tobias, the man had been buying up businesses and making promises ever since the railroad extension had stopped only a short stagecoach ride outside of Lawless. Yet something about the way Clanton had gone about his offer didn't sit well with Blaaze.

The brewery owner had tried to scare Mary Catherine into making a hasty decision, which made Blaaze wonder just how fine and fair his offer to buy had been. Blaaze also wondered why Clanton was in such an all-fire hurry to get the transaction done and settled so quickly.

This second issue in particular made Blaaze's senses twitch. The same senses had kept him alive on the trail of more than one outlaw. A bounty hunter—or marshal, *ugh*—needed to be able to sense danger before he could see it. A man often got dead before he saw trouble coming. And Blaaze's intuition said Clanton, despite his charm and show of manners as proper as Miss Templeton's, was trouble and more.

He recognized that maybe some hypocrisy was at play in his considering. After all, Blaaze had done basically the same thing to the woman when bartering the window repair for a room. The twinge of guilt he'd felt when recognizing his own devious tactics had, in part, been the impetus behind his agreement to pay a higher price for the room.

But to offer cash on the spot for the saloon? No questions asked?

Clanton was rumored to be a shrewd and unrelenting businessman with enough hired muscle to help him intimidate the uncooperative. So was he simply driving a hard bargain with Mary Catherine or was there more to it?

Seemed asking some questions about Clanton might be in

order.

With a sharp shake of his head, Blaaze pulled his mental figurings up short. *What the hell was he thinking?*

He adjusted his Stetson and reminded himself that this matter was none of his business. Underhandedness or criminal activity in Lawless was not his assignment, and he needed to leave well enough alone.

He was retired.

The woman currently held only one interest to him: a temporary room. He needed a room until he could raise a roof on his own place out on the acres of land he'd bought to start raising and training horses. Other than that, she was none of his concern. And he intended to leave it that way.

She'd soon figure out how to handle Jake Clanton. Or not. In a few weeks, maybe she'd actually be gone. With Clanton's money in her pocket, she'd have no reason to stay, and the saloon could go back to the haven it had been.

Mary Catherine gathered her notebooks from the bar and hugged them to her chest. "Fine. You can stay. But Mr. Lassiter?"

He gave her his full attention.

"You might want to make use of a tub if we have any on premises." She paused to make sure her comment hit the mark. "And mind that I'll expect you to follow the house rules," she added before heading toward the back.

Ignoring the barb about a tub, Blaaze watched her walk away. His eyes strayed to the sway of her hips, noticeable despite the unflattering presence of the attorney's suit coat.

He ignored the smirk Babs directed his way when she caught where his gaze had landed. He was too busy thinking about Mary Catherine's last words.

The house rules? He wondered what in the dickens those

could possibly be.

~

Three days later, Mary Catherine dragged herself back to her room and dropped her field notebook on the desk in the corner. She was exhausted. After poring over the saloon's books for two nights straight, spending several days doing inventory of all supplies on hand, then taking time to count the many rooms in this place as well as survey the town itself, she'd worked up a plan to bring more dining business into the saloon.

During that time, she'd only had brief moments to talk with a few of the serving ladies about wearing less revealing clothing. They'd looked at her quizzically but hadn't argued much. She'd wanted to speak to Barbara Jean about the situation, but the older woman had gone visiting in a neighboring town and wasn't due back until tonight. Charlotte hadn't been around either, which was unfortunate because Charlotte's wardrobe particularly needed work.

To add to her current challenges, Mary Catherine had learned that several of the women didn't own any conservative dresses. She'd have to add some dresses to the purchases she planned for tonight's supper sitting. The ladies would need to be well presented for her dining plan to work. She'd have to approximate sizes, but anything was better than what they'd been wearing.

She walked over to one of the open account notebooks she'd pored over last night. Some of the notations still didn't make sense. Shorthand had been used to indicate some paths of income, but what the shorthand stood for wasn't readily apparent. For instance, certain rooms were coded with a

"BH." Those rooms must be the smaller rooms on the middle level because their nightly income was substantially less than the rooms marked "SR."

This wasn't standard bookkeeping notation, and she'd been unable to surmise what the letters could be shorthand for. Plus, those noted with an SR didn't appear to make the same income each night. The amounts varied by week and sometimes from night to night even when all the rooms were occupied. Some nights the figures were so high, Mary Catherine was certain someone had made a notation error.

Friday nights especially were profitable but Sundays hardly ever. Maybe establishments had slower business on churchgoing days. That would make sense for a business based primarily on the sale of spirits like her saloon.

But what about the weekdays? The numbers simply didn't add up.

Mary Catherine snapped shut the notebook she perused. Her shoulders rose and fell with the huge breath she inhaled and pushed out through her mouth. With a tug, she freed the gold chain around her neck from beneath the collar of her dress and pulled out the watch dangling between her breasts. Etched on the front with gold filigree flowers, the watch had been a gift to her mother from her father on their tenth wedding anniversary. The inscription on the back read, *All my love. Always.*

Mary Catherine kept it close to her heart as a memento of them both. It was her way to have something of them with her since she'd had to leave everything else behind in Cleveland until she could return to redeem her family home and appropriately provide for the future maintenance of the property. All she had to do was make this business a success.

Absently, she worried the chain of her mother's watch

and pondered her predicament. She could ask the lawyer if he knew what the notations meant, but she'd rather stay in the dark than give him the satisfaction of thinking himself right about the business being "a bit much" for her to handle or that she'd be "overwhelmed" by the details. She'd considered asking Charlie, who had apparently been managing the saloon since Lila's passing. But the last thing she wanted was to have another man assume she couldn't handle the management of her business or the accurate keeping of books of account.

The employees needed to have some confidence in her abilities to run the saloon. They'd given every indication she looked like a fish out of water. She had no intention of proving she *was* a fish out of water.

Even now, more than a week later, she could still hear the condescending tone of that pompous, last bank executive back home when he'd explained her *supposed* lack of suitability for the employment she had gone to seek. He'd rambled on and on about some foolishness, but she had stopped listening to his words after a minute or so. She'd heard it all before at every other bank at which she'd sought a position.

His interview had been her third bank that month and the last major bank prospect in the city. The responses to her bank applications had all been the same. No one wanted to hire a woman—especially a Colored woman—to handle monetary accounts. Plus, it didn't help that the bankers in town knew of her arranged betrothal to Mr. Beauregard III and considered her search for employment a mere distraction until she started a family.

Her father's arrangement of marriage for her into a family of the Beauregards' status and wealth before he'd succumbed to his illness had been his well-intentioned attempt to secure a good life for her. As heir to a clothing business started by a great-great-and-more-greats grandfather who had emigrated from England to the northern colonies as a free man, her fiancé came from a family that had never known enslavement. Their family business had thrived generation after generation until they were one of the wealthiest families, of any race, in the east.

The abandoned Jeremiah Dixon Beauregard III cut a swarthy figure for sure, but he was as traditional as a man could come and had never understood her desire to work, and in banking no less. She had great affection for Jeremiah. Their families had been friends long before she'd been born. Regardless, she'd made it perfectly clear more than once she had no intention of marrying the man.

He remained content to ignore her. He'd given her space after the last of her parents had died, convinced she'd simply needed time to grieve and come to her senses. After all, what woman of right mind would turn down the chance to be wife and mother to the next generation born into the Beauregard textile empire?

Well, her apparently.

Admittedly, she'd considered a time or two—or a dozen—that perhaps she was being foolish. But in her heart, if not her head, the same question repeatedly arose to taunt her: How could she even consider marriage to a man who would never see her as an individual but merely as an extension of himself?

While her family had been free for over a hundred years prior to the passing of the Thirteenth Amendment, the men in her family had worked primarily in physical labors until her father's father and her father himself had become learned men and educators. The Templeton women comprised a long line of strong and strong-willed leaders of their families, but none had gone to college or desired to work outside the home—until her.

The division of labor her female ancestors upheld to prosper the families of each generation had made sense for them. Mary Catherine was looking for something different—something more. She hadn't studied for years to earn a bachelor's degree in mathematics so she could only become some prosperous man's housekeeping and childrearing wife. Maybe that made her not completely right and proper, but she had nothing against housekeeping or childrearing.

Women who aspired to dedicate themselves to hearth and home were an inspired and stalwart lot. Her mother had been one such woman. But Catherine wanted—deserved—a profession and a life she could direct on her own.

If she could do that *and* be a wife, she'd likely have no objection to a traditional marriage. As it stood, most of the women she knew back in Cleveland had little voice or partnership in their marriages and certainly no control over money, not even their household funds. By Mary Catherine's way of thinking, a man who was afraid of a woman with a learned brain, capable of handling money on her own, and maybe espousing an opinion or two, wasn't a man one wanted to share a roof with for the rest of one's life.

A woman might as well make her own way.

She'd always been good with numbers and found she had a knack for ciphering, even large figures, in her head without need for pencil and paper. Add that to her aptitude for financial matters and business, and she could have been an outstanding bank employee. In fact, she'd always thought she would take Mr. Bishop's, or some man's, executive bank position one day.

Mary Catherine Templeton, Bank President. She smiled to

herself. It had a nice ring to it.

But it was never going to happen.

Accepting that reality, she looked back down at the closed account book, and her smile vanished. Now she was Mary Catherine Templeton, Saloon Owner. This business was all she had to secure the future she wanted, and she needed every bit of her mathematical acumen to decipher its financial mysteries.

She'd figure it out somehow. The business terminology and various income streams would become clearer as she observed the workings of the saloon on a daily basis. They had to. Despite the mounting difficulties of managing the ladies, looming debts, and dealing with ruffians, she had to stand firm on her refusal of Jake Clanton's purchase offer, no matter how tempting.

Money alone would not give her what she wanted. The sale profits wouldn't last forever. She would still have to find employment befitting her expertise someday or marry. If men weren't willing to let her work in a business owned by one of them, she'd build her own, whatever the challenges.

Checking the time, she noted she only had a few hours before she needed to have the saloon ready for the evening patrons. Releasing the watch chain and allowing her mom's watch to hang free, she opted to push her ponderings aside for now. She'd head over to the mercantile for the items she needed. The trip should distract her enough to temporarily ignore the unshakeable feeling that whatever those codes were about to reveal might be something she didn't actually want to know.

The upstairs rooms seemed to hold the key to this place's profitability. One way or another, tonight she'd set herself to uncovering exactly how.

CHAPTER 8

BLAAZE SAUNTERED TOWARD THE mercantile, needing to pick up some packages he'd ordered in Kansas City for delivery here. Straight from the barber's, he rubbed a hand over his close-cropped mustache and smooth jaw. It had been a while since he'd had a shave. He'd been mostly wild and uncivilized for so long, he felt almost naked with a clean-shaven face.

He'd taken care of that first full bath the night he arrived. Mary Catherine's quip about a tub aside, even he hadn't been able to stand the smell of himself long enough to eat dinner. No way could he have slept that way. He'd waited for a shave, though. Since he'd done practically nothing but sleep for forty-eight hours straight, sitting through a shave would have been a waste of time and good money.

A few doors down, he saw Mary Catherine approach the mercantile's door. He hadn't seen her since that first night they'd gone head-to-head. He found he liked the look of her—dry attire notwithstanding. It was curious. She was of medium build and lithe, not usually the type of woman who caught his eye or warmed his bed, even without the smart mouth. He liked someone voluptuous and soft to sink into. He couldn't understand the allure.

Two women walked past her. Apparently not as appreciative of her look as Blaaze, they shot her disparaging looks. Word must have gotten to the town biddies that Mary Catherine now owned the saloon, and the social shunning had begun. He wondered if the easterner had any clue she'd soon be branded Lawless's next immoral outcast.

Head high, Mary Catherine's eyes met theirs with a bold stare. "Ladies," she said in a brisk tone that almost dared them to say words that matched the message in their glares.

Blaaze shook his head. The woman presented with a soft, ladylike vulnerability, but she had a backbone of steel. The contradiction intrigued him, though he still couldn't understand why a woman of her obvious breeding would want to run a saloon and deal with all that came with it. He understood it had been a bequest, but with an offer to purchase on the table, one would think she'd be ready to run back east as fast as she could.

He entered the mercantile a few steps behind her. A bell attached overhead jingled when the door swung open.

The shopkeeper he'd never met looked up as he approached and nodded a greeting. "Mr. Lassiter, I have a package waiting for you. One moment."

Blaaze acknowledged the man's comment with a nod of his own, noting he'd not had to give the man his name. God love a small town. Word got around faster than an influenza epidemic.

He turned to look around the shop as he waited. He spotted Mary Catherine immediately. She sorted through a rack of ready-made dresses. He found the action curious. The mercantile wouldn't have anything near the caliber dress she was used to. Surely, she hadn't run out of her own spiffy clothes in two days.

Then another thought tweaked his conscience. Maybe he'd ruined her yellow outfit when he'd knocked her—*accidentally*—into the trough. He hated to think he'd been the cause of her need to replace attire. She had a large account to settle with the brewery owner and expending funds on a new dress most likely was not included in her budget. The thought fled when he noticed her place several dresses over her arm. No woman needed that many dresses at once, regardless of her status in the community, and certainly not with debts to pay.

"Here you go, Mr. Lassiter." The shopkeeper returned and put a small, brown paper package on the counter.

"I need a few more items. Give me a minute." Blaaze walked away to acquire the items he needed and noted Mary Catherine stood staring at him from behind the dress rack.

She looked much like a deer sighted into paralysis by a wolf: a bit shocked, a bit nervous, and a whole lot of want-to-run.

Acknowledging her, he tapped his hat brim with two fingers, then moved to the rack behind her that held a few of the items he needed. "Miss Templeton," he said in greeting.

Her body tensed at the sound of his voice, and she stared at his face but didn't speak.

He waited for a return greeting. When one didn't come, he asked, "Something wrong?"

The temporary fog lifted from her stunned eyes, but she only managed, "Wh-what?"

Her gaze trailed down his body in a slow scrutiny then settled back on his face. "Mr. Lassiter," she finally replied, an unsteady edge to her voice unlike the termagant he remembered from the other day.

The reply was more question than greeting, but he'd take it because he recognized that look in her eyes. She wasn't simply stunned by his presence. She was stunned by his appearance.

He fought to hold in a grin. Miss Templeton liked the look of his clean-shaven face. He'd been on the receiving end of enough female appreciative looks to recognize the reluctant one she tried to hide. Nice to know he had the ability to get under her skin too.

Brushing behind her, he grabbed the items he needed off the shelf above her head and loosed his satisfied grin behind her back. When he turned around, Mary Catherine had moved to the counter. She stacked the six dresses she'd gathered on top of a stack of folded white linen. The linen sat next to a pile of food staples he suspected she needed for the saloon kitchen.

He sauntered back toward the counter.

The shopkeeper riffled through the garments laid on the counter, then looked up. "Miss Templeton, are you aware these dresses aren't all the same size?"

Mary Catherine looked at Blaaze when he stopped near her shoulder to await his turn. Her hand trembled slightly as she ran a finger down the list she held. Seeming to verify the items against her list, she replied to the man, "Yes, I know. I'll take them all anyway."

The shopkeeper calculated her tab and handed her a receipt. Apparently, Miss Templeton had sorted out the particulars of starting an open account at the mercantile. Blaaze wondered if she'd yet figured out that the store kept a stock of glass panes in the size she needed to replace the saloon window. Lila had always made sure the glass stayed in stock. One never knew when a brawl or a misthrown bottle—or man—might end up taking out the pane.

Accepting her receipt, Mary Catherine thanked the shopkeeper and moved to collect her purchases.

"Wait a minute, miss." The shopkeeper signaled the shop boy. "I'll have the boy bring those over for you. Never you mind."

Mary Catherine nodded her goodbye and headed to leave. Before she crossed the threshold, she hesitated then glanced over her shoulder. Her gaze met Blaaze's and held. Something in the look she gave him—half curious innocence, half unwitting desire—made his pulse leap, as well as the member in his pants. He found he couldn't look away.

She wasn't even wearing see-through clothing today, only a simple gray dress that covered her from neckline to the ankles encased in another pair of those fancy, heeled boots with beads and whatnots all over them. Her sleeves formed loosely over her arms, which appeared shapely enough, but a man didn't get a hard-on from ogling a woman's arms.

Or did he? Blaaze briefly took close stock of her arms. Nice arms, all right, but not a turn on that he could see.

Breaking her visual hold on him with effort, he dug coins out of his pocket and paid his tab. He wasn't one for accounts on credit. He preferred to pay as he went. When he glanced at the door again, Mary Catherine was gone.

So much the better.

He needed to remedy his lack of companionship situation pretty darn quick so that whatever it was about that prim and too-proper Templeton woman that made his blood rise could be put to sleep once and for all. Thing was, the situation might not be such a quick fix. When he'd ridden into town, the only perk of civilization that held as much appeal as a drink of whiskey was laying in the soft cradle of everything female. Yet the only womanly vision that kept coming to mind was one of Mary Catherine Templeton drenched, irritated, and nubile straight from an unexpected douse in a watering trough but with the presence of spirit to stand up to a man she felt had done her wrong.

Another twitch in his pants indicated that even the thought of such a vision stirred his pot. Half-erect, he went to gather his purchases then paused. His conscience got the better of him, and he decided he couldn't let her establishment continue with a boarded window. He turned back and paid for a pane of glass to be delivered to the saloon in the morning.

Blaaze would make arrangements with Miguel to install the new pane as soon as possible. Now that the railroad extension had stalled in this part of the state, Miguel and other traqueros had made a small homestead outside the current environs of the town. The work would be welcomed by Miguel and his brother Edmundo, and Blaaze could stop feeling like a cad for breaking the Templeton woman's window then making her live with it like that for several days longer than she truly needed to.

His good deed for the day done, he held his purchases before him to mask his current semi-indisposed state while he exited the mercantile. Without his duster on, he was liable to give some poor woman an eyeful and cause the full-on vapors. The damn thing between his legs must be temporarily faulty.

Of all the women in this town who would welcome him into their beds, his johnson was fixated on the one who definitely wouldn't. Not that he wanted her to want him.

Woman probably gave orders in bed. Not an experience he'd relish.

His side wound was feeling better. Better enough that he need no longer torture himself with abstinence. A mental inventory of past bedmates scrolled through his brain. As he headed for Tobias's, he contemplated whether the energetic Widow Chandler might be up for a visit tonight. Not without note, his partial cockstand immediately softened at the speculation.

Yep, his cock had gone faulty. And he had that city gal to blame.

Intent to put the new saloon owner out of his mind, when he got to Tobias's, Blaaze dumped his mercantile purchases unceremoniously on the shelf Tobias had cleared for him. Time to clear his mind and focus on nothing but some quiet relaxation. Until he got his first herd of horses in, he didn't have much to do in the way of livery business. He was set to build out the stables and paddocks on his land starting next week. Today and the next few days, he had no plans but to take it easy, do some reading, and maybe try a little whittling.

He'd always wanted to take up whittling.

Seemed like the kind of thing a fella did when he retired.

Blaaze checked in with Tobias and went over some of the future plans for expansion of the livery stables. A little later, he pulled an old spindle-backed chair out front. He sat down in a shaded spot and tilted, chair and all, backward against the doorpost. He peeled the brown wrapping off the two novels he'd picked up at the mercantile. It had been a long time since he could lie back and simply enjoy a good read.

Deciding to go with the lighter read, he set aside *Life and Times of Frederick Douglass,* the autobiography of the great orator and statesman from the District of Columbia. He'd heard about the novelist and humorist Mark Twain while passing through Missouri, so he'd also ordered a copy of *The Adventures of Tom Sawyer.* As someone who'd led a predominantly vagabond life since leaving home, he figured he might appreciate the mischievous adventures of young Sawyer.

Barely past the second page, Blaaze heard a commotion up the street. Looking up, he noticed a small gathering of fellas outside the saloon. It was suppertime on a Friday evening. With money in their pockets from their ranch pay, locals who frequented the saloon usually didn't gather at the saloon door. They were generally too busy trying to be the first in line for their sportin' woman of choice and a bit of grub to boost their stamina for the frolicking and the bedding to come.

Deciding that whatever was going on was none of his concern, Blaaze dropped his eyes back to the page. He'd no sooner finished a paragraph when a loud shout drew his attention away from that very same page.

Tobias stepped out, a blacksmith apron covering his overalls, wiping his hands on a rag. "What's happenin' up there?"

Blaaze pushed his hat up so he could see Tobias without having to adjust position. "Don't know."

"Aren't you curious?"

"No." Saloon business weren't none of his business. As long as whatever was going on didn't affect his sleeping quarters tonight, Blaaze had no interest whatsoever.

"Sounds like your missus might be having a little trouble."

Blaaze grunted. "She's not my missus, and it's not my business to worry about her troubles."

Tobias gave him a doubting look.

Blaaze yanked his hat brim back down to ignore the look and returned to reading his book. A loud crash interrupted his concentration before he could get past three sentences.

Jumping up, he slammed the closed book onto the chair. "Dag burn it!"

Ignoring the grin leveled his way by Tobias, Blaaze stomped toward the saloon. He pushed past the onlookers at the door and entered the saloon to find it nearly completely transformed.

Some type of cloth covering wrapped around the front of bar. The wood top was still visible, but a vase of flowers sat at each end. The dining tables had been arranged in neat rows of three-by-four, and white linens covered each table, except for one. That table laid overturned in a heap with Cyrus Duncan sprawled across the underside of the upside-down tabletop. One arm curled around a table leg. His free hand clutched a bunch of white cloth.

Duncan had apparently passed out and knocked the whole lot—tablecloth, chairs, and all—to the ground. The mess accounted for the loud noise Blaaze had heard. No one seemed inclined to assist Duncan from his impromptu resting place. The man would likely be left snuggled in that spot to sleep off his souse until he awoke on his own.

The rest of the men sat decorously with napkins across their laps or tucked into the collars of their shirts as if they awaited a meal at a fine restaurant. Once down El Paso way, Blaaze had eaten at a fine restaurant. He'd felt like a wild stallion caught in a lasso for the first time, and that's exactly how these men looked.

What was this woman thinking? If she planned to turn the saloon into some version of a citified tavern she knew back in Cleveland, she needed a good butt whipping. If she were a man, he'd consider taking off his belt and exacting the mind-correcting discipline himself.

Just when he thought he couldn't get any more surprised, two of the serving women came out and issued hand cloths to the men seated at the tables. The women were dressed in new—and boringly reserved—dresses. Guess he knew now why Mary Catherine had purchased multiple dresses in different sizes.

"What'd'ya 'spect me to do with this here, gal?" a white-haired Jed Tuttle asked while accepting one of the cloths. His eyes widened when he touched it, and he jostled it a tad before quickly dropping the cloth onto the table. "The darn thang's hot!"

Somewhat taken aback by Tuttle's tone, the sweet, quiet gal known as Macey Tucker replied softly, almost apologetically, "Um, I believe you wipe your hands on it to clean them before you eat."

"Wipe my hands!" Tuttle picked up the cloth and flung it at Macey. "I've been eatin' here on and off since this place opened. Never had no complaint about the state of my hands before. Go tell that new lady boss of yours iffin' she don't like the state of my hands then she don't need the state of my coins." He pushed back his chair and snatched the napkin from his neck simultaneously. With a disgruntled huff, he vehemently tossed the napkin onto the table before he stormed from the place.

Macey flinched, the thrown cloth pressed against her chest with one hand, before looking over her shoulder. Blaaze presumed she searched for Mary Catherine.

Lucky for Mary Catherine, she was nowhere to be seen because Blaaze sensed a mini revolt about to erupt.

After Tuttle's outburst, several other men began to

grumble among themselves. A few actually rose and followed Tuttle out.

White table linens?

Damp, heated hand cloths?

Really?

Blaaze looked around at the dazed faces of the men remaining in the saloon. Those who weren't grumbling sat in baleful silence. He'd never seen a more confused—and annoyed—bunch of joes in his life.

First, she got his randy urges discombobulated. Then, she ruined his only drink in months *and* interrupted his first reading time in over a year. Now, she was defiling his favorite saloon.

Oh, hell no, his brain roared. This woman definitely had to go.

He'd been prepared to stay neutral in the matter and let the woman find her own way right—right out of town, that is. But by the time she came to her senses, she'll have left behind a wake of chaos that would ruin Lawless for decades to come. It was time the little lady learned what was what, and he was just the man to teach her.

CHAPTER 9

WIPING HER HANDS ON a dry towel, Mary Catherine left the kitchen to enter the main room of the saloon with Barbara Jean at her side. Other than Cyrus Duncan still passed out by the boarded window, the place looked good. She'd been worried about the man but had been assured by multiple people that his current situation was not unusual. She didn't think she'd ever get used to that, but she'd have to deal with Mr. Duncan later.

Focusing on the task at hand, she surveyed the room. She'd left detailed instructions for how she wanted the room rearranged, and everything had been in place when she returned from the mercantile. All she'd had to do was cover the tables with the new white linens she'd bought. Barbara Jean had returned from her trip shortly thereafter and been surprised by the new look of the tables and her two coworkers.

"The tables look nice in the new setup," Mary Catherine said, quite satisfied with what she and the other women had managed to accomplish in an afternoon.

Barbara Jean followed Mary Catherine's gaze and cleared her throat. "If you say so, young lady."

Her smile seemed genuine enough, but Mary Catherine got the feeling a subtle message hid behind the knowing eyes that accompanied the response. Barbara Jean was the eldest of Mary Catherine's female employees and seemed to be the only one with an even disposition. Maybe two decades or so older than Mary Catherine's own thirty years, Barbara Jean acted as the matron of the group from what Mary Catherine could tell. Everyone else called her Babs, but Mary Catherine couldn't bring herself to use the nickname.

"I know the linens need to have their edges sewn to be proper tablecloths, but everything in its time. All in all, I'm quite satisfied with the results." Mary Catherine faced the older woman.

"I still say you're going about this all wrong," Barbara Jean replied.

"You'll see. Once word gets around that we offer a fine table, we'll get a bigger crowd. Perhaps attract more couples on the weekends when wives will want a break from cooking themselves." It was a fine plan in Mary Catherine's opinion.

Barbara Jean patted her indulgently on the forearm. "You've clearly overlooked the nature of our lifestyle here. You and I need to have a little chat when the supper crowd thins out."

Before Mary Catherine could respond, grumbling male voices caught their attention. She and Barbara Jean spied Macey's concerned face across the room.

Mary Catherine walked over to the woman. "Macey, is everything all right?"

"I don't think the men like the hand cloths, Miss Templeton." Macey dropped her voice to a whisper. "They've been flinging them back at us."

"Flinging them back at you?" Mary Catherine stood stunned. "Certainly not." But she looked around in time to see a red-haired gentleman toss his hand cloth at Barbara Jean.

True to the unflappable nature she'd displayed since Mary Catherine's arrival, Barbara Jean didn't let it rile her. She simply caught the rag one-handed and yelled at the culprit. "Jimbo, you might want to work on that arm. I've seen six-year-olds throw harder than that."

The men around Jimbo laughed, but Mary Catherine found nothing funny about the lack of manners. When Janey ended up with a rag on top of her head from an unknown location and stood with tears threatening to spill from her eyes, Mary Catherine had had all the misbehavior she intended to tolerate. She headed toward Jimbo's table.

Someone stopped her with a hand to her arm.

Whirling to chastise whoever dared get familiar with her that way, she came face-to-face—or more like face-to-chest—with Blaaze Lassiter.

"Unhand me, sir." She jerked her arm, but he held firm.

"Just what in the name of all that is holy do you think you're doing?" His words came out between clenched teeth, but his voice kept that low, gravelly edge he never seemed to lose.

"I'm going to instruct that gentleman on proper manners and ask him to refrain from assaulting my serving ladies with the hand cloths."

Blaaze's glance flicked to Jimbo then returned to her. "Why on earth are you handing out hand cloths? And what's with the tablecloths? This is a saloon not some hoity-toity restaurant back east." He released her. "Did you forget where you are?"

"Forget where . . . Of course not. I wanted to spruce up the—"

"Spruce up?" His eyes narrowed. "What? Us frontier folk not good enough for you the way we are?"

Her eyes widened at the ludicrous statement. "N-not good enough? I never said anything about anyone not being good enough." She took another glance around. "I merely wanted to set a good table and set us apart from the other eating places. People like to know they're dining in a clean establishment, and the white table linens will give them peace of mind."

"Lady, we're not *people*. We're Kansans. And in Kansas, we like our saloons to look like saloons. If you're planning on starting a hotel with a fancy dining hall *then* you can put fancy white cloths on your tables. Otherwise, plain old wood tables and hands however we bring 'em in needs to suit you just fine."

"There's nothing fancy about white linens," she said.

Someone harrumphed behind her. Searching out the culprit, she found the men all staring at her. Some found her tiff with Blaaze Lassiter amusing. Others looked as if they wanted to call malarkey on her "not fancy" comment.

Another survey of the room revealed it did look pretty fancy compared to what it had looked like when she'd arrived. With many of the men seeming ready to storm out of the place, she considered whether her choice of atmosphere had been too much too soon. She needed all the business she could get tonight. She couldn't afford for these men to leave without taking in a meal or ordering a drink or several.

"Look," she said to Blaaze. "I've got accounts to cover. In addition to the brewery account, I now have the account at the mercantile. It's simply good business to have a nice look. I thought the table linens and finer touches would make this place stand out. I can't take anything for granted. Miss Eileen's serves three meals a day." She glanced around the patrons thoughtfully. "Miss Eileen's crowd is likely a bit more circumspect than my regulars since she doesn't sell alcohol, but I can't take any chances."

In addition, a small café operated two blocks up and across the street. The café sold mostly sandwiches and coffee and didn't have much room for sit-down service, but Mary Catherine wouldn't overlook the establishment as possible competition. Still, she couldn't let the mistreatment of her serving ladies pass.

"Surely you understand it's basic manners to wash your hands before you eat? I don't care if we're in Cleveland, Ohio, or Lawless, Kansas. If these men are going to eat here, they're going to come to my tables with some manners and clean hands. They can clean them before they come, or they can use the cloths. I don't really care. But what they are *not* going to do"—she flicked her rag hard against his chest, working herself into a full steam—"is throw them at my staff."

Her hands fisted on her hips and the flicking rag went with them to hang down her side.

She whirled toward the rest of the room. "Do you understand me, gentlemen?" she said with a tone of finality she channeled from childhood days of being called to task by her mother.

Two men stood and threw their napkins on their table. As for the others, almost in unison, they mumbled acquiescence and looked down at their tables discomfited.

Mouth open, Blaaze stood beside her, a look of amazement on his face.

"There." She spun back to Blaaze and reached up to place

a bent finger under his chin, much like he'd done to her that first day. She pressed up to close his mouth. "Problem solved, Mr. Lassiter." She walked away before her satisfied grin spread from understated to boastful.

She dared not get too cocky. The divine had a way of dealing with those who wallowed in conceit. She had a long way to go yet, and she need not tempt fate. All the same, she was pleased with herself. Head held high, she moved toward the kitchen to see if the beef stew was ready and mentally crossed her fingers that nothing else was about to go wrong.

~

Mouth once again hanging open, Blaaze glanced around in disbelief to see a room full of some of the orneriest cusses he'd ever met look down at their tables embarrassed and kowtowing to the eastern troublemaker. It was the darnedest thing he'd ever seen.

Quickly, he made to follow Mary Catherine before she could get too far away. Taking her measure for the second time that day, he considered the simple gray dress and schoolmarm demeanor. All she needed to make the image complete was a wooden ruler.

"You can't be serious," he said in a low voice as he followed behind her. They'd given the boys enough of a show. "You plan to continue serving meals this way?"

"Absolutely."

"And what about the women?" He stopped at the entrance to the back hall and waved a hand in the direction of the two women still standing in the dining area.

Mary Catherine's gaze followed his hand movement. "What about them?"

"Those dresses. How on earth do you expect a man to get excited over those dresses?"

Behind them Babs coughed twice to cover what sounded suspiciously to Blaaze like a chuckle before she walked away.

Mary Catherine simply looked at him with wide, appalled eyes. "I don't expect the men to get *excited* by my serving women, Mr. Lassiter. In fact, that was the very thing I was trying to *avoid*." Her eyes cut to Charlotte who climbed the stairs with a gentleman grinning broadly behind her. "As much as I can."

Blaaze noted that Charlotte wore her usual skimpy getup. So Mary Catherine hadn't been able to corral that gal into abandoning her sportin' woman attire. Why Mary Catherine would even want to, given the money she was trying to raise, puzzled Blaaze to no end.

The proper miss sighed. "Charlotte's giving me some resistance, but I'll speak with her again later tonight." She glanced once more toward the stairs.

Charlotte had reached the top and, giggling with her handsy gentleman in tow, entered the room assigned to her.

"Besides," Mary Catherine added, "I'll have to find a way to keep her from taking so many breaks."

"If you're not expecting the men to get—" Blaaze blinked in confusion. "What did you say?"

Mary Catherine lowered her voice. "The breaks. They're out of hand. Not that they're very long, but I can't have the ladies running upstairs so frequently to take time behind closed doors."

Breaks? Is that what we're calling it now? He almost said the snide thought out loud until a wild supposition crossed his mind.

Surely . . .

He didn't get a chance to complete the thought. Jake Clanton strode in with the sheriff a step behind him.

Clanton took a glance around the place and an appreciative smile spread across his face. "Well now, Miss Templeton, I see you've made some improvements." He removed his hat. "Linen tablecloths. What a nice touch."

Blaaze wanted to punch the man. Clanton knew as well as he, these cowboys didn't give one hoot about linen tablecloths. The touch Clanton appreciated was that Mary Catherine would run the saloon into the ground if she kept this up, and Clanton would get to swoop in and buy the place for a song.

Mary Catherine stiffened beside Blaaze. Her outward demeanor remained calm, but Blaaze could sense the tension vibrating through her.

Unnecessarily wiping her hands on the rag she held, Mary Catherine addressed the man with an even voice. "Good evening, Mr. Clanton. Have you come to join us for some refreshment this time?"

He grinned at her. "Why, no ma'am. I came by to see if you decided to exercise your woman's prerogative to change your mind. But it looks like you've decided to hunker down."

"Mr. Clanton, I told you yesterday that I wouldn't change my mind. And you gave me thirty days to pay down my account."

"So you did. And so I did." His grin widened. "And I'll honor my word. But not for one day longer." Clanton placed his hat back on his head. "Guess I'll be seeing you again in a few weeks. I hope you'll be able to square your account then. I'd hate for the sheriff here to have to seize your assets to settle up with me."

Sheriff Brennan looked a might chagrined at the

comment, but he spoke for Clanton's interest anyway. "Sorry, Miss Templeton. I don't want to have to get involved in this, but Mr. Clanton will have a claim if the account's not settled. I only came along today to make sure Mr. Clanton gave you upfront notice that he intended to seek legal recourse in the event of your failure to pay. I wouldn't want there to be any surprises."

The two men turned in tandem to leave, and a rumbling started through the supper crowd who were close enough to overhear the warning. News would soon spread that the saloon might be losing its assets, which would put its special offering at risk. The special offering the city gal didn't seem to know was a part of her business.

If Mary Catherine didn't know about that aspect of the saloon, then who was minding the entertainment particulars?

Blaaze closely surveyed Mary Catherine's stoic face. She hid it well, but Clanton's visit had shaken her. She worried her hand along the gold chain attached to the watch she wore around her neck. He could see the cogs turning behind her deep brown eyes. Her brain was already calculating and figuring what she could do.

She didn't say much. Actually, she said nothing at all, and Blaaze decided to sit on the stool at her hip and let her do her figuring. Now didn't seem like the right time to enlighten her about the complete workings of her *Den of Spirits*. So he motioned for a drink and held his peace while he watched her hands fiddle and that pretty face ponder.

Eventually, Mary Catherine stepped behind the bar to fuss with the glassware and wipe down the surface of the already clean bar top.

A bit later, a glance up by Blaaze caught Charlotte emerging from the upstairs bedroom. She stopped at the banister, and her grinning companion dropped his lips to nibble her neck while his hand firmly cupped her ass.

Charlie had indicated the other day that Blaaze should see Miss Charlotte if he was interested in entertainment. Which made Blaaze wonder. Was Charlie or Charlotte or both running lead on the upstairs amenities? If so, what were they doing with the money they collected if no one had been paying Clanton for liquor?

While the food sales Mary Catherine was trying to take fancy might not work out so well, men being men, the upstairs fun should have a decent amount of activity. Whether things would stay that way with the church-lady attire Mary Catherine had some of the ladies wearing—or if her standoff with Clanton meant she ran out of spirits to serve before and after the romping—remained to be seen.

In the meantime, the question remained. Where was that particular money going?

If Mary Catherine didn't know what all the upstairs amenities involved, she probably wasn't aware of the payments those activities brought in. She needed to account for every dollar if she truly intended to keep this place.

No. She needed to go home, his brain interrupted.

His body flinched at the thought. An unknown force inside him warred with the underlying thought, but the voice in his head kept chiding he needed to stay out of this and let matters lie. Clanton's seizure of the saloon's assets would take care of getting the city woman on her way back home.

Yet and still, he couldn't shake the feeling that something was off about this whole deal. What it was about Clanton that bothered him he couldn't put his finger on, but his gut told him the man wasn't shooting straight or playing fair, and he never failed to listen to his gut. Seemed mighty coincidental that Lila met with a fatal accident, Clanton hired on the men who'd been hassling her soon after the accident, and now the brewery owner wanted not simply to buy out Mary Catherine but push her out of business if necessary to get his way.

Marshal Bridger Malone always said there were no coincidences, and any lawman worth his salt always remembered that. Not that Blaaze was a lawman . . . anymore. Well, not hardly. Nonetheless, Blaaze's lawman ways of thinking were sparking back to life, and he found this coincidence darn suspicious.

Damn that Malone.

It was one thing for Blaaze to want Mary Catherine out of his hair. It was another entirely for him to see her cheated or bullied out of his hair.

He placed a hand over the petite one of hers that scrubbed past his elbow for the dozenth time and leaned in to minimize the possibility of being overheard. "Listen, if you're serious about keeping this place and not selling to Clanton, then we need to talk about this 'taking breaks' nonsense."

She ran her other hand up her chain then back down. "What exactly is there to talk about?" Her tone was clipped, a clear indication she was revving to get her back up.

He didn't care about her contrariness. They had to settle this. "Are you telling me you seriously think the gals are going upstairs to take breaks? With men in tow?"

Mary Catherine blushed. Remembering the flush that had covered her down to her chest the other day, Blaaze tried to keep his eyes on her face, but it was difficult. Not that he could see much given her buttoned-up dress covered everything up to the hollow of her throat. He stared at that hollow and swallowed, overwhelmed by the desire to trace a finger down that tempting notch.

And wasn't that the darnedest thing?

"I'm not going to speculate on what might be going on between the ladies and their . . . um . . . beaus," she said, keeping her voice low.

His eyes returned to her face.

She leaned closer and whispered, "That's between them. I'm not one to judge. I simply require they be more discreet and not do it during our busy time."

"Mary Catherine—" He stopped in exasperation. Ignoring the shocked look on her face at his use of her given name, he pulled his hand away and ran it down his face before he asked, "Just what do you think is going on up there?"

"Well, I-I . . ." That blush rose again.

He snatched up his glass with a clenched grip and drank deeply to distract himself from the view.

"I noticed the women, or sometimes a gentleman, adjusting their clothing when they come out of the rooms. So I figured maybe they were . . . napping or—"

With a choked cough, he spewed a mouthful of whiskey all over her clean bar. "Nappin'!"

He leaned back and stared at her in amazement, slowly wiping his mouth with the back of his hand.

His mind reeled. *Was she serious?*

Her naiveté was almost too much to believe. He didn't want to hurt her feelings if he could avoid it, but . . .

He glanced around to see if they were garnering any attention.

Satisfied when the few folks who'd looked up at his unfortunate waste of whiskey swiftly turned back to their own business, he narrowed his eyes with his best don't-lie-to-me look and asked softly, "You truly think they're going up there to *nap?*"

"Okay . . ." She tucked her lower lip into her mouth and chewed delicately before she met his eyes again. "I have noticed some of them finish too quickly with their beaus to get an honest *nap.*" The words came out in a rushed stream. "I mean, I guess it's their beaus." She fought to keep her budding embarrassment from showing on her face. "So I know it may be more than napping. I was trying to be gracious. A lady doesn't talk about these things. And especially not in mixed company." She snapped the last part in a hushed whisper.

"I see," he said in a slow drawl, not taking his eyes off her.

Unnerved by his silent perusal, Mary Catherine picked up the abandoned rag from the bar and began to swipe at the droplets of whiskey he'd spit all over it. That she failed to take him to task for the mess served as testament to how uncomfortable this conversation made her. Her bottom lip tucked back between her teeth, and she worked hard not to look at him.

What her teeth were doing to her lower lip brought naughty thoughts to mind. Momentarily distracted, he almost missed her next comment.

"Regardless of how we refer to it, the ladies engaging in personal recreation during the workday is completely inappropriate."

Personal recreation?

The idea was so absurd he once again wondered if she could possibly be jesting, but one look at her earnest face quashed that notion. His rising ardor immediately cooled. He had no business lusting after such an innocent, and he needed to have all his blood up top to get through what he had to do next.

He stood and pushed his hat back on his head because he wanted to make sure she could see his face clearly when he laid out the facts plain and simple like. Then he lightly put his hand over the wrist of her scrubbing hand. "Stop, Mary Catherine."

His inadvertent liquid mess was long gone.

She stopped but didn't look at him.

He didn't know how her proper sensibilities would react to the news he was about to impart. He considered whether he should lead her to a back room or at least step behind the bar before delivering what he suspected would be an unwelcome revelation. Deciding on the latter, he released her long enough to step behind the bar.

With hands on her upper arms, he maneuvered her so her back was to the room and let his size block anyone's ability to see her reflection in the mirror behind him. He didn't want the men to be able to see her reaction to his impending news. He'd only known her a few days, but everything he'd seen from her made clear she was a proud woman. Despite her being out of place in Lawless, he'd not be the one to take that away from her.

Her gaze flicked to his hands on her arms then quickly around the bar. He waited until her anxious, wide-eyed gaze lifted questioningly to meet his. What he was about to tell her outweighed whatever concerns she had over his breach of etiquette in touching her so familiarly.

"I hate to disabuse you of your illusions, Miss Templeton—from Cleveland, Ohio—but ain't no nappin' or *personal recreation* going on upstairs." He slid his hands down to brace under her elbows to be prepared in case she was the swooning type. "Sugar, I'm sorry to be the one to break this to you, but you are the proud owner of a saloon—"

"Yes, I know," she huffed and tried to tug away with an impatient roll of her eyes.

For a change, he couldn't repress his grin. Maybe he wasn't so sorry after all. He held firm, pulled her closer, and whispered in her ear, "And this town's one and only whorehouse."

CHAPTER 10

A WHOREHOUSE? MARY CATHERINE tried to tell herself she hadn't heard him right. Perhaps her confusion was brought on by that devastating grin of his.

Lila would never . . .

No. No way.

Mary Catherine closed her eyes and tried to fight back the feelings of horror and shame that rose within her. She could not be party to women selling their bodies to be used for sex. No wonder the ladies had looked at her like she was an idiot when she'd told them they needed to dress more modestly.

Modesty for what purpose?

They were only going to go upstairs and pull most of it off so some man could rut between their legs . . . for pay.

She glanced around the room.

For the first time, she truly understood why the only women in the place worked for her. The women back home would never have frequented a house of spirits. In fact, many such places didn't even allow women admittance. Considering this one offered more than simply spirits, most ladies would absolutely eschew entrance.

A wave of nausea hit her, and she felt dizzy. Turning to reach for the bar, she swayed. A strong arm encircled her.

"Whoa, there, now." Blaaze's deep, lazy drawl grounded her back to the moment. "We best not let you end up on the floor."

She looked into his eyes and his physical touch dispersed from where his fingers held her waist throughout every cell of her skin. The sensory overload was too much. She was deep in debt, owner of a whorehouse, and had to endure a grinning, touching Blaaze.

Given all she'd been through in the last few days, how significant was it that of the three, the grin had hit her the hardest?

Blaaze slowly eased her around the bar and onto a stool. He held on a few seconds to make sure she was steady. "You good?"

She continued to stare at him but didn't really see him. She couldn't bring his face into focus, so she simply nodded.

Gently he took her hands and turned her on the stool to plant both her palms flat against the edge of the bar. Her hands gripped reflexively, and she held on as if her life depended on it.

And maybe it did.

She was doomed.

The way Jake Clanton kept referring to her that first day as not seeming to be a woman who would run "a saloon and such" now made sense. And it was the *and such* that was the problem. Back home, she would never have walked within ten blocks of a whoreh—

She couldn't bring herself to even think the word.

Now she lived in one.

Her parents . . . *Goodness gracious!* They both had to be rolling over in their graves.

Surely, her cousin was above laughing right now. The irreverent, non-conforming Delila Sarah Templeton had never met a rule she dared not break nor a social norm she dared not defy. Mary Catherine had been, and was, the exact opposite. As someone who staunchly followed the rules, her most adventurous action encompassed nothing more than getting a college degree. She'd think this was all a cruel joke at her expense, except Lila didn't have a mean or petty disposition.

Full of boisterous life, Lila's jolly spirit and defiant nature had been antithetical to the Templeton way of life. Though Lila's pastor father had gotten her first and middle name from the Bible, Lila had never liked her given name. Considering the Reverend Joseph Aaron Templeton had never failed to remind Lila of her Biblical namesakes' many downfalls, her cousin's hatred of her name was understandable.

Imagine being a daughter named by a pastor father for two Old Testament women who were known betrayers. Biblical Delila had coaxed her lover to disclose the secret of his strength only to reveal the confidence to his enemies. The doubting Sarah had failed to have faith in the word of God and coaxed her husband to lie with a maid in betrayal of his marriage vows to have his promised son.

When her cousin turned fifteen, she stopped answering to her given name and dubbed herself "Lila." Uncle Joseph had refused to accept the nickname. Two years later, after a night the pair had fought fiercely, her cousin disappeared.

Disappeared to come here?

Fled to become a madam and maybe even a scarlet

woman herself?

The act would have been the ultimate rebellion against her father. But why leave the place to Mary Catherine? Sure, they were family, but Lila of all people understood Mary Catherine's penchant for being the rule follower, the do-as-you're-told daughter, the one least likely to rebel against authority or defy societal standards. Her college education gave many pause, but that wasn't so much defiance on her part, simply an uncommon pursuit.

Squeezing her hands against the wood beneath her palms, Mary Catherine fought not to hyperventilate.

Blaaze lifted one of her hands and pressed a glass of water into it. With a long, firm finger, he touched the bottom of the glass and pushed it toward her mouth. "Drink, Mary Catherine."

In the midst of her inner turmoil, an inappropriate pulse of delight flashed inside her chest. He'd called her by her first names again. It wasn't proper, but she loved the sound of it in the gravelly croon of his cowboy voice.

She momentarily squeezed her eyes shut. Just sitting in a whoreh—a *brothel*, yes that was better—a brothel was turning her into a shameless wanton. She was going to hell.

Bringing her other hand up to surround the circumference of the glass, she took a long drink. *No. Not hell,* she thought. She'd done nothing wrong. *Yet.*

She wouldn't—couldn't—let these women continue to live a life of . . . of . . . f-fornication for profit.

Her profit.

The thought made her want to run and hide or maybe bury herself beneath bed covers for the next decade. She groaned softly and dropped her forehead against the bar. Still clutched in one hand, her half-drank glass of water followed after with a clunk.

"No. No. No," she whispered, head still down.

How could she face the people of this town ever again?

Blaaze awkwardly patted her back, a quiet presence that only added to her embarrassment. She wasn't sure if he stood by because he feared she would pass out or perhaps descend into hysterics. He didn't speak. He didn't have to. She'd seen the look on his face when she'd mentioned the women were taking too many naps.

Naps, for goodness's sake, of all the idiotic rationales to suggest.

She'd known in her gut the ladies had to be up to more upstairs, but she'd not wanted to let her mind go where it had been leading her. That she'd not immediately understood the signs of the upper-level activities would be a source of humiliation that would follow her all her remaining days in this community. In her mind, the only thing worse than being wrong was having others bear witness to your mistake.

The sounds of grumbling men shattered her descent into self-pity. A few tin cups, now empty of coffee, began to bang against a table on the far side of the room. The clomps of beer mugs and empty highballs quickly joined the commotion. The men were hungry. She'd never made it back to see Cook about the pot roast.

Her head popped up. "Oh no."

Hopefully, the man had not let it burn. Witnesses to her naiveté wouldn't matter if she failed to pay off Jake Clanton, because her days in Lawless would be numbered. Messing up dinner would put a big hole in her revenue generation plan.

She scampered off the stool and rushed to the kitchen. "Jonas, how's the roast?"

Cook turned at the sound of her frantic voice and gave

her a look of exasperation. "The roast is fine, of course. What were you expecting?" His disgruntled look suggested he knew exactly what she'd been expecting, and he didn't appreciate her lack of confidence in him.

Smoothing the skirt of her dress with both hands, she gathered her composure and let her heart rate settle. "The men are hungry. We need to begin serving immediately. Would you begin dipping out the pot roast, please?"

Placated by the respect shown in her use of the word "please," Jonas went to do as she bid.

"I'll need to get the girls . . . um, ladies . . . um, women, to pass out the filled bowls."

Blaaze had followed her into the kitchen, whether out of concern for her distressed behavior or mere curiosity at what other missteps she might make this day, she didn't know. She tried to ignore his bigger-than-life presence looming nonchalantly against the wall, arms and ankles crossed. He watched her silently and appeared to get much amusement out of her struggle to figure out what to call the women now that she knew what they did to make the bulk of their earnings.

Not that they weren't also serving girls. But they were a whole lot more than that. And the whole-lot-more-than-that still had her flustered.

She needed to address the women's secondary employment services—which she was terminating *immediately*. She didn't know how she would have that conversation with them when she wasn't sure she'd ever be able to look them in the eyes again, but she'd find a way. She usually did.

Smoothing her skirt once again, she audibly puffed air from her cheeks and firmed her shoulders. First, she had to deal with the evening meal, then she could deal with the other issue.

~

Blaaze pushed off the wall and fell into step behind Mary Catherine when she exited the kitchen.

She stopped abruptly and spun on him. "Are you planning to shadow me all night?"

With suppressed amusement, he shrugged. "A man's got to eat. Thought I'd head back out and make sure I got a taste of that pot roast along with everyone else." He had his doubts about the quality of that pot roast if she'd overseen its preparation. She seemed to lean toward intellectual pursuits rather than domestic services, but he'd braved greater disasters.

Deciding to ignore him, Mary Catherine continued into the main hall. She looked around the room before asking, "Do you see Barbara Jean?"

Blaaze didn't.

Unable to locate Babs, Mary Catherine caught Macey's eye and signaled her over. "Macey, would you ask the women to help Cook serve the dinner, please? We need to quiet these men before we have a riot." She glanced over at Blaaze. "Heaven forbid they start throwing things and break a window or something. Oh yeah." Her index finger found her chin. "That's right, we have no window to break, do we?"

Blaaze indulged her sarcasm with a blasé smirk. "Don't worry, Miss Templeton. You'll have your window back by supper tomorrow then maybe we can move past this little misunderstanding."

Mary Catherine blinked at him. Clearly, that wasn't the response she'd expected. She'd likely thought she'd be living with that boarded window for days to come. Truth be told, that had been his intention. He still didn't understand what had moved him to change his mind.

While she stood gaping at him, he reached for a loose strand of her hair. His fingers brushed lightly against the tip of her ear as he tucked the stray curl behind it. The feel of her soft skin against the pad of his index finger enticed his hand to linger along the outer curve of the dainty ear then trickle down the feminine jawline set with determination. His eyes met hers, and a question shifted across her face.

Macey approached and broke the spell that wove around them. Blaaze leashed the overwhelming desire to kiss her, which had ambushed him upon the feel of her skin, and stepped back, allowing his stoicism to shift back into place.

Breaking eye contact with Mary Catherine, he said to Macey, "Sweetheart, when you get a chance, would you bring me one of those bowls? What with all the excitement around here and women nearly fainting," he nodded his head toward Mary Catherine, "I plumb forgot I haven't eaten all day."

Macey giggled and headed for the kitchen. He went the opposite direction and took a seat at a back table. Macey eventually served him off the second tray she brought from the kitchen. The other women helped serve the other men, all except Charlotte. Charlotte grabbed hold of the corded tie of the cowboy she stood next to and pulled him from his seat.

No longer having any misunderstanding of where this was headed, Mary Catherine moved to cut off the path to the stairs. "My apologies, young man," she said to the young cowboy Charlotte had in tow. "We've had some urgent saloon business come up. Charlotte . . . er, actually none of the ladies will be available tonight."

"What! What do you mean I won't be available tonight?"

Voice loud as usual, Charlotte looked fit to be tied.

The patrons at the tables closest to the stairs all looked up to see what the fuss was about.

"I'm sorry for the inconvenience," Mary Catherine said to the cowboy. "I'll have the barkeep pour you a glass of whatever you'd like. No charge."

The cowboy looked at Charlotte with disappointed longing that would have made a puppy envious. After quick back-and-forth glances between Mary Catherine and Charlotte, who continued to hold tight to his tie, he must have decided Mary Catherine represented the bigger concern. With an unmanly blush, he cleared his throat and said, "Yes, ma'am."

Mary Catherine's ability to diffuse the situation impressed Blaaze. He pitied the young man who'd had to face the schoolmarm version of Mary Catherine as she interrupted his plans for an evening romp. Sportin' life crisis soundly averted, *this* time.

Though that was not to be her last challenge of the night.

Blaaze watched Mary Catherine flit about the room running interference every time she thought a patron was headed upstairs to take part in the upstairs amenities. Amid the bustling, she looked around in time to notice Macey hand Franklin, an old cowboy, a bottle of ketchup. A look of utter horror crossed Mary Catherine's face.

She hurried to the table and jerked the ketchup out of Franklin's hand before he could open it. "What do you think you're doing?"

He looked up and frowned at Mary Catherine. "What does it look like? I'm putting ketchup on my dinner."

"You haven't tasted it yet. How do you know it needs ketchup?"

"Sweetheart, most everything in this place needs ketch-up," Franklin answered with a perplexed frown.

A mumble of agreement came from the men at the adjoining tables, and the old man reached for the ketchup again. Mary Catherine held the bottle above her head, out of his grasp.

"Or maybe some salsa," his young table companion added with an enthusiastic smile.

"Salsa? Boy, you been eatin' with your traquero buddies again?" Franklin shook his head. "I done told you those hombres ain't gonna let you court that sister of theirs, so's you might as well stop sniffing around."

His young charge grinned bashfully. "Who said anything about the sister?"

Franklin scoffed. "Boy, I wasn't born yesterday. Besides, you know what salsa is don't ya?" He grabbed the ketchup from a distracted Mary Catherine, whose eyes were on one of her ladies flirting in the corner. "It's mushed tomatoes with a bunch of tiny chopped vegetables and some spices. Fancy *ketchup*. That's all'n it is. This old cowpoke don't need no fancy ketchup. This here regular ketchup's gonna do me right fine." He unscrewed the cap on the bottle of regular ole ketchup.

Mary Catherine snatched it back before he could use it. "That's my grandmother's recipe, and my grandmother's pot roast don't need no ketchup."

Blaaze's brows rose at her use of poor grammar. She was insulted enough by the old coot's suggestion to slip into frontier speak without the bat of an eye. Less than a week in Lawless, and she'd already begun to talk like a local. Her pot roast recipe *don't need no* ketchup, huh? The woman was full of surprises and not a little bit of spunk.

She motioned to Franklin's bowl with a nod of her head, clearly intending he try the dish before she'd consider returning his coveted red elixir to him. "How's about you give it a taste before you start throwing in things you don't need?"

With an approach-to-the-gallows expression, Franklin lifted his spoon then dipped up a mouthful of the roast surrounded by a light broth full of potatoes and simmered carrots. The men near them watched him closely without lifting their own spoons. The group meant for him to be the sacrificial lamb for the new owner's dish. Like everyone else in the place, Blaaze hovered in quiet anticipation to see Franklin's initial reaction.

The old man sucked in a deep breath before he took his first mouthful. Then his brows shot up and he chewed vigorously. He gave Mary Catherine a look up and down, a light of admiration lit his eyes.

"I didn't figure you for a gal what knows her way around the kitchen. This here's even got a little kick to it." He dipped up another spoonful, and his head began to nod up and down in an endless bob. "Not bad, Miss Mary. Not bad at'all." Then he dug in, forgetting she stood there.

Franklin's nod of approval caused a collective sigh of relief to rise in the saloon. Skeptically, Blaaze lifted his own spoon and dipped up a mouthful of the steeping roast. His own brows lifted. It was good. *Real* good.

He immediately dipped up another spoonful to make sure he'd not overestimated the dish simply because he was so hungry he'd damn near eat his boot right now. He spooned in the mouthful. Nope. Still good. A hum of appreciation accompanied the thought.

Mary Catherine put out her hand to Franklin. He slid the ketchup bottle cap he still held into her hand with a sheepish grin.

Triumphant, Mary Catherine chided, "That's what I thought."

A hush fell over all the tables while the men, including Blaaze, lapped up their suppers. Nothing could be heard but spoons scraping against bowls and tumblers periodically hitting tabletops, and perhaps a slurp or two.

Intending to stash the confiscated condiment out of sight, Mary Catherine headed for the bar. On the way, her gaze landed on one of the younger girls who was making nice with a dark-haired gentleman. Blaaze chuckled under his breath when he saw Mary Catherine change direction.

She made a beeline for the couple and mumbled determinedly under her breath, "I don't think so."

Chapter 11

THE NEXT MORNING, BLAAZE sauntered into the kitchen in search of Cook. It was early yet and no one other than a few boarders were about. The saloon didn't get many patrons until around lunchtime. Not planning to wait for lunchtime to get another helping of Mary Catherine's pot roast, Blaaze searched out Jonas intending to coax the cook into heating him up a bowl of leftovers instead of the eggs, ham, and biscuits the man usually served.

When Blaaze emerged from the kitchen in success, he spotted Mary Catherine. She herded the sportin' women toward the back parlor. Curious, Blaaze followed, a bowl of pot roast cradled in one palm while he spooned into the tasty fare. Each dip of the spoon elicited an enthusiastic hum.

Hearing the sounds, Mary Catherine glanced over her shoulder. "Would you mind doing that a little quieter, please?"

"What?" he said around another mouthful.

She lifted her eyes dramatically toward the ceiling, seeming to say a silent prayer. Perhaps for patience. The thought tempted Blaaze to smile, but he suppressed the urge by shoving another spoonful of roast into his mouth.

"And don't talk with your mouth full."

Blaaze shot her a rebellious glance over the spoon in his mouth, perturbed by her bossiness. It wasn't that he didn't know the proper way to behave in public or didn't have any refined manners. His parents had taught him well enough. He simply liked playing the uncouth, backward lout. He'd learned early on how easy it was to get the upper hand when people underestimated you.

Nonetheless, for her, he attempted to curb his rough behavior. Focused on his silent enjoyment of his morning fare, Blaaze continued to follow Mary Catherine and almost ran into the back of her when she stopped unexpectedly.

She turned to face him. "Where do you think you're going? This is a *private* matter, Mr. Lassiter. You need to stay out."

Ha! Like that was going to happen, he thought to himself.

To her, he said, "Not on your life."

She pursed her lips. A pouty Mary Catherine was a beauty. Too bad the poutiness was out of annoyance with him and not the flirty come on she inadvertently displayed.

Ignoring her peeved expression, Blaaze trailed her into the back parlor. Not wanting to poke the bear too much, he took the hint and wandered over to a chaise in the far corner. He sat down and propped an ankle over a knee. He felt like a man about to enjoy a theater dinner show. Except this entertainment was unlikely to unfold pleasantly.

This is going to be a disaster, he thought and watched with bowl in hand while the women gathered.

"Ladies, thank you for giving me your time this morning," Mary Catherine said primly, as if she were addressing the local

Women's Association. "I want to clear up a matter that has come to my attention."

"Clear up?" Blaaze queried from the corner. "I thought we established exactly what was going on here. You need more clearing up?" He sat his empty bowl aside and made to rise.

Mary Catherine whirled on him. "Don't you dare move. Stay seated or get out."

His brows shot up at her tone, but he flopped back into the chair. His lips twitched, and he worked hard to corral a rising grin. He'd been feeling amused a lot lately. Yet another mystery surrounding the affect the proper miss had on him.

When she turned back to the ladies, they were all staring at her in amazement. Charlotte gave Blaaze a long, curious glance before giving Mary Catherine a thorough study. The boss lady's verbal set down of Blaaze had made an impression.

Not likely an impression Mary Catherine wanted. Charlotte's worldly, speculative gaze implied suspicion as to what might be going on between him and Mary Catherine. He doubted Miss Manners noticed her shortness with him gave others the impression of a familiarity between them beyond mere acquaintance.

She cleared her throat and regrouped. "As I was saying, it has been brought to my attention"—she kept a watch on Blaaze out of the corner of her eye—"that we . . . I mean that you . . . well, that you all accept payment for . . . um . . ."

Blaaze watched Mary Catherine struggle for the right words to describe the activities of her sportin' women and offered helpfully, "Cleaving the pin?"

Unsurprisingly, the woman shot a baleful glare at him. No way would her proper upbringing allow her to use an undignified term like "cleave the pin."

"Pully hawly, perhaps?" he volunteered as an alternative.

A flush began to rise across her cheeks at his use of the expression for having a series of affairs. Oh, how he enjoyed the appearance of that comely flush so easily coaxed from the woman, and the thought of getting to see just how far down her chest it went began to play across his mind.

Because Mary Catherine remained too flustered to speak, Blaaze took the opportunity to poke at her sensibilities one more time. "No? Perhaps the term you're searching for is blanket hornpipe?"

The vulgar euphemism made her grimace, but she finally found her tongue. "No, it's not," she snapped. "And you be quiet!"

"Then what would you call it?" He waited expectantly for her answer, mirthful anticipation undermining his ability to maintain the stoic facade he was known for.

All the women in the room stared expectantly at her as well. He could tell she hated him making her give it a name. They all knew what she was talking about, but if she was going to manage a business based on sexual favors, shouldn't she be able to say what was what out loud?

"Well, the technical term would be fornication," she finally replied without a blink or a blush, having regained her composure.

His mouth dropped open in mock shock. "Oh my!" He covered his mouth with the back of his hand. "Not fornication," he said behind his knuckles before dropping his hand to his lap. "So we're going with the technical *biblical* term, then." He crossed his legs in the opposite direction. "The old biddies in town will be happy to know you agree with their assessment of the situation."

Mary Catherine blinked at him, openly clueless. *Old biddies?* Her look seemed to say. *What old biddies and what assessment?*

What she said aloud, however, was, "I've made no assessment of any kind. I simply cannot allow the practice to continue in my saloon."

"Yet you selected the term associated with improper copulation," a miffed Charlotte said. "The term people use for those they consider engaged in immoral, sinful, and in some states, illegal sexual activity. Are you feeling a bit immoral by association, Mary Catherine? What, with all this going on in *your* saloon."

"I—" Mary Catherine's mouth stalled open then closed.

The easterner hadn't let anyone forget that the saloon was absolutely hers. Blaaze had wondered if anyone else had noticed. Charlotte's words left little doubt that they had, and Charlotte apparently retained enough anger from the disruption of her activities last night to voice her disgruntlement aloud.

There was a story behind Mary Catherine's possessive need to publicly claim her ownership repeatedly. Maybe one day Blaaze would find out what it was. For now, he hoped she hadn't meant to be judgmental in her choice of words. She didn't seem like a vindictive woman. To intentionally lord a sense of superiority over these women, who were simply trying to earn a living, didn't seem her style.

Before she could regroup, Babs decided to interject. "So you see us as fallen women," she said. "Loose hussies with no soul who wallow in the pit of the Devil's playground. Is that it?" Babs's literal words were harsh, but her tone and expression revealed the implacable mirth of a woman who clearly cared naught what others thought of her or of her way of life.

A horrified expression flashed across Mary Catherine's face.

Babs saw it and took pity on her. "I'm just poking a little fun, Miss Mary Catherine. Honey, I had no idea until yesterday that you didn't understand what Lila's joint was all about. When I said we needed to have a talk, I didn't think it would be with an audience, but here we are." She moved to stand beside Mary Catherine. "I understand this may be a bit of a shock for your ladylike ways, but any cousin of Lila's who has the courage to come all this way to Kansas to be an independent woman of business has got to have some gumption in there too. How 'bout we refer to me and the ladies' doings as 'amorous congress' or perhaps 'convivial relations' instead?"

"Yes. Convivial relations." Obvious relief overtook Mary Catherine at the proffered euphemism. "We could say that."

Amorous congress still had too much of fornication implied, Blaaze thought, but he opted to keep quiet this time.

"So you're going to throw us out, Miss Mary? Is that what you've brought us here to tell us?" Greenleigh asked. She was a quiet one, but her quietness was not to be confused with meekness. Greenleigh had always been able to hold her own.

Shocked, Mary Catherine turned toward the young woman. "Gracious, no, Greenleigh. I'm not throwing anyone out. And no one calls me Mary."

A low snort shot from Blaaze in his corner perch. "Seems fitting to me," he mumbled under his breath. Except for a few glances, no one acknowledged his comment.

"But you said you weren't going to allow any more . . ." Macey's face bunched as she tried to remember the acceptable term. Giving up, she finished a little more circumspect than

Charlotte and Babs. "Allow us to do our upstairs business anymore."

"That's ridiculous, Mary Catherine," Babs said. "I don't know what all Charlie has been doing with the house's share of the money we bring in that he's needed to run a tab with Clanton, but this here saloon doesn't survive without the upstairs business. And I don't mean the boarding rooms."

"Barbara Jean, try to understand." Mary Catherine's hands spread almost in supplication. Her gaze moved from Barbara Jean's face to each of the faces of the other women in the room, searching for understanding and at least one ally. "I went to college so I could pursue a life outside the home. I thought I'd be working in business, specifically banking. That didn't work out for me, but I can adjust to running a saloon. Alcohol and boarding rooms, I can manage. As for the other, I can't. I can't be a party to . . . to that."

~

A hush came over the room. Mary Catherine felt cornered and alone. She'd never had many friends, and women friends especially had been scarce. Navigating a focused conversation with any group of women would have been challenging. Navigating one on such a delicate topic felt absolutely torturous.

As an introverted bookworm, she'd spent more time in her room with a book than socializing. When she did socialize, she had a hard time finding anything in common with her peers to discuss. Once she went to college, her classes had been filled with men. Mathematics wasn't popular with the female students. On the rare occasion she did have a female classmate, they generally studied math and science on the path to medical pursuits and were as bibliophilic as her.

The silence of the room broke when Barbara Jean asked, "A party to what? No one's asking you to join the puttin' out business. Lila never did. But she understood the value to the town and to us ladies of having a thriving brothel."

"How could it possibly benefit you ladies to sell yourselves to the men in this town?" Mary Catherine was truly and genuinely baffled.

"Hell, without us, there'd be no town." Barbara Jean waved a hand to encompass the other women in the room.

Most of them nodded in agreement.

"You think these men are sticking around to build and extend the frontier without a little womanly comfort along the way?" Barbara Jean snorted. "Ha! A dozen men to each woman means eleven of those men aren't getting hitched, and therefore, aren't getting marital congress. They've got to get their jollies somewhere. They ain't stayin' iffin' they don't have somewhere to sheave their pistols every once in a while. We're here to service that need but not for free or not in exchange for a mere roof over our heads and a passel of kids. But for a *price*.

"As long as men can get their *convivial relations*, they're gonna keep coming out west, and the town's gonna keep growing. That makes us enterprising women who offer a valuable service to this town. That there also gives us independent money. We have control over our own lives, our own money, and our own destinies."

Mary Catherine wasn't convinced. "I believe that we can make this saloon work without the need for you to sell your bodies," Mary Catherine told her. "The dinner business will pick up, and I've got other ideas. I'll, of course, continue to pay you, and you will all work downstairs exclusively from now on." She turned to Charlotte. "But you must be properly clothed during your service for me. No more attire appropriate for . . ." She flushed again.

"Prostitutes," Charlotte said unceremoniously.

Babs hitched a hand high on her hip. "I prefer the term sportin' woman, if you please. Prostitute is so mundane."

"Well, I will not be party to sportin' women operating out of my saloon." Mary Catherine's tone of finality brooked no argument. "We'll do things my way, and we'll be fine. You'll see."

Unimpressed with Mary Catherine's bravado, Charlotte rose and flounced out of the room. Macey sat looking as if someone stole her favorite puppy. Most of the other women looked to Babs for guidance. Babs simply shook her head in pitying disbelief at Mary Catherine's mandate.

Eventually, Babs looked over at Blaaze and said, "Maybe you can talk some sense into her, cowboy. She's consigning us to a life on the street or forcing us to look elsewhere for work. Don't see how she's going to pay Clanton back that way." Babs turned and left the room.

The other women slowly followed her out one by one.

Blaaze sat in his chair and, like Mary Catherine, watched them all depart. When she stood alone, he said, "No way you're going to keep this business going without those ladies doing what they do upstairs. You're shooting yourself in the foot."

She turned to him. "Since I don't carry a gun, Mr. Lassiter, I won't be shooting myself anywhere and most especially not in either foot."

"All the same, Babs is right. How do you expect to pay back Clanton and keep this business going without that additional money?"

"That's not for you to worry about." She lifted her chin and crossed her arms.

He stared at her resistant posture then stood. "Looks like in another few weeks Clanton will take hold of most of the saloon's assets and neither one of us will have to worry about it anymore." He touched his fingers briefly to his hat with a tilt of his head. "You have a good day now, *ma'am*."

Chapter 12

BLAAZE LEFT THE SALOON wondering at the woman's lunacy. He admired the directness with which Mary Catherine had approached her concerns over supporting one of the world's oldest professions. She might be fierce in her determination, but she knew nothing about running a saloon in a town like Lawless.

The men of the town were going to want her head, and she was going to drive herself right out of business with this move.

She hadn't a clue.

But far be it for him to push when she didn't want to be corrected about her mistaken position.

That prim sass of hers was an acquired taste. He found he was beginning not only to appreciate her knack for it, but to like it. Dangerous territory for him to be in.

In fact, territory he needed to avoid altogether.

So he'd leave her to it.

Like she said, it wasn't his business to worry about.

No more sportin' women. Let's see how this was gonna

play out. Tobias had thought him ticky after his first run in with Mary Catherine Templeton. Blaaze predicted they were about to have a whole town full of ticky men.

Thinking of Tobias, Blaaze headed to the livery stable. He found Tobias in the back eating a plate of ham hocks and beans. The big man looked up when Blaaze walked in.

Tobias motioned with his plate. "You want some beans? Still hot. I only just made them."

Blaaze shook his head, still full from Mary Catherine's grandmother's pot roast. He wandered over to the seat opposite Tobias and sat silently while Tobias partook of his meal. It had always been thus between them. No need to fill silence just to fill silence. It was one benefit of Tobias's friendship Blaaze truly appreciated right now. He needed to think some things through, and Tobias's place was as good a place as any.

The clank of a spoon scraping against an empty plate eventually broke the silence.

Blaaze leaned his chair back and propped his feet on a bale of hay. "I believe that's empty. You can stop scraping at nothing."

With a big grin his direction, Tobias gave the plate another long, deliberate scrape then licked the back of the spoon before he set the tableware aside. "Now, it's finished."

Blaaze chuckled. "Ya think?"

Tobias chuckled in return. "I think." He rose and headed for the back shelf. Along the way, he picked up an empty glass and motioned with it toward Blaaze, a silent inquiry as to whether Blaaze was interested in joining the smith for a drink.

He was. He nodded as much to Tobias, who grabbed an extra glass and moved over to the back corner to fill both glasses half full with moonshine.

When Tobias handed Blaaze a glass, he asked, "So what's on your mind?"

Blaaze didn't bother denying the inquiry. Tobias knew him too well to have bought the denial anyway.

"Our Miss Templeton just decided there'll be no upstairs services at the saloon any longer."

Tobias's glass stalled halfway to his mouth. "No upstairs services. You mean, she's shutting down the brothel?"

Blaaze took a sip and nodded. "That's exactly what I mean."

"Whoa." Tobias sunk to a hay bale stacked against a column and leaned back. "The boys aren't gonna be happy about that."

"My thoughts exactly."

Tobias's expression turned pensive. "The next nearest house is about two days ride over by Edgewater. It's not impossible to make that a regular thing, but it'll sure take some advance planning. I mean, there's always Beulah's place on the outskirts of town. She's been trying to turn that mammoth boarding house of hers into more for a while now, but she never could quite compete with Lila and her ladies. She can't seem to keep any gals worth beddin' long enough to make a true run against the saloon's business.

"Of course, now that Clanton's been trying to back Beulah in turning her place into the area's first hotel, that may change. I suspect he's not interested in a purely reputable hotel 'cuz Beulah's latest female employees have a bit more charm to them. I'm sure that's Clanton's doing. Guess this change in the saloon's gonna make him all the happier." Tobias stretched his legs out in front of him and crossed his ankles.

He started to take another drink then his hand stalled.

"Wait. I thought Mary Catherine owed that man lots of money."

"She does."

"She done paid him off?"

"Nope."

Still without taking a drink, the smith's drink hand dropped to his thigh and his empty hand settled in the crook where his leg met his hip. "Well, how the blazes does she plan to do that if she's cut off her best source of cash?"

"Exactly." Blaaze raised his glass in mock toast. "The woman just sealed her fate. She claims she's got other ideas about how to make the saloon profitable, but I got my doubts. I think she's bought herself a sheriff's seizure and a ticket out of town."

Nodding, Tobias went to take a drink again. Once again, he stopped before the glass got all the way to his lips. Blaaze found the bit comical. At this rate, Tobias was never going to get in a drink.

Tobias's eyes narrowed on him. "Am I missing something?" he asked. "I thought you wanted her to leave town. So isn't this whole debacle gonna get you exactly what you want?"

Was it? Blaaze was no longer sure. He was torn. He wanted her gone not simply for his peace of mind but her own safety. This town was going to chew her up and spit her out. "Yeah, but this feels too much like she's being run out of town, and that doesn't sit well."

Somehow, he'd feel better about the whole thing if she actually made the choice to leave. He wasn't quite sure what difference it should make to him why she left town as long as she left. The look on Tobias's face told him his pal was wondering the same thing.

"I think you're splitting hairs, Lassiter. And you sure are twisting yourself up in knots over Jake Clanton's plans for the lady and her saloon. Those lawman instincts you're trying to pretend you don't have and don't want are screaming at you that there's foul play afoot. I can see it in your eyes. And as much as you're a man to stand up for the underdog, it's also time you admit it's this *particular* little underdog of a filly that has you and your protective instincts knotted up the most."

"You're overselling it." Blaaze took a drink. "It's simply my life—and everyone else's around here—would be a whole lot simpler, and I could focus on easy living and retirement, if that woman would be reasonable and recognize she has no business in a ratchet town like Lawless. Certainly not as the owner of the town's only saloon and established whorehouse. Or rather, the town's only saloon since it looks as if the whorehouse is no more."

He pushed up the brim to his hat and shook his head. "She has the education to figure out a fair price for a buyout. She could negotiate a deal, take her money, and head back east better off and none the worse for wear. Instead, she's decided to go up against a man who appears to have the scruples of a heretic. Makes no sense."

"Makes sense if you like to keep what's yours. And I figure she's got a right. You don't?"

Blaaze scratched at his hairline while he thought about it. A brewery, the town's saloon, a hotel, and one or both of the latter run as part of a brothel. Seemed Mr. Clanton had big plans for Lawless. Blaaze was beginning to wonder exactly what the man would do to anyone who got in the way of those big plans. "Clanton seems to want a piece of everything in this town. I'm not partial to him trying to take advantage of Mary Cate, that's all."

"Mary Cate?" Tobias went on alert.

Dammit. He'd never meant to say that out loud, and certainly not in front of Tobias. The man would read more into it than was there. Blaaze had taken to referring to the hellion side of the Eastern Miss as Mary Cate in his head. That fiery, imperious side of that personality of hers put him more in mind of a regal Kate or Katerina, and certainly nothing like the prim and proper *Mary Catherine* she tried to maintain in public.

He ignored his buddy's speculative perusal at his slip-up and turned the conversation back to Mary Catherine's nemesis. "I'm beginning to wonder just what Clanton would do to make sure he got that piece of everything."

Glass at the edge of his lips, Tobias sat motionless for a minute. He smirked at Blaaze's sidestep of his pet name observation then gave Blaaze a considering look. "You thinking about finding out?"

Blaaze gave a noncommittal shrug and downed the rest of his moonshine. "It was just a thought."

"Uh-huh." Tobias finally threw back his bit of moonshine and finished it in one swallow. "*Ahhhh* . . . Goes down right smooth if I do say so myself." He dropped his glass with a clomp onto the upside-down barrel beside him then looked up at Blaaze. "Just a thought, my ass."

Blaaze spread his hands. "Hey, what kind of talk is that? I was simply speculating out loud. A man can't speak his mind to a friend anymore? Geez."

He tilted his hat down and settled in for an afternoon nap. He'd had enough of Tobias's speculating at his expense. He'd help Tobias shoe some horses a little later. Once the sun set, he could do a little reconnaissance.

When night finally arrived and he'd completed his share

of the livery chores, Blaaze headed for the door. "I'm out of here. Think I'll swing by my place and take a look around."

"Really?" Tobias followed him to the stable where Scout was boarded. "Gonna swing by mostly empty land this time of night with a perfectly good bed awaiting you up the street? Who you think you're kidding?"

"Don't be so suspicious." Blaaze began to saddle Scout. "I don't see the problem with a man going out to check on his own property."

Once he finished with the saddle, Blaze swung himself up. With a tap of his hat at Tobias, he cued Scout into a trot. If he happened to take the scenic route home and pass by the Clanton spread on the way, that'd simply be a bonus.

~

The next afternoon, Mary Catherine set about the task of coordinating a more conservative look for her female employees.

"I'm not wearing that!" Charlotte shouted loud enough for people to hear her in the next county.

"I'm standing right here, Charlotte. You don't have to yell." Mary Catherine tried to hold on to her patience, but her patience was wearing thin. "Ladies do not raise their voices. At least try it on." She held out the simple beige day dress again.

Charlotte ignored the offering.

They'd been at this for over an hour. Between the additional dresses Mary Catherine had bought at the mercantile and the dresses some of the women already owned, the revamping of her serving ladies' appearance had gone better than Mary Catherine expected. Most of the women had cooperated . . . to some point. But Charlotte and two others had decided to make things difficult.

Those three had taken the new rules about the style of dress when in the saloon as an affront. They didn't agree with the cancelation of the upstairs services and kept giving Mary Catherine looks like she'd grown two heads. The women might not understand her need for them to be more circumspect, but no way could she allow skimpily clad ladies to represent her and her establishment. Besides, with no more brothel services, the need for such alluring attire no longer existed.

The evening crowd would begin to trickle in soon, and Mary Catherine wanted this dress business settled.

Barbara Jean came to her aid. "Come on, Charlotte, try not to be such a princess." She took the day dress from Mary Catherine and held it out to Charlotte.

Charlotte crossed her arms, an obstinate look on her face, and shook her head.

Mary Catherine sighed. "You don't have to wear this particular dress, Charlotte. If you don't like the color, we can find something else. But I need you to try it on so I can get an idea of the fit. I don't have a measuring tape, so I need to approximate sizes."

Mary Catherine had discovered that several women had dresses of their own that would serve nicely for working the floor. Macey, in particular, had seemed gratified to be able to wear her regular clothes. Thank heavens. Mary Catherine wasn't sure her tab at the mercantile could take outfitting the entire rest of the group.

Charlotte, unfortunately, did not have a suitable garment of her own. Her clothes all looked like undergarments standing in for outer garments. Everything the woman had shown Mary Catherine seemed to scream, "Imagine what I would look like without any clothes on!" Propriety was definitely not a part of the woman's vocabulary.

"I'm with Charlotte," Grace, one of the detractors, said. She couldn't be more than eighteen years old. "I'm not taking advice on wardrobe from a woman who dresses like a prudish old maid."

The barb strung, but Mary Catherine would never let the girl or any of these ladies see it. It wasn't the first time she'd been made fun of for her clothes and probably wouldn't be the last. Given the life and fiancé she'd left back home, she'd most likely end up an old maid despite Mr. Clanton's high opinion of the bachelors Lawless and the surrounding environs had to offer. Though she'd like to think there was nothing prudish about herself.

She'd worn one of her nicest dresses today. While it covered her to the ankles and had a circumspect neckline unlike Grace's attire, Mary Catherine thought the lines and embellishments quite stylish. She looked down and brushed her hand self-consciously against the soft, cotton fabric of the gray dress's skirt.

"That's enough, Grace," Barbara Jean said. "No reason to be rude. You might want to remember this here gal is now the boss. So's you might want to be holdin' that there tongue of yours or you might end up back on the streets where Miss Lila found you."

Although not fond of the girl's unflattering comment, Mary Catherine would be loath to put anyone out on the streets. "Listen, Grace"—she turned to Charlotte—"and Charlotte, I understand this may not be the way you're used to doing things. But I need you to cooperate. As long as everyone works together, no one's ending up on any streets.

Trust me to know what I'm doing."

Grace scoffed. "Lady, if you're not gonna let us show off the wares, then you don't know nothing about men. Whether they're spending on liquor or women." She snatched the conservative dress from Barbara Jean. "But iffin' you want us to dress like nuns? *Fine*. I'll dress like a nun. Just don't come complaining to me when the money for the night comes in low."

Some establishments made it so their serving staff made nothing except the tips bestowed on them by the patrons. From what Mary Catherine could tell from the records she'd reviewed, Lila had paid a fair wage, and Mary Catherine had no intention of changing the practice. That is, she intended to pay as fair a wage as she could depending on the daily take of the place, so Grace's jibe hit home.

Without even a hint of modesty, Grace dropped the shin-length dress she wore into a pool at her feet. The girl had nothing on underneath except stockings, short bloomers, and a corset that curved mostly *under* her breasts. Blushing, Mary Catherine looked away from the girl's bare nipples, not looking back until the girl had pulled the new dress over her head and smoothed it down.

Grace stepped away from her floored dress and made a quick twirl in a circle, arms out wide. The dress had come from Mary Catherine's personal wardrobe and fit the girl well. So they must be the same dress size. Mary Catherine jotted a note to that effect in her notebook then looked at Charlotte.

Charlotte huffed and headed for the door. "Not happening, lady. I dress the way I dress." She stopped at the threshold and looked back. "You don't like it? I can always find myself another house." With a flounce, she stormed out of the room.

A gentle hand touched Mary Catherine's shoulder. "Don't worry about her none," Barbara Jean assured Mary Catherine. "Not too many places round here that will put up with the likes of her, lessen the twit finds some old coot wanting to keep her as a mistress."

Mary Catherine certainly hoped it wouldn't come down to anyone needing to serve as some man's mistress. She understood tight times, but she still couldn't imagine a woman bartering her body in such a way. With only about three weeks to put together the money she owed Jake Clanton, Mary Catherine was facing tight times of her own. The sum she needed to pay off her debt was substantial indeed, to use Jake Clanton's words. If Blaaze hadn't given her a large portion of his room payment in advance, she wouldn't even have half of what she needed.

The bounty hunter had surprised her when he'd agreed to her double room rate, but she'd readily taken it. His money would help tide her over until she learned the full workings of this business and figured out how to make it more profitable. She needed to figure it out in the next week or two to take care of Mr. Clanton, but she also needed to figure it out in the long term to take care of herself.

She looked around the room. She was now an employer, so she also needed to take care of these women. The business was a means to not only her independence but theirs as well. She had no experience connecting with other women, but she could certainly share the basic concepts for establishing a thriving enterprise with them.

She tucked her pencil into the top of the bun at her nape then gathered up her notes. "Okay, ladies, everyone remember what I said about the importance of looking our best. I'll have dresses this evening for those of you who need them. Everyone else be sure to dress in the garment we selected for you."

"Why do we have to wear ugly dresses when Charlotte doesn't?" one of the younger girls whined.

Before Mary Catherine could answer, Macey put an arm around the girl. "Because we've got more sense than Charlotte and know to do what we're told," she said as she led the girl from the room.

Women who do what they're told, wasn't that the way men wanted the world. Well, she wanted to be the one to do the telling, at least as it related to her business and her life. So if she didn't want to be a woman forced to do what a husband told her to do, Mary Catherine was going to have to make this saloon more profitable.

The pushback from the women wasn't the worst of it. She still had to decipher certain entries in the saloon's notebooks that failed to reconcile. She spent last night factoring and figuring over the books. Now that she understood the full nature of Lila's—*her*—business, the codings made sense. She had boarding rooms notated by "BR" and sportin' rooms abbreviated as "SR." The fluctuation in the revenue for the SR rooms from night to night also now made sense.

The rooms for boarding had a modest, steady intake. The income from the brothel rooms varied by day. The books showed high revenue on Friday nights during Lila's tenure because, Mary Catherine had learned, that was the night the ranch hands got paid.

Last night had been Friday night, and her intake had been abysmal. This was mostly due to her elimination of the brothel activities, but careful calculations showed those numbers were suspiciously low after Lila's death even with the brothel still in full operation. Somewhere she'd lost substantial cashflow, and she didn't know how or where.

She made a mental note to speak with Charlie. After what Barbara Jean told her yesterday about Charlie's responsibility for handling the revenue and purchasing the supplies, she had some questions for the bartender. That was on her agenda for later.

At the top of the day's remaining agenda was another pass at the saloon's records to see what she might have missed. She glanced up the stairs, a twinge of anxiousness making her inexplicably wary. It was foolish to let some paper and scribblings unnerve her, but what if there were more debts than the brewery? What about other capital issues?

With an internal pep talk, she shook off her hesitancy and grabbed the railing to ascend. Now that she'd thrown away what was likely her business's most profitable offering, no time like the present to figure out how lively her future livelihood was truly likely to be.

Chapter 13

THE SUN SHONE BRIGHT as Mary Catherine headed toward the mercantile for the third time since her arrival. Her second jaunt into the store had been to acquire the additional dresses she'd needed for the serving women and some toiletry items for herself. While she walked, she practiced a speech under her breath she hoped would sound persuasive to the proprietor, Mr. Ludtke.

She needed a few more items, but she needed him to extend her credit until she settled up with the brewery owner. It was an embarrassing situation to be in. A week had passed since she had her encounter with the ladies over the upstairs amenities, and since that time, her profits had plummeted. She hated to admit that Barbara Jean and Blaaze had been right, but the proof had been staring at her from the pages of her account books this morning. The intake from the boarding rooms combined only with spirits and food sales wasn't enough to chip away at her debt to Mr. Clanton.

On top of that, she had received a telegram yesterday from her banker back home. She hadn't been able to send the promised payment on the mortgage she'd taken against her parents' home. If she didn't wire at least one payment by the end of the week, the bank had threatened to take the house. She'd hoped life in Lawless would net her a living that would allow her to maintain her independence *and* her parents' home. Right now, that wasn't working out so well.

To avoid colliding with Bernice and her daughter Chastity on the boardwalk, Mary Catherine took a step to the side. Bernice ran the Women's Suffrage Association and made quite a big deal about furthering the position of women in Kansas. She'd been lobbying for women's suffrage for quite some years from what Mary Catherine had heard.

She smiled at the ladies as they passed. Neither smiled back. Chastity dropped her eyes and Bernice gave a rather loud "harrumph" before she grabbed Chastity's arm and pulled her away like Mary Catherine had the plague.

Mary Catherine kept her aplomb. The rude behavior wasn't new. When she'd first arrived in Lawless, she'd received many a speculative stare from the women of the town. She'd chalked it up to curiosity about a stranger. But after the first week, she'd noticed many of the looks morphed from curious glances to rude stares and now to outright female hostility.

She sighed internally. After what she'd learned about the saloon's upstairs business, their behavior should come as no surprise. The female leaders of the town were unlikely to welcome the town madam into their inner circle. Didn't mean it didn't hurt.

Stepping into the mercantile, she saw the proprietor stocking shelves near the back of the store. She walked up behind him. "Good afternoon, Mr. Ludtke. I wonder if I could speak with you for a moment."

"Well, good afternoon, Miss Templeton." He stepped down from his stool. "What can I do for you today? You come to settle up your bill?"

Mary Catherine fought to keep her face neutral. "Actually, Mr. Ludtke, I was wondering if I could have a few more weeks to get you that first payment."

His brow puckered. "Well . . ."

She jumped in before he could continue and tell her no. "I know you—and everybody else in town—have heard by now that I have to settle the saloon's brewery account with Jake Clanton in about two weeks."

He nodded. "I've heard."

"The thing is, that's a substantial sum, and I've got to settle that in order to keep the saloon open. If I lose the saloon, then I'll be unable to pay my account with you at all."

"Well, see, that's the thing, Miss Templeton." He scratched the top of his balding head. "If Clanton takes your business, then where does that leave me? I don't expect you have another source of income?" he asked almost hopefully. "Maybe family back east who could send you some money?"

If only, Mary Catherine thought. There was Jeremiah. If she wired him, he'd surely send her the money. Of course, Mr. Beauregard would also take it as an indication she intended to honor their betrothal despite all her prior words to the contrary. He didn't even know where she was. She hadn't left him word upon leaving, and asking him to wire her money would likely bring him to town. Bring him to town with expectations that their wedding would not only happen but happen quite soon.

She couldn't do that. It'd be the equivalent of giving up. She hadn't even been in Lawless a full month. She needed time. If she had more time, she could do this. She could turn her saloon into a financial success. She knew she could.

"Mr. Ludtke, I just need a little more time. How about this? I promise that I'll pay you first. When it comes time to pay Mr. Clanton, if I don't have enough to pay his debt in full, I'll pay you off the top and take my chances with Jake Clanton." She handed him a list. "Right now, I could really use these items."

The list consisted mostly of cleaning supplies and a few ingredients for a new menu she was considering. She'd have to deal with Cook's persnicketiness about fooling around with his kitchen, but she'd deal with that when the time came. Mr. Ludtke looked over the list then scratched the top of his head again. She could see part of him wanted to help her, but another part of him questioned the soundness of such a risky business move.

She understood. If she were on his side of the equation, she'd likely not extend herself the additional credit. That didn't mean she wasn't going to try and convince him to take the gamble. "I've got to keep the boarding rooms clean and tidy. I've also got to keep the meal services running. By adding breakfast for more than my boarders and a few lunch specials, I'll be able to increase business. And I've noticed a lot more of the railroad workers are coming into town for meals at the saloon. That means more patrons for other businesses in town as well, including your mercantile. With more people spending more time in town, that means more time for them to shop."

His lips curved upward at her spiel. "You're quite the businesswoman, aren't you Miss Mary?"

She blinked at his shortening of her name. More and more people kept calling her Mary, the biblical name associated with purity and innocence. She could still hear Blaaze's mumble about how appropriate the appellation was given her decision to terminate the brothel services the women used to offer.

Mr. Ludtke chuckled, amused with himself over his businesswoman comment. "Okay. Truth be told, your account isn't that high compared to most in this town. A few more weeks isn't going to do my bottom line much harm."

He moved to grab some of the items on her list from the shelves closest to him then walked around the store gathering the other items. After he stacked everything on the counter, he calculated her total and bundled them in a woven brown basket to make them easier for her to carry. He started to hand her the basket then yanked it back when she reached out her arms.

"Know," he said with a stern look, "I'm going to keep you to your word, Miss. When it comes time for you to pay Clanton, you either pay us both or pay me first. I'm doing fine by my standards. But if it comes down to Clanton's bank balance or mine, I dare say that not getting your payoff isn't gonna hurt Clanton none. Me on the other hand, I can't afford to be giving away my store. You understand?"

"I understand." She quickly grabbed the bundle of goods when he moved to hand them to her a second time, not wanting to give him another chance to haul them back or change his mind. "And don't worry. You have my solemn word."

Besides, Clanton had a secondary recourse. If she didn't pay him, he could seize part or all of the saloon's assets to make himself whole. She just had to make sure it didn't come to that. If he did and the bank seized her home, she'd be totally destitute. At this point, she could likely save one or the other. Time made that calculation easy. She'd increase her odds of success with the longer of the two deadlines.

Sorry, mom and dad, she thought, fighting back tears and a deep-seated melancholy.

She headed for the saloon but almost changed course when she saw the cluster of six women up ahead, five of whom were white. They appeared to be waiting for her, which did not bode well. Already emotionally raw from humbling herself before Mr. Ludtke and facing the permanent loss of her childhood home, she had no desire to have what looked to be an upcoming confrontation. Straightening her spine and making sure to suppress her momentary lapse of self-possession, she staunchly maintained her course nonetheless.

"Look what we have here, ladies," Elizabeth Duffy, chairwoman of the Lawless Women's Council, said. "If it isn't our local saloon mistress."

"Ladies," Mary Catherine said affably, trying to remain cordial despite the snide tone in which she was addressed.

She'd understood when she'd first arrived in Lawless that the townspeople were not happy to learn their precious saloon had transferred to another woman. The men especially had been concerned when they realized she was without any frontier experience. She'd been winning over the men with the new recipes she'd added to the saloon's normal fare, but cutting off their access to the women had set her right back where she'd started. Maybe even further back.

"Ladies? No sense putting on airs, missus. No self-respecting lady would own a den of spirits. You should be ashamed of yourself. Encouraging drunkenness and condoning fornication. How dare you lure our men into lascivious and sinful behavior. We don't need the likes of you in town. Why don't you go on back east."

"She's as bad as that tramp cousin of hers," Elizabeth's

sister Alice added.

Three of the women with them nodded in agreement.

The insult to Lila made Mary Catherine compress the bundle in her hands. The brown basket crumpled inward beneath her squeeze but didn't break. Maintaining her composure was going to be harder than she'd thought.

Face tight, she replied stiffly, "*Ladies*, you do realize that even if I were to leave town, the saloon isn't going anywhere? Someone else would simply take over and run it. What difference does it make if the someone running it is a woman or a man?"

Calliope Watson, who had remained silent up to this point, stepped forward. As the pastor's wife, Calliope held a lot of influence in town despite being a Colored woman. "I don't know how they do things back in Cleveland, Miss Templeton, but here in Lawless, we have standards of propriety. We're working to bring the federal vote to Kansas. We already have some of the first laws in the country that allow women to vote in local elections. Why we've gotten Susanna Madora Salter of Argonia elected the first female mayor in the country. We can't have fallen women traipsing about town or furthering improper businesses. It undermines all the great work women of Kansas are doing, especially the Lawless Women's Council and Bernice's Women's Suffrage Association."

Mary Catherine stiffened at the implication that she was a fallen woman. It was a lofty speech, especially considering Bernice's Women's Suffrage Association didn't include women of the Race.

"I heard you graduated from college?" Alice asked, as if she didn't believe it.

"*Hmpf.*" Elizabeth made a big show of looking Mary

Catherine up and down. "Only makes her think she's better than us." She stepped in close and got in Mary Catherine's face. "Well, Miss Know-It-All, you ain't no better than us."

Alice put her hand on her sister's arm and pulled her back. "Shush, Beth." She looked Mary Catherine in the eyes. "My point is, if you have that kind of education, you could be of great service to the woman in this town. That is if you weren't set on running an improper enterprise for a woman."

Fallen woman. Miss Know-It-All. Cousin of a tramp. Proprietor of an improper enterprise. Mary Catherine had had all the caterwauling she was going to take from these women. No wonder Blaaze referred to them as old biddies. They had notions right out of the '60s.

"Actually, there *ain't no*"—she purposefully glanced at Elizabeth upon repeating the poor grammar—"improper enterprise for a woman. A woman can—and *should*—be allowed to run any business a man does. It shouldn't matter what kind of business I, or any other woman in Lawless, might run. We can still assist with the advancement of women in Kansas and this town. So I'll thank you to keep to yourselves your ideas about what's appropriate for me and my college degree.

"You all are the ones who should be ashamed of yourselves. We're *all* in this struggle for financial and voting rights. Women should stick together. It's not as if the men are working hard to give us rights equal to theirs. All you're doing is playing into their hands by picking and choosing who gets to be part of the fight. The segregation of our suffrage efforts and pitting certain women of the town against others is a strategy that works in their favor; it's known as divide and conquer. With your divisive attitudes, good luck accomplishing your goals." She adjusted the bundle in her hand.

"Oh, and, Alice . . ."

Whatever look Mary Catherine had on her face made Alice take a huge step backward, but Mary Catherine didn't let her retreat.

She got within slapping distance of the woman but didn't strike. "Don't let this college education and eastern upbringing mislead you," she said, exaggerating her diction and her accent. "If I ever hear you call my cousin a tramp again, or speak ill of her in any way, I'm gonna channel a little bit of our prizefighter great-grandfather and knock your judgmental teeth right down your throat."

Alice and her entourage collectively gasped, and the mouth of the church matron dropped open. Satisfied her message had been clearly received, Mary Catherine stepped past the bunch. She looked ahead only to see Blaaze watching her from two doors down.

One shoulder perched against the column in front of the barbershop, he was all long and lean and hatted handsomeness. He looked calm and relaxed, but the demeanor was a facade. She'd figured out in her short time in town that Blaaze Lassiter's insouciant manner hid a sharp, attentive mind that missed nothing and governed a predator always ready to strike.

He nodded at her, a small upturn to his lips. He must have heard what she'd said to Alice. She returned his nod and gave him a looked that dared him to say anything about the encounter. His mouth spread into a full grin, and he lifted his hands in mock surrender.

How the arrogant cowboy always managed to show up whenever there was the slightest altercation involving her, she couldn't fathom. However he managed it, this time, she didn't care if he'd seen and heard her entire encounter with the women. He and they could all go stuff themselves.

As if it was her fault those ladies' men came to town to drink and philander. Uppity biddies. And they called her a know-it-all. She might appear not to have the worldliness required to live on her own and manage the most popular hangout in town, but that was about to change.

Go back east. *The heck if she would!*

She braced herself as she got closer to Blaaze. No telling what the man might have to say.

His low, insolent drawl stroked over her as she approached. "Well done, Miss Templeton."

Her steps faltered. His lips spread into a wider grin at her reaction. That certainly had not been on her list of possible greetings. The unexpected praise was all the more unnerving said in that deep, resonant voice that somehow washed a calm over her and made her heart race simultaneously.

Amused by her look of shock, he winked at her, pushed off the column, and headed into the barbershop with that smug grin firmly fixed on his face.

A smug, sexy grin.

Mary Catherine stood in place, momentarily unsettled by the magnetism of the rugged cowboy. Too bad he was as annoying as he was good looking. Her gaze strayed to the seat of his pants, where the tight denims gripped his firm, rounded backside. Slightly bow-legged, the man sauntered more than walked. The thought of all that tight, firmness beneath her hands sent a hot flush through her.

With a start, Mary Catherine shook herself and quickly headed on her way before someone caught her gaping at the man's butt. Maybe even the man himself. *And wouldn't that beat all,* as the locals liked to say.

Two weeks ago, when she'd looked up at the body hurling

toward her through the saloon window and seen his face, she'd been stunned. He'd been dispossessed of the hat that had been low over his brow when he rode in, but she'd recognized the villainous-looking character who had ridden past her boarding house window earlier in the day. The way he'd held his body, the swagger in his stance, and that long coat—that made him look every bit the outlaw—could not be mistaken.

Up close, the scruffy beard and dusty clothes he'd had on did little to staunch the dangerousness that surrounded him. The muscles and strong physique that resided beneath that full-length coat were evident not only in his appearance, but also in the easy strength he'd used to pull her from her watery trap. The trickle of awareness she'd experienced when he'd set her on her feet and looked deep into her eyes had unnerved her. She'd been forced to take a step back, afraid she was being sucked into some unexplainable maelstrom that would leave her scorched and mindless and possibly lifeless.

The fear had been real, but she wasn't sure the fear had stemmed solely from concern over the mortal repercussions tangling with a man like him could have. Most of her adult life, Mary Catherine had suffered exposure to a wide variety of controlling and powerful men, and they weren't her type. She preferred the studious, romantic type.

Certainly a man from wild country who looked as if he made his living using a weapon for nefarious purposes shouldn't be the first man she met who made her feel *very* female . . . and unavoidably delicate. In a town reported to have at least a dozen men for every woman, surely she could find a safer prospect to involuntarily awaken all the biological underpinnings that evidenced she had physical parts in need of stimulation other than her college-educated brain.

They didn't breed men like that back in Cleveland. And if she didn't want to end up with only enough money to make it back to Cleveland, where she'd likely have to give in to Jeremiah to avoid homelessness, she'd better figure out her current financial situation fast.

Chapter 14

UPON REACHING THE SALOON, Mary Catherine stashed the food stuffs in the kitchen then climbed the stairs to her room. She dropped her personal purchases onto the small desk where the most recent account book still laid open to the page she'd last reviewed.

She'd tried to supplement the meal income by adding lunch specials that came with a free sandwich. It had brought in additional men for lunch, but none had eaten or drank enough to make up for the sportin' rooms being closed. Her fist tightened at her side. This would never do.

After today's run-ins with the town's society women, she was more determined than ever to make a success of the legacy Lila had left her. She ran her finger down the most recent column of figures. No way she'd manage to pay off Jake Clanton with these numbers. She was barely able to pay the women the wages they were due.

Deciding not to dwell on what was not and work on what could be, Mary Catherine returned to the kitchen. Cook didn't particularly like people in his kitchen, but the lunch hour was about to begin, and this was as good a day as any to try out her new special. She'd posted bills along the street advertising that patrons got a free lunch with any drink order. Today's lunch cost more than one drink, but the hope was men would stay longer and drink more if they could do so over a heartier lunch.

She'd carefully planned today's special: succulent, sliced beef between two slices of fresh baked bread. Mary Catherine would bake the bread herself. It was one of the first items her mother had taught her to make. Momma's bread recipe was stellar. It baked up light and had a bit of a sweet to it due to a few special ingredients. Mary Catherine had made a bit of an investment in those additional ingredients, but she needed to increase her income and the added expense seemed worth the risk.

This lunch special needed to draw in more patrons during the afternoon hours. That was her slowest time. Business boomed pretty steadily at night, but the current income from nights wouldn't get her out of her bind.

She'd given up on the white table linens and hand cloths idea, wanting to make sure the men felt welcome here. Unfortunately, she was beginning to realize that the brothel formed an essential part of this community. The sportin' enterprise went well beyond her original perceptions of it as mere obscene behavior and sexual lewdness. She puttered around the kitchen letting her turbulent thoughts run amok.

Finally driving Cook crazy enough to boot her out of the kitchen, Mary Catherine took her worrying brain into the main hall. Looking around the room, she was surprised to see a woman walk into the saloon. She was tall—very tall—and dressed in a buttoned shirt, denims covered by leather that had fringes on the sides, and a pair of boots that looked suspiciously like snakes. She wore a hat with a rounded brim and braided leather trim. Two leather straps dropped down beside her ears and were joined together where they dangled under her chin.

Though her clothing was not the traditional dress of any woman Mary Catherine had ever met, the clothes were cut for the woman's shape. This wasn't a woman trying to dress like a man; this was a woman embracing the practicality of cowboy attire while leaving no question she had a womanly shape underneath. That shape was solid and curvy. Mary Catherine suspected this woman could handle herself as well as any man around horses or on a ranch.

She was definitely a woman who'd draw attention, and Mary Catherine was fascinated.

The stranger stood in the doorway and took a long look around the saloon. Satisfied by what she saw—or didn't see— the woman stepped up to the bar and flipped her hat off to dangle at the back of her shoulders. The hat sat atop a long, single braid that hung to her midback. She sat down.

"I'll have a whiskey," she said to Charlie, who stood behind the bar gaping at her.

He gave her an odd look before he dropped a glass in front of her and picked up a bottle of whiskey. "You sure you don't want me to have them bring you a cup of tea from the kitchen, miss?"

She flipped a silver coin onto the bar. "Do I look like the kind of woman that drinks tea?"

At that, the barkeep grinned. "Nope. But I was trying not to make assumptions."

The woman chuckled at that. "Fine. I'll try not to take offense. Now, how about that whiskey?"

He poured her a finger of whiskey, but she waved him to

keep pouring. After pouring in another finger, he stoppered the bottle and went back to what he was doing. When the woman lifted her glass to take a drink, she noticed Mary Catherine watching her.

They stared at each other for a few seconds, then the woman gave Mary Catherine a salute with her glass. Mary Catherine nodded at her in return, unable to shake the feeling there was something familiar about this woman, though she was certain she'd never seen her around town. The woman would have been hard to forget, and as the only Colored woman to enter the saloon besides Mary Catherine, Barbara Jean, and a few of the sportin' women, the woman would certainly have been the talk of the town if she were a regular.

Knowing there was nothing else for her to do in the saloon, Mary Catherine took one last look at the stranger then headed back upstairs to calculate what she needed her take to be for the rest of the day. She'd gotten some basic figures from Charlie about his collections and purchases over the last few months. Annoyingly, he hadn't bothered to write anything down, so she had only the notes she taken during their conversation. What she'd learned was Charlie was a lousy business manager.

Tonight, things had to change. Back in her room, she drummed her fingers distractedly against a ledger cover. She probably needed to add something to her offerings better than a free sandwich. Something that would draw a big crowd, a big paying crowd. There had to be a way to draw in the men with something other than food and drink alone—something other than the services that shall not be named.

Her fingers stalled when a crazy idea came to her. It was a little risqué but didn't come close to selling sexual favors. At least not the hands-on kind of sexual favors. She'd read in some of the papers she had shipped from Kansas City, Wichita, and even as far as Sioux Falls, that many establishments had added dance hall girls. While the town "respectables" probably wouldn't think dance hall girls were a proper business for her to run either, it was better than running a whoreh—*no!*—a brothel.

If she got really creative, she might be able to not only easily pay all the ladies of the house but double up on her savings for Jake Clanton. Mary Catherine ran through the possibilities in her mind and a smile slowly surfaced. What she had to do required her full focus and ingenuity.

She wanted to be sensitive to the ladies' situation lest they think her casting prolonged judgment on their previously chosen lifestyle. While she was certain her pastor uncle and churchgoing parents would find such prior lifestyles inappropriate, Mary Catherine tried very hard to live by the basic tenet of judge not lest ye be judged. She probably hadn't done a good job of that the other day. Now, she had a chance to make it up to them.

First, she had to find out if any of the ladies could sing or dance. Even if they couldn't, how discriminating of a crowd could there be in Lawless, Kansas, of all places. The men would absolutely love it.

How hard could running a dance hall be, after all?

~

A few days later, Blaaze sat at the livery stable finessing his latest whittling project.

"You simply going to let that continue?" Tobias motioned to the sheriff sauntering across the street from the saloon to return to the jail.

Blaaze shrugged and considered his next scoop of wood.

It was the second time he'd tried to make a horse, but it was starting to look like a deformed cow. "Not my business," he said dismissively while he pondered how to take the face in the wood block from bovine to stallion.

Tobias turned to look at him dead on, a red-tipped rod hot from the fire held high in his big grasp. "That little eastern filly ain't your business?"

Blaaze leaned backed and cocked an eye beneath the brim of his Stetson. "Don't let her hear you call her that."

Tobias grinned before getting back to the business at hand. "You know that brewery man aims to take her business or run her out of business."

"It won't come to that."

"Horse shit. And that sheriff's not gonna do a damned thing. Clanton owns him lock, stock, and barrel. Don't you think it's time you stopped acting like the town grandpa and become the peacemaker you signed up to be?"

With a contemplative gaze, Blaaze intentionally laid his lazy drawl on thick. "Just how do you figure?"

"Don't give me that innocent look. I'm getting tired of looking at you. Get off your ass and do something, Lassiter. You've got more authority than that useless piece of fake lawman."

Blaaze glared at his old friend.

Tobias shoved the hot poker into the cooling pit. "You forget I was here when Malone tapped you?" He sat down the iron he'd just shaped, pulled off his gloves, and came to stand in front of Blaaze. "I know about that star you keep hidden away for lord knows what reason."

Blaaze started to speak, but Tobias held up a hand to silence him.

Arms crossed, Tobias snarled at him. "You need to stop

playing helpless and shut this crap down. This town won't be worth a damn if Clanton gets control of it, and it looks like he's already got control of the sheriff."

Blaaze continued on with his carving, but a part of him knew Tobias was right. Clanton was up to no good, and that useless piece of sheriff kept the town under control by preventing the men from wearing weapons. Knowing he couldn't count on the law to be the law was going to cause a long-term problem for Blaaze.

He had no intention of picking that star back up. That didn't mean he couldn't do a little more snooping tonight to make sure he wasn't caught unaware whenever Clanton decided to make his move. He'd keep that bit to himself. Tobias need not be the wiser. The man would be impossible to be around if he thought he'd inspired Blaaze to get involved. Blaaze had already traveled out to the Clanton place and the brewery to get the lay of the land. The ruffians he'd spotted at both places didn't seem the kind of fellas an upright businessman associated with.

Ignoring Tobias's lecture, Blaaze set his whittling aside and tilted his hat down over his face to settle back for his afternoon nap. After his nap, he slipped away and did a little more scouting. Near noon the next morning, he dragged himself to his room.

He'd snooped around the Clanton spread most of the night. He'd also taken a swing by Beulah's place, curious to see what the woman had going on that warranted Clanton's scheming to make her place the first hotel within two hundred miles. Best he could tell, her place would be the closest lodgings to the planned Lawless railroad stop, assuming construction on the railroad ever resumed.

Tossing off his clothes, he dropped into bed. All he could

think about was sleeping till sundown. Unfortunately, the sound of a crash woke him from a sound sleep only a few hours later. Jerking up in bed, Blaaze let his eyes adjust to the low light of drawn curtains. With a frustrated curse, he plopped back against the pillow. It was way too long before sundown.

No sooner had his head hit the pillow than a loud, long scream came from downstairs, followed by a man's shout. When another crash that sounded like a breaking table made the floor shake beneath him, he sprang from the bed and grabbed his pants. He quickly stuffed each leg into his denims, threw on his boots, and yanked on his shirt, not bothering to button it before he snatched open his bedroom door and rushed out into the hall.

A quick glance over the railing revealed complete chaos. He couldn't believe his eyes. At least two dozen men had descended into pandemonium. Max Davenport, the area's largest ranch owner, was yelling at Mary Catherine, and God bless her heart, she stood toe to toe with him, yelling right back. Blaaze's eyes scanned the room to find Charlotte leading a very happy Willis Montgomery up the stairs. Clearly, she thought to take advantage of Mary Catherine currently being otherwise engaged.

He didn't see Babs, but Greenleigh struggled in a corner with a bloke who tried to whisk her toward the back stairs. She wore a purple and black dance hall dress with layered ruffles to her knees in the front and down to the floor in the back. He wondered if that had been a Mary-Catherine-approved wardrobe choice.

What the Devil had happened here? A man decides to take a well-deserved nap through the afternoon, and all hell breaks loose. All he'd wanted was some peaceful shut-eye until the late evening. No such luck. He couldn't seem to catch any rest in this place, despite the outrageous price he was paying for the privilege of trying.

This saloon and that woman—he took another quick glance at Mary Catherine—were screwing up his nice, quiet retirement. He hadn't had a moment's peace since he'd gotten to town. All because misfortune had seen fit to have Miss College-Educated Lady-From-Back-East arrive nigh on the same day.

He surveyed the room again. What the dickens had she done now? Because however this mass chaos had evolved, he had absolutely no doubt it had been started by the little hellion with the pencil sticking out of the bun at the back of her head.

Then again, maybe not. Blaaze's gaze settled on several cowboys he'd seen hanging out at Clanton's place during his nightly sojourns.

The tallest one picked up a man Blaaze didn't recognize and threw him over the bar into the shelved bottles of spirits. Two full shelves crashed to the floor. So maybe Mary Catherine had had a little help getting things started.

His eyes swung back her way. Whatever Max said to her made her eyes go wide, and she began to vehemently shake her head. Max grabbed her arm and tried to lead her toward the parlor. When Mary Catherine resisted, he shook her hard enough for a tendril of her thick, wavy hair to come loose and dangle against her temple. Mary Catherine struggled against his hold to no avail. Deciding leading her along wasn't going to get him anywhere, the man lifted her off her feet with one arm, braced her kicking body against his hip, and continued his path toward the parlor.

Blaaze knew a rage he'd never felt before. He sprinted to the top of the stairs. When he reached the landing, he didn't bother to descend. He simply vaulted over the stair rail and landed deftly beside Max and Mary Cate with bended knees and a steadying hand against the floor. Max's eyes widened in surprise, and Mary Catherine's showed visible relief.

Blaaze straightened to his full height. "Going somewhere, Max?" he said with a menacing step forward.

"Lassiter." Max's jaw tightened. "This is none of your business. Get out of my way." He tried to take a step, Mary Catherine still pressed against him, though he'd lowered her feet to the floor.

Blaaze cut him off. "Well, Max, that's where you'd be wrong. 'Cuz it seems to me you're holding on to a woman who doesn't want to be held on to."

"*Exactly.*" Mary Catherine jerked to pull away from him, but he pulled her back.

"What's it to you?" Max said to Blaaze, easily corralling Mary Catherine once again.

Blaaze tucked a thumb into the waistband of his denims. "It's the funniest thing. I seem to have this problem with women being forced to do things they don't want to do."

Max mugged at him. "Now, you see, that's where you'd be wrong. Me and Miss Templeton here have some business to take care of. She was being a might difficult at first, but I think we've come to an understanding. At least, we're gonna get to an understanding after we have a chance to discuss things privately over in the parlor."

"Oh, now I get it." Blaaze made as if to consider Max's words. "You're simply planning to go discuss some business. Privately." He quirked his head. "In the parlor. And Miss Templeton decided she couldn't walk there on her own and needed you to carry her?"

A chuckle rumbled behind Max's closed-mouth smirk.

"Something like that."

Blaaze glanced at Mary Catherine's face. "Is that the right of it, Mary Cate?"

Max's eyes narrowed at his use of such a familiar address with Mary Catherine, and she gave Blaaze a look that could melt steel as sure as any forge Tobias had in his smithy before she shook her head in the negative. The head shake was followed by a tilt of her head that telegraphed *Quit goofing off and get me away from this cretin.*

"Hmm." Blaaze ignored her smart-ass expression and rubbed his chin in false thoughtfulness. "Well, Max, we seem to have a problem. The lady doesn't agree with your take on the matter."

"Isn't that unfortunate," Max said with a glare.

"Yeah, for you." Blaaze threw a quick jab that knocked Max backward. Simultaneously, he grabbed Mary Catherine around the waist and snatched her from the rancher's grasp.

Max stumbled a few steps then wiped at his mouth. A trickle of blood dripped from his split lip. A flinch under his eye was Blaaze's only warning before the man charged.

Blaaze shoved Mary Catherine toward the stairwell wall and ducked the punch Max threw. A fairly large guy, Max could probably hold his own in a fight, but Blaaze was currently angrier, meaner, and deadlier. So the matter finished in pretty short order. With a three-punch combination, Blaaze had Max laid out on the floor unconscious.

Mary Catherine moved to walk away, and Blaaze pulled her back just as a chair came flying past and crashed against the wall beside them. He looked around at the continued bedlam throughout the main room. Chairs flew, bottles shattered, tables crashed. The noise level had nearly doubled. If this wasn't put down immediately, Mary Catherine wasn't going to have much of a saloon left.

He shoved her down beside a wood hutch. "Stay put," he said with a pointed finger to emphasize his seriousness.

Assured she intended to stay where he put her, he dove into the fray.

His first stop was to free Greenleigh from her overzealous suitor. Then he grabbed two scuffling cowpokes who were doing more damage to the nearby tables than to each other. Intent on shoving them outside, he only made it halfway there before a chair smashed against his back and knocked him to the floor amidst its shattered shards.

Blaaze rolled to avoid being stomped on and quickly grabbed a stool to pull himself up. He wobbled to his feet facing the bar. Years of survival instincts made him whirl to get the brawling mob from his back, but he'd barely made the turn when two gunshots rang out.

Chapter 15

COMPLETE SILENCE DESCENDED ON the saloon.

Expecting to see the sheriff, Blaaze glanced toward the entrance only to find Marshal Bridger Malone, his gun aimed toward the ceiling and badge gleaming prominently against his vested chest.

The lawman lowered his gun and pointed it toward no one in particular. "Next man to move gets a bullet in his gut," he warned.

His eyes scanned the crowd and the damage. When his gaze found Blaaze, he studied Blaaze's open shirt, bruised temple, and jeans stained with whatever he'd rolled in a few minutes ago. "Having a little trouble, Lassiter?"

Blaaze scowled at his buddy. "Quite the entrance, Malone. It's about damn time you showed up. I sent that first telegram weeks ago."

"I was busy." Bridger holstered his weapon and took an amazed look around the room. "Where the hell is the sheriff?"

"That's a good question," Blaaze responded. He'd been wondering the same thing.

Convenient how the law couldn't be found when some of Clanton's men and a passel of roughnecks decided to tear up the saloon.

From the corner of his eye, Blaaze noticed Mary Catherine rise from her crouch next to the hutch he'd stuffed her beside. She stared at the man in her doorway wearing a badge that identified him as a deputy US marshal. From the look on her face, Blaaze suspected she'd never seen a man of the Race wearing a badge.

It wasn't a usual sight, but ever since Judge Parker commissioned two hundred deputy US marshals back in 1875 to serve in Indian Territory, times had been progressing some. One of the two hundred was the first-ever Black marshal, Bass Reeves. Reeves was making a name for himself down south with his sharpshooting skills and his—so far—perfect record of bringing in his man. With Reeves standing as a stellar example of what men of the Race could do if given the proper chance, more and more Colored men were getting appointed to serve as lawmen.

"Where's the proprietor?" the marshal asked him.

"That's her over there." Blaaze motioned toward Mary Catherine with his head. "Excuse me for a minute." He walked over to her and used a finger to slip a loose curl behind her ear.

"Well," she said softly, sounding a bit whipped.

This time, he found it difficult to resist his persistent urge to touch her. He studied her face, calculating her possible reaction, then decided to risk the censure. He cupped a palm around the back of her neck and brushed her cheek with the side of his thumb. "Are you all right?"

"I'm fine," she said, not pulling away. "I guess I owe you a thank you."

Her body contradicted her claim of being fine. She trembled, so he put an arm around her waist and pulled her closer. She reached up a hand and lightly touched his temple. He winced when her fingers found a tender spot beside his left eye.

"You should let me clean that for you." Her voice came out in a rote tone, but active concern showed in her eyes. Her fingertips came away covered with a smidgen of his blood.

"Maybe later." He held her in place when she made to move away.

Taking hold of the heel of the hand she'd used to touch him, Blaaze rubbed her fingers against his denims to clean them. Still holding her close, he raised their joined hands and trapped them against his chest by pulling her tighter against him.

Their gazes connected and held, eyes staring into each other rather than at each other.

For the first time since they'd met, no animosity or baiting or gamesmanship clashed between them. And for the first time, he noticed something different when she looked at him: unshielded desire. The realization made his heart pound. The undercurrent of mutual attraction that pulsed between them made him want to carry her upstairs and explore all the fiery temperament she hid beneath her prim and proper exterior.

The lust she unfailingly awakened in him eased into a foreign and unrecognizable tumult. The rising emotions included concern and caring and even tenderness, yet went beyond that into unfamiliar territory pretty close to possessiveness. The thought unnerved him.

His chest tightened as he fought to ignore the strange sentiments. He needed to get a hold of himself and focus on her. "Mary Catherine, you are not okay."

"I'll be fine. It's just . . ." She gave a slow, pained look around. "How am I ever going to pay for this?"

The soft despair in her voice rocked him. He could physically feel her pain. The damage done today would be a big burden on top of what she already owed Clanton, and he suspected Clanton had planned on as much. She currently looked disheartened, but she was a woman of strong will and determination. She could bounce back from this, and if he had to, he would temporarily lend her his strength to help even the score with those who set themselves against her.

Her palm flattened against his chest, cool against the heat of his skin. Her gaze darted back to his when she noticed the hard thudding of his heart. He wondered if she suspected that it was her causing his heart to pound and not the physical remnants of the altercations he'd recently escaped.

Her fingers flexed, and their tips brushed lightly over his pecs. The feminine touch slid his body into that unavoidable pang of arousal he constantly battled around her, and the urge to kiss her exploded through him like a burst from an unexpected cannon fire.

Luckily, he remembered they weren't alone. So instead of kissing her, he asked her the question that had been on his mind since he was so rudely awakened from his interrupted nap. "What happened?"

"*She* happened," Max Davenport snarled, staggering up behind him. The rancher held his jaw with one hand, gently moving it back and forth to test its working order.

Blaaze watched him warily, but the man did not attempt a hostile strike. He simply glared at Mary Catherine.

"How so?" Blaaze asked.

"She's got her women teasing my men by strutting around waving flouncy skirts and showing off ankles and legs and garters. My men haven't had female consort in over a week. Last payday, they came to town only to find out she'd closed the upstairs rooms. I've had more fights and mishaps on my ranch in the last seven days than I've had in the last year. If these boys don't find a way to let off steam soon, I'm not going to have much of a ranch left."

Blaaze thought about the purple and black dress Greenleigh wore. *So it* had *been approved wardrobe?*

"Just because a lady shows a little leg when she's dancing doesn't mean she's set to be mauled by a bunch of men," Mary Catherine lectured at Max.

Now, they had Blaaze's full attention. "Um, Mary Catherine, you had the women put on some kind of show?"

"Yes." Her clipped response held all the righteousness of a woman who believed wholeheartedly in her course of action. Her shoulders went back, and she stood up straighter. The overwhelmed Mary Catherine fled, and the decisive, in-charge Mary Catherine roared back to life. "It was simply meant to be a bit of entertainment. It's becoming quite popular in saloons west of the Mississippi. The men get to hear several ladies sing or watch them dance, and they can buy dances with the other ladies."

Blaaze scratched his chin and stared blankly at her. "You tried to sell them dances instead of . . . um . . ." He cleared his throat, trying to be circumspect and not embarrass her since they had an audience in Max.

"Yes, *dances,*" Max spat. "Can you believe that!" He shoved a finger in Mary Catherine's face. "Lady, the only dancing these men want to do is on top of bedsheets. We're not interested in this dance hall nonsense."

Mary Catherine slowly pressed his hand away from her face. "I told you before, Mr. Davenport, I am not gonna allow myself to be bullied by you or anyone else."

Blaaze noticed the grammar slip but ignored it to step between the pair. The last thing he needed was for a new disagreement to ignite between the two of them. The barroom brawl would start all over again. "Mary Catherine, you can't go picking fights with men twice your size."

She bristled at his words. "I didn't pick a fight with him. He picked a fight with me. And told me if I couldn't provide the entertainment the men were expecting then I should pay him back for the time and damages I caused on his ranch. *I* caused. What nonsense! Said if I didn't want to pay, he and I could fight things out on the sofa in the back parlor."

Max had the good sense to take a few steps away from Blaaze at Mary Catherine's last revelation. He threw up his hands in defense. "Look, I didn't mean no real harm, Lassiter. I wouldn't have actually hurt her. I was simply hot under the collar and wanted to scare her smart. This here gal needs to understand what she's done to this town."

"Once he got started with his demands," Mary Catherine added, "the other men joined in, and soon fights were breaking out all over the place."

Blaaze rubbed a hand down his face. So Max had gotten things started, and Clanton's men had likely seen it as an opportunity to escalate matters.

"Max." Blaaze took a deep breath and let it out slowly before he continued. "I think it's time you took your leave."

"Look, Lassiter—"

"Nope." Blaaze threw up a hand. "You've said your piece, and you've certainly done enough. You might want to get out of here before I think too hard on what kind of fighting you really intended to do with Mary Catherine back on the parlor sofa. Then I'd be obliged to defend her honor by calling you out to the middle of the street."

Max blinked quickly, not mistaking his threat to challenge him to a shootout. Blaaze wasn't reckless or cocky about gunfights. He had a fast enough gun, but he wasn't foolish enough not to recognize there were men faster. Somewhere. But not this man. When it came to a contest between a man who'd spent his whole life ranching and a man who'd spent the last fifteen years tracking and apprehending the worst of the worst, everyone knew in which direction the deadly bullet would fly.

Backing away from him, Max raised his hands in surrender once more. "No need for threats, Lassiter. We're all just a little testy. Won't happen again."

"See that it doesn't." Blaaze watched him gather his men and leave the saloon. He'd be following up with the rancher later about a donation to cover the repairs for his share of the damages done tonight.

When he turned his dumbstruck attention back to Mary Catherine, she had an obstinate look on her face.

Before he could speak, she snapped, "Button your shirt."

He blinked hard twice. "What?"

They were already back to the bossy, Mary Cate? That was sure quick.

"Button. Your. Shirt." She crossed her arms and squeezed her hands against her biceps, bracing herself for some expected onslaught. "I can't think with you walking around half naked. If you're about to give me a lecture, you need to do it with your clothes fully on."

~

Mary Catherine didn't like the knowing grin that spread across

Blaaze's face at her admission, but at least the man buttoned his shirt. She could still feel the smooth strength of his chest beneath her fingers, and it bothered her that she desperately wanted to touch it again.

She even liked the way he smelled. A hint of bar soap mixed with the scent of fresh air and leather. Being close to him tonight had been a whole lot different from the first time they'd met. The smell and attire of him at their introduction hadn't been anything to get close to, let alone entice a woman. Those intense eyes, on the other hand; those were one and the same. And, now, they seemed to be quietly laughing at her.

"Wipe that smirk off your face and say what you're going to say."

"Now, Mary Cate—"

"Stop calling me that! That's not my name."

He leaned in. "But that's *my* name for you," he said in a deep, growly voice that went straight to a hollow low in her abdomen.

Her breath stalled, and she suddenly felt lightheaded. Her eyes strayed to his full lips. A brain fog descended, and it no longer mattered if he called her Mary Cate or Mary or simply Cate. He could call her whatever he wanted if he'd lean in a little closer, let her touch him once more, maybe lay those lips against hers. She involuntarily tilted toward him. Blaaze's eyes dropped to her mouth, and he seemed to move closer without noticeably moving.

"Lassiter! I haven't got all day," the marshal called, breaking the moment between them.

She jerked away.

Blaaze's eyes squeezed shut for a second. "Hold your horses, Malone! I'll be right there."

While Blaaze gathered himself, Mary Catherine reined in the floozy he seemed to bring out in her and put a respectable distance between her and temptation.

"My lands! What in the dickens happened here?" Barbara Jean swept into the saloon, mouth agape. She gave the marshal an appreciative glance as she sashayed past him and made her way over. She was all dressed up, with a fancy hat, white gloves, and an elaborate red and gold embroidered hand fan that matched her dress. "A gal takes a few days off and all hell breaks loose. What did I miss?"

"The new floor show, apparently," Blaaze replied.

"Floor show?" A perplexed Barbara Jean moved her gaze from the chaos of the destroyed room to Blaaze's face.

"Yes, it seems Miss Templeton decided introducing dance hall girls to the saloon's offerings might help turn things around."

Barbara Jean stared at her in amazement. "You've deprived these boys of convivial relations—"

Three hard coughs burst from Blaaze at Barbara Jean's use of the euphemism they'd come up with during the *we-can't-have-any-more-whorehouse* meeting.

Barbara Jean swatted him with her fan before she continued. "You deprive these boys of convivial relations over almost two weeks then flaunt women kicking up their skirts and waving flouncy dresses in front of them? Miss Mary Catherine, are you out of your mind?"

"I-I wasn't flaunting anything." Mary Catherine was taken aback by Barbara Jean's words.

"Sure you were," Blaaze interjected. "That was like waving a red cape at a raging bull. Actually, it was more like waving a red cape at a *herd* of raging bulls. And last time I checked, you didn't look much like a matador." His expression—and tone—changed to something akin to a parent teaching a child a hard lesson after some prankish faux pas. "Sugar, these men are downright horny. If you'll excuse the frank talk. And you just had Greenleigh and whomever prance around in front of them and remind them exactly what they weren't gonna be getting anymore." He shook his head. "By the way, where'd you get the purple dress?"

"Greenleigh already had it," Mary Catherine said.

"Really?" That surprised him.

"Yeah." Barbara Jean pulled out her hat pins and removed her hat. "Greenleigh used to be a singer. She was headed for California to make it big when she was robbed along with others on a train and couldn't make it the rest of the way there. She ended up a few train stops before the one outside Lawless. Tried to make it on her own as best she could but found there weren't many options for an unmarried woman who didn't know how to do anything but sing and dance. Found many men were willing to help her if she did a little something for them in return. Said she held out as long as she could and was near starving before she decided sacrificing her body beat dying of hunger."

"That's horrible. She didn't tell me that." Mary Catherine glanced over at Greenleigh, who was being comforted by Macey and several other of the women.

"What'd she tell you?" Barbara Jean asked.

"Well, I came looking for you to share my idea."

"About the dance hall girls?" Barbara Jean laid her hat on one of the few remaining upright tables and removed her gloves.

Mary Catherine nodded. "You weren't around. When I told her why I was looking for you, she got really excited. Told me she'd once danced in a show in St. Louis, and she still had several of her costumes. She thought it was a grand idea."

"I bet she did." Barbara Jean chuckled. "Honey, you asked a performer to do what they do best. Perform. Be the center of attention. Greenleigh was probably in hog heaven tonight."

"Until some man tried to carry her off." Blaaze leaned a hip against the table holding Barbara Jean's accessories.

"What!" Barbara Jean stared at him incredulously. "He did not."

"Yeah, he did. And Max Davenport tried the same with Mary Catherine," he volunteered.

Mary Catherine made a face at him. He didn't need to replay every detail. He'd already made clear his disapproval of her activities. He didn't need to gloat over her mistake.

"Max said he wouldn't have actually done anything," she explained to Barbara Jean. "He only wanted to scare me."

"Ha!" Blaaze made a doubting face. "And you believed that malarkey?"

Barbara Jean picked her fan back up and began to fan herself. "Lord Almighty. We've got to fix this. In fact, that's where I went today. To the bank over in Hicksaw. Thought I'd try to get a loan to buy the brothel from Mary Catherine. That would have solved two problems: given her money for Clanton and let us women get back to what we really do instead of her paying us money she can't afford to pay to do work she really doesn't need us to do. I'm not one for charity."

Mary Catherine took offense at the words. She understood about not wanting to accept charity. That Barbara Jean thought her capable of undermining their pride in such a manner did not sit well. "I'm not handing out charity. I told you I'd find a way for all of us to be okay. You all work here.

I simply changed the nature of the work."

"You changed the nature of the work by giving us pretend work that it don't take half of us to do." Barbara Jean's words didn't have any real bite. She smiled genially at Mary Catherine as she said them.

The words stung nonetheless.

Blaaze touched Barbara Jean's arm to draw back her attention. "You said you *thought* you'd get a loan. I take it things didn't go well."

"No," Barbara Jean replied.

"Why didn't you try the bank here?" Blaaze asked.

"I did. I went to see Basil over at Lawless's State Savings Bank first. He turned me down. Said he couldn't loan money to a woman without her husband's consent. He's visited me enough times he knows well and good I don't have no husband. A fact I thought I could use to persuade him, but he wouldn't budge." Barbara Jean closed her fan. "So I thought I'd try my luck over in Hicksaw but didn't have any better luck there."

"Guess them boys going to be tearing up the town a bit longer." Blaaze gave an amused glance at Mary Catherine.

"This is not my fault," she said adamantly. She was tired of people blaming her because the men in this town couldn't control their urges.

"You sure about that?" Blaaze's grin widened. "Max sure thinks it is."

Ignoring the way that devastating grin made him all the more handsome, Mary Catherine began picking up debris around her. "He had no right to accuse me of that or treat me the way he did. I have a right to run this place as I see fit. This is *my* saloon."

"So you keep reminding us. But is it, really?" Blaaze stood.

"Think about it, Mary Catherine. It's also their saloon. I realize this is now *legally* yours to do with what you want, but understand this establishment used to be the men's sanctuary. A place for a man to come drink, eat, and yes, even find comfort with a woman. You can't sweep in and take that away from them and not expect some frustration. If you're not interested in running this as a brothel, then maybe you do need to consider selling the business to someone who is. Especially when there are women here who are willing to provide the services these men so badly want. It doesn't have to be Clanton. There are other choices. Babs, here, has just expressed interest. The two of you are clever enough to figure something out."

He gently took hold of Mary Catherine's arm to halt her haphazard straightening. "Look, I heard you tell the women on the walk the other day that a woman should be able to own any business she wants. Did that apply only to you? Or does it apply to all the women in this town, including the ones who work for you?"

She gave no immediate response to the question.

"Right now, you may be doing what you think is right, but is it really right for everyone? There are women who make their living as sportin' women by their choice. Not just here, though this saloon has been the main house since Lila started it. Know that if you continue with this, your ladies will be forced to go elsewhere. Going it alone as a courtesan isn't exactly safe, and other house owners may not be as nice to work for. So make sure this is truly the stand you want to take—for yourself and for them."

Looking around the room, Mary Catherine considered his words. She was so used to going it alone she hadn't considered that what she deemed the right path might be the right path only for her and not the right path for everyone. When she returned her gaze to Blaaze's face, he was watching her.

He studied her face before he released her arm. "I need to go take care of something with Marshal Malone. I'll send some people over to help you clean up."

"The ladies and I can handle the cleanup." She didn't want any more of his help today.

"You'll need help moving the big items," he said, heading toward the stairs.

"We'll be fine. I know how to take care of this." Her frustration began to rise again. Was the man hard at hearing?

He stopped and stared at her. "Mary Catherine."

"What now?" she huffed, less politely than was proper.

"I realize you like to do things your own way, but you don't have to take on everything by yourself." He walked back to her. "Let me help you, woman."

She took in his exasperated expression and blew out an unladylike breath. "Fine. Send someone to help with the big items."

He nodded then heading for the stairs, he yelled across the saloon, "Hey, Malone! Let me change my pants and grab my hat. I'll be right back."

God forbid the man go anywhere without his hat. She was surprised he hadn't burst from his room earlier wearing it.

Mary Catherine started to stalk away but stopped. Following his approach to the stairs with her eyes, she called after him. "Hey, Blaaze?"

He came to a dead stop and glanced her way. Something flashed in his eyes that she couldn't read. "Yeah?"

She hesitated. With all the frustration he'd brought her, it felt odd to not be peeved at him but in his debt. Yet, indebted she felt, and she owed him her genuine thanks. "Thank you for intervening."

His head tilted, and he regarded her speculatively. "You're welcome, Mary Cate," he replied in a deep croon that heated her insides to near melting.

He turned to dash up the stairs, and Mary Catherine's lips curved up at his use of the pet name he'd given her. She didn't bother to complain this time. She'd have plenty of time for that later, assuming she could figure out a way to pay for this mess and continue to keep her business open. She still had a lot more cash to save to be able to stave off the brewery owner.

With a glance at Barbara Jean, she let reality take hold. Unfortunately, she had a pretty good idea exactly what she had to do to salvage her future.

Chapter 16

MARY CATHERINE AND THE women took to cleaning up the saloon after all the men left. Blaaze's words were bouncing around in her head. Had she been myopic in thinking she was saving the women from some ill-fated lifestyle?

She understood about making unconventional life choices. It had only been in the last few years that woman were allowed to work inside a bank. Even with that, they were limited to administrative positions that kept them in the back away from clients. Mary Catherine's decision to pursue a client-facing position was an unconventional career for a woman and was what had landed her here in the first place. Well, that and deciding to buck convention even more by refusing to marry a man who was considered a very good match by all the standards Ohio society set for matchmaking.

The final bank interview that had dashed her last vestiges of hope for a financial career stood out clearly in her mind. She had entered that final bank only to be encouraged by its puffed-up bank president to give up "this nonsense" about banking and pursue the path expected of her gender—go marry a nice man. In her case, he'd had the audacity to add, the man she was already engaged to should do nicely.

Deciding there was no need to continue the farce of an interview, Mary Catherine had risen from the guest chair and departed the man's office—and the third largest bank in Cleveland—without a look back. She was perfectly capable of doing the bank manager job she'd applied for. In fact, she had no doubt she could have done it better than the pompous male who had given her the condescending lecture on the improperness of her employment inquiry.

But employment in banking was not to be. As Barbara Jean had indicated, women weren't even allowed to avail themselves of banking services without the aid of a husband or male family member. How could they expect to pursue employment there? At least not as something more than a secretary.

Despite that reality, could she really consider work providing carnal favors the equivalent of bucking society to get a job in banking? She surveyed the women around her. She truly didn't understand why they'd want to do that work.

She looked over at Barbara Jean. "You ladies have so many other choices. Why on earth would you sell yourself?"

Barbara Jean set down the chair she had just righted. "Honey, reality isn't always what you want it to be. Sometimes you have to do what you can to survive. This is me. Us." She waved a hand to include the other women in the room. "This is us doing what we can to survive. And this here gives *us* the choice on how we live."

"This was your *choice*?" Mary Catherine understood about hard choices, but she still couldn't quite wrap her mind around this particular option. She looked around the room.

"All of you? You all came here and made this choice of your own free will?"

"Well, you heard Greenleigh's story. I think if she could go back to dance hall days, she would. And then there's . . ." Barbara Jean trailed off and looked over at Macey.

"It's all right, Babs. It's not like everyone else doesn't already know my story." Macey went over and took a seat next to where Mary Catherine stood. "I didn't exactly plan on being a . . ." Like Mary Catherine, Macey had trouble talking frank talk. "You know."

Mary Catherine nodded.

"I arrived in Lawless to be a mail-order bride, but it didn't work out."

Barbara Jean scoffed. "Ha! That's one way of putting it. It didn't work out because that no-good scoundrel who advertised for a wife up and married someone else before she arrived. The lout got himself another woman, and when Macey stepped off the train expecting to be met, she was left standing there all alone for hours. When the sheriff heard her story, he went and found the bum, Wayne McHenry, and brought him to the station. Wayne made it pretty clear that he was already married and couldn't exactly marry her too. He had absolutely no remorse. Told her she'd simply have to take the train back home."

"Only problem was," Macey said, "I didn't have the money to take the train, or anything else, back home. I'd spent my money to get to Lawless. All the money I had. It was why I answered the ad for a mail-order bride in the first place. My folks were dead. I didn't have any siblings. I couldn't find a teaching position. I thought coming out west to be wife to a man who wanted a wife bad enough to advertise in the paper was a good way to make a life for myself."

Mary Catherine was appalled. "He broke his word to you then left you without recourse? He didn't even offer to pay for you to return home?"

Macey shook her head solemnly. "The sheriff took pity on me and let me stay the night in the jail—"

"In jail!" Mary Catherine exclaimed.

"Yeah." Macey smiled solemnly. "That wasn't going to be a long-term solution, just something to give me time to figure out what to do. After a few days, Lila heard about what happened to me and offered me a room here. She didn't ask anything in return. I think she thought in a few days, I'd find some work to do and would be able to afford a boarding room of my own. It didn't work out that way."

"To make matters worse, that scoundrel Wayne comes slinking in here some weeks wanting to buy time with Macey. The varmint." Barbara Jean feigned spitting on the ground.

"He does not!" Mary Catherine's hand flew to her mouth.

"He does!" all the women exclaimed in unison, then broke into laughter over the coincidence.

"But surely Lila could have found something else for you to do besides work in the upstairs rooms?" Mary Catherine asked Macey.

"I have no real skills," Macey replied. "Outside of housekeeping and baking, that is, but Lila already had a cook. So she didn't need me. It wouldn't exactly have been fair to fire Jonas and hire me anyway. Besides, I don't do full meals too well. I mean I can cook and all, but not like Jonas. I couldn't feed big crowds full meals with any real skill. But breads and pies and cakes and biscuits, those I can do real well."

That was definitely something. Mary Catherine looked at Macey in a new light. The saloon patrons often had sweet tooths. "Biscuits and pies and cakes . . . *hmm*. What about rum cake? My mother had a recipe for rum cake that she could change up to add all kinds of yummy flavors."

"Sure." Macey shrugged. "I don't see why not."

Pensively, Mary Catherine considered Macey. "Are you really that good at baking?"

Macey looked back at Mary Catherine with a steady gaze. "Yes. Is that so surprising?"

"It's not that it's surprising, but it might be part of the answer to my problem." Mary Catherine rethought her words. "*Our* problem. We could start selling sweets. Not just as desserts, but all day long. We can have biscuits. And maybe muffins?" She looked hopefully at Macey, who nodded. "We could serve those as breakfast, grab-and-go style. The men wouldn't have to come in and sit if they didn't want or didn't have the time. They could come in, grab breakfast and maybe some coffee, then off to their work or chores. With this new source of income and the lunch specials I've been trying, I could possibly double the revenue from the food services."

"That'll be real grand, Mary Catherine," Barbara Jean said. "But you and we all know that sweets aren't going to pay off months of brewery credit. If you have any prayer of paying Jake Clanton by the deadline, you're going to have to reopen the sportin' rooms for business."

A Templeton running a brothel; Mary Catherine couldn't fathom it. Her parents would be appalled. Her entire community back home would be appalled. She wasn't sure she wasn't appalled herself at the thought, but Barbara Jean was right. Mary Catherine couldn't afford to be too self-righteous about this. She'd realized that tonight. Her survival, and as she'd recently learned, the survival of these women depended upon her making this establishment work, upstairs and downstairs.

She sighed. "Barbara Jean, I don't know the first thing about running a brothel."

With a huge smile, Barbara Jean squeezed her shoulder. "Don't worry about that none. I know enough for the both of us. You let me handle everything." Barbara Jean considered for a minute. "Of course, we could square things quicker if we didn't have to deal with the few bums who took forever to finish their business."

"You mean they can take as long as they want to get to the, hmm, er, end?" Mary Catherine asked delicately.

"Yes." Jessie rolled her eyes. "The last time Charles Barrett came through he kept stopping himself. Said he wanted to make it last as long as possible. Cost me two patrons by the time he was done." Her tone lured the other women into disgruntled agreement.

"Yes, he did." Charlotte sashayed into the room rubbing her cupped fingers against her breast in a triumphant gesture. "And I appreciated the extra income that day."

Jessie glared at her, but Charlotte returned the animosity with a cat-that-ate-the-last-mouse grin.

From the interaction, Mary Catherine assumed Charlotte had managed to snag Jessie's missed callers. As shocked as Mary Catherine was about the nature of these women's business, a clear inequity existed in what they got for what they gave. It seemed to her, if a man wanted to take more time, then he should have to pay more.

She shook her head, unable to believe she was seriously considering how to improve this trade instead of leaving it shut down. But the more she got to know these women, she understood they were good people. Many had found themselves in dire circumstances they couldn't avoid, and rather than give up they'd made the best of them. That was something she understood.

If they had to work in a brothel to survive, and that brothel was going to stay a part of her saloon, then the least she could do was consider ways to improve how the business transactions were handled. She needed to keep these ladies safe. And just as important, she needed to make sure they made the most money for what they bartered. Gentlemen unilaterally extending sessions, women unwillingly losing clients to one another, and men wanting to partake of women they'd forced into this profession, these were conditions she could not—*would* not—let stand.

That said, when it came to a brothel, Mary Catherine was totally out of her element. She'd been fairly stoic and independent about the challenges of running the saloon. She had absolutely no personal reference from which to manage these other services. She was willing to give it a try, but she needed to be open with these women about her limitations.

She took a big breath and looked around the room. "Ladies, I've got to admit, back home, I wouldn't have come within ten miles of a brothel. Now, I'm living in one, and you want me to serve as its proprietor. Or rather, its madam." She might as well call it what it was. "As if it were some everyday occurrence."

"Well, honey, out here it is," Barbara Jean said. "That's just the way life goes. Men outnumber us by the dozen, but not all of 'em want to do the respectable thing and marry a woman. Men are pretty simple and can be lumped into one of three categories." She held up her hand and ticked off her fingers. "They want to marry us so they can bed us whenever they want. They want to keep us as a mistress so they can bed us whenever they want but not actually have to live with us.

Or they simply want to bed us."

Barbara Jean dropped her hand to her waist, and her hip canted to the side as she got into her telling. "Now, out here ain't enough of us for them to get that last without the marrying or the mistressing, so's the men are willing to pay for it. With the paying, they get whatever they want but don't have to put too much effort into it because they know they're gonna get it whenever they want as long as their coins are good."

Barbara Jean simply shrugged when Mary Catherine's mouth dropped open in shock and continued. "With the marrying kind, they've got you stuck so not much effort usually goes into that marriage beddin' either. Lessen a gal gets lucky. But, then again, iffin' a husband don't put too much effort in, he may not get that beddin' as often as he likes."

Still floored by the woman's sex talk, Mary Catherine sank into a chair without taking her eyes off Barbara Jean. She could find no words.

"We gals still got our ways." Barbara Jean winked at her. "Now, with the mistress-keeping man, he's got to give somewhat of a good beddin' or a mistress is going to be looking for another beau. That, or he's got to be generous with the gifts. Many a mistress will overlook a shortcoming or two in the bedroom—you know, when a man doesn't know what to properly do with his tools—if a man is showering her with jewels and fancy dresses and nice tidbits like chocolates shipped from back east."

The gold, bejeweled necklace Charlotte sometimes wore popped into Mary Catherine's mind. The saloon books laid out what each woman received in wages. Charlotte made a healthy enough living but didn't make quite enough to buy herself such trinkets. Even if the jewels weren't real, a piece like that would cost a fair sum. Of course, Charlotte was popular with the men. But that popular? She wondered if Charlotte served as some man's mistress outside of her sportin' transactions at the saloon.

"Now when a man knows what to do with his equipment, whew, chile!" Barbara Jean fanned herself with her hand, then pumped her hips to accentuate her words. "Ding. Ding. *Ding.* It's like the ringing of a bell."

Jessie and Charlotte fanned themselves as well. "Amen," they said in unison.

"Too bad we don't get to hear that bell ring too often," Charlotte said, taking a seat next to Jessie.

Jessie grinned at her, all animosity seeming to have passed. "If only."

The two burst into a fit of chuckles that had them leaning against each other.

Mary Catherine simply stared. *The ringing of a bell?*

Noticing Mary Catherine's expression, Barbara Jean added, "Don't you go frettin' none. I'll take care of everything. In fact, I'll make you a deal. You take care of the downstairs business and the boarding rooms, and I'll take care of the upstairs business."

That sounded like a fine idea. Everyone could go back to the way things were, and the women could do what they wanted. Except for Macey and maybe Greenleigh.

Mary Catherine didn't see why she couldn't keep the dance hall show if she was bringing back the sportin' rooms. Greenleigh could do what she loved and maybe even make more money than she did upstairs. And she could put Macey to work baking. If the woman was as good at it as she claimed, maybe Mary Catherine could finally compete with Miss

Eileen's pies. It was certainly worth a chance.

"Okay, Barbara Jean." Mary Catherine stood and, with arms akimbo, sold her soul to the Devil. Or so it felt. "We'll do it your way."

"Good. That's settled." Barbara Jean patted her on the shoulder. "Oh, and we're going to need more sponges."

Mary Catherine looked around at the half-cleaned mess. "I know we've got a ways to go to get this mess cleaned up, but I just bought cleaning products. Why do we need sponges?"

Charlotte gaped at her. "Really? You don't know much about lying with a man, do you?"

Mary Catherine could feel a blush rise.

"Be quiet, Charlotte." Barbara Jean glared at the girl. Looking at Mary Catherine, she said, "Honey, now don't let your eastern sensibilities take this the wrong way." She cleared her throat and scanned the faces of the other women in the room. "But have you ever laid with a man?"

Mary Catherine stiffened, and her spine straightened. "I know the ins and outs of . . ." She hesitated then finished with a matter-of-fact tone, "what happens between a man and a woman." Books were amazing teachers, and some even came with rather explicit pictures.

A smirk spread on Charlotte's face, and she said in a sultry tone. "The *ins and outs*, huh?"

All the ladies in the room laughed. Mary Catherine went right past blush to full-on embarrassment. She didn't need a looking glass to know her well-bred purity showed all over her face.

"Sex." Charlotte placed a hand on a cocked hip. "It's called *sex*." She chuckled. "Hell, Miss Mary, you can't even say the word, so I'm pretty certain that you've never indulged. A fine lady like you would have considered any premarital relations against the church's teachings and all."

"And if you're going to have sex, you need sponges." Jessie delicately motioned pushing something into her privates. "You know, to make sure you aren't in a family way when it's all over."

Mary Catherine was aware of plant-based practices, such as ingesting herbs, to guarantee a woman's regular cycle but not the use of sponges as a barrier to a man's seed. Coming to Lawless was expanding her education in whole new ways. Many of these frontier revelations weren't things women of her upbringing would have discussed openly, the way these women did. Mary Catherine wasn't sure if that was good or bad. She was beginning to think it was the latter.

"Um." Barbara Jean stared consideringly at Mary Catherine "It seems we have a madam with a virginity problem."

Macey giggled beside her.

Mary Catherine looked around the room. All the women were watching her with grins on their faces, but these weren't malicious grins. They weren't laughing at her. They were simply amused by her situation.

In the midst of this blossoming camaraderie, she considered whether it was time she let herself fully live her own life and not the life willed to her by a community and society to which she no longer belonged. She'd stepped out of tradition with her pursuit of a college education and a desire for a career in banking, but she'd not truly become her own woman. She'd not truly stepped away from all the inequitable confines society placed on her gender. There were so many other things she wanted out of life than mere survival, and she could have them. She could have them all if she reached for them.

She'd been avoiding marriage to Jeremiah to get what she wanted. She'd never really considered whether she would eventually marry someone else. Most likely not. Not that she didn't expect she'd want companionship as she got older. But marriage? The more she thought about it, the more she didn't see the point for her.

Since she hadn't chosen the path of educator, her goals made her an uncommon woman. She had enterprising plans that most men likely wouldn't go along with for their wives. It took a certain kind of man to accept a wife with her level of education and want her to do anything more with that education than further his own pursuits and position in society while raising socially acceptable children. She had no confidence in finding such a man.

If she weren't planning on marriage, then what on earth was she saving her virginity for?

Having an enterprising nature didn't mean she didn't want to experience all that a man and a woman could share. The memory of the warmth of Blaaze's arms around her earlier and the feel of his hot skin beneath her palm made that hollow he'd stirred low in her abdomen hungry for more of what a man—what *that* man—had to offer.

There was no real reason to deny herself—besides the strictures of society's rules of propriety, that is. If she were discreet outside of this close-knit group, it truly was no one's business anyway. Besides, how could she even begin to understand how to make things better for these women when she wasn't knowledgeable about the ins and outs of what made their business so important?

The internal pun made her grin openly. "It seems we do."

Everyone laughed good-naturedly at her admission.

Glancing around the room, she said unabashedly, "Ladies, I think maybe it's time I do something about that."

CHAPTER 17

A FEW HOURS LATER, Blaaze sat at one of the few remaining tables at the back of the saloon with Tobias and Marshal Malone. He and the marshal had paid a visit to the jail only to find the sheriff was nowhere to be found and Blaaze's prisoner had gone missing.

None of them were happy about the current situation. Blaaze made sure his pearl-handled beauties were nearby, but he hadn't worn one into the saloon. After this afternoon's fiasco, he'd decided he couldn't afford to get caught completely unarmed in this town again. His life, and Mary Catherine's welfare, might depend upon it.

For the time being, he'd settle for Malone's guns. The marshal was as fast and sure of shot as any man Blaaze knew. Someone had to be ready to counter the sheriff's incompetence—or *intentional* inaction. If Dunst Huntley had gotten free and was still lurking around, no one was safe in this town. The man was a violent robber with a penchant for assaulting women.

"I'm concerned about Dunst not being in the jail."

Malone took a drink of his beer and looked at Blaaze. "The sheriff did know you'd sent for a marshal?"

"He knew. I told him I was sending you a telegram." Blaaze leaned back in his chair, trying to keep his attention on the conversation and gaze off Mary Catherine, who flitted around the bar counting and tidying like she was expecting the president to stop by.

Tobias hid a knowing, and annoying, grin behind a sip of bourbon then addressed them both. "The sheriff doesn't exactly run things around here according to regular rules."

"Oh yeah?" Malone gave him his full attention. "Exactly how does he run things?"

"According to Clanton's rules," Tobias informed them.

Malone studied Tobias a moment, then asked Blaaze, "Who the hell is Clanton?"

"Local, wannabe big shot," Tobias answered before Blaaze could. "The man's looking to make his mark on the world by buying up what he can of Lawless and building what's not available to buy. Everyone suspects he's got the sheriff in his pocket, though Brennan's been careful not to make it obvious."

"Well, Sheriff Brennan better have my prisoner safe and secure or he's going to find out what it's like to be holed up with the kind of scum he's been elected to corral." An angry twitch started in the lawman's jaw.

Malone had been after Dunst and his gang for over four years now. The bunch had started off robbing banks but had since moved on to other outlets. No matter, they'd looted one bank in particular that would have Bridger Malone on their tails until they were all behind bars or sent to hell. Blaaze sure hoped Sheriff Brennan hadn't let Huntley get away. Otherwise, Brennan might be joining the dastardly group in the pit fire Malone was intent to send them to.

Blaaze's gaze strayed over to Mary Catherine again. Her evening's toil had taken a toll. Smudges covered her dress, and a mess of her hair had come loose, mostly in the back but several springy curls dangled in the front across those gorgeous cheekbones. The status of her hairdo didn't seem to matter; her beauty shone all the same. She tucked a wayward strand of hair behind an ear and glanced around, taking note of the sparse crowd.

He, Malone, and Tobias were amongst the few currently in the saloon. Most townsfolk had heard about the goings on earlier, and the saloon's usual patrons had decided to stay away for the rest of the evening. A situation that wouldn't help her bottom line.

She began to wipe her hands on a rag. Her hands stopped when her gaze found his. He nodded sociably at her. She took in his tablemates before she returned her gaze to him and nodded in return. He should probably look away, but something about the way she watched him made him curious. She had something on her mind, and he wondered what that something had to do with him.

"Am I keeping you from something, Lassiter?" Malone's chiding voice intruded on Blaaze's thoughts.

"No," Blaaze said matter-of-factly, still looking at Mary Catherine.

"Then perhaps I might get half as much of your attention as the proprietress," Malone quipped.

Tobias chuckled at Malone's gibe and clinked glasses with the marshal.

Blaaze turned his gaze to Malone.

Malone shared a conspiratorial smirk with the smithy then took a drink. He sat his glass down, and his expression returned to serious. "We do still need to figure out what happened to Huntley and where the sheriff has made off to."

"Looks like you guys won't have to look very far." Tobias motioned with his head toward the entrance to the saloon.

Sheriff Brennan strutted in, hand on the butt of the one revolver he wore holstered at his hip. He took notice of Blaaze and Tobias, then zeroed his attention onto Malone. His eyes narrowed when he noticed the two weapons attached to Malone's sides. Unlike most men, Malone preferred to wear a double holster setup rather than tuck a spare gun at his back. From time to time, he actually wore two individual gun belts on opposite hips. He said he liked to be able to take one off when he wanted, but always liked to have a spare on-hip when hunting the worst criminals.

The sheriff sauntered over and stopped in front of Malone. "Boy, I'm gonna assume perhaps you can't read. So you must have missed the message on the sign outside of town that required you turn your weapons into the sheriff upon arriving."

Malone's grip tightened around the glass he'd been about to pick up when Brennan had appeared in the doorway.

Uh-oh, this was not going to end well, Blaaze thought. He remembered what happened the last time he was with Malone and someone had called him "boy." If he didn't know how contained Bridger could be, he would be tempted to move his seat back to guarantee he stayed out of the upcoming fray.

"I read just fine." Malone, deceptively even-keeled, took a slow drink. He stared at the sheriff over the glass's rim the whole time.

That wasn't the reaction the sheriff had expected, and he didn't much like it from all appearances. "I'll take those weapons now."

"I don't think so." Malone didn't raise his voice or move, other than to replace his glass on the table.

"Boy, I'm the—"

Malone's right gun whipped up into the sheriff's face and paused a hair's breadth underneath the man's nose. The marshal pulled his gun so fast, no one saw his hand move. He stood slowly, lowering the gun at the same pace until it rested against the front of the sheriff's shirt at his gut. "You want to call me *boy* again?"

"*Shit.*" Tobias's awed expression mirrored that of everyone else in the place, few that they were.

Blaaze simply shook his head. He'd seen it all before. The marshal was fast. Maybe one of those gunmen who were even faster than himself. Since they were friends, Blaaze counted himself lucky he'd never have to test the matter. Needless to say, he intended to make sure he always stayed on Marshal Bridger Malone's good side.

"I'm the sheriff—"

"I know who you are." Malone pulled back his duster and revealed his star. "And I'm US Deputy Marshal Bridger Malone. Where's my prisoner?"

The sheriff blinked twice quickly. "That real?"

A puzzled look crossed Malone's face. "Of course it's real. Why would I bother wearing a fake star?"

"Maybe you're just trying to intimidate me," the sheriff said with more bravado than his face showed he felt.

"I don't need a fake star, or even a real one, to intimidate you." Malone poked gently at the sheriff's gut with his gun. "Now do I?"

The sheriff swallowed audibly.

"I'll ask you again, sheriff. And this time, I better get an answer." Malone's voice turned menacing. "Where's my prisoner?"

"W-well, there seems to be some q-question about Mr. Huntley's status as wanted."

That rubbed Malone completely the wrong way. "I'm going to assume Mar—"

Blaaze coughed hard.

Malone's shoulders lifted with an exaggerated sigh. They'd discussed Blaaze's intent to be done with this marshal business. He'd already given Malone his star. The marshal had accepted it under protest, but as far as Blaaze was concerned the matter was a done deal, and the people in this town didn't need to be the wiser about his temporary walk on the law side.

"I'm gonna assume *Mr.* Lassiter," Malone corrected, "gave you the wanted bill for the man."

"Sure, but I—"

"Sheriff, there are no buts here. The man is wanted by the law, and if I don't have him to take before Judge Parker at Fort Smith when I ride out of town tomorrow, I'm taking you before the judge in his stead."

The sheriff bristled under Malone's threat. "On what charge!"

"Aiding and abetting." Malone shifted his stance but didn't take his gun off Brennan.

"Aiding and abetting?" Brennan looked at Blaaze as if to check that the marshal was being serious.

"Sounds right." Malone twirled his gun and holstered it in one smooth move. "What say you, Blaaze?"

Brennan eyed the marshal warily, careful to keep close watch on the man's hands. Blaaze had known Malone a long time. Despite the man's poker face, from the look in his eyes, he was beginning to enjoy rousting the sheriff.

Blaaze might as well play along. "Aiding and abetting

sounds about right. A man works hard bringing in a criminal, don't make no sense the outlaw's allowed to simply walk away. And by the sheriff no less." He made his best put-upon face. "Tsk, tsk."

Malone tried to hide his grin at Blaaze's dramatics, but he couldn't quite keep the edge of his lips from turning up slightly. "So, sheriff, seems you need to go find an outlaw. I suggest you have him in the jail when I come by tomorrow morning. Else you and I will be taking a long ride." Malone sat down, picked up his glass, and drained the remainder of his drink. He waved the sheriff off dismissively with the back of his hand. "Sheriff, I believe you have work to do. Best be on your way."

The sheriff stood frozen in place. His glare darted between Blaaze and Malone. He seemed to notice Tobias for the first time, and a look of embarrassment slid across his face. Looking away from Tobias, his gaze crossed over Blaaze again, and he frowned. His look suggested he blamed Blaaze for this comeuppance he'd experienced in public, and he started to say something.

Malone stopped him before he could. "Don't worry about him. He's with me." Bridger leaned back, legs stretched in front of him, and laced his hands across his stomach. "Good day, sheriff."

Brennan gave him one last glare. The experience of having a gun almost shoved up his nose stopped him from challenging Malone, but Blaaze suspected the sheriff would come looking for him once the marshal left town. Just like Malone. Stir up trouble then leave Blaaze to deal with the fallout.

When the sheriff spun and walked away, Malone looked at Blaaze. "Where do you think he's headed?"

"Straight to Clanton's," Tobias said.

Malone's brow rose. "Hmm. You figure?"

"Yep." Tobias picked up his glass and stared disappointedly into its emptiness. Setting the glass down, he continued. "Based on what Blaaze told me about this Huntley character, only one man in town would be interested in having an outlaw like that around. And there's only one man in town Brennan would trust to have his back if any hassle arose from Huntley's being free."

"Clanton," Blaaze finished.

Tobias nodded his head. "Clanton."

"Good evening, gentlemen." Mary Catherine approached the table. She held a bottle of bourbon in her hands and refilled Tobias's glass.

Tobias smiled at her. "Why, thank you, Mary Cate."

She smiled back at him. Blaaze growled under his breath. Mary Catherine didn't hear him, but Tobias did. The big man hid his grin behind a sip of fresh bourbon.

"Her name's Mary Catherine," Blaaze barked at the smithy. "Use it. Or better still, Miss Templeton will do right fine."

Tobias merely grinned at him and winked at Mary Catherine, who seemed surprised by Blaaze's tone with the man. Malone looked between him and Tobias, trying to figure out what exactly was going on. Blaaze ignored both men and Mary Catherine's chastising expression.

That was his name, and only his name, for her. By outward appearances, she preferred he didn't call her that. That had been part of the reason he'd initially kept using the nickname. Now, he felt it suited her. Prim and proper Mary on the outside—all pure and virtuous as the virgin mother—with a whole lot of fire underneath, the Cate in her. And the

Cate in her was meant only for him.

His Mary Cate offered the marshal a refill. Malone declined.

"Are you sure, marshal? It's on the house. I must say the best part of this extremely long and extremely miserable day was watching you make that man squirm. He's a weasel."

Blaaze gave her a mock look of shock. Name calling was not her usual behavior.

"What?" She challenged him with a look of her own. "Am I wrong?"

"You're not wrong." Tobias cheerily backed her claim.

"Happy to oblige, Miss Templeton, but I've had my limit for the night," Malone assured her.

Blaaze suspected he wanted to keep his wits unsoused in case he had to deal with any later fallout from his run-in with the sheriff over Huntley.

"Well, then, how about a piece of pie?" Mary Catherine countered.

Malone perked up. "Pie?" The man had never met a piece of pie he didn't like.

"Yes, apple pie made fresh this morning. How about I bring you a piece? On the house, of course."

"That, I won't turn down, Miss. Thank you." Malone's mood had clearly taken a swing for the better.

The saloon slowly emptied of other patrons, and Bridger polished off the pie he received in short order. After the men chatted a bit more, the trio eventually rose to head out. Blaaze and Bridger decided to follow Sheriff Brennan's trail to find out where he'd gone and make sure Huntley made it back to jail by morning. Tobias headed back to the livery ahead of them to ready their horses.

When Blaaze walked toward the door, Mary Catherine

rushed around the bar and followed after him.

"Hey," she called.

He stopped, waving Malone on ahead. "I'll catch up with you."

Once they were alone, she asked, "How come you don't like it when someone else calls me Mary Cate? You do it all the time."

He moved close enough to touch her but didn't. Instead, he cocked a thumb on his belt to keep himself from reaching out. "Because I know you secretly like it."

Mary Catherine rolled her eyes. He stepped even closer and stared deep into those huge pools of brown. He could tell her nerves raced liked an out-of-control stampede thanks to the throbbing vein in her neck. But she didn't look away. What he read in her eyes suggested things his mind told him he needed to say no to, but his body definitely wanted to say yes.

Blaaze gently dropped an arm around her back and pressed a kiss against her temple. "You're going to have to stop looking at me that way, Mary Cate, or you're going to be in a whole different kind of trouble than you already are."

"What way?" Her voice held an innocence her eyes didn't convey.

Nonetheless, he doubted she understood exactly what her demeanor offered.

Pulling her closer, he dropped his voice to a husky whisper. "Like you're giving me an invitation to join you in one of the upstairs rooms."

Every part of him stiffened at her next words.

"What if I were?"

~

Mary Catherine watched Blaaze's eyes turn molten. She couldn't look away. She stared up into those intense, dark brown eyes and stood mesmerized.

She'd read about cobras who could fixate on their prey with unblinking eyes. Common theory suggested they charmed their prey into a hypnotic state, making them easy marks for a deadly strike. The scientific reports she'd read explained it otherwise. They indicated no such magic hypnosis actually happened. The prey simply became paralyzed with fear, recognizing the superior predator, and wait unmoving for that predator to devour them.

Blaaze's eyes drew her and made her want to surrender to his arms. Lean against him. Feel what it was like to have a man hold her, cradle her, make love to her. She sensed this man would devour her . . . but in a way she'd thoroughly enjoy.

"Careful, little miss," he warned. "You're playing with fire."

"I'm not a little miss," she said and slid one hand up his chest to rest over his pounding heart. "I'm a grown woman and the madam at this here brothel."

He grinned at her. "Face it, sugar. You look more like a schoolmarm than a madam. All you need is a long, wooden ruler to go with that pencil in your hair and the image would be complete."

She stiffened and opened her mouth to say something, but words would not come.

A schoolmarm? she thought, utterly speechless.

He clasped two fingers on a stray curl from her destroyed bun and slid them down its length. "Even the way you talk reminds a man of his schoolhouse days."

The way he looked at her, the way he touched her,

suggested nothing so innocent as schoolhouse memories.

"What's w-wrong with the way I talk?" she finally managed despite tightened lungs.

He moved his lips to the edge of her ear. Lowering his voice to its deepest baritone, he whispered, "You talk like you swallowed a dictionary."

The way he said it made it sound almost a compliment rather than criticism, but her ego couldn't definitively decide which while he held her this way. The wild, pulsating feeling in the hollow of her abdomen that only he'd ever caused started up again. People talked of butterflies in one's stomach, but these pangs were too intense to be butterflies. They reminded her more of the wild stallions she'd seen roaming amongst the rolling hills outside her train window on the way to Lawless.

Hard, galloping lust that ran free without restriction. That's what she felt. No, that's what she was.

Something shifted in his eyes, and Mary Catherine suspected he'd seen into her thoughts and deciphered the uncontrollable emotions assaulting her. Like earlier this evening, her body gravitated toward him. This time, he didn't hesitate.

The space between them disappeared. His lips brushed hers, a light touch that felt safe and gentle but promised a thrill beyond its simple contact. His hand went to the back of her head, and he gently shifted its position to tilt her lips to an angle that allowed him to slip his tongue deep inside her mouth. An easy frolic enticed her own tongue, and she moaned as she gave over to the call to play. Lifting her arms to his neck, she melted into him. Despite the liquid feel of her spine and legs, he kept her upright with a hand at the small of her back.

He pressed her firmly against him, sheltering her even as he thrust her into a maelstrom. Slowly, he tasted her mouth from every angle. The pressure, the stimulation, the erotic thrill of the kiss intensified. Built. Soared. Mary Catherine lost awareness of everything around her except Blaaze's touch, the feel of his hard body against hers, the taste of his lips and tongue.

The languid nature of the kiss slid into urgency. He began to consume and not simply taste. A promise eased from his lips to her core. She reached to grasp that promise by pressing herself more firmly against him and consuming him right back. His answering moan threw them both into a frenzy that threatened to escalate to behavior not proper in a public place, despite no public currently being around.

A door closed somewhere, and the kiss became an eternity and an instant all at once. Blaaze lifted his head to stare down at her. No words emerged from those lips that had tantalized and schooled simultaneously, but a lifetime of conversations flashed between them before he reached up and removed one of her arms from his neck. She allowed the other to slide down the front of his shirt before she dropped it to her side.

After a flash in his eyes that resembled regret, he kissed the back of her hand. "You're not for me, little darling. Save that for a gentleman, someone worthy of you."

Without waiting for a response, he sauntered away.

Mary Catherine's hand went flat against her belly, and she pressed in. Her eyes focused on the firm backside molded by the seat of his denims, the long legs with the slight bow, and the lazy sway of arms that evidenced a confidence and competence that no man—or woman—could easily ignore. Her eyes slid closed.

Little did he know she was already deep into that whole different kind of trouble he'd mentioned.

Barbara Jean walked up beside her. "I've heard of playing with fire. But, Mary Catherine?"

She turned unsure eyes Barbara Jean's way.

"You best consider that man's name might be Blaaze for a reason." Barbara Jean chuckled and shook her head. "Honey, I've got to say, when you set your sights on something, you certainly go big, and I admire your gumption. I'd be remiss, however, if I didn't mention that he's a mighty big target to aim for to solve your particular problem."

Mary Catherine opened her mouth to say something, but Barbara Jean held up a hand to stop her.

"Now let me finish. I'm not saying he's a man to be wary of. Only he's known to be a might stingy with his favors. He's a discreet and discriminating sort. When you live by the gun the way that man does, prudence demands you not be one to spread yourself around willy-nilly, hopping into bed with whomever. Discriminating or not, I will say, the way he moves"—she glanced toward the closed door Blaaze had exited through and gave an appreciative shake of her head—"I'm absolutely positive he's one man who knows exactly what to do with his equipment." She headed for the stairs and said playfully over her shoulder, "You make sure and let me know."

"Barbara Jean, wait." Mary Catherine dropped her hand from her belly. "I'm not sure he wants me that way. He just turned me away."

Stopping at the base of the stairs, Barbara Jean turned and looked at her. "Oh, he wants you all right."

"How can you be sure?"

"Because," she said, eyes twinkling, "of the way that man

looks at you when he thinks no one's paying attention. Least of all you."

"How's that?" Mary Catherine gave her an inquiring look.

"Like you're a well-cooked steak, and he's a man who's been starving for weeks."

Mary Catherine gave the woman a dismissive wave of her hand. "Pfft! Half the time he acts like he wants to strangle me."

"Yes," Barbara Jean replied. "But that doesn't mean he doesn't spend the other half of his time thinking of ways he could make you purr."

Mary Catherine gaped at Barbara Jean. Her? Mary Catherine Templeton, a well-cooked steak? "You have to be joking?"

Maybe the man had thought of Lila that way at one time. Lila certainly had had that effect on men. Mary Catherine had always been the studious one in the background. No one had given her much attention until she'd started her college studies and her engagement to Jeremiah had been announced.

She knew Lila and Blaaze had been close. Exactly how close? Had they been lovers? She'd considered it when she'd first met the cowboy. Even then, the thought hadn't been a pleasant one. It bothered her more now.

Schoolmarm. That's what he'd called her. A schoolmarm who talked like she'd swallowed a dictionary. That's exactly what he thought of her.

Didn't sound particularly alluring. How could she compete with the women of his past or the memory of her cousin? She understood the ways plains society held different mores than back home, but to consider Lila freely sleeping with Blaaze whenever she wanted made Mary Catherine's stomach churn. And this time, not in a good way. She couldn't sleep with her cousin's former lover, no matter how attracted she was to the man.

Could she?

"Hey, Barbara Jean, did Blaaze and Lila ever . . .?"

"Nah, honey," Barbara Jean said as she ascended the stairs. "They were close and all, but Miss Lila had her own man. The couple started this place together."

Relief coursed through Mary Catherine. That was one ghost she didn't have to expel.

"I wouldn't worry about it too much. It's not as if he's going to let any other man get close to you. It's only a matter of time before you bring that gunfighter to heel." Barbara Jean climbed to the top of the stairs and stopped when she got to the landing. "I tell you this, if I had a man like that stare at me every time he saw me as if he was starving and I was supper, I know exactly where I'd be going to get my introduction to womanhood. So, honey, you go right on ahead and follow your instincts. Trust me, that man wants you. It's up to you to make sure he gets you."

Barbara Jean entered her room and left Mary Catherine alone downstairs. Mary Catherine locked the front doors. She wasn't as sure of herself or Mr. Lassiter's interest as Barbara Jean seemed to be.

Sure, he'd kissed her. And boy, could the man kiss. But it wasn't the first time a man had kissed her without attempting to do more. Even her fiancé had been content to wait until after their vows before he'd do more than kiss her chastely from time to time. He hadn't found her much of a temptation beyond that either.

Well, there was that one time Mr. Beauregard III had lost his self-control. He'd recovered—rather easily—before things went too far. So . . .

She thought for a minute about what had transpired with her once-betrothed for that one time but had to let it go. That didn't matter anymore. Now, what she had to do—what she wanted to do—was figure out how a right and proper "schoolmarm" like herself could possibly be the one to tame a larger-than-life, gun-toting bounty hunter like Blaaze Lassiter.

The man had once called her clever. She pulled the pencil from her bun and let her cleverness run free while she tapped the pencil on the nearest table.

Once. *Tap.*

Twice. *Tap.*

Three times. *Tap.*

Pondering Barbara Jean's last words, a plan of action slowly formed in her mind, and for the first time that day, a smile eased across her face.

Mary Catherine Templeton, erstwhile schoolmarm, knew exactly how she planned to entice the recalcitrant Mr. Lassiter to change his mind.

Chapter 18

MARY CATHERINE SAT AT her desk the next day scribbling lists and double-checking figures. On top of the personal problem she had with a particular cowboy, her revenue had not increased to necessary amounts yet, and parts of the account books still did not add up. After decoding the mystery notations for the brothel business, she found the take from the bar did not square up with the amount of alcohol withdrawn from the inventory. Another problem she had to solve.

She slapped the current account book closed. Hopefully, word would get around that the terminated upstairs personal amenities were no longer terminated, and things would begin to turn around. She'd also gotten Macey to bake more pies with some fresh apples they'd commandeered from trees on Jonas's land. Jonas was a bit of a grump, but somehow Macey managed to handle the man's mercurial moods.

Between the lunch specials, the pies, and the news that the upstairs business was back, Mary Catherine prayed the next five days provided a windfall. That's all the time she had left to earn enough money to pay off her brewery bill. She rose and went downstairs to help with the next meal service.

After making sure Jonas had all he needed to finish putting together the sandwiches along with fresh servings of squash and beets, Mary Catherine removed her apron and headed for the main room. A few men had straggled in, so that was a good start.

She glanced to where Charlotte stood grinning at a gent who sat at the bar with an empty shot glass in front of him. Mary Catherine hoped Charlotte's smile led him to refill that shot glass frequently. Or perhaps . . . Mary Catherine tried not to think about the other thing that smile of Charlotte's might lead him to want. Mary Catherine had still not quite come to grips with this whole brothel notion. She'd made a few changes to the upstairs procedures, but otherwise she was going to make do and leave all that entailed to Barbara Jean.

She glanced over to Blaaze's favorite table. There he sat, legs stretched out over another chair, boots crossed, chin to his chest, and that ever-present hat tilted down over his face. He acted as if he didn't have a care in the world. He'd come down, had breakfast, then passed out lazily in his chair. He'd made no acknowledgment of their kiss. It was as if it had never happened.

"Irritating man," she grumbled under her breath.

Macey came from the kitchen carrying a fresh-from-the-oven apple pie. She placed it behind the bar. They'd decided if they kept a few warm pies behind the bar, the smell might entice more men to buy a slice . . . or two.

Deciding to ignore the annoying cowboy snoozing in the back, Mary Catherine headed for the bar to cut into the pie. Might as well give the aroma a boost. She'd just loaded a piece onto a plate when she heard a man upstairs yell.

"I'm not finished yet! You can't kick me out." The loud thud of a boot hitting the hallway floor followed the yell.

"You're finished all right, Lucas," Jessie yelled right back at him. "Your time is up. We've got time limits now. No more dawdling all afternoon as if a girl ain't got other business to do."

"Time limits? How's a man supposed to thoroughly get in the mood when someone's standing outside the door marking time?" Lucas hitched up his pants and pulled on his one missing boot.

"Hey! I wasn't done yet." Another man shuffled backward out of Grace's room a few doors down from Jessie. He stumbled then danced on one foot when Grace threw his boots out after him, managing to hit one of his socked feet in the process.

Lucas pointed at the man. "See there! A man can't be rushed in these things. He's got a right to finish his business and get dressed with dignity. *Privately.* What kinda malarkey is this?"

Lucas grabbed for a girl standing close by with a clipboard, and Mary Catherine stepped from behind the bar in case she had to intervene. She needn't have worried. Jessie was having none of it.

Jessie jumped in front of the girl. "Don't you touch her."

A young girl of only eighteen, Beth had been given the job of tracking each man's time. She'd seemed to Mary Catherine too skittish and unsure of herself to work behind closed doors. So Mary Catherine assigned Beth the task of keeping track of each patron's time, and the girl had gladly accepted.

The time limits were part of Mary Catherine's new protocols. The women were allowed to set the maximum patrons they would service each day, and each man had a time limit. When a patron had only ten minutes left, Beth tapped a light warning on the bedroom door. Once the ten minutes were up, the ladies had the right to kick them out. No more of this taking as long as they wanted business.

"Lucas, you go on," Jessie admonished the man. "Or this will be the last day you get any of my time."

"Aw, Jessie, come on now," he whined. "Don't be like that."

"I'm serious." The look on Jessie's face convinced him she meant it. "Maybe next time you'll put some effort into it so a girl don't spend all her time staring woefully at the ceiling."

Turning beet red, Lucas finished fastening his pants and stormed down the stairs in a huff. Jessie patted a wide-eyed Beth on the shoulder, and Beth gave her a grateful smile. With a slam of her door, Jessie ensconced herself back into her room. Beth looked down at her clipboard then walked to the end of the hall and rapped decisively on the last door.

A masculine protest answered. "No! Not yet, not yet. Oh oh ooooooh . . ."

Beth stifled a giggle, and Mary Catherine said her blessings that the crisis of the moment had been averted. That was, until Lucas reached the bar.

He stopped in front of Mary Catherine and pointed in her face. "*You* are a menace. Who ever heard of time limits in a brothel? You don't know the first thing about running a saloon or a whorehouse. Time you went back east where you came from."

She calmly palmed his finger away from her face. "Well, if you ask me . . . Lucas, was it?"

He nodded.

"You don't seem to know the first thing about pleasing a woman. If you did, you'd still be behind closed doors. Apparently, the ladies of this establishment don't believe you're capable of . . ." Heat rose to her cheeks. She couldn't bring herself to say the words out loud. "Well, you know."

His expression turned perplexed. "Capable of what?"

"Capable of . . . of . . ." Mary Catherine thought about Barbara Jean's little performance the other day and finished with, "Ringing any woman's bell." She didn't have the gumption to add the hip movements, but whatever he saw in her expression got her point across.

His eyes widened when he finally understood the reference. "Why you . . . you . . ." Irate, he took a step forward. "Who the hell do you think you are, insulting a man that way?"

Mary Catherine nervously reached behind her and surreptitiously grabbed the neck of an empty bottle of whiskey that had been left on the table. "Well, haven't you heard, honey?" She put her other hand on her hip and summoned her best impression of Barbara Jean's sass. "I'm Miss Cate, head whore. My establishment, my rules."

She heard Blaaze cough at her claim of being head whore. He nearly fell over as he made to put his feet down and sit up. So much for him being asleep.

Gripping the bottle behind her tighter, she warned Lucas, "You have two choices. You can head over to the bar and have a drink on the house for your inconvenience, or you can simply remove yourself from the place. What you won't be doing is making a ruckus, threatening my ladies, or threatening me. Choose."

Lucas finally noticed her hand behind her back and narrowed his eyes while considering her intent. If he decided to push the matter, the bottle likely wouldn't be enough. Didn't mean she wasn't going to use it as best she could.

Turns out, she didn't have to. Lucas looked over to where Blaaze now stood, leaning lazily against the back wall watching them, and decided he'd take the drink. He grunted at her, gave one last glance Mr. Lassiter's way, then stepped to the bar.

Mary Catherine heaved a sigh of relief and dropped the whiskey bottle back on the table. A quick glance at her hands revealed a noticeable tremble in her fingers. Looking put upon that his nap had been interrupted, Blaaze sauntered toward her. She made fists to hide the tremors from his too-alert eyes.

"Head whore, huh?" he said when he reached her, the amusement in his deep voice unmistakable.

"Not yet, but I'm working on it." She busied herself collecting the dishes left on the abandoned table and refused to look at him. It was all bravado on her part. Lawless had broadened her horizons much since she'd arrived, but not enough for her to take on such a brazen role, now or in the future.

"Mary Catherine, you have to stop saying things like that."

"Why?" She knew why he thought she should. His presence painfully reminded her that last night he'd turned down what she had to offer.

"Because some man is going to take you seriously and decide to accept your proposition."

"Good. That's exactly what I want." She wasn't a woman who liked to ask for help. She'd been subtle when she'd broached her proposition with him. She'd never been the flirty type, and it wasn't as if she had the courage to come right out and say, *Excuse me, sir, would you mind taking me to bed?*

He grabbed her arm and spun her to face him. "No, it's not."

She yanked her arm from his grasp. "Yes, it is," she snapped in the face of his annoyance.

Men were always questioning her choices for herself. Was it so hard to believe she knew her own mind? She'd traveled across the plains alone to get here. She had some fortitude. Maybe she was more straitlaced than the women he was used to, but that shouldn't make her less desirable. His ability not to take her seriously about this grated.

"You've made it clear you're not interested in me. That's okay. I'll take my vocabulary and schoolmarm ways and find someone who is. I'm sure in this dozen-men-to-each-woman town some man will find my offer appealing."

"You can't be serious, Mary Cate. It was one thing for you to mess with me the other day. And I can't say I didn't find every second with your lips time well spent." He tilted his head down and dropped his voice to a low, warning whisper. "But now, sugar, you're being an outright tease. And it isn't funny."

"I'm. Not. Laughing." Nor was she interested in being a tease.

He looked at her doubtfully, returning himself to his full height.

How hard could it be for a willing woman to lose her virginity? She intended to start a campaign to find out. She wanted her first time to be him. Perhaps he'd change his mind when he realized she'd decided to find his replacement. Maybe she'd even start her search with his buddy Tobias.

"Think about it," she said. "What self-respecting madam doesn't know how to pleasure a man?"

He didn't hesitate. "One who shouldn't be a madam." He

gave her a thorough once-over before giving her a doubting expression.

"Don't give me that look." Mary Catherine crossed her arms and leaned her bottom against the table. "There are some advantages to being a learned woman. Books are amazing teachers. I know things."

He wandered closer. "What I have to show you, you can't learn in any book. You simply have to feel it. Firsthand," he drawled in that growly voice that always made her feel like his words were caressing her body and not simply her ears.

Mary Catherine repressed a shiver. Steeling herself against his charismatic lure, she retaliated with the best weapon at her disposal, a verbal parry. "Empty words since I'll never find out." She grabbed the dirty glassware off the table and once again worked to channel a little bit of Barbara Jean's gumption. "I'm beginning to think you're more talk than action. Maybe all that bounty hunter bravado is to make up for a lack other places." She made a pointed glance at the front of his jeans and tried hard not to blush.

He didn't seem to notice the flush she was trying hard to repress because shocked outrage exploded across his face. His mouth opened and closed a few times as if he couldn't quite figure out where to even start with a retort. Immense satisfaction swirled in Mary Catherine's chest. It felt good. It felt really good to, for once, have a clever comeback and say it instead of censoring herself to satisfy the mandates of a society that only within the last two decades considered her a person—because of the color of her skin—and still considered her nothing but the extension of a man due to her gender.

He yanked the glassware out of her hands and dropped them onto the table. "Enough of these games. Come with me." Taking giant strides, he tugged her along behind him.

"Where are you taking me?" Mary Catherine nearly had to jog to keep up with him.

"We're going to settle this once and for all." He pulled her through the kitchen, clearing out all its other occupants with a gruff, "Out!"

Ignoring the now-cleared room, he kept moving till they reached the spacious pantry, tugged her inside, and slammed the door closed. He pressed her up against the wall to the left of the door, not with any malice but with enough determined impetus she dared not budge from where he'd put her.

He took a step back, a tense vibration radiating from his tall, gorgeous frame. When his gaze swept over her from head to toe, Mary Catherine knew a slight moment of fear. Not a fear born of impending violence or harm. This fear thrummed with an anticipatory anxiousness mixed with a heavy dose of doubt. She wasn't sure she was ready for whatever he had in mind "to settle this once and for all."

Blaaze yanked off his ever-present Stetson. It should be a sin for a man to look so temptingly good in denims and a brimmed hat.

He rubbed a huge hand down his tense face. "You know," he said, dropping his hand. "For a prim and proper miss, you sure are quite a tease. Did they teach you that, too, at that fancy college you attended?"

He studied her as if he thought he could figure out the answer to his question simply by looking at her.

He tossed his hat onto a nearby shelf, ignoring baking ingredients spilled about, then stepped in close. "How to make a man squirm and yearn till he damn near bursts the front seam of his pants at the sight of you?"

The statement—*question?*—drew her gaze downward.

Before she could check the truth in his words, he pressed against her. The hard ridge she felt along her abdomen provided the verification she sought and sent a prolonged thrill of anticipation up her spine.

Her eyes closed, and Mary Catherine tried not to think about the promise of what that hardness would provide rubbing against her . . . pushing inside her. She hadn't simply relied on books. She'd been intellectually curious enough to touch herself experimentally. As pleasurable as the self-fondling had been, what she felt behind the crotch of his denims promised an immensely different experience.

The sounds she'd overheard from Charlotte's room last evening came back to mind. All the moans, the groans, the rattling of the bed frame, and the feral, female cry when whatever ecstasy Charlotte had been chasing finally got caught reverberated through Mary Catherine's head.

"Oh, *my*," she breathed and fought a cry of her own.

She'd asked for this, wanted this, or so she'd thought. Was she really ready for everything this cowboy had to give?

Blaaze rubbed a bent finger along her jawline. "You want to know why I keep saying no to you, Mary Cate?"

Her eyes popped open at the sound of the nickname only he got to call her. The nickname he'd claimed as his alone and adamantly refused to allow anyone else to use.

She nodded in response to his question. She currently did not trust herself to speak.

"Because a woman like you isn't fated to simply pleasure a man. You're the kind of woman a man marries. The kind of woman who accomplishes great things and moves the Race forward. You're too good for a man like me. A man who's done unfathomable deeds to catch the foulest of vermin. A man who's half outlaw himself. Hell, you're too good for every man within five states and three territories."

His hips moved, and she could feel his turgid length through the folds of her skirt and the underlying petticoat.

"I'm not asking you to marry me," she said in a low, breathy voice.

He had to sense the budding need beneath the control she desperately tried to hold on to but was fast losing the battle against.

"No." He bent his knees and dipped his hips lower until he lodged himself between the apex of her thighs. "You're asking me to debauch you and go about my way with a clear conscience."

He ground against her woman's center and a bolt of lustful lightning shot through her. This time she couldn't suppress the sounds of pleasure that squeezed from her lips.

"I may have lived my life by the gun, but I'm not completely devoid of morals." He moved his hips against her again. "Is that what you really think of me? That I could use an upstanding woman like you to satisfy my needs then just walk away?"

The pace of his grinding hips increased. Mary Catherine grabbed his forearms and squeezed hard.

"Come on, Mary Catherine, is that what you really want from me? Tell me the truth. 'Cuz if that's what you really want, I'm prepared to give it to you."

The physical taunt had become too much. Her hands tightened more on his arms. "Blaaze, *please.*"

"Please what, Miss Templeton?" He planted one hand above her head against the wall and pressed in harder.

"Don't tease me. I know you don't like my being here very much, but don't torture me. You don't have to be cruel."

A light flashed in his eyes. "Cruel? Sugar, I'm not trying

to be mean, and the only torture I want to give you is the kind that'd make you scream my name so loud they'd hear you all the way down at the livery stable."

His other hand went above her head, and he started a slow consistent grind. Her fingers began to cramp she held to him so tightly. She wanted nothing more than to let him strip her bare from the waist down and show her what this would feel like with nothing on between them.

"Ever thought about what it would be like to be deflowered against a wall, Miss Templeton?"

She simply blinked. No, she hadn't, but now that he'd mentioned it, it really didn't sound all that bad. "Is that what this is about? I challenged your manhood. Now, you think you can intimidate me into backing down by manhandling me in the back of a pantry where anyone in the saloon might hear us?"

He chuckled. "Intimidate you? You think that's my plan? So you do think me a scoundrel."

"*No*. That's not what I meant." And it's not what she thought. She'd originally thought him gruff and without manners. Even dangerous. But she'd learned he was not the miscreant her first impression had suggested.

"No? You sure about that?" He increased his slow, consistent grind. His breathing became slightly labored, and a gruff half-hum half-moan eased from his throat before he resumed his taunting. "Because I assure you, I have nothing in mind but taking care of that proposition of yours."

She blinked up at him, the budding sensations between her thighs making it difficult to think straight, let alone speak. The man couldn't be serious. Not right now . . . in a pantry? "H-here?"

"No time like the present. I thought you wanted me to . . .

what did you call it? Ring your bell?" He chuckled again, only this time it sounded a lot less like mirth and a whole lot like devilment. "The other day, you didn't specify it had to be in a bed. And by now, you should know I'm not the type of man to let a little thing like properness or rules keep me from completing a challenge." He dropped one hand to the back of her thigh and squeezed gently. "Spread your legs wider for me, sugar."

His hand twisted in the folds of her skirt, and he began to tug upward. He watched her eyes. She suspected he was waiting for her to object, but she wasn't going to object. She'd been waiting for this moment from the time she decided she was getting rid of that pesky virginity problem of hers. She'd known at the start the only man she trusted to give her the full experience—the kind of experience a woman needs to place her on the true path to ecstasy—was the man currently pressed up against her. Everything this man did, she had no doubt he did with passion and thoroughness.

Shoot those guns he'd been wearing the day he'd rode into town.

Put down rabble-rousers during a brawl.

Initiate a virgin . . . *Oh, yeah.*

She couldn't wait to feel what that thoroughness might mean for a woman who graced his bed. Okay, so they weren't exactly in a bed. But she could manage to accept it up against a wall if that's where he deemed to give it to her.

She'd been bold enough to get on a train with the last of her money in her purse. She'd been bold enough to take over a saloon no one in town seemed to want her to own. She'd been bold enough to continue a brothel despite social conditioning that had indoctrinated her to see such goings on as contrary to proper womanhood.

Whatever this man wanted to give her, she'd be bold enough to grasp with both hands. All she wanted was to stop this ache inside, a needy ache that had been created the moment he'd hauled her out of that watering trough. It now flared to near inferno as he stoked her with a firm grind against a pantry wall.

When her skirt was at her hips, Blaaze rocked against her core once more, and one of the buttons beneath the flap down the front of his jeans found her pleasure point. When she whimpered, he crooned softly and ground in the exact same spot again. Nothing but her bloomers and his jeans stood between his engorged penis and the damp, throbbing place between her thighs. Gracious, how she wanted him to touch her there.

"Ring your bell. Is that what you want me to show you right now, sugar? How it feels when a man brings a woman to ecstasy so hard her whole body trembles?" He dropped his lips to the line of her neck and began to nibble.

Mary Catherine's head went back. The mere thought of experiencing the release his words promised made her want to weep. Anything would be better than this half-rapture she could barely endure but didn't want to stop. "Yes. That's exactly what I want."

A growl reverberated low in his throat, and he snarled against her skin, "You can't mean that, Mary Cate." His voice turned chiding and almost desperate. "Tell me no. Tell me to stop. For all that's holy, woman, you have to come to your senses."

"What I'm going to tell you is . . ."

He raised his head and stared into her eyes.

"Don't. Stop." The punctuated order rasped through shaky breaths.

He said nothing for seconds. Then she saw the moment his resolve snapped. Her anticipation, along with her heart, soared.

A predatory gleam entered his eyes. "Well, okay then, sugar. Whatever you say."

Ith both hands under her thighs, Blaaze lifted Mary Catherine and secured her against the wall. He planted himself firmly at her core then grabbed one of her calves to curve her leg around his back, encouraging her to wrap both her legs around him. Everything in him wanted to be skin to skin with this woman, preferably in a humongous bed made with soft sheets.

But that wasn't happening today. No matter what the crazy, obstinate, bossy woman said.

Nonetheless, more than one way existed to "ring a bell," and he was fine using the buttons behind the panel on his jeans to strategically hasten that along. He'd seen the look on her face when he'd ground against her woman's pearl earlier. He had the perfect tool to lure her honey from its comb and send her into a climax worthy of shooting stars.

"Please don't stop." Her soft plea wrapped in accented properness sent a tremor through the base of his spine.

How could she sound so dignified at a moment that felt like he was battling five mavericks at the end of one lasso?

He fought to control the growing release building through the tremors unleashed by her enticing voice and the feel of her body against his. He managed to growl into her neck through gritted teeth, "Mmm . . . no. Not stopping."

He couldn't stop if he tried.

That train had left the platform, and there was no calling it back.

The scent of her skin filled his nostrils, and he wondered why he'd never noticed she smelled like sugar. He worked his hips, every bit as dedicated to this wall dance as he'd be if they were horizontal in a bed and he were buried deep inside her. A keening sound started low in her chest and rose to a deep, throaty hum that pushed him further toward the brink of control. He slammed his lips against hers, to catch the rising sound as much as to taste her sweetness. His tongue slid deep, and he rode her sweet spot with slow and steady pistoning hips.

She began to move with him. She was close, but so was he. If he didn't send her over soon, he was going to lose it in his pants.

He brushed his lips along her neck to her ear and coaxed, "Let go, Mary Cate. Feel me here." He lifted her legs higher, opening more of her to his covered erection, and pumped his hips. "Imagine all of this deep inside you. Ride me, my darling. Find that spot that makes you feel like heaven, and take what you need."

Her arms tightened around his neck, and her hands slid to the back of his head. She pressed his face closer, and her legs tightened around him. Her hips became wild, grinding in rhythm with his. Soft cries poured from her in staccato coordination with each of their thrusts, and he fought to keep himself from going over the edge.

"Don't hold back any longer, Mary Cate," he near pleaded. He couldn't hold back much longer. He struggled on the verge of release. "Let." He thrust harder. "*Go.*"

She did.

And so did he.

Her head flew back against the wall, and her thighs trembled. She shook against him, her sounds changing to soft sobs somewhere between joy and true weeping. He pressed in and held, struggling to separate which trembles were truly hers versus his own.

He pulled his chest away from her and simply stared at that overwhelmed—*and overjoyed?*—beautiful face. He couldn't believe what he had just done with her. Worse, he couldn't believe what he'd just done to himself.

Part of him couldn't help but be satisfied that she looked so thoroughly stunned.

Ring her bell? *Yep. Ding, ding!*

Ring his bell? *Dammit.*

He released her and stumbled back. *Yep. Ding* fucking *ding.*

Grabbing his hat, he registered in passing the mess of white powder coated along the bottom of the rim. He couldn't think straight enough to care. He needed to get out of here, before he recovered and started all over again. Only this time, with his pants around his ankles and his cock buried deep inside her.

To regain some teensy bit of control, he dismissively swatted his hat against his leg. He ignored the puff of flour that flew off and stuffed it on his head. Another small cloud of whiteness wafted down as the hat met his hair. Once again, he ignored it.

With one last glance at Mary Catherine—

No, *Mary Cate.* Because there was nothing prim and

proper about the woman who leaned dazed against the wall. The woman who had taunted him into debauching her in a pantry. Well, the pantry had actually been his doing. Still and all, he was now certain this woman would have had no qualms letting him have her innocence right here against that pantry wall.

What shook him most was he was also now certain she wouldn't have regretted it. She appeared completely satisfied with herself and no what-have-I-done hysterics were anywhere on the horizon.

Him? He would have felt like a cad had he taken her completely. Would have felt like he'd taken advantage. Now, he wasn't certain who had taken advantage of whom.

He yanked the door open and hastened out of that small space that suddenly felt a lot smaller than it had only three minutes ago. He sensed he appeared to be fleeing.

Hell, maybe he was fleeing.

This woman was more dangerous than he'd originally thought.

He looked up as he nearly crashed into Cook. Jonas's startled expression made Blaaze pause.

"I was never here," he grunted at the man.

He waited for some acknowledgment. Slowly, Cook nodded his understanding. It would have to do. Blaaze felt a nudge of chagrin hit him. He was leaving Mary Catherine to face her employee on her own. No way to prevent what came next, though, so he kept moving. He had to get out of here. All the way out.

Macey nearly crashed into him when he hit the kitchen doorway. She startled then gave a perplexed glance at his face. He had nothing for her. No words. No warning. Macey was so sweet; any words from him would likely send her into a swoon anyway.

He made a beeline to his room. Torment chased him. Safely behind a closed and locked door, he leaned on straight arms over the washstand, head down. He fought to stave off the shakes. He recognized a feeling similar to that which often assaulted him after a gunfight. He was headed for a massive energy crash. Worse, his encounter with Mary Catherine had resulted in a temporary euphoria that was anything but euphoric.

What his body wanted was fighting what his mind kept telling him, and his mind kept telling him, *No. Not this one. This one's not for you.*

The dampness in his drawers told him otherwise and annoyed him to no end. He'd been unable to stop himself from exploding in his pants like some inexperienced adolescent. That hadn't been part of the plan.

He'd never in his life been unable to control his release. Granted, he'd not gotten around to checking on the Widow Chandler. Still, long abstinence had never equated to loss of control. Until *her.*

A panicked thought resurfaced. *I've got to get out of here.*

No way could he stay in this room tonight. He wouldn't be able to resist that lovely temptation who'd be asleep down the hall. No force on earth would be able to stop him from slipping to that woman's room and sliding between her thighs all night long.

It wasn't logical. They made no sense together, but it didn't seem to matter to his churning brain. He glanced down at the front of his pants, to the damp spot transferring from drawers covering the limp, but very happy, appendage between his legs.

He yanked off his hat and tossed it toward the bed.

Glancing into the oval looking glass mounted above the washstand, he took note of the flour dusting his face and the front of his shirt. A languid breath pushed from his nostrils, and his shoulders dropped. No wonder Cook and Macey had stared at him so strangely.

After removing his bottoms, he grabbed a cloth and cleaned up. Then he changed his drawers and pants, still mentally thrown by what had transpired for him to need to do so. He didn't bother with the shirt. He simply brushed away as much of the condemning powder as he could then hastily threw a few necessities into his saddlebags. He made sure to grab the whittling supplies wrapped in oil cloth. He'd need those later to settle his nerves. Then he exited the room like demons were on his heels.

He ignored the real voices calling after him once he hit the downstairs area and headed straight for the saloon doors. He glanced toward the livery stable, then decided no way would he bunk there for the night. Tobias would take one look at him and know something was up. What that something was, Blaaze didn't want to talk about.

Tobias's voice rattled around his memory. *There's only one thing a man wants to do with a woman who makes him feel that way. Strangle her or bed her until neither one of them can walk. Which way you leaning?*

Guess that question had been answered. He definitely couldn't face Tobias tonight, the jackass know-it-all.

Blaaze stomped straight to the stable where Scout boarded. After saddling the stallion, he threw himself up. "Come on, boy. We need to head home."

Seemed they were both sleeping in a barn tonight. Time he stopped playing with that citified woman and got busy building a house on his own property. He was retired. He didn't need to be tied up in her problems with Clanton or with running a whorehouse or with losing her status as a damn virgin.

What the hell had the woman been thinking? *Head whore, indeed.*

She needed to go home. Blaaze had no doubt she would be headed back east soon, especially if Clanton got his way. She was no more qualified to run a saloon and whorehouse on the plains than Blaaze was qualified to be a friggin' dance hall girl.

Putting time limits on the men's visits upstairs made about as much sense as the white table linens. Her learned brain wanted to run her own business. Maybe he got that. On the one hand, she was trying to make conditions better for her women. On the other hand, she was outmatched.

Clanton wouldn't play fair. He didn't want her money; he wanted her business. He wanted Beulah's business. He wanted control of all the service businesses in town before construction on the railroad resumed and allowed the rest of the country to stop right at the town limits of Lawless.

Once progress came, more people would come. Along with more people would come more money. That's what Clanton wanted, control of the money. So the last thing he wanted was for Mary Catherine to make things work, upstairs or downstairs. Any success of the saloon meant a cut into Clanton's money grab.

Blaaze's outing with Malone the other night had ferreted out the sheriff's nefarious connection to Clanton. With the law behind him, Clanton could do about anything he wanted in this town. The brewery owner had thought to use Huntley to further his underhanded activities, but Malone had put a quash on that by scaring the sheriff into reclaiming the outlaw from Clanton's spread. The vermin had been secured back in jail by the morning, and Malone had left town with the prisoner the next day. Neither of them had let on to the sheriff that they were onto his crooked dealings.

The sheriff intended to help Clanton drive Mary Catherine out of business. If that didn't work, Blaaze wondered if the brewery owner was capable of getting rid of her all together. Blaaze's gut fairly screamed at him, and it screamed, *Yep. Yeah. And heck yes!* And he didn't think that meant simply putting her on a train back to Cleveland. The man wouldn't have needed Huntley for that.

He needed to find out for sure what Clanton had planned for his next move. Otherwise, he'd have none of the peace and quiet that was supposed to be his nice, relaxing retirement from taking down bad guys. Men who were scum, it occurred to him, exactly like Clanton.

Double dammit, he cursed to himself then kicked Scout into a gallop, recognizing no matter how fast he raced toward home, what he fled—who he fled—burned under his skin. Perhaps permanently. And more than he needed her gone, he needed her safe. Even if the man he had to be to keep her safe was a man she was unlikely to feel comfortable alone in a room with ever again, a man as much outlaw as bounty hunter.

But if he had to choose between never seeing her look at him again like she did tonight or pushing back at those who endangered her, the choice was easy. The man who returned to the saloon tomorrow would be as ruthless as the men who threatened her livelihood.

~

Mary Catherine lingered against the wall of the pantry in a daze of contentment long after Blaaze departed. Her legs felt wobbly, and her mind couldn't form any lucid thoughts. Cook eventually walked in, arms full of vegetables to shelve. He stopped when he noticed her. He glanced back over his shoulder toward the door then back at her, but he didn't say a word.

One thought finally crossed her mind. She should feel chagrin. Maybe embarrassment? Something other than this satisfied bliss. One of her employees had entered the kitchen shortly after she'd frolicked with a man in the pantry. No way he'd not seen Blaaze vacate the room minutes ago. Mary Catherine was decently dressed—although quite a bit wrinkled. Cook had not seen anything inappropriate, but he had to have an idea about what he'd missed.

What he had missed was not right and proper behavior for a Templeton, but she couldn't repress a grin. She didn't particularly care. It felt really good not to worry about being right and proper for once. It didn't matter if Cook had an indication of what she and Blaaze had been up to amongst the potatoes, cured meat, and bags of flour.

Her eyes dashed toward the stores of flour. The spilled detritus of an open bag spread across the nearest shelf and a dusting of whiteness covered the lower shelves, plus the floor immediately below. The look on Blaaze's face when he'd pulled his precious hat from the higher shelf covered in baking ingredients crossed her mind.

Her grin grew wider.

The man was persnickety about that hat. She'd never seen him so dismissive of its care as he'd looked when he'd brushed ineffectively at the mess and thrown it on his head like he couldn't get away from her fast enough. She didn't think he realized that in addition to the flour on his denims, he'd had flour dotted across his forehead and one cheek when he'd vacated the room.

Her gaze moved back to the immobile Cook. He took another glance over his shoulder then back at her. He glanced over her skirt, and his brow puckered before he raised his eyebrows at her in silent speculation.

Yep, wrinkles spotted. *Oops!*

She almost wanted to chuckle. Clearly, not the behavior he expected from her if the look he gave her was any indication. Her fingers flexed against the wall below her hips before she pushed herself off. Regardless of her most recent behavior and the half-confused, half-disapproving look she was getting from Cook, she was a lady. She would walk from this pantry with dignity. After all, she was the boss, and Jonas had not the right to question anything she did.

Of course, he and the others at the saloon had recently become more friends than employees. That didn't mean she didn't have a certain authority she'd not allow anyone to question. Despite her inner pep talk, she couldn't stop her hands for straying to brush the wrinkles on her skirt when she passed by Cook. With a courteous nod of her head, she continued out into the kitchen to seek her bedroom as quickly as possible. A cloud of satisfied delight flowed out with her.

She could feel Cook's eyes on her back when she walked past. Her step faltered but a second when she noticed Macey near the kitchen entry. Macey gave her a curious look but said nothing. Mary Catherine sped up, wanting to be anywhere but there as potential spectacle.

No one gathered in the main hall, and she made her way to the stairs without any further witnesses. Almost running now, she fled toward her room. She wanted to hold on to this feeling she had, and she didn't want to have spectators while she basked in the fading glow of what had been her first true intimate encounter. Her first orgasm brought on by a man. And she'd been right. It was totally different than exploring her own anatomy, and they hadn't even gotten to the full act.

Rushing through the bedroom door, Mary Catherine closed it absently with a backward flick of her hand and threw herself face down across the bed, flipped immediately over, and stared blankly at the ceiling, her arms spread wide.

Barbara Jean's voice drifted through her consciousness, *. . . if I had a man like that stare at me every time he saw me as if he was starving and I was a well-cooked steak, I know exactly where I'd be going to get my introduction to womanhood.*

Mary Catherine grabbed at a pillow and hugged it to her chest. The ghostly feel of Blaaze Lassiter grinding intimately against her made her squeeze her thighs together, pull her knees up, and roll onto her side. She knew what man she wanted, but for some reason, he didn't want to solve her little problem.

Not true. He wanted her. What happened between them tonight proved that. He didn't want to want her—obstinate, judgmental male that he was—but that didn't mean he'd be able to not give in to her if she persevered in the matter.

She popped into a sitting position, thrown by her last thought. She'd been going about this the wrong way. She'd been begging and pursuing. How pathetic. She was smarter than that.

Barbara Jean was right. If Mary Catherine had learned anything about men since her sojourn in the Kansas plains, it was that men were simple. They were obscure equations to calculate, but once you knew how to move the right exponents around, each equation was pretty easy to solve.

She had Blaaze's numbers, but she'd been trying to work them in the wrong sequence.

Time for her to recalculate and regroup.

Chapter 20

BLAAZE STOOD AT THE mouth of the livery stable two days later, leaning against the entrance post with a water canteen in his hand. He watched men trickle in and out of the saloon. Word had finally spread wide that the saloon had a new owner—a new *female*, unmarried owner.

Every unattached male in the area apparently wanted to come take a look-see. His eyes narrowed when he watched the recently returned mayor leave his office, head toward the saloon, then adjust his vest and hat before entering the establishment's double doors. If the mayor was taking a look, likely before his horse had even cooled down, this was getting serious.

"What's wrong with these men?" he grumbled aloud. Didn't they realize a woman like her didn't belong in this half-civilized, off-the-beaten-path frontier town? That she was too good for the lot of them?

"What's gotten you riled already today?" Tobias stepped up beside Blaaze, his blacksmith apron covering his overalls.

He motioned to the crowd gathering at the mouth of the

saloon. "She's turning this place into as much of a farce as the Ringling Brothers traveling circus." Blaaze had seen the one-ring extravaganza once over in Wisconsin.

"What's it to you?"

Something about Tobias's tone made Blaaze turn his head to look at his pal. "Nothing. It's just annoying is all."

"Why? She's minding her business. Why don't you mind yours?"

Blaaze stood up straight. "What's that supposed to mean?"

"What do you mean?" Tobias leaned a shoulder against the opposite post.

Frustrated, Blaaze asked, "What do *you* mean?"

Tobias chuckled sardonically. "I asked first. Seems you've been awful interested in what Miss Templeton does with her saloon. What's your deal?"

Blaaze scoffed. "It's not her saloon she's minding. She's turning our watering hole into a den of chaos, and now it looks like it's becoming a courting service. Every unattached guy in town, and a few not so unattached ones, have filed in and out of that saloon in the last couple of days."

"It's to be expected. A woman like her is the kind a man can marry. Men out here don't get much opportunity like that without writing away for a mail order bride or some such. Fellas would be plumb stupid not to take advantage of a filly like that."

Blaaze whipped around, so riled up he ignored the livery owner's regular habit of referring to everything female as a filly. "Are you out of your mind? A woman like her doesn't belong here. The last thing she needs is to marry some homesteader or wannabe rancher. She needs to take herself on back east to her cushy life before this frontier eats her alive." He turned back toward the saloon. "Besides, given the business she runs, do you really think all those men are actually after marriage? Some are probably looking for a much more casual relationship and"—he motioned with the canteen—"that lady there is too green to know it."

"Seems to me you're making a whole lot of assumptions about that lady there."

"Assumptions, my ass." Blaaze took a sip from the canteen. "Lila ran that saloon like a personal entertainment palace. Mary Catherine couldn't find a good time with both hands and a personal guide." When he remembered how she'd managed to corral him into giving her a good-time grind against the pantry wall the other day, he scowled. He'd been avoiding the enticing siren ever since.

"She's not Lila, Blaaze."

"*Exactly*. And she has no more business taking over Lila's place than a nun."

"That's not what I meant." Tobias grabbed the canteen from Blaaze's hand and took a long pull. "Why don't you stop comparing her to what she doesn't have and start looking at what she does have."

Blaaze looked at him inquiringly.

"She doesn't have to be a Lila. You and I both know that Lila was one of a kind with more grit and gumption than most men. But maybe Miss Templeton is too if you give her a chance. She's already proven she's got grit. After all she's faced so far with that saloon, if she were a dainty flower, she would have already hightailed it out of here. You're so busy focusing on who she's not that you've yet to appreciate who she *is*."

Blaaze glared at the big man then turned his back on him. Digging around in his saddlebag, he made a show of ignoring the man. Tobias eventually walked away shaking his head. Blaaze pulled out his whittling supplies and took a seat. He'd been working on this particular carving for a few days, and it was finally coming into shape.

He understood why his dad had been such a fan of the hobby. Whittling helped settle the mind. Not that Blaaze was much good, yet. He'd get there now that he had time to do nothing but practice, raise horses, and read.

His dad was a master whittler. The old man could turn a piece of wood into exact replicas of animals, plants, or whatnot, and had taught Blaaze the basics. In the past, Blaaze had always been too impatient to develop much talent for the wood art and way too fond of mastering his gun draw. Now that he was older and needed to put a certain saloon owner and her troubles out of his mind for a bit, shaping wood with his jack knife drew his brain into quiet repose.

About an hour later, he looked up when he heard the crunch of steps coming his way.

Well, damn. So much for ridding his mind of the saloon proprietress. Mary Catherine Templeton advanced toward him. Her fancy boots took small, graceful steps that lent an enticing sway to her hips. When their gazes met, she offered a hesitant smile.

Blaaze pushed back his Stetson and dropped his hands and wood work to his lap. "Miss Templeton, how might I help you this morning?" A devil crawled up on his shoulder, and he couldn't prevent himself from adding, "You wouldn't be looking for help with any bell ringing this fine morning, now would you? I thought we'd settled that matter the other evening."

The embarrassed flush that covered her from neck to cheeks made his cock perk up and reminded him how much he'd wanted a second round of that bell ringing challenge. A thought that equated to being speared by the tines of his own devil's pitchfork, which made his contrariness rise up.

"Actually, I was looking for Mr. Craig." She took a quick survey of the surroundings. "Is he around?"

"He sure is." Tobias stepped from the back rubbing his hands on a rag. His smile spread wide when Mary Catherine looked his way. "Good morning, Miss Templeton. Something I can do for you?"

"Why, yes," she said demurely. She shot an uncomfortable glance in Blaaze's direction before she continued. "Is there a place we could speak privately?"

With a nod, Tobias led her toward the private back room where he kept his business papers and personal items. Mary Catherine stepped in behind him and closed the door all but a crack. The move irritated Blaaze. It wasn't as if he planned to eavesdrop or anything.

He picked up his whittling, wondering what could be so all-fired important she needed to take the big man behind a nearly closed door to discuss it. Chips of wood flaked off wildly as he attacked his unfinished basswood carving with punishing scoops. Not the technique he'd been taught, but his mind had slid from its settled state the moment he'd noticed Mary Catherine walking his way. His current rile eliminated the cockstand that had risen in his crotch, and he silently stewed over what the dratted woman could be up to and what in tarnation it might have to do with Tobias.

"Thank you so much, Mr. Craig. I'll see you tonight for dinner." Mary Catherine came from the back room with a smile on her face. She stopped beside Blaaze's chair to stare at the carving in his hand. "That's a really nice dog, Mr. Lassiter. You're quite good at that." She nodded genially at

Tobias then headed up the street.

Blaaze glanced at the carving in his hand. "It's a horse," he muttered to her retreating back. He watched her hips sashay all the way back to the saloon. When she went inside, Blaaze finally looked over at Tobias.

The man was watching him and grinning like a loon.

"You gonna tell me what that was about or you just gonna stand there looking like a clown at the rodeo?"

Tobias's eyes twinkled at the obvious irritation in Blaaze's voice. "Well, you heard. Miss Templeton has invited me to have dinner with her tonight."

"Dinner? Why?" Blaaze couldn't think of any ironwork at the saloon she'd need fixing. "What's she want you to do for her? She doesn't have a horse."

"Nope." Tobias propped a shoulder against the doorway side post mimicking his earlier stance, and his grin got wider. "It's not a horse she's interested in having me service."

It took a minute before the look on Tobias's face helped Blaaze catch the underlying meaning of the blacksmith's words. Blaaze shot to his feet. His whittling knife and carving hit the dust. "She did not!"

A mischievous twinkle entered Tobias's eyes, and he gave an extremely slow confirming nod. "She *did.*" His hand went to his chin, and he rubbed it thoughtfully. "At first, I told her I was flattered by the consideration, but I didn't think you'd be too happy with either of us if I took her proposition seriously. Then she said the most curious thing." He crossed his arms and stopped talking.

Blaaze fisted his hands at his side. "Well, you gonna tell me what that was?"

Tobias made him wait a beat before he answered. "Said she'd already discussed the proposition with you, and you'd turned her down."

Blaaze's mouth dropped open. That woman was not going around town telling people she'd wanted him to bed her but he'd refused. She didn't have a lick of sense for a college-educated person. He'd been trying to protect her reputation and here she was dragging her own name into the mud.

"That woman is not staying in town. She's going back where she belongs with the fancy people she's used to so she can eat off linen tablecloths and use heated hand towels and sleep in places that don't double as a brothel." Blaaze began to pace.

He needed her to leave. She couldn't go on living in the same town as him. He'd not be able to resist this pull between them forever, and she'd never survive plains life attached to a no-good rascal who had people all over the country after his head or looking to test the speed of his gun.

"Seems she's decided to stay."

"She's not staying!" Blaaze flexed and released his fingers. He could feel all his usual cool unraveling, and he grappled to keep the unfamiliar feeling at bay.

"She was pretty adamant about that. Doesn't strike me as a woman easily taken to changing her mind." Tobias eyed his fume with something like pity in his eyes. "Seems she's decided to take on a companion, and she's holding interviews this week to make her decision."

"Interviews! She's holding . . . *interviews*?" Blaaze stopped pacing, lifted his hat off his head, and scratched his scalp with the fingers of the same hand. "With that woman's poor discretion and bad luck, she'll end up unwittingly picking the worst scoundrel in town." A scoundrel who'd be worse than him because the varmint wouldn't have the decency to leave her alone.

Blaaze slapped his hat back onto his head and stomped over to the shelf where he'd stashed his gun belt in a crate. Putting it on, he grumbled, "That woman is going to get herself hurt."

"Or bedded."

Blaaze's hand whipped instinctively to the butt of his Colt.

Tobias's hands shot up. "Whoa there, cowboy. Don't go shooting the messenger. Literally."

Blaaze blew out a long breath and lifted his hand away from his gun. With a chagrined look, he made a big deal of showing spread-wide fingers. "Sorry."

Tobias silently acknowledged his apology. "I don't get it. Why'd you turn her down? You clearly want her. She seems to want you back."

"I told you. She's leaving." He'd make sure of it.

"And?"

Blaaze simply stared at him. The answer to that should be obvious. "She'll not want to go back home ruined."

"*Ruined* is such a judgmental word."

Blaaze huffed out another big breath. "Fine. Unfit for marriage."

"She made it pretty clear she's not looking for a husband. She's looking for a *companion*. So whether she takes a lover and stays in town or takes a lover and eventually leaves town, what's the difference to you? You've never been interested in taking a wife. She doesn't seem interested in being a wife. I don't see the problem."

Blaaze said nothing. He'd didn't have an answer, so he picked up his carving and jack knife from the ground. He wiped them on his jeans then bundled them back into the oilcloth he used to protect them.

Tobias, being Tobias, didn't let it go. "Unless . . ."

Blaaze straightened. "Unless what?" he asked warily.

Tobias studied him. "Well, I'll be damned."

Hands back at his hips, Blaaze snarled, "What? Spit it out, you old coot."

"You've fallen for that gal. Fallen hard from what I see." Tobias burst into deep, raucous laughter. "Kind of difficult to think about taking her casually to bed when the heart's involved." Still laughing, he pushed off the door post.

"Knock it off! You're crazy. I have *not* fallen for that buttoned-up, city priss."

"Oh yes, you have, and it's all that prim and proper, citified priss with the accented, college vocabulary that's got you all in a twist." The big guy hunched over and slapped his knees, laughing even harder. "Well, I'll be double damned. Who'd have thought."

"I said, knock it off!" Blaaze was about ready to go for his gun again.

"Don't get mad at me because you're gonna let that woman choose another man to initiate her into womanhood."

"Womanhood? Now who's talking judgmental bull. She's already a woman. Taking a man to bed isn't going to make her any more of a woman than she already is."

"Fine." Tobias said, echoing Blaaze's previous response. "Then initiate her into the pleasures of the flesh. How's that?"

Blaaze didn't like that at all.

"Guess we'll see who's the winner of Miss Templeton's *companionship* at the end of the week." Tobias turned to go back inside. "Best go make sure my good denims are clean for tonight."

Blaaze called his buddy's name in a low voice that came out with a slow growl. "Tobias . . ."

The blacksmith looked over his shoulder, a smirk firmly in place. "Yeah?"

"You show up at that dinner tonight, and I *will* shoot you." Blaaze had never been more serious about anything in his life.

The big man burst into laughter again and kept walking.

Snatching his pearl-handled Colt from his holster, Blaaze flipped open the barrel and gave it a spin to check each hole for a bullet. Satisfied he was fully loaded, he twirled the Colt back into its holster.

Determined to put an end to this interview nonsense, he stalked toward the saloon intent on finding out whom else he might have to shoot today.

~

Mary Catherine had lunch spread out on the round table where she'd sat when she'd first met with the attorney-at-law not so long ago to discuss Lila's estate. Today's meeting was quite different than her original business at this table. So she'd made the additional effort of adding one of the white linen tablecloths she no longer used out front. She'd had the linens hemmed, and the effect was quite lovely. Whatever the preferences of the saloon menfolk, she'd set her own table as she deemed appropriate.

After all, it wasn't often a woman of her upbringing chose to pick her own male companion rather than having a husband chosen for her by a father or other guardian. Something she wouldn't have had the courage to do back home out in the open like this. Plains rules for women were a little more lax.

Standards of propriety still existed, but myriad opportunities also existed. Women could own businesses outside of laundry, food service, and seamstress, even a saloon, without being thought complete pariahs . . . mostly. And since many saloons also doubled as town halls for social and political gatherings, women could even enter those establishments—at certain times of day—without tongues wagging, except maybe by the staunchly religious.

She ignored the internal voice that wanted to remind her that she was once one of those staunchly religious individuals. Now? She didn't quite know what she was. Her Bible upbringing was hard to put totally aside, but the possibilities of living a life by her own dictates outside a community heavy with expectations of her based upon her family name and connections was a temptation she was finding hard to resist.

Carefully, she moved the blue and gold painted china tea service she'd found in the glass-front cabinet against the back wall onto the table. The teapot was warm and full with a fresh brew of black tea. Here she was taking a step that felt monumental, if not a bit scary. A twinge of uncertainty hit her briefly when she thought about the fiancé she'd rejected back home, but she set it aside. She'd decided to build a life here in Kansas, whatever that brought, and she'd not succumb to second-guessing herself or allowing fear to send her into the arms of a man simply out of familiarity when she knew he wanted her to be someone she couldn't be for him.

She smiled welcomingly at her guest, a charming farmer only a few years older than herself named Drew Johnson. He smiled expectantly back at her from the chair opposite hers. She'd only just sat down herself when a looming figure shoved unceremoniously through the ajar parlor door. The door rebounded against the adjacent wall, and Blaaze Lassiter propped a raised hand against the portal to keep it from ricocheting back into his face.

Palm still resting against the door and the heel of his other hand on the butt of the gun holstered at his side, he surveyed the scene then flashed a menacingly goofy grin at her. "Is it tea time?" he asked, releasing the door. He cocked a hip brazenly and hooked the thumb of his free hand into the corresponding front pocket of his denims. "Well, I'll be. I arrived just in time," he said in a lilting falsetto that made him sound like one of the town biddies excited to sit for tea and biscuits with her gossipmonger friends.

He entered the room and gave Mr. Johnson a false grin that did little to counteract the dangerous saunter created by the continued placement of one hand on his gun. The farmer's eyes skirted to that deliberately placed hand then darted to Mary Catherine's face uncertainly.

Mary Catherine glared at Blaaze. "This is a private sitting, Mr. Lassiter. If you wouldn't mind taking your refreshment in the outer hall."

"Oh, but I do mind." He stopped between them, eyeing their lunch spread. "This looks so much more appealing. I don't remember you ever breaking out the good china for a sitting with me."

She'd never had a sitting with him, so the comment was absurd. Before she could point that out, he removed a biscuit from a plate in the center of the table and took a large bite. Ignored crumbs sprinkled down the front of his shirt.

He hummed in appreciation. "Oh, yeah. This is really good," he said with his mouth full. Then he dropped the uneaten portion of the biscuit on top of the others on the plate and made a big show of slapping his hands together to rid them of any residual morsels.

An affronted gasped escaped Mary Catherine, and she popped up from her seat.

With a quick hand to her shoulder, Blaaze pressed her firmly back down into her chair.

Drew Johnson grabbed the napkin from across his lap and stood, finally finding his voice. "Mr. Lassiter—"

"Sit *down*," Blaaze said abruptly. His eyes flashed, all playfulness gone.

"Now, see here!" The farmer threw his napkin down on the table, but the bravado didn't last long.

Blaaze drew his gun lightning fast. "You can sit down or you can leave. Either way, I can't promise I won't shoot you all the same."

"A-All I was trying to say is ... um ..." Mr. Johnson swallowed and took a deep breath to regroup. "What I believe the lady was trying to tell you diplomatically is that she and I have private business to discuss."

"Your business is finished." Blaaze cocked the hammer of his pistol with a loud click that reverberated its threat through the room.

Drew Johnson's Adam's apple bobbed. "But ..." He glanced at Mary Catherine.

She didn't know what to say to the man. The last thing she wanted was to get him shot, and Blaaze Lassiter looked every bit as if he intended to do just that.

In the face of Mary Catherine's silence, the bounty hunter motioned with his gun for Drew to scoot. Drew glanced once more at Mary Catherine, but she could do nothing more than shrug apologetically. They were all clearly at an impasse, and the man with the gun had the upper hand.

After straightening his shoulders, Drew Johnson walked stoically from the room without another word. Mary Catherine couldn't really blame him. Blaaze was a formidable man to stand up to. Still, he'd had no right to interrupt her luncheon. She'd been planning to get to know the young farmer. She'd drawn up a list of questions to use with each of her potential suitors and had been prepared to select a bed companion other than Blaaze in case she couldn't get the bullheaded bounty hunter to come around.

He'd come around all right, toting a pistol. That was not what she had in mind, and that he'd done so made her fuming mad. He'd probably scared the bejesus out of Drew. The man would likely never talk to her again.

Gun back in his holster, Blaaze moved to take Mr. Johnson's empty seat.

His bottom had barely touched the chair when she snapped, *"Get out."*

His head cocked at her tone, and his eyes squinted. Slowly, he said in a deep grumble, "You want to say that again?"

She stood, pressed her hands against the table, and leaned toward him. "How dare you interfere that way and pull a gun on my guest. You had no right!"

He stood and, mimicking her posture, shouted, "I had every right! You fool woman are going to get yourself into a lick of trouble you won't be able to undo."

"It's my life and my decision what trouble I get into." She pushed away from the table and him. "I made you an offer; you weren't interested. So don't stand there and try to dictate what I do or with whom."

He came around the table toward her. "You listen here—"

"No." Her hand shot up as a blockade. "Don't come near me."

Her gesture and firm tone stopped him in his tracks.

"I'm not doing this with you again," she managed to say

with less vitriol. Holding back tears of frustration she'd never let him see, she wrapped her arms around herself as if that might contain the anger and roiling emotions assaulting her. "Get out."

He stood staring at her, his chest heaving. In anger? With a bit of the frustration she felt herself? She wasn't sure.

His eyes held an intensity that reminded her of how he'd looked at her after their interlude in the pantry. She could now recognize it for what it was. He wanted her, but he was perplexed by his wanting of her. She felt almost sorry for him. She'd endured that same brand of confusion the first few times she'd encountered him and his unfathomable allure. Battling that serpent had made her feel raw and vulnerable.

Nevertheless, she wouldn't continue to accept his insulting need to treat her like some damsel he had to protect even from herself. She was a grown, fully intelligent woman with natural wants and needs. Wants and needs he'd been the one to awaken. They could approach this matter practically, like everything else she did in her life.

She'd weighed the pros and cons for herself and calculated the best way forward. It seemed like a perfect proposal where a man was concerned, especially for a man who seemed to be physically attracted to her. She'd get the experience she wanted, and he'd get a liaison without extended obligation. His unceasing resistance to her proposal didn't make sense, and she couldn't let this push and pull continue unacknowledged between them.

Her voice softened, but she tried to conceal the glimmer of hope her next words represented. "Have you changed your mind, Blaaze? Have you changed your mind about trusting me to know what I want from you and giving it to me?"

He lifted his hat with one hand and slowly rubbed the

other over his closely cropped hair. He looked down at his Stetson with a deep sigh, turned it a few times, then shaped the crown absently. After deliberately placing the hat back on his head, he shook his head no.

"Mary Catherine . . ." He began to move toward her again.

She took a big step back, afraid to let him touch her lest she lose her nerve over what she had to do. "No."

Her heart hurt at his answer. If he didn't want to be with her, she didn't want him around. She couldn't have him around. She'd be unable to function with him around as a constant reminder of what she craved but could not have, a constant reminder of his rejection of her.

She took another step back. "Leave now. In fact, Mr. Lassiter, leave for good."

CHAPTER 21

MARY CATHERINE STOOD BEHIND the bar counting bottles of spirits. It was early yet, after breakfast but not quite time for the afternoon crowd to wander in. Two of the elder males of the town dozed at separate tables near the back, and Charlie, the barkeep, had wandered out for a while to take care of some personal matters.

It had been days since she'd seen the elusive Mr. Lassiter. On one hand, that should have been a good thing. That's what she'd told him to do: disappear. On the other, she hadn't counted on how much she'd miss seeing the cowboy, his annoying behavior notwithstanding.

Barbara Jean sidled up beside her behind the bar. "No matter how many times you count those bottles, the tally's gonna come up the same as it did yesterday and the day before that." She took the current bottle from Mary Catherine and returned it to its crate. "You know, moping around here pretending to be busy isn't fooling anyone."

Mary Catherine stopped herself from making a pouty face. "I'm not moping."

"Sure you are, honey. And everybody knows why." Barbara Jean chuckled lightly. "Or should I say knows *who* is responsible for this forlorn mood of yours."

Before Mary Catherine could challenge that comment, a familiar round-brimmed hat dropped onto the bar in front of them. The cowgirl from the other day plopped down on a stool with a totally exasperated look. She'd been in the saloon several times over the last few days, but she generally skulked in the back as if she was waiting for someone . . . or perhaps avoiding someone. Maybe even a little of both.

"I need a room," the cowgirl said bluntly.

Surprised, Mary Catherine put down the bottle she'd removed from the current crate of inventory she was inspecting. "I don't think you want to stay here, miss."

"I just said I did." The woman's eyes narrowed. "You have a problem renting me a room?"

"No, it's . . . um . . ." Mary Catherine thought of a way to state what had not been so obvious to her upon her arrival. "You do know this isn't only a boarding house, right?"

The cowgirl looked around then back at her and shrugged. "No matter to me. As long as no one expects me to join in, live and let live I say."

Mary Catherine couldn't believe the woman would be that blasé about it. She glanced at Barbara Jean, who simply shrugged.

"Have you tried Miss Eileen's place, down a ways on the other side of the street?" Mary Catherine suggested.

"You trying to get me jailed, Miss Templeton?" The woman leaned an elbow on the bar.

"W-what?" Mary Catherine startled at the nonsensical question and at being called by name. The two of them had never been introduced.

The woman smiled, and like before, Mary Catherine had the distinct impression she should know her.

"Surprised I know your name?"

Mary Catherine nodded.

She chuckled. "You do know that you're the talk of the town? A person can't get too far around here without hearing about the city woman who took over the saloon. I figured most of the talk I'd hear around this town would be about that scoundrel Lassiter. But you've got the town tongues wagging something fierce."

"Blaaze?" Mary Catherine looked down and scribbled her last count into her bar ledger to hide the effect hearing the man's name had on her.

The cowgirl perked up. "Yeah, you know him?"

Looking up, she ignored Barbara Jean's knowing expression and said, "Yes, I do. He has a room here in fact."

Or did he? His room was paid up through the end of the week, but he appeared to have packed up and left like she'd told him to do.

A worried expression flitted across the woman's face before she could suppress it. She looked every bit as if she might get up and leave, but then her shoulders rose and fell as if she'd come to a decision. "Hmm. Thought I'd have a few more days to get the lay of the land before I had to face that ornery cuss, but might as well bite the bullet." She took another long look around the saloon. "What's he doing rooming here? Thought he'd bought a passel of land here abouts."

Barbara Jean chimed in. "Yes, well, word is there's nothing much on that land right now but a barn and a paddock."

The cowgirl shook her head. "Figures. Guy always did

love horses more than people. We're gonna have to fix that housing situation, though. Arrange a roof raising for him. Gal can't be sleeping in a barn long-term."

Barbara Jean glanced at Mary Catherine, but Mary Catherine simply blinked and tried to keep her expression stoic. The thought of this woman staying with Blaaze brought an unwelcome feeling of possessiveness, but no one needed to know that.

Despite her best efforts, whatever expression Mary Catherine made had the cowgirl studying her closely for a moment.

"You okay, Miss Templeton?" the woman asked after a few seconds.

Mary Catherine laid down her pencil. "Um, yes. I . . ."

Barbara Jean took pity on Mary Catherine and took over the conversation. "You planning on sleeping out at Mr. Lassiter's? Even without a house and all?"

The cowgirl laughed. "Oh that." She waved a hand. "Don't worry none. I've slept in a barn or two in my time if it comes to that, but I'd thought when I set out to track him here that the man would have a roof I could sleep under."

The comment bothered Mary Catherine. This woman had searched Blaaze out and followed him here? And she expected to stay with him. Who was she to the bounty hunter? He'd always acted the aloof, loner type, but here was a woman attached enough to him to track him down across the plains.

Even more curious now about the woman's statement about trying to get her thrown into jail, Mary Catherine asked her what she'd meant by that.

"Have you ever met Miss Eileen?" The cowgirl eyed her sharply.

That made Barbara Jean laugh. "Oh yeah, we have."

Mary Catherine smiled. "Why, yes, when I first arrived in town."

"Then you know." The woman made one abrupt nod. "And iffin' I have to spend another second in that woman's presence, the sheriff will be hauling me in for murder."

"We certainly can't have that," Mary Catherine said in all seriousness, completely understanding the thought. She'd place the woman in an upper room, but not too close to Blaaze's room in case he returned. She had no right to interfere with whatever was between the bounty hunter and the cowgirl, but that didn't mean she had to make it easy for the woman to do . . . whatever she wanted to do with Blaaze. "Barbara Jean will have someone set you up in the last set of rooms on our upper floor. I have some nice tea brewing in back. I could have a cup sent up for you."

"Tea again." The cowgirl gave Mary Catherine a look of utter amusement. "What's with you people? Do I look like the kind of woman who orders tea, let alone drinks it?"

Mary Catherine grinned remembering the woman saying the same words a few days ago. "How about a cup of coffee then? I'll warn you it's awfully strong because that's the way the men like it."

"Now *that* sounds right heavenly. Coffee I'll take."

"I'll have that sent right up, Miss . . .?"

Her expression became guarded. "Just miss is fine . . . for now. And I wouldn't mind having that coffee right away, if it's all the same."

Mary Catherine sent back to the kitchen to have the coffee prepared, and Barbara Jean went off to arrange for the preparation of the woman's rooms. Moving back to the crates before her, Mary Catherine restarted her review of the dollars made versus the bottles of spirits that remained. The revenue collected was significantly below what should have been given the number of bottles withdrawn from the inventory. She had only a few more days to meet Jake Clanton's deadline, so every penny counted.

Income had picked up nicely since Barbara Jean started running the upstairs amenities, but it still bothered Mary Catherine that the liquor tallies were off. It was one of the reasons she'd been spending more time out front. She'd likely already have her account with Mr. Clanton settled by now if the bar credits and debits actually reconciled.

The cowgirl moved to the end of the bar with her coffee and quietly watched while Mary Catherine did her inventory counts. The pensive gaze unnerved Mary Catherine. She was too aware of the woman's presence, and the possibility of what her relationship might be with the town's sullen bounty hunter disturbed her.

After uncharacteristically miscalculating her totals not once but three times, Mary Catherine stuffed her pencil into her bun with a sigh. She'd not solve this dilemma with a certain cowboy and a mysterious cowgirl invading her thoughts. She glanced over at the woman, who gave her a silent salute with her steaming cup. Something about the amused look on the woman's face suggested she was aware of Mary Catherine's discombobulation.

Her gaze was too sharp. An unmistakable intelligence hid behind her eyes. As a tall, full-figured woman with a pretty face and an air of fearlessness, she was the kind of woman who would appeal to a rugged man like Blaaze Lassiter. He'd not look at this woman and think schoolmarm, that was certain.

The flair of jealousy surprised her. She was done with the man after all. Except . . .

Was she?

Her aching heart seemed to feel otherwise. She *had* been moping for days, as Barbara Jean had pointed out. And if she continued to mope rather than take some action, she might be clearing the field for this woman to take up with the man Mary Catherine wanted for herself.

She snapped her ledger shut and grabbed it up with her miscellaneous notes. Self-righteous pride be damned. She went determinedly in search of Barbara Jean. If the elder woman knew about Blaaze's land, maybe she also knew where it was.

He'd stormed into her tea the other day intent on disrupting her life.

Now, it was her turn to disrupt his.

~

Mary Catherine drove the one-horse wagon she'd borrowed from Barbara Jean toward the Lassiter homestead. The ride wasn't as smooth as the buggy she'd learned to drive back home, but the mare was mild and responsive. The closer she got to Blaaze's land the more nervous she became. She'd convinced herself she needed to clear the air with the cowboy, but maybe she was simply a glutton for punishment.

When he'd come into the saloon parlor and interrupted her lunch with Drew Johnson, she'd been peeved at the man's audacity. She could still see Mr. Johnson's face when Blaaze had waved a gun at the farmer and threatened to shoot him if he didn't leave. Drew had tried to be brave in the face of the gun and a man known to take down outlaws for a living, but he'd abandoned her without a backward glance. She couldn't really blame the farmer. Blaaze was a formidable man to stand up to.

Still, he'd had no right to interrupt her luncheon.

After what he'd done, Mary Catherine didn't see how she'd convince anyone else to meet with her. And if she was honest with herself, she didn't want to sit down with anyone else. Only one man stayed on her mind. She'd hoped her interview plan would be successful in either forcing the man to change his mind or allowing her to find a suitable replacement. She hadn't counted on Blaaze being motivated to threaten—or do—fatal harm to the other suitors.

She felt a little bad about that miscalculation.

Looking around, she spotted the large tree and boulder Tobias had told her marked the turnoff to Blaaze's land and steered the wagon onto the dirt lane that would lead up to the ranch house. Her heart began to pound. She'd thought confronting the man in private would be the best option for addressing everything they needed to work through. Now, she wasn't so sure.

When she got farther up the lane, she noted no completed ranch house stood on the property. A large barn appeared with a huge paddock not too far away. Blaaze's horse grazed on some hay dumped inside the open paddock. The paddock had fresh rails and posts. The house stood framed but not yet erected. The foundation had been set and stairs led up to a porch and the open wood beams for walls, but that was it.

So Barbara Jean's information had been right, which explained why Blaaze had been sleeping at her saloon despite having property of his own.

The crunch of gravel beneath the wagon's wheels interrupted the peaceful silence of greenery rimmed by full trees. The whack of a hammer echoed into the quietness, and she scanned for the source of the sound. Her gaze landed upon Blaaze atop the barn, shirtless.

Shirtless.

Goodness.

His brown skin glowed with a sheen of perspiration. Solid, muscled arms flexed when he lifted a board and carefully placed it into position. He hammered the board into place before he looked up to scan her approaching wagon.

Even with his hat brim pulled low to shield his eyes from the sun, she could tell he wasn't pleased to see her. Her nerves got more agitated. Was she out of her mind coming here like this?

She'd let the arrival of the no-name cowgirl goad her into an action she might regret.

Blaaze had made it pretty clear he thought her a complete idiot for interviewing for a companion. His words had stung until she'd rationalized that he wouldn't have been so upset if her plans didn't bother him on some personal level. But maybe she'd been wrong.

She watched him watch her approach. She pulled the horse to a stop, set the handbrake, and climbed down from the wagon. By the time she dismounted and turned to face the barn, Blaaze had descended a ladder and stood a few feet in front of her. His eyes shuttered, and he rubbed a large cloth across his face. When he lowered the cloth to wipe his sweat-dotted chest, her eyes followed the movement.

The man was beautiful. All rich brown skin, muscles, and attitude. The vision was enough to make a woman swoon, assuming said woman were the swooning type. Which she wasn't.

At least, she didn't think she was.

He might be the impetus to prove herself wrong.

"Is there something I can do for you, Mary Cate?"

Her gaze flicked to his at the sound of the nickname. His cocky expression made clear he'd noticed her appreciation of his show of drying himself off. And she had little doubt it had been an intentional show.

Her gaze dropped to his chest once more, and she momentarily lost her train of thought. "I, um . . ." She attempted to clear her throat, but dust—yeah, dust—was making it difficult to talk.

Blaaze laid down his cloth and stepped over to pick up a canteen from a long table propped against the side of the barn and covered with tools and building materials. He handed the canteen to her. "Here, try this."

Their hands touched when she took the canteen from him. Nerves, or something heavier, flitted around in her stomach. He was standing too close, yet simultaneously too far away.

She took a big drink and handed the canteen back to him. "We need to talk."

"About what?" He gave her a perplexed look.

She wasn't buying it. "You know about what."

"Thought we'd said all we needed to say the other day. You're the one who told me to leave. For good." He sat the canteen down. "I left. Matter done."

She closed her eyes briefly and pushed out a deep sigh. "You were waving a gun and threatening a very nice man because of something I'd done. Something, I might add, that was none of your business. Then you proceeded to treat me like a child who didn't know her own mind. My parents are dead, Mr. Lassiter. Trust me, you're no substitute."

He raised his hands, palms out, as if conceding her point. "You're right. None of my business. You go right ahead and continue putting yourself on the auction block. Not like our people didn't fight for years to avoid such a fate."

"How dare you! That is *not* what I was doing. Besides, you know after word gets around what you did to Mr. Johnson, none of the other men will show up."

He shrugged. "There's still Tobias."

She gave him a calculating stare. "Is there?"

An angry glint flitted across his face. "Don't. Go. There."

"Then stop it," she snapped.

His eyes narrowed, but he didn't speak.

"Stop with the tough guy act."

He tilted his head. "Act?"

"Okay. So it's not an act. At least, when it comes to men." She lifted her chin. "But I've never seen you be other than a gentleman with a woman."

He treated Barbara Jean like his favorite aunt. He went out of his way never to speak too harshly in Macey's presence, knowing the timid woman scared easily. He even showed respect when in the presence of the town biddies, despite not having a high opinion of their character.

"Every woman, that is, except me," she added softly.

She leaned wearily against the side of the wagon. She couldn't do this battle of wills with him much longer. She was tired. Tired of having to fight Jake Clanton. Tired of fighting to stave off insolvency. Tired of having her morality questioned and being looked down upon because she'd inherited a brothel. Tired of not knowing what was what with this man.

"*Please*, Blaaze. Talk to me straight."

He perched against the table behind him and crossed his arms over his bare chest. He hadn't bothered to put his shirt back on, despite it lying easily accessible on the table beside his hip. A calculated move on his part, she suspected, after her admission following the barroom brawl.

Silently, he watched her. She pressed her hands against the side of the wagon bed at her back and said nothing in return. They stood that way for minutes before she visibly saw his internal shield come down.

When he finally spoke, his voice was almost a whisper. "Why are you fighting so hard to stay here, Mary Catherine?"

"Where would you like me to go?"

"Don't do that. You wanted straight talk, so answer me straight. Your parents are dead, but you obviously came from a good family. Which means you were likely part of Cleveland society. You have a college education. I can't believe you couldn't find a beau and have a nice easy life back in Cleveland."

She repressed the urge to get defensive at his suggestion that she have done nothing with her education except start a family and blend into society. He was right. She'd asked for straight talk. She needed to give him straight talk.

"I wanted to use my degree to go into banking. Unfortunately, there were no women in banking in Cleveland, and no one was interested in letting me be the first. I . . ." She looked away from him for a minute. Her failure to make things work in Cleveland still left a raw feeling in her chest. "I tried to support myself as best I could while finishing my studies, but I had to take a bank loan against my parents' house to do it. I'd already missed one payment and was close to missing another when I got the correspondence about my bequest from Lila. It was take my chance here in Lawless or give up and marry the man my parents promised me to."

He stiffened. "You're . . . *engaged?*"

<h1 style="text-align:center">Chapter 22</h1>

Blaaze held himself rigid as he waited for Mary Catherine to answer his question.

"No." Mary Catherine looked away. "I mean, yes. Sort of."

He tried to hang on to the inexplicable betrayal rising within him. He had no claims on this woman, but somehow, he felt duped. "How does one 'sort of' be engaged?"

She had the decency to look at least somewhat repentant, but the chagrin didn't help his mood. *She was engaged?*

"I called it off." Her gaze met his again. "He's from a prominent family. The last thing he needed was the scandal of having a wife who worked, especially one who worked in an unusual career for a woman. And I didn't want to give up my banking dream to only do philanthropic work and raise children."

"But . . .?" He was sure there was more to this story.

"But Jeremiah's a lot like you."

She certainly had his full attention now.

"He's stubborn. He's convinced I'm making a mistake,

and he's going to save me from myself by making sure we honor our parents' desire for us to be man and wife. I disagree."

"Of course, you do." He uncrossed his arms and gripped the front edge of the table with both hands. His grip was so tight he felt he could snap the table in two. "Talk about stubborn."

She stepped over to him. "Is that the problem? I'm too headstrong for you? Not that I haven't heard that before. Jeremiah never said as much out loud, but I'm pretty sure he got frustrated with me at times."

He ignored her question, curious about this fiancé of hers. "This Jeremiah Whomever, what's this prominent family of his do?"

She hesitated, as if trying to decide whether or not to give him the man's background. "Jeremiah Dixon Beauregard III. His family has owned a clothing business since at least the early 1700s."

"Always free?"

She nodded.

"Well, if this fiancé of yours is any kind of man, he'd send you the money you need if you ask him."

"He's not my fiancé. But, yes, he would. He runs his family's textile business. What I need would be but a pittance to him. But he'd take my request as confirmation that we're still betrothed and of how much I need him to take care of me. Which would lead to an expectation that I be grateful enough to go through with the marriage. Knowing I won't, I can't take his money. Either I'm going to be dependent upon a man or I'm not. I can't do both."

She stepped between his legs and touched her palm to his chest. "Now, answer my question."

He stood and moved away from her. He had to escape the burn of her touch against his bare skin, the burn of her admission that she had a wealthy man from a good family waiting to take care of her. This was a man her parents had approved of, no less.

He'd never been jealous of another man in his life. Never considered himself less than or not good enough to be around anyone under any circumstance. But today, Blaaze found himself teeming with jealousy that somewhere out in the world lived this Jeremiah Dixon Beauregard *the third*, who had the right to claim this woman as his own.

Knowing that a ruffian, a killer, like himself would be beyond the pale of an acceptable mate where her parents were concerned, Blaaze turned his back on her, snatched up his shirt, and stuffed his arms through the sleeves.

"Oh." She took a big step back. "Okay."

A glance over his shoulder showed her eyes starting to glisten with what looked dangerously like tears she was trying not to shed.

Hell. His hands stalled on the halves of his shirt. He'd never been able to handle a woman's tears, and this woman's tears would gut him.

Forgetting about the need to fasten buttons, he whirled around and pointed at her. "Don't. And don't look at me like I just kicked your puppy. You belong to another man."

"I do not. I don't *belong* to anyone." She took another step back. "Only I can make the choice to marry, and I've made it perfectly clear to him and to you that betrothal to him is not my choice. You heard me perfectly fine." Her throat worked, but she held her composure. "Clearly, you're using this as an excuse. An excuse not to tell me the truth." She quickly spun to walk away and, with her back to him, said in a clipped voice,

"I won't bother you again."

Impulse made him grab her wrist. "Mary Catherine, wait."

She yanked at his hold but didn't turn around. "No. Let me go."

He tugged her around and pulled her to him. He swallowed, trying to hem in the tension that had accosted him when she'd meant to walk away . . . from him . . . maybe truly forever this time. The pain in her eyes matched the angst in his chest.

"Think about what you're asking of me. I'm just a tired, cranky bounty hunter, set in my ways. I'm looking for nothing more than to raise horses and live quietly in peace for the rest of my days. I don't currently have a house or even a bed . . . to take you to." He brushed a few stray hairs from her eyes and stared deeply into them, feeling a vulnerable truth pull from him despite himself. "You're not too anything for me. Except maybe too good."

"You said I talk like I swallowed a dictionary," she whispered with a hitch in her voice.

"You do." He chuckled softly, brushing her cheek. "I never said I didn't like it."

Eyes now swamped in unshed tears and total confusion, she stared at him.

He placed both palms against her cheeks. "For a smart woman, you're being extremely dense right now."

"W-what?"

He lowered his head and kissed her. It was a soft, slow, thorough kiss.

When he lifted his head, he said, "I want you more than I want to see the sun rise every morning. If you're set on giving yourself to a man, know I'm not going to let any man touch you but me."

She placed her palms flat against the bare skin beneath his unbuttoned shirt. "Then touch me, Blaaze."

Lightning struck his heart at the way she said his given name. From the first time she'd done it after the brawl in the saloon till now, the impact affected him the same. To hear his name from her lips made him feel claimed, branded, and forever owned. And damn, if he didn't want to be owned by this woman.

Her eyes reflected the vulnerability he felt, and she stepped closer and dropped her head against his chest, hiding her eyes from him. "I can't stop thinking about you," she confessed. "I can't stop thinking about what happened between us in the pantry. I'm restless at night. If you feel even a small part of what I'm feeling, how can you continue to say no to me? Don't you think we deserve to be with each other?"

No, he didn't. She deserved better than him, a man who had lived by the gun and chased outlaws so long he was mostly outlaw himself by now. He was a man who'd picked this half-built town on purpose to lay low from scum and scoundrels who'd likely come gunning for him if they knew where he was. He shouldn't pull an angel like her into his world, but as he savored the sound of her words through a raspy tone of feminine desire, he began to unravel.

"I don't want you to regret this." He wrapped his arms around her. Pulling her closer, he tucked her head under his chin, and said with earnest fire, "I don't want you to regret *me*."

Her arms came around his waist. "I could never regret you." She tilted her head back so she could see his face. "Don't you see? My only regret would be to rattle around alone in my apartments above the saloon without telling you the truth. Trust me to know who I am and whom I choose."

Her hand rose to his jaw. "I choose you. Choose me back."

He hesitated only a few seconds to savor her raspy tone of indisputable desire before he dropped his head and kissed her again. This time he held nothing back and let all his own desire and want filter through his lips into hers. He was in for a lot of "I told you so" from Tobias, and for the first time, he didn't care.

Dropping a finger to the ruffle that edged her dress along her bosom, he rubbed the rough pad of his fingertip slowly back and forth along the soft, female skin plumped enticingly above the ruffle line. A mere fraction of an inch of fabric kept the modesty of her budding nipple from his eyes. It dawned on him that if he took her at her word, he now had permission to view—even touch—that nipple, and he was immediately and completely hard.

He slid his finger beneath the dress collar and the annoying corset beneath but held back from the nipple. The sound of her labored breaths increased his arousal. He dared not look her in the face. If he did, he was certain he'd not be able to control his urge to take her fast and hard right here on top of his worktable. Though she'd offered herself to him without any obvious reservation, he understood that she was not the carefree wanton she intended to portray.

Bold? Yeah, she was definitely that.

But wanton? No.

Experienced? Definitely no.

Blaaze thought to agree to this madness to protect her from herself and from other men who would abuse the trust she was offering her first lover. But who was going to protect him from her?

One night with this woman would change him forever.

He knew it.

There was no going back from here. No going back to the man he was before she'd stepped in front of his human projectile and ended up in that watering trough. The man who'd rode into town seeking to put gunfights behind him and to disconnect from responsibilities—and people in general—couldn't hold his own against the man she needed to protect her from the bad elements of this town, including her brave but misguided self.

Even knowing this, he couldn't stop himself from taking what she offered.

He slid his finger along the curve of the dress top until he reached her shoulder. He slipped the fabric down and pressed a lingering kiss to the bared shoulder. He allowed the tip of his tongue to brush her skin. She trembled beneath his finger and tongue. He tugged harder on the dress edge, pulling her corset along with it. Her undergarment released more easily than he had expected, and he wondered in passing why her corset was once again so loose it was easily movable.

Dismissing the brief, distracted thought, he tugged until nothing but the tip of her right breast held the top of her dress in place on that side. Anticipation spurred him to fully expose the treat, but the thrill of the wait caused him to pause.

He glanced into her eyes. "You sure about this, sugar?" He rubbed the tip of her naked breast with the back of his finger crooked into the edge of her bustline.

A raw, throaty moan squeezed from her throat, and her eyes became hooded. A soft whisper of words came out barely audible. "Blaaze . . ." She stopped and licked her lips as if she couldn't get her tongue to work right and her throat was as parched as a desert in the New Mexico Territory.

"Yeah?" he whispered back.

She blinked up at him but did not speak. He wasn't sure

she could. Somehow, the thought excited him even more.

Whatever her original intent in coming here, this was not the straightforward, practical trade-off it had started out to be—a night of pleasure for him in exchange for providing a new carnal adventure for her. This lady desired him. She may not understand the depth of the desire she displayed.

Hell, with all his experience, he didn't understand this pull they had toward each other. Her fancy, city ways made no sense mixed with his cowboy lifestyle and frontier living. With all her intellectualizing, she had to know that.

Her hand rose, and she tightly wrapped her fingers around his wrist and squeezed.

Dread seeped in. The gentlemanly thing to do was give her the chance to back out of this interlude, but the possible disappointment if she came to her senses drove deep into places he dared not examine too closely.

"Stop teasing me and get on with it," she scolded.

He lifted one brow in mock censure, even as relief filled him. Those weren't the words of a woman about to change her mind. He'd already sensed that the bossy, eastern miss would want to give directions even in lovemaking.

"What's the matter? Afraid you're not up to the task?" she quipped at his brief delay.

He chuckled lightly. "How would you know the difference, my little maiden?"

She smiled at him, a mysteriously worldly smile given all she'd never experienced. "I run a brothel. Remember? Surely, you don't think I could live above a house full of sportin' women—my personal den of iniquity—and not have learned a thing or two about pleasure."

Of course, she had. But it was time she understood that book knowledge and platonic learning held very little on the ecstasy between a man and a woman when pleasures of the flesh were done right.

"There's only one way to truly know about pleasure. Which is exactly why you came here."

"Maybe," she conceded. "But that's only if you're up to snuff." She tilted her head sideways. "Are you?"

God, he loved it when she spoke like a local in her proper accent. *Up to snuff* sounded almost sophisticated instead of like the callout it was. He got impossibly harder.

Almost nothing thrilled him more than a challenge, except maybe the feel of a woman's soft curves beneath him . . . or above him. He'd never been particular about position. Good thing, since they didn't have a bed and he was going to have to get creative.

He flicked the back of his finger against her nipple again. This time her head lolled back. He dipped his hand fully into her gown until the fabric gave way on one side and sloped to reveal the full of her breast. He cupped the heavy roundness then tweaked her beaded nipple between his thumb and forefinger.

She moaned again.

He slid his other arm around her back and pressed closer. "Let's just say . . ." He pushed up her lovely brown nipple for easier access. "I'm looking forward to ringing your bell a second time," he said gruffly before he took her nipple deep into his hovering mouth.

Mary Catherine grabbed the back of Blaaze's head when his lips encircled her budded nipple. Despite the ecstasy coursing through him, he became conscious of their standing in the open. He had a large plot of land. It was likely no one would even come by, but the thought that someone could pulled him out of the erotic haze to one of reality right before she pushed his head up.

In a breathy voice, she asked, "You don't intend for us to do this out here . . . in the open, do you?"

"No one's around for miles and miles." He chuckled at her even though he'd had the same thought.

"Yes, but . . ." Her eyes revealed her doubt about how this would transpire. She looked around and eyed the wagon.

He caught her expression and laughed. "No. No way." Taking her hand, he pulled her into the barn. "Come with me."

When he got her inside, he looked around. They were secluded from prying eyes, but the available bedding spots left something to be desired.

"This is not exactly the way I envisioned being with you the first time. Or any time, really."

His words seemed to surprise her. "You've thought about sleeping with me?"

"Trust me, we were not *sleeping* in any of my thoughts. Or any of my fantasies. Or even my dreams." He pulled her into his arms. "We've got painfully few choices of where to make this happen. You sure you don't want to wait until we get back to our rooms at the saloon?"

She vehemently shook her head. "I'm not giving you the chance to change your mind."

"Sugar, there's no way I'm changing my mind."

Slowly, she smiled. "Good. Then come with me, cowboy." She tugged his hand.

Ignoring the hay piled high beneath the barn loft, Mary Catherine led Blaaze toward one of the side walls. He watched her curiously but followed without a word.

"I've been wondering, since that night in the pantry . . . um." She blushed prettily and tucked her bottom lip between her teeth. "What that would have felt like without any clothes between us." She stopped and placed her back against the wall. "W-wanna show me?"

He studied her seductive lean. Her dress covered her breast again, but she still made a luscious picture. He considered her offer. It was intriguing, but not without its problems.

"That wall is too rough for your delicate skin. You'll end up with scratches and splinters."

"Surely, a man like you has more imagination than that." She raised her hands to the center of her neckline and released a hidden fastener beneath the ruffle.

He watched the female clothing secret being unveiled to him. *Who knew?*

Slowly, she released several fasteners hidden beneath the fabric down the center of her bodice until her dress gaped open to the waist. Deliberate fingers did a delicate dance downward freeing the tiny buttons on the front of her corset from their loops one at a time until the sides fell open and loose. Her performance mesmerized him. He'd like to remove all that fabric all together, but being able to view the essentials would have to do.

Blaaze stood taking in those glorious breasts, rounded and full. Their darkened tips had been the source of many an uncomfortably erotic dream since the day he'd pulled her from her impromptu bath in the trough. When he finally moved, he stepped to her and pushed her legs wider using one well-worn leather boot against the dainty, fabric, button heels she liked to think of as boots.

His hands went to her breasts and he cupped them reverently.

Her hands went immediately to his belt buckle.

"Whoa." He grabbed her hands to stop her. "You're moving a little fast there, sugar."

She freed her hands and pushed his shirt from his shoulders. "No," she breathed out in a breathy sigh. "You're moving a little slow there, cowboy."

Okay then. He noticed the shelf to the left of her shoulder and grabbed the pinch of his Stetson to remove it.

She stopped him immediately. "Leave it on."

"Excuse me?" Flabbergasted, he didn't protest when she raised her hands to his brim and gently repositioned the hat on his head.

"Leave the hat on," she said in a husky voice, her face completely flushed.

He stared into her eyes. The fire alight in their depths consumed him.

Well, all right, he thought.

If the little miss got excited by him wearing his hat, leave it on he would.

Grinning, he said, "Yes, ma'am."

CHAPTER 23

MARY CATHERINE WATCHED BLAAZE'S beautiful brown eyes darken. His pupils had already been nearly fully dilated. After her comment about the hat, she could see very little of the brown that reminded her of luscious, melted chocolate.

She didn't know where the hat comment had come from or where she'd found the impetus to be this bold with a man. She didn't recognize herself. She wasn't certain what it was about this particular man that brought out the brazen in her. She was finding she liked it. She liked being his Mary Cate very much. And Mary Cate *needed*. Every pore in her body craved being filled—filled up—with this man, by this man. Flesh to flesh, skin to skin.

Dare she admit to him or anyone else that she'd studied tomes in the college library on the anatomy and mechanics of human coupling?

It had not been the appropriate part of the library for a woman, but she'd managed it. Considered the domain of the scientists and aspiring doctors, that part of the library had contained many of the informative texts on women's reproductive anatomy, female hysteria, and treatments through the ages to resolve that latter feminine affliction. A fake need to check out a book in an adjoining row and a quick hand when no one was watching often served a girl well.

Now that she'd experienced firsthand some of the more intriguing aspects of bringing a woman to completion, lust overpowered her. A lust that surely couldn't be normal. If this is what they meant by hysteria, no woman would ever want to be permanently cured of it. Repeated trips to the doctor for some stimulation by hand or a handheld implement that vibrated against her clitoris. *Yes, please!*

She stared at Blaaze, an exceptional specimen of male virility, and thought, *Dr. Lassiter.* The dampness between her thighs increased, and her swollen pearl throbbed. What she needed right now was a bit more haste than this particular doctor was habitually known to exert. She reached for his pants again, and this time, he didn't fight her.

Relieved, she whispered, "Blaaze, I can't wait much longer. I'm about to perish from the wanting. I need you to touch me somewhere. Maybe everywhere."

Reaching under her dress, he murmured, "Shh, Mary Cate, I don't like to rush. How 'bout I help this along by giving you a bit of head start."

His hand slipped under her dress and inside her bloomers. He found the core of her. When he felt the dampness waiting for him, he groaned long and deep. "Good gracious, woman. You're soaked." He pressed in one finger then two. "I . . ."

Her legs began to tremble at the invading pressure. She clenched around his fingers and made him groan again. His lips slammed down on hers, and he pressed a thumb against her clitoris and began to circle. She whimpered. He increased the pressure and began to alternate pumping fingers and circling thumb.

An explosion built within Mary Catherine. Knowing what it would feel like after his initiation in the pantry, she chased it with accelerated hip thrusts against his fingers. When the explosion became inevitable, she grasped him around the neck with both arms, careful not to knock off his hat.

In a gruff voice, he demanded, "Let me go, Mary Cate."

She couldn't unclench her arms or her thighs. Her orgasm gripped her fiercely, and she didn't think she'd ever regain control of her own body.

"Let *go*," he pleaded.

He pulled his hand free of clenched thighs and wrenched his shoulders from the clutches of her arms. He bunched the sides of her dress and anxiously offered them to her. "Hold this up for me. I've got something very important to take care of."

He dropped to his knees, whipped one boot off her foot, and yanked down her bloomers like the pantaloons were on fire and he needed to save her from scorching. With a hand braced under her knee, he lifted her unshoed foot free of the bloomers and over his shoulder. With one hand on his hat, he shocked her by attaching his mouth to her most private part with a greedy hum.

"Oh my!" The feel was exquisite. She nearly lost hold of the dress but held firm and instead lost all sense of self-consciousness.

His tongue repeatedly took slow licks along the entirety of her folds, and she began to writhe to the accompaniment of her own sounds of pleasure.

He chuckled. "If you're going to be this active, you might want to hold on to this hat you were so intent I wear."

She hummed an acknowledgment and allowed her skirt to perch on the edge of the crown of his hat, covering his face from her view. She placed one hand delicately against the back edge of the Stetson, enough to keep it on but not damage its shape.

Blaaze grabbed the back of the thigh of her standing leg with his liberated hand and pushed the thigh on his shoulder outward to spread her wider. He proceeded to pump his tongue deep into her. Curling it on the way out, he did it again and then again and again, driving deeper the more emotive she got.

In and out.

In. Out. Swirl.

It felt so good. Nothing might ever feel this good again.

"Yes," she cried, working herself on his tongue.

When he unexpectedly drew her swollen bud into his mouth and sucked, she shattered. Tears burst unbidden from her eyes this time, and she screamed so loud, she suspected they could hear her all the way back in town. Her standing leg went weak. She wasn't sure she'd be able to stay upright, but Blaaze held her firmly against the wall with one hand pressed against her abdomen and continued to lap gently at her pulsing womanhood.

He reminded her of a hungry man at his favorite meal, intent on taking his time to finish his plate. She repressed a giggle when Barbara Jean's comment about him watching her like he was starving and she was a well-cooked steak crossed her mind. Seemed Miss Babs knew exactly of what she spoke.

When his face emerged from her skirts, he situated his hat with one hand and slowly fisted the bare erection he'd freed from his pants sometime during his adventures under her clothing. A bare-chested, Stetson-wearing Blaaze with his manhood free and rigid for her was about the most glorious sight she'd ever seen. She finally understood why painters preferred the naked human form to feed their muse. The naked body was the most beautiful of all the Divine's creations, and this one was all hers to appreciate. At least, for tonight.

The urgency in his face thrilled her and unnerved her simultaneously. She didn't know if she could survive a full coupling with this man or if she had another orgasm to give. How many times could a woman even do that in one night?

Blaaze wasted no time. He shucked her other shoe from her foot and yanked off her bloomers. Rising, he made certain his hat was stable then lifted her. She knew what to do without prompting this time and wrapped her legs around him. His large palms cupped her bare buttocks. The wicked warmth of his hands against her backside, lifting and spreading her thighs, made her flush with a want so intense she began to tremble.

He wedged her against the wall and demanded, "Move your skirt." His voice hungered out in a vibrato more rasp than words.

She gave her skirt a frantic tug. A longing she'd never experienced or suspected existed made her impatience rise to match his.

As soon as he had a free path, he placed himself at her entrance and made a slow, deliberate thrust. His long firmness slid through her damp folds and planted deep. So deep she felt its tip knock against the inside of her. No more depths to reach, no more room to press. The length and breadth of him filled her completely. She cried out. Shock, pleasure, and an odd, comfortable discomfort mixed together to unsettle her.

Her cowboy groaned like a wickedly triumphant villain,

but managed a gentle, "You all right, sugar?"

Locking her ankles behind his hips, she said between short, bracing breaths, "It feels almost too full, too much. But it also feels a little good."

He gave an experimental pump. "Just a little good?"

"Oh!"

He chuckled and did it again.

"Oh!" she exclaimed again, this time louder.

"Yeah, that's what I want. A lot good?"

"Yes, a whole lot good . . . now." She managed to smile in the face of his cockiness. She should have known that even in this he'd be irreverent and arrogant, and why she enjoyed that about him she couldn't fathom. She'd never much cared for arrogant men, not until him.

His hips picked up their pace, and Mary Catherine's stray thoughts were drawn back to focus on nothing but the pleasure building between her thighs and low in her abdomen. He hit a spot high inside and her clitoris at the same time, and her arm went wide, knocking the shelf beside her.

The resonant clang of a bell sounded, and Mary Catherine thought she was hearing things. When Blaaze did it again, her arm hit the shelf a second time and another clang sounded. Her wild arms and his driving pumps made her shoulder slide closer to the shelf and bump it over and over again.

The clanging started to sound with every thrust, and Mary Catherine eventually discerned a cowbell lied somewhere upon the shelf. She began to giggle. Blaaze looked up startled. He thrust his hips, and when the cowbell sounded once more, Mary Catherine couldn't suppress a moan wrapped in a boisterous laugh.

Blaaze slowed but didn't stop his hip movements. He frowned at her. Apparently, it was not good form to laugh while engaging in intimate relations with a man, but she couldn't help herself. The next time the bell sounded, he noticed it too and a lascivious smile played across his lips.

Intuitively understanding what she found so funny, he worked to sync his thrusts so she hit the shelf and forced a syncopated din from the bell. The hilarity of the move, and his delicious rhythm, snuck up on her. The barn filled with her delighted moans, his intense groans, and the intimate sounds of their joined bodies.

Her flesh gripped at him. Ecstasy began another rise, and Blaaze became equally wrapped up in its clutches. His thrusts became faster. And deeper. Her thighs started to tremble, and his breath panted against her ear.

"Ah, hell, Mary Cate," he said on a ragged breath. "I can't hold back. I need you to let go. Let go, now, or I'm—"

He didn't get to finish his statement before he exploded inside her. A long, slow groan poured from him as his hips spasmed against her. Finally, his forehead hit the wall beside her ear, and his hat popped off, having gone loosely askew during their vigorous, vertical romp.

"Damn," he muttered and pressed deep inside her to ride out his release.

He grasped her buttocks firmly and ground against her. After a few intense rubs of his pubic bone against her bud, she grasped for the shelf as a renewed burst of pleasure hit her. She grabbed the shelf so hard it came free of the wall, and all its contents hit the floor. The elusive cowbell bounced against the ground, sounding three loud and exuberant clangs before it went silent and still.

Blaaze gave a muffled chuckle into her shoulder over the sound. He didn't seem to mind the mess about their feet, but when he finally looked into her eyes, a worry showed on his face. "Sugar, I think we may have a problem."

~

Blaaze grabbed a fresh blanket from a chest on the other side of the barn. He spread the cover across a corner of the hay pile beneath the loft. He picked up his hat and another stray item, dusted them off, then placed the stray item in his pocket and his hat on the shelf above the one Mary Catherine had pulled from the wall.

Chuckling softly, he retrieved the cowbell that had humored her during their coupling and handed the noisy trinket of oxidized copper to her. She shook it and giggled at its clanging. The sound of her laughter sent warmth through the center of his chest.

He'd never heard her laugh until today. She'd been in the midst of one trial after the other since her arrival in Lawless. Knowing he'd been a part of something that had lightened her spirits enough to genuinely laugh felt real good.

Lifting her into his arms, he walked her to the blanket and laid her down. He fastened his pants up to all but the top button, then retrieved a clean bandana from his saddlebags. Returning to her, he slid his hand underneath her dress and wiped between her legs and her inner thighs. She watched him warily.

He deserved the mistrust.

He'd failed her.

For the first time in his life, he'd released inside a woman without precautions. Now they had to deal with the possible repercussions of his irresponsible behavior. Perhaps their encounter in the pantry—and his resulting premature ejaculation—should have schooled him. When it came to this woman, he had no control.

Together, they righted most of her clothing, but he stopped her from closing the bodice of her dress. Pulling her into his arms, he distractedly began rubbing one of her breasts while he gathered his thoughts. As they laid quietly, Scout wandered into the barn on his own from the paddock. The stallion walked over to their pallet and gave them each a brief snuffle before he decided he was unimpressed with the two humans infringing on his domain and walked to his stall.

The sky outside had turned dusky and full dark would soon descend. He needed to get Mary Catherine back to the saloon. He didn't want to release her from the shelter of his arms, but he wasn't sure she'd be able to find her way at night. All the landmarks she'd used to get here wouldn't be as visible.

"What are you worrying about?" She pushed up slightly and laid a hand on his bare chest. "Having regrets so soon?"

Her question surprised him. "No. Are you?" He watched her face closely, looking for signs of feelings she might not want to reveal.

"No." She propped her chin on top of her hand. "I have no regrets. Nor will I have them later. Give me some credit for knowing my own mind. Remember?"

"I do." He lifted his head and gave her a light peck on the lips. "Or we wouldn't be here like this."

"Then what's going on? I can see concern of some kind churning behind your eyes."

Her hair was in total disarray. As many strands fell around her face as probably remained in her messed-up bun. Yet, she was the most beautiful woman he'd ever seen.

Funny. He'd never really thought about her physical beauty. He'd wanted her. He'd been fascinated by her brain and turned on by her accent.

Objectively, he understood she had a pretty face that would draw a man's gaze, but tonight her loveliness hit him like a bullet through the lungs. The impact spread in an unsettling tightness that was not so much pain as an odd mix of being unable to breathe and breathing fully for the first time. And every breath was because of her, about her, for her in a way he didn't clearly understand. All he knew was if he'd added to her trials, to her challenges, in any way, he'd never forgive himself.

He lifted a hand toward her and a slight tremble in his fingers made him clench and unclench his fist before he tried again.

"Mary Cate," he said quietly, toying with a tendril of her hair, "during all this learning you've been doing in your den of iniquity . . ."

She smiled at his use of her phrase for the saloon, and he momentarily lost where his thoughts were leading him. She noticed, and her smile grew into a wide grin. He chuckled at his obvious slip of being captivated.

Clearing his throat in a dramatic regrouping, he returned to the issue at hand. "Did you happen to learn anything about womanly . . . precautions?"

Her eyes lit with amusement. "Oh, now I understand." She rolled onto her back and looked up at the ceiling. "Barbara Jean made sure I knew about my options."

He leaned up on an elbow and stared down at her. "She did, did she?"

"Yes. I put in a sponge before I came." Her gaze cut back to him. "And to be doubly sure, I'll make some of Barbara Jean's special tea before I go to bed tonight."

"That sounds as if . . . as if you were certain you'd get your way with me, little miss." His frown was only half playful, because he wasn't quite sure he liked being thought a sure lay.

She laughed. "More like me simply being prepared. I like to always have a plan."

He laid down and pulled her back on top of him. "Do you, now?"

"Yes." She settled against him. "Although I think there may be something else we have to worry about."

"What's that?"

For the second time that afternoon, she tucked her bottom lip into her teeth, which made Blaaze antsy about what she might be about to say.

"A woman came into the saloon looking for you." She watched his face closely, clearly looking for his reaction to the news.

He had no idea what woman would come looking for him in Lawless. He'd told no one this was his final destination. "What woman? What's her name?"

"She didn't want to give me her name, but she seems to have plans to come out here and stay with you."

He laughed softly then. "Oh no she doesn't. I don't take in women."

Mary Catherine pushed up with a hand to his chest and hovered over him. "You sure about that? I don't want to come between you and a lady friend or a mistress or something . . . more." Her voice trailed off in a querying tone.

"Mary Cate . . ." He stopped himself from replying in jest.

Her expression showed her obvious worry over the prospect that he'd coupled with her but might toss her over immediately for this mystery woman, whomever she might be. He owed it to her to assuage her fear unequivocally.

"I don't have a 'lady friend,' and I certainly don't have a

mistress. My line of work makes either a bad idea." The two of them would have to deal with the truth of that soon. "I don't know who this woman is, but whoever she is, I guarantee you the only woman I want in my arms or in my bed is you."

Without warning he yanked her down on top of him.

A gasp of surprise pushed past her lips. She wiggled to right herself and yelped when her elbow bumped his pocket. "Ouch. What was that?"

He shooed her hand away as she felt for the object. "Nothing."

She looked over to the few shelf items still left of the ground. Her eyes became contemplative. "What was wrapped in that cloth you picked up? It had something shiny poking out." She rubbed her elbow. "Something shiny and apparently hard."

"Nothing important. Something I need to get rid of. I forgot I'd stuck it up there."

"Let me see." She reached into his pants pocket.

He placed his hand over hers, trapping it inside the pocket. He waffled over letting her pull out the pouch. He'd shoved the unwanted trinket into the pouch and pulled the drawstring tight before stuffing it carelessly into his jeans. There had been a reason that weighty hunk of metal had been stashed away in this barn. That reason hadn't changed, so he saw no need to start showing it around.

"Mary Catherine, it's not that important."

She studied him. "I think it is because you're edgy about letting me see it. Why? What could you be hiding that could be of such significance?" She tugged beneath his hand for release.

He sighed and let go.

Cautiously, she pulled out the pouch and opened it. A shiny star embedded on a circle of silver slid onto her palm. Her gaze met his. "Is this the marshal's?"

"Yep. Just not the marshal you're thinking of," he said simply.

Her eyes widened. "You're a US deputy marshal?"

Sitting up, he took the star from her hand and slid it back into the pouch. "No. I used to be a US deputy marshal. For a period. To help Malone chase down a particular pack of scoundrels. I'm retired. For good. Nothing's ever making me put that star back on. Malone, the stubborn mule, was supposed to take it with him and end my commission. He managed to leave it behind."

"On accident?"

Blaaze scowled. "An on-purpose accident."

She watched his expression while she tried not to laugh. "There's no such thing as an on-purpose accident, Blaaze. Either it was on purpose or it was an accident."

"Exactly." He wondered if he sounded as perturbed as he felt.

"Ah. Marshal Malone doesn't want to end your commission." She sat up next to him.

"He's going to have to replace the sheriff when he returns. I think he believes with me here, he's got an automatic replacement, but that's not happening." He propped his arm over a bent knee. "I've had a near lifetime of shooting people and having people shoot at me. This last time was close. Had I not been near friends in Indian Territory when I got shot, I may not have made it. I've nabbed my share of scoundrels. I'll leave the rest to the others."

She placed a palm against his far cheek and turned his face to look at her. "So you don't like wearing guns?"

"Wearing guns is part of life out here, sugar." Placing his palm against the back of the hand against his cheek to hold it in place, he turned his face and placed a lingering kiss on the warm center of her hand. Still holding her hand, he said, "A man can't build much on the frontier without being able to handle a weapon. But being a bounty hunter—or a lawman— is different. You make enemies. Men come gunning for you. Sometimes to settle a score. Sometimes simply to see who has the fastest gun. I figured I'd quit while I'm still fast enough to best my enemies and live to grow gray rocking in a chair on my own porch."

He studied her face. He needed to make sure she understood and had no illusions about the man that he was. Looking into her eyes, he said, "Make no mistake, Mary Cate. I'm not some hero or saint content to bring people to justice. I'd just as soon shoot 'em dead and collect the price on their heads. I figure it saves our courts the trouble of a trial only to hang 'em anyway. I've spent most my life killing people for a living, and I'm good at it. In fact, I've killed a *lot* of people. Which is why there are a lot of men out there, maybe even a few women, who would love to see me dead."

Blaaze wondered briefly if his visitor at the saloon was one such woman, maybe come to avenge her man. He'd have to figure that out later. For now, Mary Catherine was his only concern.

"I came to Lawless because that's a life I no longer want. I'm tired of looking over my shoulder." Softly, he admitted, "I'm tired of anyone I might get close to being at risk of danger or foul play because of me."

He placed another kiss in the center of her palm. Marshal Malone had learned that last lesson the hard way. Blaaze had no interest in finding out how it would feel to lose this beautiful woman from the world simply because she'd made the mistake of attaching herself to him. He'd managed to walk away from that life, and he planned not to go willingly back into a way of living where people would as soon shoot him as look at him.

"I'm done with that life for good, whether Marshal Malone is willing to accept it or not. This star's staying right where it is, trapped in this barn, until that hardheaded cuss takes it back or it turns to rust."

She frowned down at the bagged star in his hand. "Then why did you put your gun back on the other day?"

Not releasing the hand he held, he slid a finger of his other hand across her forehead to tame some loose hair and tucked the wisps behind her ear. "Does it bother you to know I could shoot a man?"

"N-no." Her gaze dropped to their joined hands. "I mean, I wouldn't want to see a man get shot. But, of course, I understand sometimes it might be necessary."

Might be necessary. She hadn't looked at him when she'd said those words. He didn't believe her "no." In her world, bad people received trial before meeting their justice.

He released her hand. "Yeah, sometimes it might be necessary. That's why I had my guns close by. I don't trust Clanton, and the sheriff'll be no help if Clanton steps out of line. Your farmer just happened to be in the wrong place at the wrong time."

"Clanton's not after you. He's after me," she said matter-of-factly before her expression turned stern. "And Mr. Johnson isn't a criminal. He didn't deserve your threats at gunpoint."

"What Mr. Johnson deserved is up to me to decide." He laid on his back and folded his hands behind his head. "As far as Clanton's concerned, I intend to make sure he plays fair."

She began to shake her head, starting to see the way of things. "Oh no. You're not taking this on because of my mess. I'm not going to let you sacrifice your retirement for me."

"Too late. It's already happening. Besides, I was never giving up the guns. Only what I do with them."

"Blaaze—"

"Shh." He reached up to slipped a hand behind her head to loosen what remained of her bun. "I don't have to put on a badge or carry a wanted poster in my pocket to protect the prettiest lady from the meanest men for however long she's in town." Separating her fall of thick curls around her shoulders, he decided he'd had enough talk of guns, killing people, and Jake Clanton. "Enough talking. I've got a few more lessons to teach you about pleasure before I have to take you back."

Blaaze pressed Mary Cate onto her back. He hesitated only briefly to savor that all her womanly glory belonged to him for a little while longer. Then he proceeded to show her he was as good ringing bells laying down as he was up against a wall.

CHAPTER 24

MARY CATHERINE FLOATED ON a cloud of contentment from Blaaze's lovemaking for several days. They hadn't been able to stay apart the last two nights. Blaaze had come creeping to her room in the wee hours each night to show her how much more fun they could have using a bed.

Oddly, Charlie hadn't showed back up for work over the last few days, so Mary Catherine was doing setup herself. She stood shining glasses and smiling to herself when the cowgirl, whose name she still didn't know, came down from her upstairs room. The woman greeted her and asked that breakfast be sent to her at a back table.

The woman had been oddly missing during the evenings when Blaaze had been at the saloon. He'd been spending more time on his land during the days, working with Tobias, Miguel, and a few other men to finally raise the roof for his house. So Mary Catherine still hadn't figured out the woman's relationship to Blaaze, and he didn't seem in too much of a hurry to find out.

After taking care of the cowgirl's order, Mary Catherine sat at a table at the edge of the bar to review her ledgers once again. She'd figured out exactly how much was missing from her bottom line. If she didn't know better, she'd think someone was skimming her profits. She didn't truly believe any of her employees would do such a thing, but she needed to be vigilant to make sure she had enough to pay Jake Clanton by the end of the next forty-eight hours and still pay her bill at the mercantile as she'd promised Mr. Ludtke.

She'd started to make nice additional money by helping several of the merchants in town with their books. Once word got around that she had experience with accounting and finance, she'd been approached for everything from balancing accounts to checking the accuracy of bills of lading and verifying interest charges by the bank. It was a nice sideline business, and she enjoyed using her degree to support other merchants in town.

The extra work had given her the idea to help Macey start her own business selling baked goods. Mary Catherine covered the ingredients for Macey's baking, but they split the profits instead of Macey taking a straight wage. Once the saloon was back on solid footing, Mary Catherine would help her move into her own storefront.

For now, she needed to make sure she had enough funds on hand to cover the rest of the women's wages, except for Charlotte's, who had disappeared shortly before Charlie. Mary Catherine wasn't surprised by Charlotte's mysterious departure. They'd never completely found their footing with each other.

If she couldn't take care of the mercantile owner and the ladies who were still around on top of paying Mr. Clanton, she'd have to let the brewery owner confiscate most of the saloon's assets. As if her thoughts had conjured him up, Jake Clanton barreled into the saloon with Sheriff Brennan and a younger man on his heels.

The brewery owner flashed papers at her. "I heard you had some trouble the other night, Miss Templeton. I've come to protect my investment."

Mary Catherine took the papers from Jake Clanton's hand. "What is this?"

"A list of the damages to this place. No way you're gonna be able to do business and pay my bill with these expenses. I'm here to cut my losses and confiscate the remaining liquor and whatever furniture pieces will settle up the balance."

"You'll do no such thing." Mary Catherine came away from the table beside the bar, quickly skimming over the list.

The itemizations and losses were oddly accurate, which made her wonder from where—or from whom—he'd gotten his information since he hadn't been in the saloon since their last encounter. Angry at his intrusion and this new ploy to take what was hers, Mary Catherine charged up to the man. She flicked the list dismissively at him, but he didn't take it back.

Squeezing the paper until its middle crushed in her fist, she said. "I have two more days, Mr. Clanton, and the damage done to this place the other night doesn't change that."

Three armed men entered the bar, two toting empty crates. Mary Catherine eyed them as she fell into a stupor of disbelief at the audacity of the increasing number of unwelcome men. She faintly registered the bustling sounds of the awakening town, along with its subtle, townsfolk chatter and the clomp of footfalls along the wooden walkways. Somewhere down the street the jangle of distant spurs reached her ears, a taunting reminder that she'd intentionally chosen to move to this frontier town where fairness, manners, and cordiality mattered less than domineering power and the armed backing of a crooked lawman.

Without a word, the latest arrivals headed straight behind the bar. They started filling the crates with bottles from the shelves that hadn't been broken during the brawl.

"Put those back this instant!" Mary Catherine whirled toward them, intending to put a stop to the seizure, by force if necessary.

The sheriff grabbed her arm to stop her. "Now hold on there, Miss. Mr. Clanton has a right to recoup any losses he might suffer." He started to say something else and got distracted when he noticed Cook watching them from the kitchen doorway.

Jonas stood quietly, wiping his hands on a rag. When Macey stepped up beside him, he whispered something in her ear. Macey nodded and scampered out of the saloon, making sure to give Jake Clanton and his men a wide berth.

Taking advantage of the distraction, Mary Catherine snatched her arm from the sheriff's grasp. "He has a right to recoup his losses only if I don't pay my balance in two days. Not a day before."

"Now that there's subject to speculation." The sheriff hitched up his pants and laid the heel of his hand against the butt of his holstered gun. "Seems to me a man can't be expected to simply sit by and let good money dwindle away due to your incompetence."

"Incompetence! You're one to talk," she hissed and snatched her arm loose.

Antagonizing the sheriff was not her smartest move she realized upon noticing the glare the man leveled at her insult. She took a deep breath and gathered herself to try an attempt at diplomacy.

In a business-like tone, she addressed Jake Clanton. "We had an agreement, sir. An agreement that quite a few people witnessed, including you, sheriff." Her sober gaze met the lawman's. "He can't back out of that agreement simply because a few patrons got rowdy. That's the nature of this business. Spirits can sometimes bring out a boisterous nature. As I'm sure Mr. Clanton is aware given the nature of his own business."

Jake Clanton smirked at her. "You mean spirits and a horny disposition, seeing as how you cut off the boys' carnal delights."

She stiffened. "What I do in my saloon is none of your business, Mr. Clanton. However, know that I've remedied that particular situation."

This news surprised him. "Really? I hadn't heard." He looked around for the ladies who worked the saloon, but none of them had yet come down for the day. He did a double take when his glance slid over the cowgirl sitting quietly in the shadows. From his expression, he wasn't too impressed with her womanly appeal.

The woman gave him a snarky salute with her fork and went back to her meal.

Frowning at her gesture, Jake Clanton turned his attention back to Mary Catherine. "A wise move, Miss Templeton, but one that may be too late. Beulah's already started offering the boys an alternative down at her place. Now, she's only got a few ladies and hers aren't as popular as yours. Yet. But it's a good start now that Charlotte's joined the house." He gave a cheeky grin. "And once I finally persuade Beulah to join with me in building up this town, we'll turn that place into a fully-fledged hotel with a bar of its own. We'll have to change the name, of course. Clanton's has such a better ring to it. Don't you think?"

The man was a blooming egoist. Everything centered around him, and his revelations about Beulah's meant her issues with him were only beginning. Worry invaded Mary Catherine. New brothel competition close to the town environs might be why her upstairs crowd hadn't completely returned to normal. Not that she paid too close attention to who came and went. Since she and Barbara Jean had come to an agreement about the elder woman managing the upstairs amenities and compensating Mary Catherine with a percentage of the take from each of the rooms the sportin' women used, Mary Catherine only paid attention to the rents she received from Barbara Jean. The money was good but by no means back to the levels prior to Lila's passing.

Plus, Charlotte had been popular with the men, despite all her difficulty to work with. Her change of house would affect overall profits. In the long run, if those profits didn't pick up all around, things weren't going to be good for the saloon or Barbara Jean's brothel services even if Mary Catherine managed to pay off Clanton, especially if he intended to open another bar in town.

"So you see, Miss Templeton, you've done too little in the time I gave you," Jake Clanton told her. "I aim to collect my due now." He motioned to the men behind the bar to continue.

They finished their packing and picked up the loaded crates to head out of the saloon. Trying to figure out what she could do to stop them short of flinging herself at men more than a head taller than she and wearing guns, Mary Catherine's brain distracted to that jangle of spurs, closer now somewhere along the wooden walkway right outside and accompanied by the synchronized, ominous echo of heavy footfalls.

The clomp-jangle grew louder, and she had the irrational thought that she wished she were a man of size and stature capable of making those heavy footfalls. She needed the might to fight back, and her intellect didn't hold the threat she needed in this particular situation. She needed a weapon of a whole other sort.

The metal clink of the spurs jangled right up to the saloon's double doors and stopped. Everyone looked over. Blaaze Lassiter stood blocking the exit of the men with crates, a scowl on his face and a gun belt on his hip. Over his shoulder, Mary Catherine could just make out the top of Macey's head as she rose on tiptoe to survey what was happening inside.

The bounty hunter's assessing eyes raked the room before settling on the men before him. "Put. That. Down."

A relief she couldn't name washed over Mary Catherine. Facing challenge after challenge for this new business was wearing on her. By no means was she ready to give up, but seeing Blaaze arrive bolstered her spirits.

The sheriff, however, looked none too happy. The lawman's shoulders bunched upon hearing Blaaze's words, and he looked miffed and a bit surprised to see the imposing cowboy blocking the wide-open doors. Like Mary Catherine, he must have thought Blaaze out building on his ranch this morning.

The sheriff recovered quickly. He straightened his posture and puffed out his chest. "See here, Lassiter, we won't be having no interference from you. This here is all right and proper like." Sheriff Brennan stepped toward Blaaze. "My deputies have every right to confiscate certain items of value that will be applied against the outstanding debt to Mr.

Clanton."

"Deputies? Since when?" Blaaze stared at the four lemmings accompanying the sheriff and the brewery owner.

"Don't you worry none about that," the sheriff told Blaaze. "Like I said, Mr. Clanton has every right to confiscate certain items of value that can be applied against the outstanding debt owed to him."

Blaaze glared at the sheriff and plied him with a long, slow, "Really?" He drew the word out across several seconds and tilted his hat off his brow with a pointed index finger. "So you got a writ and all from the judge then, I assume."

Sheriff Brennan glanced a bit nervously at Clanton, who glared back at him with a silent message that amounted to *take care of it, you idiot.*

The lawman took a deep breath. "You know we won't have a judge 'round here till summer hangin' season, Lassiter. As the law in these parts, I can't let this go that long. Mr. Clanton is entitled to redress for what that lady owes him."

Blaaze took a menacing step forward, and his voice dropped at least an octave to a gravelly growl. "That lady?"

With a quick step back, Sheriff Brennan cleared his throat and corrected himself. "Um, I mean, Miss Templeton."

Barbara Jean appeared from somewhere and sidled quietly up beside Mary Catherine. She hid a chuckle behind her hand. Softly, she said for only Mary Catherine's hearing, "Seems your man isn't going to tolerate any disrespect to you."

Mary Catherine jerked her head Barbara Jean's way, ready to deny the classification of Blaaze as her man.

With a squeeze to her shoulder, Barbara Jean cut off the intended protest. "No sense denying it, honey. No matter how much you two think you're sneaking around."

Heat settled across Mary Catherine's cheeks, and a grin

spread across Barbara Jean's lips.

Watching Blaaze, the elder woman added, "I always did like that young man. Gruff as he tries to play it, there's a heart of gold under that bounty hunter exterior. Doesn't mean the man's not deadly as any outlaw, though. The sheriff might want to pick his side wisely today."

Boots clomping and spurs jingling, Blaaze came the rest of the way into the saloon. "Redress, huh? I find it mighty interesting you waited until the marshal left town to come for that redress."

"Um, well . . ." The sheriff looked at Clanton again. "After I delivered Huntley to him, the marshal had important business elsewhere. I didn't see the need to trouble him with such a simple matter."

"What I'm hearing is you've decided to take a bit of a skirt around the law, sheriff. Because you think you can since nobody appears to be watching."

"Wait just a minute! This here is on the up-and-up. You were here when we warned that gal—"

Blaaze shot him a glare, starting to look every bit the outlaw Barbara Jean had referred to.

"Um . . . Miss Templeton. When we warned Miss Templeton if she couldn't pay off her brewery tab, we'd have to seize her assets to cover the debt."

"I was here, all right. I don't remember you saying anything about seizing those assets without a writ from the judge." He shot an evil look over at the two men who were inching closer to the door. "I said put . . . that . . . *down.*"

Mimicking the sheriff's earlier move, Blaaze cocked a hip and placed his right hand on the butt of his holstered gun.

"Blaaze," Mary Catherine said worriedly. The last thing she needed was for him to get shot trying to help her. He'd made clear his stance on getting shot at again. No matter what he'd said about protecting her, she'd not be the reason injury happened to him again. She'd rather the morons took the alcohol. She'd find a way to replace it over time. She hoped.

The targeted deputy focused on the position of Blaaze's hand then glanced at the sheriff, awaiting instructions.

The sheriff's eyes narrowed. "What'cha doing wearing those guns in town, b—?"

The edges of Blaaze's lips twitched when, clearly remembering what happened the last time he'd called a Colored man with a gun "boy," the sheriff stopped himself from finishing.

Annoyed with the cowboy's knowing look, the sheriff roughened his voice. "The marshal's gone. He can't protect you from town rules anymore."

This time, Blaaze let free the grin he'd been repressing. "I don't need the marshal to protect me. I do right fine all by myself." With a showy flare, Blaaze whipped his gun from its holster with a spin and aimed it at the immobile deputy closest to the door.

The deputy flinched when the gun stopped pointed at his chest.

"See," Blaaze added with an insouciant smirk.

"Now, see here," the sheriff huffed. "Put that gun away, Lassiter."

Blaaze shrugged, gave the gun a twirl and holstered it in one smooth move, almost as fast as he'd pulled it.

The sheriff took that ill-advised moment to pull his own gun.

Blaaze's expression went from amused to lethal in an instant. "That's a mistake, sheriff."

Feeling cocky now that he had a gun drawn on the bounty

hunter, the sheriff scoffed. "You're outnumbered, Lassiter. Take a look around."

Blaaze took a slow glance around the men accompanying the sheriff and Jake Clanton. He didn't look too worried. Unnerved by his nonchalance and fearing he'd do something rash, Mary Catherine made to move, but Barbara Jean clamped down on her shoulder and held her in place. She glanced questioningly at Barbara Jean, who admonished her with a sharp look and a tight shake of the head.

The sheriff unleashed his own smug grin. "The only mistake being made here is you thinking you can push around the law. Even you can't handle four men at once."

Blaaze casually dropped his gun hand to the side of his holster. "You sure about that, sheriff?"

The sheriff eyed Blaaze's hand at the ready then checked the positions of his backup, not too sure of himself now despite the gun in his hand. "W-Well . . ." Opting not to take anything for granted, the sheriff conceded, "We've got civilians around, so this is no time for a shootout. But you best be coming by my office before the end of the day to turn in that weapon. I'll have no more of this."

Clanton's face turned bright red. "You cowardly buffoon," he said to the sheriff. "If you're not going to do your damn job, we'll do it for you." Clanton motioned to one of his men.

The man without a crate in his hand went for his gun, but Blaaze was faster. Blaaze snatched the sheriff in front of him, simultaneously grabbing the lawman's gun fast enough to shoot the hired man's revolver from his hand then whirled toward a crate-toting gent when he heard the man's crate crash to the ground. The man's gun hadn't even cleared his holster when the sheriff's commandeered gun aimed square at his chest. The man's free hand went up in surrender, and he stood awkwardly with three fingers on the gun he'd only managed to get halfway out of his holster.

By the time Blaaze spun to keep the sheriff positioned between him and the third armed man, the sound of glass breaking and a loud thud caught everyone's attention. Mary Catherine looked at the last deputy laid out on the floor amongst the shard remnants of one of her whiskey glasses. His crate sat neatly on the floor beside him, and he had his gun in his hand, but he was out cold. A large, red bump sprouted on his forehead.

Her gaze swung to the cowgirl who now stood behind the bar holding an empty glass in one hand and playfully tossing and catching another in her other hand.

Blaaze's eyes widened at the sight of her. "*Addison?!*"

She gave him a cocky smirk, and Mary Catherine figured out why the woman had looked so familiar.

Without taking her eyes off Blaaze, the cowgirl said to the sheriff, "I think that'd be two against four, sheriff. We'll take those odds all day. Won't we, big brother?"

Mary Catherine's mouth dropped open. She stared at the woman's once-serious brown eyes in a shade and holding an irreverent joviality exactly like a certain bounty hunter's, a bounty hunter whose smirk her mouth mirrored exactly.

Everyone was so caught up in the showdown between Blaaze, Clanton's men, and the cowgirl—*Addison*—no one noticed a stranger enter the establishment until he spoke.

"What's going on here?" asked a distinguished male baritone.

Oh no. Mary Catherine knew that voice. Her eyes squeezed shut, and she must have made some sound because when she opened them, Barbara Jean stared at her with a worried expression.

Mary Catherine slid her gaze toward the entrance, and yep, there he stood with what looked like half the town behind him, including the mayor and Tobias.

The last person she'd ever expected to see in Lawless, Kansas, was here in Lawless, Kansas.

Mr. Jeremiah Dixon Beauregard III.

Chapter 25

BLAAZE STUDIED THE WELL-DRESSED stranger and Mary Catherine's wide eyes. This could only be one person: the fiancé.

The man was as tall as him and solidly built beneath the expensive clothes. Whatever he did for his family's textile business involved more than simply sitting behind a desk. The quiet, bookish, and perhaps dandified image Blaaze had held in his mind when he'd thought about the fiancé Miss Templeton had left back in Ohio burst and shattered into sharp shards of petty annoyance.

The man's alert eyes glanced around the room. He took in the bloody-handed deputy, the unconscious victim of glassware assault, the gun-toting Blaaze, and finally over to Blaaze's newly-arrived, pain-in-the-ass sister. When the man's gaze settled on Mary Catherine, it scanned over her in obvious concern before he pinned her with a relieved but narrowed-eyed stare.

Just what Blaaze needed to add to his day, Mary Catherine's past come to find her and half the town looking on, likely drawn by the gunfire. Ignoring the fiancé and the spectators for the time being, Blaaze surveyed the mess himself. Two of the injured men were Clanton's lackeys. The other two were locals. The younger of the two, with the knot forming on his head, had to be Clanton's son. They looked too much alike. Only an idiot made a man like that a deputy. He'd abuse the power for certain.

Blaaze motioned with the gun he'd confiscated from the sheriff for the hands-up deputy to surrender his weapon. Not knowing what to do, but clearly fearing the reprisal from Blaaze more than the sheriff, Clanton's man dropped his gun and scurried out of the saloon. Blaaze walked over and retrieved the abandoned gun.

Two down, Blaaze thought after double-checking that the man whose gun hand he'd shot was doing nothing more than standing uselessly dripping blood on the floor. Blaaze had had about all he was going to take of this nonsense from Clanton and the sheriff. Breaking the law in the light of day, with no consideration at all that anyone would object. And as far as Blaaze could tell, no one would.

On the one hand, he shouldn't be surprised. He had selected this town because of its quiet, unassuming citizens. As his daddy always said, live and let live. That ought to be the Lawless town motto. Maybe they should paint that on a sign outside of town instead of that ridiculous warning telling people they couldn't wear guns.

On the other hand, people here needed to stand for something or this little town wasn't going to keep its quiet, unassuming way. If Clanton had his way, no one would be able to do anything in this town without paying homage, and lots of money, to him. And that way lies serpents.

"Sheriff," he said into the man's ear before releasing him.

"I suggest you advise Mr. Clanton that he needs a writ from a judge to seize any property Miss Templeton hasn't agreed to voluntarily forfeit to him. Until then, he needs to come back in two days." With an intentionally flashy twirl, Blaaze flipped the sheriff's gun and offered it to him butt first. "Otherwise, I'm likely to get antsy."

The sheriff's jaw tightened at the threat. He took the proffered gun and began to coerce a grumbling Clanton toward the door.

Clanton shouted over his shoulder. "This isn't over, Lassiter."

"Trust me, Clanton, I'm counting on it," Blaaze replied.

"Wait a minute." The fiancé stepped in front of Clanton. "What's this about seizing Miss Templeton's assets?"

Mary Catherine raced over and put her hand on the fiancé's arm. "Jeremiah, I'll explain everything to you later."

He placed his hand on top of hers. "Explain it to me now, Catie."

Blaaze tensed. *Catie?*

Clanton decided to enlighten the gentlemen himself. "She owes me money for several months' worth of credit to this establishment that hasn't been paid. Her time's about up."

"*This* establishment?" Surprise flashed across the newcomer's features, but he schooled it quickly. "How much money?"

Clanton told him.

Jeremiah reached inside his jacket and retrieved a leather wallet. He handed it to Mary Catherine. "I'm sure you'll find more than enough inside."

Her hands flew behind her back. "No. I'm not taking your money."

Jeremiah grabbed one of her wrists and pulled the hand

from around her back. He placed his wallet in it. "It's not my money. It's *our* money. Once we get married it won't matter, but if you insist on paying me back, you can do so after the sale of your parents' house goes through."

Mary Catherine's face fell. "I'm not selling my parents' house."

"That's not what the bank manager told me." To his credit, the man stepped closer to her and lowered his voice before continuing, "This isn't the place to have this discussion, Catie. That we *can* talk about later."

"Hold up." Babs sashayed forward. She stopped to whisper something to Mary Catherine, who became extremely agitated. "I'm not taking no for an answer, young lady. It's time we settle this matter and get rid of this varmint for good. So stop mouthing off to your elders and go do what I told you."

Blaaze had never heard Babs use that scolding tone with Mary Catherine before, and using the "elders" line was playing dirty. Mary Catherine felt it too. Her frustrated frown said it all. Nonetheless, she disappeared into the back parlor to do what Babs had told her. When she emerged, she handed Babs a large brown envelope.

Babs stepped behind the bar and pulled a stack of paper currency from the envelope. She counted the lot. Then reaching into her generous bosom, she pulled out her own stack of bills and counted a wad onto Mary Catherine's pile. She folded what remained of her stash in half, stuffed the bills back down the front of her dress, and put the counted stack of bills into the empty brown envelope.

Babs handed the envelope to Clanton. "There you go, you no good swindler. Saloon bill's paid in full. Don't bother to come back. You can send our future orders with one of your men."

Brows puckered, Clanton pulled the bills from the envelope and made a big deal of counting every one. When he was done, his frown deepened. "So it is, *Miss* Forrester," he said sarcastically using Babs's surname. "But let's be clear. I didn't say anything about paying *down* the saloon's account."

Mary Catherine came to stand beside Babs. "What do you mean?"

Exactly what Blaaze was wondering.

"I never expected you to pay off your account. I expected you to give up and sell me the saloon. Now that your account's paid in full, your account with me is closed."

Working up a full steam, Mary Catherine stepped forward. "You can't expect me to pay cash in full for all my future orders. Those aren't normal terms, Mr. Clanton. You know it, and I know it. How am I supposed to manage that?"

"That's not my concern, Miss Templeton. I made you a fair offer for this place. I'm a businessman. It makes good sense for me to combine a saloon with all my current business interests and the hotel I plan to build in anticipation of the railroad being extended. They'll be starting construction back up anytime now and plan to have a stop right on the Lawless border. Business is going to get good around town with all the people that'll be coming. Homesteaders. People on the way to California. Heck, even more of your folk are coming up from down south. You've got an established, popular operation here. No sense for me to start from scratch."

A low rumbling started through the meager crowd inside the place and the spectators gathered at the door. News would make the rounds quickly that the saloon was about to lose its supply of alcohol. That would leave Mary Catherine with only one offering—other than a few boarding rooms—to draw patrons in.

Clanton gave the place another good look and shrugged. "If you're not willing to sell, I guess we'll be doing business against each other. It wouldn't be very smart of me to supply my competitor with their spirits, now would it?" He shoved the payoff into its envelope and stuffed it all inside his vest. "Besides, a saloon is no place for a lady like you anyhow. I figured we could do business together. I buy. You sell."

Blaaze couldn't see Mary Catherine wanting to remain the owner of an establishment that was only a brothel. It was one thing to let Babs pay her for use of the upstairs rooms to add to her overall profits. It was quite another for her to truly become the "head whore" she'd postured as to make a point.

His fists clenched at his sides. Seems Mr. Beauregard *the third* had arrived at the right moment to give her an alternative to that fate. An alternative that would take her out of town and back to a life that no longer risked destitution.

The fiancé stepped forward and took Mary Catherine's elbow. "Mary Catherine, surely you don't plan to keep running a saloon. If this man's offered you a fair price for this—" He looked around the room, noticing the suggestively clad women who had emerged along the upstairs balcony upon hearing the commotion. "Um, establishment . . . you should consider it."

Mary Catherine gave the man an indulgent smile, but she didn't move away from his touch. "Jeremiah, please, let's talk about this later. Privately."

His lips pressed into a thin line, but he nodded deferentially to her. His hand remained on her elbow, and Blaaze wanted to toss one of those glasses Addison kept playing with at the man's head. Walking over to the bar, he leaned sideways against the counter right in front of his sister, not taking his eyes off Mary Catherine and her beau. He'd let this Jeremiah deal with the offer apparently still on the table from Clanton.

"You okay, big brother?" Addison asked with a grin in her voice.

Blaaze hesitated before looking at his sister. She only called him big brother when she was up to mischief. So he knew what he'd see. Sure enough, she had a smarmy look in her eyes.

He grunted before responding. "What?" As soon as he'd said the word, he could've kicked himself for asking such a dumb question. Addison always did have a sharp eye, a sharp mind, and an even sharper intuition. She rarely missed anything, and she had inherited their mother's uncanny knack for reading him and their father like an open book. It was aggravating.

She glanced over to where Mary Catherine stood with her gentleman then gave Blaaze a speculative look. "Oh, I don't know, you just look like you want to kill that tall, handsome, city fella. And did he say something about getting married?"

A low growl escaped from his throat, and he lunged across the bar for one of the glasses in her hands, but she was quick and snatched it out of his reach.

"Nuh-uh." She laughed. "I'm not sure if you're planning to use this on him or me, but I think I'll hold on to it either way. We've had enough chaos for one morning."

"I'll say." Tobias dropped onto the barstool beside him. Looking at Blaaze, he said, "Why didn't you tell me you were planning on shooting people when you grabbed those old spurs off the tack wall?"

"'Cuz I didn't figure on shooting anybody." Blaaze grabbed up the tumbler of whiskey Addison set in front of him and took a big gulp.

"I was wondering where you got those spurs." Addison crossed her arms and leaned forward with both elbows on the bar. "You just had to make an entrance, didn't you? Was that for the benefit of the little proprietress who can't seem to keep her worried eyes from wandering over here?"

He scowled at his sister. "Why would you think something like that?"

Curious as to her comment about Mary Catherine's wandering eyes, Blaaze peeked at the new mirror behind the bar and noticed Mary Catherine surreptitiously cast a nervous glance his way before continuing the conversation with her beau. Perhaps she was worried the man would find out about their dalliance in the barn. That'd be one way for her to end her engagement. If she really wanted to, that is. His hand tightened around his whiskey glass.

Addison scoffed. "Like I don't see the way you look at her, and right now, how much you want to strangle the fella standing with her. Besides, you'd no more wear spurs on a horse than I'd run naked down the middle of the street."

Blaaze winched at her words. "Please don't put that image in my head."

Tobias stared at her as if noticing her for the first time. A wide grin spread across his face, a twinkle in his eyes as if he was indeed visualizing Addison with nothing on. "Well, hullo. When did we get such a pretty new barkeep?"

"We didn't," Blaaze growled, not liking where this was headed. "She's not the barkeep, and she's not staying in town either. So don't get any ideas, you big oaf."

Tobias ignored him, still staring at his sister with a goofy grin.

Addison smiled back at him. "Don't listen to him."

She started to offer Tobias her hand, but Blaaze grabbed her wrist and planted her palm firmly on the far side of the bar.

He looked Tobias in the eyes. "Yeah, listen to me." He pointed at Addison. "Sister. That's all you need to know. And that I still have a bullet with your name on it."

Tobias simply blinked at him. "Sister? You never said anything about having a sister."

Blaaze took another drink. "Because she's a pain in my ass, and I try not to think about her."

That wasn't the complete truth. Blaaze didn't like to talk about her because the fewer people who knew of her relationship to him, the safer she'd be. The last thing he wanted was for bad guys to go after her to get to him.

Tobias reached over and slid his palm under Addison's hand that Blaaze had just released. The big man gave a gentle squeeze before kissing the back of the hand. "Hello, sister."

Addison giggled, actually giggled. Blaaze wanted to throw up in his glass, but that would be a waste of good whiskey.

"It's Addy," she finally said to the posturing nincompoop trying to get Blaaze's goat by flirting with her.

Still holding her hand, Tobias placed his hand over his heart. "Miss Addy, you're the prettiest thing to enter Lawless since Miss Templeton came and riled up the place."

The blacksmith gestured with a cocked thumb in Blaaze's direction as he said *the place*, and Blaaze's jaw tightened.

"My name's Tobias Craig. I'm your brother's business partner. I'd say you'd definitely be worth getting shot by him."

Blaaze rolled his eyes at their flirtatious nonsense, more annoyed by their poking at his mad over Mary Catherine's male visitor. Mainly, because they were right about his disposition, and it bothered him that his current pique was noticeable. Granted, only two people who knew him as well as Tobias and Addy could likely tell, but all and still.

He took another peek into the mirror to see the goings on. Clanton and the sheriff had departed, and others were starting to clear out or head back to their corners of the saloon. Addison and Tobias kept up their annoying banter, which made him reach across the bar for the bottle of whiskey and refill his glass.

Mimicking Tobias's earlier stance, Addison freed her hand from his and placed it over her heart. "Why, Mr. Craig, how you flatter me. Unfortunately, I think you're going to have to wait in line to get shot by Blaaze." She motioned with her head for Tobias to look over his shoulder.

Following their gazes, Blaaze watched Mary Catherine lead her fiancé into the back parlor. A massive wave of possessiveness washed through Blaaze. He tossed back his drink, slammed the empty glass on the bar, and gritted through his teeth, "Yeah, you are."

Standing, he stalked after the disappearing couple.

~

"Jeremiah, what are you doing here?" Mary Catherine asked as soon as she and Jeremiah entered the parlor. She turned to close the door, then thought better of it under the circumstances. She had enough gossip about her. She didn't need additional rumors to start about her entertaining an out-of-town gentleman alone in the back room.

Jeremiah watched her with curious eyes, puzzled by her hesitation to be alone with him. No doubt he was thinking of all the times they'd been alone together back home. After all, in his mind they were engaged, as his comment earlier attested, and no one considered it improper for a betrothed couple to be alone together. She stepped away from the door, which she left half open nonetheless.

He removed his hat and sat it on the table. "I came as soon as I heard from Clifton at the bank that you'd defaulted on the loan against your parents' house. I knew something had to be seriously wrong for you to give up on that house. When he told me about the pending foreclosure, I asked him where you'd sent your last wire from. When he told me it was a place called Lawless, Kansas. Well . . ."

Stifling her irritation at the bank manager's disclosure of her loan status, Mary Catherine walked over to Jeremiah. Sure, he'd helped her secure the loan, but the reminder that others considered her under his control grated. The irritation combined with a tweak to her ego that he'd learned about her financial failings and felt he needed to come rescue her.

Right now, he seemed at a loss for words. For someone always as eloquently composed as Jeremiah, that was saying something. She experienced true chagrin that she'd likely worried him. Not enough that she could blindly succumb to his way of thinking, but here they were.

He stared searchingly at her face, looking for something he didn't seem to find. "Mary Catherine, what's going on? Why are you here in a saloon?" He cleared his throat. "A saloon that obviously doubles as something more." A disapproving grimace flashed before he steeled his features.

She turned away from him. "I don't know what you mean. I came here to run a business, of course. My cousin left me this saloon."

"You came here to run a business your cousin left you without telling me you were leaving?"

"You would have tried to talk me out of it, Jeremiah. You

know you would."

"Of course, I would! You're my future wife. Why would I want you in the middle of the plains in some half-civilized town where they settle business disputes with guns?" He paced away then came back to her. "Come home with me," he said earnestly. "Sell this place to that man and come home with me. You don't need to work. I'll take care of you. We'll redeem your parents' home and get married like we should have a long time ago." He looked as if he was going to embrace her, but he stuffed his hands in his pockets instead.

"Jeremiah, don't you understand yet? I want to work. I wanted to go into banking, but that didn't work out. Now, I want to use my education in business. Your family built their own business. I'd think you of all people would understand the legacy I want to start."

"But you can have that legacy as part of the Beauregard family." His hands came free of his pockets, and he lightly drew her to him by her forearms. "Our children will inherit my share of the business."

"So I'm only to bear you children and raise them?" She searched his face for some understanding that he knew her well enough to recognize how limiting those words sounded to her.

He released her and stepped away. "You say that like it's such a horrible thing."

Her hands went up then flopped down at her sides. "Of course not. But I don't want that to be all I do. All I am."

A pensive expression took over his face. Thoughtfully, he said, "I guess I could talk to Clifton. I'm sure I could get him to let you work at the bank for a few years until we decide to start a family."

She shook her head. "Don't you get it? That's exactly why

he wouldn't give me a job in the first place. He assumed that I'd marry you and start a family and leave. That I'd simply be Mrs. Beauregard playing at banking for a little while, and in his opinion, likely messing up accounts in the process. I'm nothing but an extension of you in Cleveland, Jeremiah. That he told you about the status of my loan is proof of that. We're not even married yet, and he's given you access to my banking information."

"Yet?" he said, a faint hint of hope in the request for clarification.

She sighed loudly. "Jeremiah . . ."

He sobered. "All right. But remember, he gave you that loan on my word. So he thought I'd want to know about its status."

That was fair. That she'd needed Jeremiah's backing had irritated Mary Catherine at the time, but she'd accepted it. No sense bemoaning after the fact the strings that came with that backing.

She moved to take a seat and noticed the shadow of a Stetson hovering on the wall opposite the parlor door. She headed that way. Blaaze must have heard the swish of her skirts, because he stepped fully into the doorway.

He looked over her head at Jeremiah before he asked softly, "You holdin' up okay?"

"Yes, I'm fine." She'd had a rough week, but at least she had Clanton off her back. She'd have to deal with the alcohol supply issue, and she'd have to deal with the Jeremiah issue. Her hands lifted to rub at her temples where a building headache throbbed. For now, she could only deal with one headstrong man at a time. She placed a hand on Blaaze's chest and pushed to back him out the door.

He didn't move, not an inch. "You don't look like you're

okay. Sounds like he's pressuring you to do something you don't want to do, and it looks like your head hurts."

"This is between me and Catie." Jeremiah took a step forward. "I'd appreciate it if you'd give me and my fiancée some privacy."

"Your appreciation isn't my concern," Blaaze said looking directly at Jeremiah. He made as if to move farther into the room, but Mary Catherine pushed hard with the hand still on his chest. He stayed in place and looked down at her.

"Blaaze, please. Let me handle this. I'll speak with you in a moment. Wait for me at the bar."

Blaaze placed his hand over the hand she had on his chest. "Are you sure, Mary Cate?"

Mary Catherine noticed he looked over her head when he called her Mary Cate. His way of responding to Jeremiah calling her Catie. A glance over her shoulder revealed Jeremiah wasn't too pleased to know Blaaze had his own pet name for her. They were like two little boys fighting over a ball. Only she was the ball, and this male tit-for-tat was making her head hurt worse.

She shoved at Blaaze. "I'm sure. Now go."

His mouth flattened in a tight line, but he left.

Mary Catherine took a seat at the table and dropped her head into her hands.

Silence filled the parlor. If she didn't know better, she'd have thought Jeremiah had also left, but she'd heard no indication that he'd moved. After a few minutes, the chair opposite hers was pulled back and he had a seat.

"He calls you Mary Cate," he said in a slow, drawn-out voice.

It was a statement.

He continued when she didn't say anything. "And you call

him by his first name."

Mary Catherine looked up, knowing what was coming next.

"You're very informal with him." His hands bunched on the table and Jeremiah's gaze locked with hers. "Tell me, Catie, what's that man to you?"

CHAPTER 26

MARY CATHERINE THOUGHT ABOUT how to answer Jeremiah's question. She didn't actually know how to classify her relationship with Blaaze. "He's a ... friend. I guess."

"You guess? Why don't you know?" Jeremiah leaned back in his chair, one hand stretched forward on the table and the other in his lap. He gave her a look that suggested he thought she was intentionally being untruthful with him.

"In the beginning, he was opposed to my being here. Blaaze thinks I don't belong in a town like Lawless and should move back east."

"Well, there's something he and I can agree on." His tone was businesslike. It was a persona she'd seen him don when negotiating a deal. It was not unlike the card players she'd watched in the saloon who tried to read their opponents during poker games without giving away any tells of their own.

Mary Catherine had the unladylike urge to stick her tongue out at him, but she summoned the remnants of whatever Templeton good-and-proper she had left and continued her explanation. "The thing is, whenever I've had a problem with Jake Clanton or someone trying to push me out of business, he's been there to help me. So I'm not sure where he stands. If he really wants me gone, then he could simply let me fail and be done with it."

An understated scoff slipped from Jeremiah. "It's one thing to convince you to sell your business and leave. It's another thing to stand by and let someone take it from you. No man who looks at you the way he looks at you would let that happen."

Mary Catherine's head jerked up. She could see his suspicions in his eyes. "Jeremiah, it's not like that. He doesn't feel that way about me. We're not . . . I mean, I'm not . . ." She looked down at the table, unable to say aloud she didn't feel that way about him because she wasn't sure it was true.

"I see." The fingers of the hand he had resting on the table curled under until he had a fist lying knuckles up against the wooden surface.

His silence lasted so long Mary Catherine couldn't bear not to know what he was thinking. When she looked back up, she could see the hurt and disappointment in his eyes.

"You've never been a conventional woman, Mary Catherine," he finally said in a low, matter-of-fact voice. "I think all these years you've thought I don't appreciate that. But I do. I'm sure being out here has exposed you to a lifestyle a lot different than how we were raised back home. The novelty and newness of it all. It's understandable, I guess, in this environment that you'd be drawn to someone else . . . someone flashy and maybe dangerous in a way a woman might find exciting." His forehead puckered, and he said almost to himself, "What kind of name is Blaaze, anyway?"

Mary Catherine's lips twitched. She suppressed a languid grin and watched Jeremiah pick up his hat and stand. He twirled the hat in his hand a few times as if considering his next words carefully. Mary Catherine watched him warily. She didn't want to hurt him. In truth, she cared for him deeply. They'd been family friends since childhood, and he'd always been good to her. He'd been her rock when she'd lost both her parents, and he'd obviously come here to be her rock again if she needed.

Finally, he put the hat on his head. "I'm staying at Beulah's boarding house on the outer edge of town if you need me. It's been a long trip, and I need to . . ." He shook his head as if the words were stuck in there and he could shake them loose, but he didn't finish whatever he was going to say. "I'll be back tomorrow, and we can talk more then."

He walked to the door but pulled up short at the threshold. His back still to her, his shoulders rose and fell through a deep inhale and slow exhale before he said, "And you're wrong about how that man feels about you." He glanced over his shoulder at her. "I've felt that way long enough to recognize it in another man. But I'm not going anywhere. I believe in our future together, Mary Catherine. I want you for my wife. You're in trouble. Trouble I could help you with if you'd let me. And I don't need to wear a gun to do it. I don't know what your real relationship is with that cowboy, Catie, but there's something you need to know."

Her head tilted. "What's that?"

"I didn't come all this way to walk away from you." He strolled out the parlor door without giving her another look.

Mary Catherine dropped her forehead to the table. Rolling her head side to side, she allowed the pressure from the press of the table to counterbalance the throbbing inside her head.

How had she managed to end up with two of the stubbornest men in the country in her life? As much as they postured with each other, it was ironic that they basically wanted the same thing. To get her back to Ohio as fast as possible.

Maybe she ought to consider it. She'd about had enough of barely having enough. She didn't know how long she could fight Jake Clanton, and if the man was set on taking over the hospitality business in Lawless, he'd always be a fight.

Who was she kidding? Despite all she'd learned in the past month, she still knew little about surviving frontier life or saloon life for any extended period of time. She'd given it her best try.

By the end of the next week, she might not have alcohol to sell out of the saloon. There was no saloon without alcohol. She wasn't sure it made any sense to keep trying. She'd witnessed a man getting shot today, for goodness's sake. The man hadn't been killed, but the ordeal had scared her. As Jeremiah had said, she now lived in a town where business negotiations were as likely to be settled by a gun as by diplomatic haggling.

Raising her head, she sighed and stared at the door. Thinking of Jeremiah, she wondered if it would be so bad to go ahead and marry him. Maybe she *could* get banking out of her system by working for a few years and then doing what most other woman of her upbringing did: start a family. They could save her parents' house and have a good life together. She had no doubt that Jeremiah would make a good husband. Maybe he could even be persuaded to let her help with his family's business. The prospects boded well for a good life.

Her thoughts shifted to a certain cowboy sitting out at her bar waiting to speak with her. The mere thought of him made her heart race. Just like it did every time he walked into a room. She'd gotten so used to his touch, the feel of him, that she hadn't thought twice about placing her hand on his chest when he'd interrupted her and Jeremiah. No wonder Jeremiah sensed there was more between them.

Of course, the more was only sexual, nothing long-term. No promises. But Blaaze made her skin sing when he touched her. He made her feel she could unleash the bit of bad girl she'd been raised to suppress, enough to pursue desires that were more than a bit scandalous. The scary part of it all was she was beginning to think she liked being that little bit scandalous Mary Catherine, liked being his "Mary Cate."

Did Jeremiah sense it had gone as far as bed? Was that something he could overlook? Did she want him to?

She'd told Blaaze she had been clear with Jeremiah about ending their engagement. But now she was beginning to wonder. Maybe she'd been selfish and not emphatically clear. Maybe she'd wanted all along to know that Jeremiah would be waiting if she failed at building the life she saw for herself. Because here she sat feeling on the verge of failing, and his plea to go home with him tempted her in the face of her current trials.

It tempted her as much as its acceptance terrified her for what it might mean for her future. And that temptation felt like a betrayal. A betrayal of who she believed she was. A betrayal of who she wanted to be, who she wanted to become.

She sat for long minutes, pondering the question of whether she'd used equivocal language in her engagement termination. Eventually, she rejected the thought. She'd been extremely clear with Jeremiah, and she'd meant every word. At the time.

Given his parting words, she better understood that it wasn't that she hadn't been clear, but that he hadn't wanted to hear her. She'd always thought he'd considered their engagement a mere obligation he had to meet. She'd never dreamed he had feelings for her beyond their long-time affection for each other. Had she known, would she even have come to Lawless? Could she have spared herself this whole ordeal?

What a mess her life had become.

Setting aside her descent into self-pity, Mary Catherine rose. She'd solve nothing sitting here wallowing in what might or might not have happened in the past or what might happen next. She'd decide what to do about Jeremiah later. She had time to think about it until he returned sometime tomorrow. For now, she needed to deal with that "flashy" and dangerously "exciting" cowboy. And maybe it was time she figured out what she intended to do with him too.

~

Blaaze sat silently next to Tobias at the bar lost in thought. Addy served drinks like she'd been doing it all her life, and Blaaze absently wondered what had happened to Charlie, the actual barkeep.

He hadn't had any more to drink. He needed a clear head for when Mary Catherine came out to finally talk with him. He glanced over at the parlor door. She still hadn't come out, even though her fiancé had left over thirty minutes ago. He held on to his patience. It was a struggle when all he wanted to do was storm into the parlor and demand some answers.

Answers to what, he wasn't quite sure. Even if he did know, he wasn't sure he was entitled to any answers. He'd wanted the woman gone from the moment she'd splashed into his life dripping water from the trough in a yellow dress that still haunted his dreams. Clanton had thrown up another obstacle to prevent her from making her saloon a success, and now her fiancé had come along to lure her back where she belonged.

Except she belongs with me. His gut twisted at the errant thought. The last thing she needed was to be trapped in a rough life when she could go live a posh life in a big house back east with her strapping city fella and raise wealthy babies.

Except Blaaze could give her a big house. Here. Right outside of town on the one hundred and sixty acres of land where he intended to established his horse ranch. He thought about the house he had finally started building on that land. It was three times larger than he needed, even to show himself as a prosperous rancher. If he was honest with himself, he'd been thinking of her when he and the men had framed up the two-story home with multiple bedrooms and a formal dining room.

As if he'd ever need a formal dining room.

Unless Mary Catherine stayed.

After that day in the barn, all he'd thought about was how nice it would be to take her inside *his* house and keep her in *his* bed until she admitted that she wanted to be *his*. And not just as a pretend madam in search of an education in carnal pleasure. But that wasn't what she wanted.

She wanted to be a businesswoman. She wanted independence. She didn't want to tie herself to a man, or so she said, repeatedly. Now that he'd seen this Jeremiah Dixon Beauregard *the third* and seen them together, Blaaze had to wonder.

Mary Catherine finally emerged from the parlor and walked behind the bar. She took one look at Addy and asked, "Still no Charlie?"

Addy shook her head. "I doubt he's coming back, Miss Mary."

Mary Catherine turned tired eyes to his sister, questioning her name choice.

Addy simply shrugged. "That's what most of the ladies call you. Seems rather appropriate to me."

Shaking her head dismissively, Mary Catherine grabbed a clean glass and poured in some whiskey. Addy, Tobias, and Blaaze watched her curiously. None of them had asked for a whiskey. When she started to raise the glass to her lips, Blaaze shot half over the bar and grabbed her wrist.

"What do you think you're doing?" he asked her.

"Having a drink of whiskey. What does it look like I'm doing?" she quipped with her schoolmarm air of consummate authority. She was giving a good show of keeping it together, but the up-and-down motion of her other hand along her mother's watch chain told a different story. "This might be the last of it in a while. Thought I should give it a try at least once before I get run out of business."

Blaaze removed the glass from her hand and sat back down. Passing the glass to Tobias, he gave the blacksmith a look that warned *if you give her back that glass, I'm done joking about your final demise.* To his credit, Tobias didn't question the message. He simply drained the glass dry. Addy removed it after he set it on the bar and grabbed up the whiskey bottle to put them both out of Mary Catherine's eyesight.

"Mary Cate, we're not gonna let them run you out of business if that's not what you want." He glanced askance at Tobias. "We can help you with the alcohol situation in the short run."

Tobias gave him a direct stare with a familiar raised eyebrow that silently asked, *Can we?* "Hmm, before you go making promises we can't keep, I'll remind you the sheriff isn't going to look the other way with my stock the way he pretended Clanton wasn't violating Kansas law."

Mary Catherine's questioning gaze bounced between them. "What are you talking about?"

Intrigued by the direction the conversation was taking, Addy stepped closer. "Boys, are you two running a little business that might involve a still?"

Blaaze considered Tobias while he pondered how, or whether, to answer Addy's question.

Tobias shook his head in dissension. "I see what you're thinking, Lassiter, but don't say nothing unless you're prepared to take care of our sheriff problem."

Blaaze ran a hand down his face. Tobias was talking about that damned silver star and putting it on again to keep the sheriff from getting out of line and playing favorites with who got to skirt around the Kansas constitutional amendment prohibiting the manufacture and sale of intoxicating liquors. It was a dance lawmen and justices of the peace did all throughout the state, but here in Lawless the dance favored Jake Clanton. Blaaze didn't care enough about that at the moment to dance back into his role as US deputy marshal, so he sighed and shook his head at Tobias.

"Then the lady's gonna have to find another solution." The blacksmith sounded almost disappointed, and the disappointment seemed to be aimed directly at Blaaze.

"You know," Addy interjected, "Anheuser-Busch has been using refrigerated railcars, like the ones created by that Georgia fella to ship peaches, to ship beer. If we telegram right away, we could probably get several kegs of beer here by the end of next week. Of course, we'd need to get some ice boxes to load them in given the distance from the railroad stop to here, but it's better than nothing."

"A lot of good beer's going to do me if I don't have a bartender," Mary Catherine said. "I wonder where Charlie went."

"I doubt he's coming back." Addy leaned forward, placing her elbows on the bar. "Since you started calculating the inventory with such interest the last few days, I suspect he's worried you're going to figure out he's been pinching off the top."

"What? He's stealing from me?" The surprise on Mary Catherine's face was clear. "How can you be sure?"

"I've watched him every time I come in. What I can tell you is all the money he collected didn't end up in the money bag. Even more interesting?" Addy paused for effect. "Part of his take got slipped to that fella Blaaze shot in the hand earlier."

"Clanton's man?" Tobias asked.

Blaaze glared at her. "Why didn't you say something?"

Addy looked affronted. "Hey, I didn't know these people. None of my business. If I'd known she was a special friend of yours, I would have said something days ago."

Mary Catherine averted her face at the use of the words "special friend," but not before Blaaze saw her blush rise.

She grabbed up the ledgers she'd left stashed under the bar. "That actually makes sense. Clanton's list of damages to the saloon was suspiciously accurate. He had to have gotten the information from somewhere."

"Charlie," Addison said with certainty.

"Maybe," Mary Catherine replied. "He was responsible for paying for supplies, including the alcohol. According to him, he didn't write anything down, but maybe that was all a ruse. He could have been working with Clanton all along. Or maybe it was Charlotte. She never liked the way I ran things, and Clanton says she's down at Beulah's now. That could be his doing. I don't know."

"Or maybe they're all in cahoots," Blaaze said. He thought about the day he arrived and Charlie's unease until the two troublemakers had shown up.

"Who knows if that brewery tab was even real," Tobias said.

"True." Nodding, Blaaze contemplated something Babs had told them the other day. "Babs said Charlie had also been collecting the house's share of the sportin' business take. If he was pocketing that money, too, or funneling it to Clanton, then they've been double tipping all the way around."

Mary Catherine flipped to a page in the notebook, and ran her finger down it. "With the twelve bottles I counted missing, and the number of glasses they each pour, that's . . ." She muttered a sum then cursed.

Blaaze gave her a chastising look. She stood her ground unapologetically. Blaaze's lips twitched. So her fatigue hadn't stopped her mad from pushing her to the point of fed up. That was a good sign. It gave him hope that the defeated look on her face was only temporary.

Addy looked at her in amazement. "Was that an approximate guess or the exact figure?"

She slammed the ledger shut. "The exact figure."

"That fast?" Addy slid the book from under Mary Catherine's hand.

Mary Catherine didn't stop her.

Landing on a page of interest, Addy ran a finger down a column of figures. "You added up all these figures, did the multiplication of glasses poured per bottle, and calculated the dollar amount that fast. In your head?"

Finally, Mary Catherine noticed Addy's curiosity was more like astonishment. "I-I'm good with numbers," she said with a shrug.

"I'll say." Addy slid the ledger back to her.

Slowly, Tobias repeated her words as if he didn't quite understand them the first time. "You're good with numbers." He looked over at Blaaze, and Blaaze could see the figurin' going on in his friend's head. The man hated numbers. He did what he had to do to track the profits from his still business, but he hated it.

Blaaze could probably take on that part of the business if he wanted to. Not as fast as Mary Catherine and not in his head, but he did quite well with figures using pencil and paper. Didn't matter, though, because he'd already told Tobias he wasn't taking over the books of account, so he knew what was coming before Tobias spoke.

"So . . . Mary Catherine, would you be willing to do that number stuff for me?" he asked hopefully.

Mary Catherine gave him a noncommittal look. "I don't see why not. I'm doing it for several other business owners in town. What would you need me to do?"

"Well, if you could keep accurate ledgers for my *special* business, I could possibly provide you with a solution to your alcohol problem." He glanced at Blaaze before he said, "At least temporarily. Now, you wouldn't be able to tell anybody where you got that particular alcohol from. But we could broker a deal so that you could keep supplying your customers until you come up with something better, and I can have an accurate account of my profits."

The ornery devil was boxing him into a corner. Tobias knew if Mary Cate accepted his offer, no matter what Blaaze had said before, he'd not let anyone—not even the sheriff—

challenge the legality of her source of supply.

Glancing at Blaaze with a mischievous grin, Tobias reached out a hand for her to shake. "What do you say, Miss Templeton?"

"I'd say, at this point, Mr. Craig, I don't have much of a choice." She placed her hand in his. "I paid off a tab I might not have owed only to find myself without the inventory to run a key aspect of my business."

They shook on the bargain.

"Seems I've managed to make a mess of yet something else," she grumbled under her breath before pulling away.

Blaaze reached for her hand, but she moved it to pick up her notebooks.

"I'm tired. I'm going to go lie down for a bit." She headed for the stairs. Without turning around, she added plaintively. "Oh, and of course, I need a new bartender."

Addy shuffled from behind the bar. "Hey, you've got a bartender. Me!"

Mary Catherine waved with the back of her hand but didn't speak or stop her ascent to the upper level.

"Does that mean I got the job?" Addy yelled after her.

Mary Catherine disappeared from view without answering, headed toward her rooms.

Addy faced him and Tobias. "Do you think that was a yes?"

Instead of answering her question, Blaaze asked her baldly, "What are you doing here, Addy?"

She looked down at the bar and began to clean. "Can't a girl come see her big brother without there being an inquisition?"

"No. Because you had to go searching to find me, which means you weren't coming to here, you were running from there. Does Dad know where you are?"

She kept cleaning and didn't look at him.

He sighed deeply. "What'd he do this time?"

"Nothing."

"*Ad-dy*." He dragged out her name in exasperation. She and their father were constantly at odds after mom died when Addy was just a teen.

She stopped her incessant fidgeting and huffed out a breath. "He keeps nagging me to get married. Says it's time I settled down. I'm not ready to settle down, especially since Clint has convinced Dad he's my best option for the settling."

"Clint Meyers?"

She nodded.

Blaaze wracked his brain. "Isn't he—"

"A whole head shorter than me? Yeah, that's the one." She grimaced.

That's not what he'd been about to say.

Tobias chuckled beside him, interrupting his thoughts about Clint.

"It's not funny," Addy scolded him. "A gal likes a man she can look up to, or at least, look straight in the eye. It's tough being a woman as tall as I am when it comes to courtin'. Most men avoid me if they see I'm taller than they are, and the others consider me some exotic challenge they want to try climbing. No, thank you."

Blaaze sympathized with his sister. She was only a few inches shorter than him, which meant she was pushing six feet tall. It had been at least a decade since he'd known her to own a dress of any kind. She preferred pants to anything else, usually jeans with a gun belt on her hip. Since she rode, roped, wrangled, and shot better than most men he knew, she'd need a man of substance to have the gumption to partner up with her.

"I could—" Tobias started to say, with a grin.

"*No.*" Blaaze grabbed his forearm and squeezed hard, shutting off whatever Tobias was about to say. "You couldn't."

He didn't care that the blacksmith was taller than Addy. Pal or not, he wasn't getting anywhere near her, not for romance or whatever else he had in mind.

"Which means," Blaaze said to Addy, not yet releasing Tobias's arm, "Dad's probably out looking for you. Great. Addy, if you bring that man to town, I'm gonna—" He didn't exactly know what he was going to do, but it wouldn't be good.

She walked away before he could think of anything pithy to say. The evening crowd had started to gather, so she went to fill an order at the end of the bar. She shot Tobias a playful wink over her shoulder as she went.

The goofy grin on Tobias's face made Blaaze want to hit him. He settled for releasing the man's arm. "You need to take me seriously."

"Yeah, yeah. Sister. I know." He raised his hands palms out. "I'm keeping my hands to myself, but you can't fault a man for looking. That's a whole lot of fine woman."

Blaaze swiveled on his stool. "Really? Must you?"

"Okay. Okay." He laughed out loud. "In all seriousness, though. You know solving Mary Catherine's liquor situation isn't going to put an end to this. Clanton was clear. He wants this place one way or the other. He's not going to let this go. He's going to use that crooked sheriff to get that gal's place once and for all."

"You know I'm not going to let that happen."

Tobias stood. "I hear what you're saying, but I need you

to think about something. It's great to have the backing of a lethal bounty hunter with a fast gun and all. But sometimes, what the little guy—or in this case, the little gal—needs is some *legal* justice. You took an oath, Lassiter. Quit running from it." He leaned in and dropped his voice for only Blaaze to hear. "More importantly, stop running from what you feel for that woman. Especially when she needs you to step up."

Blaaze watched his friend walk away. The big man called Addy's name and blew her a kiss before exiting the saloon. Addy made as if to catch it. The two of them were going to drive him to distraction.

Thinking about Tobias's words, Blaaze wasn't sure he agreed that Mary Catherine needed him, or even wanted him, to step up. She had Jeremiah Dixon Beauregard *the third* to solve her problems now that the man was in town. He glanced up the steps, wanting to follow her up and check on her. But if he did, he wouldn't be able to leave her untouched, or at all, for the rest of the night.

With Beauregard close by and adamantly claiming their betrothal, Blaaze didn't have the right to continue his liaison with Mary Catherine. Their arrangement no longer seemed appropriate. He'd never been one to poach another man's woman, and he wouldn't start now. He'd thought on what Mary Catherine said about her relationship with the man, but the two of them had unfinished business to resolve. Mary Catherine needed to sort that particular business out on her own.

Slipping off the barstool, he sauntered to his usual table in the back. He'd keep watch over the saloon. No telling what Clanton's next move might be, and Beauregard's money might entice Mary Cate but it wouldn't defend her from the brewery owner and his lemmings.

He settled in his spot and let his gaze travel the entire floor. Addy seemed to have the locals eating out of her hand. He smiled to himself. That gal always could charm the skin off a snake. Satisfied that all was as it should be, he leaned back and thought of the ways he was going to wring Charlie's neck once he found the crook and likely Clanton spy.

Eventually, he glanced once more toward Mary Catherine's rooms. He'd sleep upstairs tonight to be safe, but do his best to stay in his own bed. He just wasn't so sure how successful he'd be at that.

CHAPTER 27

MARY CATHERINE STIRRED FITFULLY in her sleep. Her mind raced. In her half-awake dreams, she watched men come into her saloon, load her liquor into crates, and begin to walk out. The image played over and over. Prodded by an awake mind, her eyes fluttered open to the bleak darkness. She rolled to her side.

If Blaaze had not arrived today, Jake Clanton would have taken her remaining alcohol and much of her furniture. It was becoming a habit with them. Her getting into trouble and Blaaze coming to her rescue. She didn't like that she had somehow become one of those women constantly in need of saving.

She'd been fairly independent for a long time. She wanted to see herself continuing to be independent for an even longer time. Yet somehow here, on the plains of Kansas, she was fast learning independence was a myth. She couldn't truly be independent and get through this life of hard living and even harder adversaries. If she were truthful with herself, she'd waded in way beyond her manageable depth.

Barbara Jean, the sportin' women, Blaaze, and even Tobias, the charming rascal, had done much to keep her from completely failing at this saloon-owner adventure she'd undertaken. If not for them, would she have already given up? She wasn't sure. But she *was* sure that if not for them, she wouldn't have what little success she'd managed till now.

Flopping onto her back, she stared at the ceiling.

Choices. She had choices to make.

Saloon. Jeremiah. Ohio. Blaaze.

Her eyes squeezed shut at the thought of Blaaze. He'd started out as a headache. Actually, he was still a headache. A lithe, gorgeous, seductive headache as dependable and protective as he was ornery and lethal. What did it say about her that she wanted to ignore the ornery and lethal part of him that used to kill people for a living? Or, maybe, still killed people for a living.

She'd seen the look in his eyes when the sheriff had pulled a gun on him today. Their taunting glibness had instantly turned deadly. Killing Sheriff Brennan had definitely crossed his mind. She'd been afraid he'd do it. Pull his gun and shoot. Worse, she'd been afraid his doing so would get him killed by one of the other armed men in the room.

That fear, the fear of watching him die, had been paralyzing. With the paralysis had come a startling realization; she would pine for this man if he were gone. She'd never once felt bereft at the thought of not seeing Jeremiah again. She had missed Jeremiah. She sometimes had wanted to be able to talk to him again. Despite their easy camaraderie and closeness, she'd never felt bereft or anxious over the possibility of separation from him.

He was safe and sure and everything a woman raised like her should want in a husband. That is if she trusted the institution of marriage to allow her to be a whole person and not merely an extension of her spouse. Of course, that had always been the problem. She didn't trust in the combination of marriage and autonomy.

She'd like not to think she was one of those women who were attracted to things bad for her simply because they brought a thrill. But there was no denying that Blaaze—the opposite of safe and sure and socially acceptable—drew her like an unworldly moth to an effusive flame. Her heart didn't care that he represented the opposite of safe and sure and socially acceptable.

Restless now, she sat up and climbed out of bed. In her bare feet, she walked over to her desk, slid open the bottom drawer, and removed a small box of Lila's she'd discovered this morning stashed in a secret panel at the back of the rolltop desk. She hadn't found time to go through all its contents yet. No time like the wide-awake present.

After lighting the desk lantern, she flipped open the attached lid to the wooden box. She peered at the array of items stashed in the box and wondered what sentimentality attached to each. Visible were bundles of letters from Lila's paramour, some pressed flowers, several miscellaneous trinkets, and the edge of what looked like a small bound journal. Mary Catherine extricated the journal. Torn between wanting glimpses of the cousin she hadn't seen since she was fifteen and not wanting to invade what had been Lila's private thoughts, she sat without opening to the pages within.

She stared at the cover until an unbanishable curiosity rose and won out.

Slowly, she opened the journal, and a folded sheet fell to the floor. She bent to retrieve it, noting the heavy texture of the linen sheet. She separated the folds and a single photograph fell into her lap. Stunned, she peered in astonishment first at the creased Kansas certificate of marriage then at the photograph face up in her lap. Lila stood in a pretty dress next to a light-haired, pale-skinned man in churchgoing attire, who smiled up from the print.

Lila had been married to the man she'd run this saloon with, not his mistress. Mary Catherine fell back in her chair. Her cousin had been married.

To a white man.

And she'd kept it a secret.

Mary Catherine wondered if the choice had been a reflection of Lila's rebel nature or out of a sense of caution.

Kansas was one of the few states that didn't have miscegenation laws. But just because interracial marriage wasn't illegal here didn't mean plenty of individuals weren't vehemently opposed to it. The violent border war, which had ensued after the issuance of the Kansas-Nebraska Act in 1854, hadn't ended so long ago. The proslavery and anti-slavery opponents who'd fought over whether the Kansas Territory would enter the Union as a free state or a slave state had waged many a bloody battle. Those we had fought for and believed in the cause for slavery still resided in and around the state.

Gently, she tucked the photograph into the fold of the marriage certificate and slid them back between the pages of the journal. A line on the pages she'd opened caught her eye. Laying the journal flat on the desk, she read the pages before her.

I'm not sure how much longer I'll be around. Clanton's getting restless, and when Clanton gets restless, people start disappearing. He took my Clive. Not directly, but he's responsible. Oh, they say it was bad luck and all, but I know Clanton arranged that shooting. I can't prove it to the law's satisfaction, but I know. And I'm pretty sure I might be next.

I've made arrangements for my cousin Mary Catherine to inherit the saloon Clive and I built. I kind of laugh at the thought of what Mary Catherine will think when she discovers what I've left her. She's the right choice, though. She won't be what Clanton or anyone else in this town expects, but she'll surprise them all.

Between the two of us, she was always the good one. Sometimes I wished I could've been more like her. People assume she's less than she is because she walks with quiet dignity, follows the rules, and plays within the confines of societal dictates. But Mary Catherine has a will of steel. She's strong. Stronger than even she knows, I suspect. Once that girl wants something, there's no turning her from her course. Oh, she'll say all the right things and present herself with deference, but therein lies her power. She knows how to go her own way while making the social mavens think she's following theirs.

I wish I could see her one more time. I've missed her something fierce. Maybe I should have written her, but I didn't want my past, especially my father, to come looking for me. Maybe she'll find this journal when I'm gone and know that I thought of her often. That she inspired me. That knowing she was going to pursue a college education and do something magnificent in the world gave me the courage to reach for big dreams in the open plains where it was okay for me to be all that I am.

If you find this journal one day, my Mary

Catherine, know I love you, and I'm watching from above as you give Jake Clanton hell. He's gonna learn one way or the other that Templeton women are forces to be reckoned with.

A tear plopped on the back of her hand. She rubbed it away and sat back. Clanton had killed to get what he wanted. Killed not once but maybe twice. Her shaking fingers balled into fists before she regained her composure and sat the journal aside.

The discovery that Lila had admired her warmed the center of Mary Catherine's chest, even if that admiration may have been misplaced. A will of steel seemed overstated as it pertained to her. Lila had more faith in her than she had in herself.

A glint of metal flashed from the bottom of Lila's box. Reaching in, her fingers caught a chain. She pulled it out and discovered a man's ring strung from its length. The ring dangled in spirals before her eyes, a wedding ring. Proof that Lila had had the courage not only to embrace adventure but also to risk her heart, despite the danger.

If what Lila wrote were true, then Clanton truly wasn't done with her. Her resistance might lead him to take drastic—and fatal—measures with her too. That thought sent a totally different feeling piercing through her chest, a feeling of dread so fierce she felt as if the walls were pressing in on her. She closed the lid to the box and pooled the chain with its ring on top of the journal.

The soft creak of floorboards outside her door startled her. She stopped in the process of returning the box to the drawer and listened. Light footfalls continued past her room to the end of the hall. It had to be Blaaze. He'd stayed close.

He'd stayed close to assure her safety no doubt.

She stared at the ring perched atop Lila's journal. The symbol of Lila's courage in seeking a new life for herself stood as testament that going your own way and being your own person could—and did—reap rewards.

Once that girl wants something, there's no turning her from her course.

What Mary Catherine wanted right now was to be encircled by the strong arms of the cowboy who bunked down the hall. She glanced at her closed bedroom door and rose on bare feet. She didn't want to feel alone, not tonight. Nor tomorrow. Or the next day. Not after what she'd been through this afternoon, not after what she'd learned from Lila's journal.

What the next days would bring, she couldn't know, but she could certainly deal with tonight. With the now.

Gathering her courage, she padded down the hall on bare feet. She stood outside Blaaze's bedroom door and pressed the pads of the fingers of her left hand soundlessly against it. She could almost feel his presence shift to her through the closed portal. A need, a desire, pulsed through her. A need so raw it transcended the sexual.

She wanted his body, sure. She wanted a replay of how they'd come together that first time in his barn. Desperate. Uncontained. All passion. No reservations. All walls down between them.

It seemed like weeks ago. Months ago. Years ago. But what she wanted even more than that, she wasn't sure she could name.

When he was around, a sense of calm filled her. The constant voices in her head quieted. The ones that told her to keep busy, to do it right, to do it again.

Don't forget to check one more time.

You have to get this right. You have to do this right.

No mistakes.

No failure.

Don't give them a reason to doubt you.

All those mantras grew quieter when she looked into his eyes. When she looked at him. They grew even quieter when he touched her.

The simple words he'd uttered the other night were more powerful than he or anyone could possibly know. She'd fought against accepting them at the time, but her resistance had been hard to maintain in the presence of his handsome face and chiding mouth.

"*. . . you don't have to take on everything by yourself,*" he'd said.

But . . . But . . . But!

She'd been taking on everything by herself for a while. Even in her younger years, when her parents had been alive, she'd tended to stay separate, alone, autonomous. Not intentionally. Not on purpose. But that burden sat on her shoulders nonetheless. Now that she'd taken conscious note of its presence, the burden felt unbearably heavy.

Taking a deep breath, she lifted the key in her other hand. As quietly as she could, she slid it into the keyhole. She gave it a slow turn and pushed the door open a sliver. Holding her breath, she eased by inches through the small opening. The cock of a gun hammer startled a gasp from her lips, and she went still.

"Dammit, woman!" The deep, quiet curse came out through gritted teeth. "Mary Catherine Templeton, are you trying to get yourself shot?" Blaaze wiped a hand down his face. Bending his elbow, he pointed his gun towards the ceiling and released the hammer.

Relief shot through her. "I-I'm sorry." She started towards him. "I didn't think you'd—"

"No!" He threw up his other hand palm facing out and sat up fully from his half-reclined position. "Stay right where you are."

She stopped immediately, disappointment racing through her. "Why?"

He gave a harsh grunt in response. "*Why? Really?*" He placed his gun on the bedside table. With a sharp edge to his voice, he asked his own question. "Where's your fiancé?"

I don't have a fiancé, she wanted to scream. Not that the two men in her life would listen to her. She took a small step toward the bed. "Jeremiah, went back to Beulah's."

Her eyes had adjusted to the low light spilling into the room courtesy of the open blinds bracketing his bedroom window. He sat bare-chested before her, and her eyes hungered over the glorious muscles of his chest. The chest she wanted to throw herself against. The chest she wanted to rub herself against.

She stepped closer to the bed. Blaaze watched her with a frown. He watched her, but he wasn't looking at her face. His gaze raked over her. She glanced down to see that the sliver of moonlight filtering through the window glowed against the whiteness of her nightdress. The outline of her naked body showed beneath the gossamer fabric. When she glanced back up, he'd pressed his eyes closed and fisted one-handed the sheets bunched low across his lap.

"We can't do this Mary Catherine." His voice was a hushed rasp. "You need to go back to your room. Whatever you need to work out with Jeremiah, you need to work it out without me in the middle."

Chapter 28

MARY CATHERINE STRUGGLED TO keep her composure. She couldn't bear to go back to her room. To go back to that room and be all alone with her thoughts.

Alone with the press of obligations she owed a man who'd come looking for her here in Lawless.

Alone with the press of what to do with her feelings for this man from Lawless who had shown her why she should never settle for an arranged relationship that lacked the passion he made her feel.

No matter Blaaze's insistence that she didn't belong here, that she didn't belong with him, their differing backgrounds didn't matter to her heart.

She stood by the bed close enough now to see the hunger beneath the annoyance she'd heard in his voice. That hunger and annoyance were coupled with something else. Perhaps, uneasiness?

But that didn't make sense. This self-assured, powerful, deadly man didn't become ill at ease. Ever. Especially not because of her. And he'd certainly never show it if he did.

A stirring beneath the sheet across his lap lulled her gaze downwards. She tilted her head in contemplation. Despite his outward behavior, he clearly had not become immune to the unfathomable pull between them.

"Don't concern yourself with that none. I've made a commitment to myself that I'm not touching you again. And you coming in here with barely anything on isn't going to change that." His face took on its familiar stoic mien.

He dropped his other hand to the sheet and fisted the top edge near his hip as if afraid leaving his hand free might tempt him to reach for her. Or, as if she might make a grab for it and divest him of his cover. She almost laughed at the absurd thought, except a part of her half wanted to try it. If him being bare to her gaze might drive him wild enough to let her stay, it might be worth the effort. But fighting over a sheet was foolishness, and she had come prepared to ask for what she wanted.

"Don't send me away, Blaaze. I—" Her voice broke, and she turned away from him. She didn't mean to beg. She didn't want to beg. She didn't want his arms around her solely out of pity.

The soft brush of strong male fingers wrapped around her wrist. Blaaze gently pulled her back around. With a concessionary sigh, he tugged her onto his lap and tucked her under his chin.

Whispering into her hair, he said, "You're so strong-willed, Mary Cate, I sometimes forget about the soft and sweet and vulnerable woman trapped inside that you don't like to let others see. What's wrong, sugar?"

"He killed her, Blaaze. I think Clanton may have killed Lila." Tears burst from her, and for the first time in her life, she didn't care if someone saw her cry.

"Shh," he crooned. "It'll be all right."

She shook her head, tears falling in earnest now, then told him about what she'd read in Lila's diary.

He pulled her down against his chest, the sheet still covering his lower half, and she told him about the hardships that had led her here. She told him about all her hopes and the accompanying doubts she'd had on her journey to Lawless, about the family home she could no longer pay for and might lose. She told him about her fears.

When she was finished, he simply held her pressed protectively against him and let her tears dry on their own. They didn't speak. His heart beat strong and steady beneath her ear, reminding her how much she wanted that heart to beat for her. Her fingers brushed lightly against the ridge of one pectoral, and she inhaled the scent of him—the allure of warm male skin beneath a hint of bar soap mixed with an overlay of fresh, outdoor air. Intoxicated, she turned her head and brushed a kiss against his chest.

He tensed. Then he raised a hand to the back of her head. His large palm brushed softly along the thick braid she'd plaited down her back for bedtime. He gave it a soft pull and made her head lift so she could look at him. "Mary Catherine, as much as I want you right now, I'm not one to encroach on another man's woman."

"I told you I don't—"

"Yeah, I know. You don't have a fiancé. And maybe *you* don't, but the man I saw today thinks he still does. Or maybe he simply hopes he does. Either way, from the look in his eyes, he still wants you to be his wife. He didn't hesitate to hand you his wallet and offer you every dollar in it to take care of Clanton. A man doesn't do that for just any woman. Mr.

Beauregard *the third*—"

Her brows rose at his trite enunciation of the regnal numbers for Jeremiah's name, which caused him to pause. She placed her chin on the back of her hand and shook her head.

He simply shrugged with a wry almost-grin and continued. "Mr. Beauregard would gladly take you back to Cleveland and take care of you. Take you back to where Clanton wouldn't be an issue. Where you'd be out of reach and safe. Why stay here after what you've learned? With all the danger you now understand awaits you? There's no shame in choosing survival over this place."

Resting her profile back on his chest, she let out a quiet breath. "Of course, I want to be safe, but I don't want to give up who I am to do it. I shouldn't have to. I shouldn't have to get married and become the extension of a man as my only life choice. No ownership of my own property. No control over my own money. No employment outside the home. I should be able to work at a bank if that's my choice. Or run a saloon here. What *I* want should matter. What I have or earn should get to be mine. Bad men should behave."

A skeptical grunt came from him. "Sugar, you're gonna be waiting a long time for bad men to behave."

Her lips curved wistfully at that. Yes, she knew that. Couldn't blame a woman for wishing, though.

The hand of the arm behind her back found her neck and his fingers played in the short curls at her nape. Her hand trailed along the contours of his abdomen then back up. Finding the bump of a male nipple, she rubbed the pad of her forefinger atop it. Intrigued when it began to plump, she shifted so she could reach his other nipple, unconsciously drawing her knee up across his thigh and brushing a stiff rod beneath the sheet.

Blaaze's breath hitched. He trapped her hand flat against his chest and swatted her butt with the hand that had been fondling her hair. "Be still," he grumbled. "If you're going to stay, you need to behave."

"No," she whispered. She didn't want to behave. And she was definitely staying.

"No?" He almost choked on the word in his surprise.

She pushed up and hesitated only a moment before adjusting her legs to straddle him. The sheet kept their naked skin from touching, but she ground against the long, thick erection beneath her. He may have promised himself he wouldn't touch her, but she'd never promised she wouldn't touch him.

Encouraged by his labored breathing, she leaned forward and took his face between her palms. "No," she repeated quietly, decisively, and dropped her lips to his.

He turned his head away. "Mary Catherine, you're scared."

"Yes." She kissed him again.

He groaned when her tongue pressed into his mouth, and he pulled away from her a second time. Gently he placed his palms at her shoulders and looked deep into her eyes. "Sweetheart, this is not what you really want. You're scared and not sure of your place right now. And you want me to make you feel better."

"Yes." She undulated her hips against him, feeling every bit of his aroused length. The pleasure building between her thighs left a damp trail on the bedsheet that covered him, and she became more determined than ever to change his mind.

He groaned, his hands now at her hips. "Not like this, Mary Catherine. You don't really want me. You just want a distraction. To maybe not think about your troubles for a while."

This time, she leaned down and wrapped her arms tightly around his neck. Continuing to grind against him, she confessed, "Yes, I want to feel safe, and I want to feel better. I want you to make me feel better. Because more than I want to feel safe, I want you."

A sound of frustration rumbled through his chest. Pressing her advantage, she took his lips with hers and kissed him deeply. His manhood twitched beneath her. Sprawled fully atop his solid, strong body, she reveled in the signs of his desire for her. The signs he couldn't shield or control even if he wanted to.

The anxiousness that had driven her here receded in ripples. When the specter of morning dawned, she'd still have to face whatever trials were yet to come, but she'd face them with the same force of single-minded resolve she intended to take her pleasure tonight. The pleasure, the source of sensual gratification, she could find with only one man. The man who laid beneath her fighting to resist himself as much as her.

Understanding he held back out of some misplaced sense of honor, she grasped the edge of the sheet underneath her. His eyes tracked her hand movement, but he didn't try to stop her this time.

She waited for his gaze to come back to hers. "You don't need to protect me from myself. From you. What I want should matter. Remember?"

His hands dropped to the backs of her thighs. He gave them a brief squeeze before he slid his fingers to the edge of her nightdress and dragged the garment up her legs to her waist. Their gazes met again. She pushed upright and removed the sheet from between them so they were skin to skin. With a deliberate roll of her hips, she rubbed her throbbing center against his naked erection.

A half croon half growl spilled from him as her essence coated his pulsing hardness, and finally, his control snapped.

~

Sitting up, Blaaze wrapped both arms around Mary Catherine and held her tight against his chest. He canted his hips beneath her, pulling her along the length of him from root to tip. The exquisite pressure of her full weight against his swollen cock felt like heaven. She covered him, surrounded him, made him want this for himself every night.

Increasing the pace, he encouraged, "Move with me, Mary Cate."

Without hesitation, she took up his rhythm, her hips rocking above his in this intimate, seated dance. The tip of him slipped inside her, but he held himself back and teased slowly out of that luscious heat. Taking himself in hand, he pressed that tip, coated in her slickness, against the swollen ball of pleasure at her center and rubbed.

Her head rolled back, and she released a slow, euphoric moan. "Aaaaahh!" Choking off a whimper, she grabbed his shoulders. Her nails bit into his skin, and her hips bucked.

He grinded against her core in a steady rhythm until her croons of pleasure became cries for more. His thumb took over for his cockhead and slid up and around her pearl of nerves. She became frantic in her need, and the urge to fill her near shattered his intent to draw out this play for her sole pleasure. He worked his thumb with deliberate slowness down the folds of her womanhood before dipping the digit inside. She purred in satisfaction but arched forward searching for a fullness his lone thumb couldn't provide.

She went up on her knees, stance wide, in pursuit of the release she needed. "Blaaze, please!"

He teased around her opening before removing his thumb and easing in two middle fingers, his palm up. Seated only to his knuckles, he rolled his wrist twice before pulling out.

A low plaintive whine escaped her, and she reached for his wrist. Squeezing, she begged in a ragged voice, "Don't stop. I need—"

His lips crushed onto hers. He claimed her mouth with a marauding and relentless tongue and thrust his two fingers all the way into the warm, wet depths of her. She cried out against his mouth, and he continued to plunder.

Her lips, her tongue, her slick heat became his only focus, his complete world. His fingers ministered within the moist arousal between her thighs. He pushed deep, filling the room with the sounds of their hunger for one another.

He pumped with abandon. In and out. Again and again. Then slowed to make languid waves against her soft, intimate flesh. When her greedy sounds pushed him too close to the edge, he found the textured sponginess at the front of her internal walls and curved his fingers to concentrate skillfully on the spot.

Mary Catherine jerked and cried out in surprise, her woman's pleasure erupting without warning.

With a wicked hum of satisfaction, Blaaze murmured in her ear, "That's my girl."

He allowed her to ride his fingers to full completion. Kissing her cries of ecstasy from her lips with soft pecks, he withdrew his fingers and gently rubbed her throbbing knob until her climax ebbed. When she went limp against him, he tucked her under his chin and inhaled the luscious scent of the oil she used on her hair, something light and sweet smelling. Content to hold her like this for the rest of the night, he reached for the covers and went to lie back on the bed, but Mary Catherine resisted.

Remaining upright on his lap, she dropped her small hand to wrap around his unspent erection and stroked. Her thumb rolled over his leaking tip, and it took all his self-control not to toss her onto her back and bury himself in her all the way to his balls.

With difficulty, he pulled her hand away. "Mary Cate," he said between gritted teeth, "you have to think about your future. We can't take any more risks in bed. Not when you may be going back home soon."

The glow of contentment left her eyes. "Why do you want me to go away so badly?"

The hurt in her eyes ricocheted and lodged in a painful twist deep inside his chest. Needing to erase that look of rejection, rejection he'd never intended, he lowered his guard and told her the truth. "It's not that I want you to go away." He placed a palm against her cheek. "I don't think this place, or this town, will ever be the same for me without you in it. But I want you—need you—out of harm's way."

What he thought—what he *knew*—but didn't say was, *Being with me might be as dangerous as standing against Jake Clanton.*

"You can keep me safe," she insisted.

"What if—" He broke off, not wanting to bring the reality of who he was into this intimate time between them. Perhaps the last such time they'd ever share. Knowing the truth existed whether they spoke of it or not, he forged ahead with the words that needed to be said. "What if the best way to keep you safe comes down to putting Clanton, or someone else, in a grave? How are you going to feel about my protection then? About being tied to a man who kills?"

Seconds of silence swirled around them.

Finally, she said, "I know what you do, Blaaze. I'm not harboring any ill-conceived notions or girlish fantasies about that." She palmed both sides of his face and looked into his eyes. Lowering her voice, she added, "But I also know who you *are*. And I'm here. I want to be here. Now, let me give you what you just gave me."

Her forehead came to rest against his, and he wanted to believe her. He wanted to believe the look in her eyes that accompanied those words. But maybe he was being selfish. Convincing himself he deserved this last night before she decided a life in Cleveland, a life with Beauregard, was simpler than the risks here. That being alive and safe was worth the tradeoff for the independence she'd been clinging to.

Raising his head and looking into her eyes again, he couldn't deny her. What he saw in those beautiful pools of brown was worth whatever pit of hell would be waiting for him for daring to reach for an angel so radiant, a soul so bright. Whatever happened, wherever she went, he needed the memory of how she felt around him when she clasped his cock with her warm sheath and shuddered around him in the sweetest grip a man could know.

With a head to the back of her head, he pulled her lips to his and drank deep of her kiss. Searing the taste of her onto his tongue, allowing her to seep through his skin, through his senses, into his very being. When her restless hips began their insistent undulations, he released her head and yanked her wrinkled nightdress over her head.

He tossed it aside and dropped his lips to one exposed breast, nipping and licking around the curved fullness. Easing to the darker skin of her aureole, his mouth found a pebbled tip, and he sucked it into his mouth. A flattened tongue laved the jewel over and over.

Blaaze drank in her throaty moans with the taste of her skin, sweet, salty, and distilled with a hint of vanilla. He followed his thirsty tongue with a gentle bite that made her head fall back. He continued until she resumed her restless wriggle on his lap. Giving her no quarter, he held her tighter and moved slowly to the next peaked globe.

He took his time, sucking and nibbling until he could feel her thighs start a steady, innate tremble that indicated her woman's pleasure was close again. Firmly, he bracketed her waist with his hands and lifted. He guided her over his stiff cock and thrust up, piercing through her tight wetness all the way to his root.

With an irrepressible groan at the carnal deliciousness, he asked, "Mary Catherine, do you know how to ride?"

"No." Her voice was breathy and tense with ecstasy.

"Time for your first lesson, my angel."

Lying back on the bed, he directed her to remain upright and planted his hands in the crook where her thighs met her torso. He pulled her forward so her pleasure point grazed along his shaft with her movement.

"Oh yeah, just like that," he said, directing her hips to rock back and forth from the front to the back. "Now, squeeze me with your thighs, sugar."

With hooded eyes, she gave him a mischievous grin. "You sure it's my thighs you want me to squeeze you with?" she asked in a husky voice that nearly made him shoot his seed way before he was ready.

Her pelvic muscles contracted and released around him. Then she did it again, adjusting their tempo as she rode his shaft towards her own fulfillment.

"Mary *Cate* . . ." His voice broke on the last part of her name. God bless an intelligent woman.

Blaaze channeled into the tightness between her heavenly thighs in tandem with her rocking pelvis. Each stroke, each pulsing squeeze, drew his elated cock to its thickest, to its longest, and their pace quickened. They punctuated the horizontal communion with a call and response every bit as joyous, every bit as reverent, as that of any Sunday service.

Her sensual sobs rose in harmony with his own deep, dirty growls of gluttony. In time, his teeth clenched as he sought to prolong the feel of her exquisiteness around him and postpone an oncoming orgasm he still wasn't ready to let erupt.

With effort, he managed to wrangle again the urge to spill his seed and reclaimed his coital self-control. Then he proceeded in earnest to teach Mary Catherine to ride—forward and backward—from an easy canter to a full-on gallop until they were both spent and limp and could no longer move.

CHAPTER 29

BLAAZE AWOKE THE NEXT morning to an empty bed. He ran his hands down his face. He could smell the hint of Mary Catherine in his bed, on his skin. How did a man ever get rid of this feeling?

The feeling that there should be something in his hands, in his arms, that he desperately wants to hold on to, but knowing it'll never be his to hold.

He still couldn't believe she'd come to him in the night.

He'd been unable to fall asleep. As he'd laid wide awake in bed, his senses had prickled. He'd sensed danger coming.

Clanton had gotten bold. To saunter into the saloon in the bright light of day and decide to simply take what he wanted had been a bold play. The brewery owner had basically flaunted his ability to get the sheriff to dance to whatever tune he decided to play.

Already on edge, the scratching sounds at his door had gotten his back up. He'd snatched up his gun instinctively. The sharp female gasp at the cock of his hammer had been all that prevented his finger from fulfilling its pressure against the trigger.

At the thought he'd almost shot his annoying, beautiful, challenge of a woman, he'd had to force down a lump of bile that had risen in his throat. He wiped a hand down his face again.

His.

Who was he kidding? Even after what they'd shared last night, Mary Catherine wasn't his.

Maybe she was no one's if her stance on marrying Beauregard was true.

Not true because she said it out loud, but true because she meant it—truly meant it—in her heart.

He sat up. His bare feet touched the floor, and he sat there, hands beside his bare hips staring at the floor. For the first time in a long time, he heard silence. Not in the saloon, the usual bedlam emanated from downstairs. Silence in his head, silence in his own heart.

To wander the land with the capacity to kill another human without hesitation or remorse was a talent that marked a man. People often thought it didn't affect you. It did. Deeper and harder than any experienced bounty hunter wanted to admit. It was likely why they were mostly quiet loners.

It took something out of you when you watched life drain over and over again because of you. Even the ones you know deserved to die had the power to siphon off a bit of your spirit and chip off a sliver of your soul. Not the worst ones, but enough of them to harden a man.

He'd thought his heart about petrified at this point. No more room at the inn, save for maybe three people: Addy, his pops, and Tobias. His lips canted at the thought of Tobias. He should have listened to the big oaf that first day. He'd warned Blaaze what was coming with Mary Catherine. How he'd seen what Blaaze couldn't on that day, he'd never understand.

He lifted his head. Listening now to identify the sounds so familiar but today grating on his sensitive ears. A few plates clattered. Breakfast was being served to the early risers. Someone clomped bottles behind the bar, likely Addison. Her bartender stint would go over real well when their father came looking for her, and come for her he would.

Uh. His head dropped to his open hands. A sort of fog shifted over him. The haze eerily remnant of the remainder of a good souse.

Was he drunk on Mary Catherine—no, on Mary Cate?

Lifting his head, he chuckled softly at his inane poetic bent. It was the flowery stuff from the tomes of poetry his parents used to share some nights out on the porch under a night sky, whether starry or cloudy. It never seemed to matter which. His mom would sit on his dad's lap and read from one of her favorite books of poetry. His dad would rock them and listen silently for as long as she wanted.

Every once in a while, his dad would take the book she was reading out of her hands, flip the pages, and read a poem back to her. He always chose the same poem. Blaaze and Addy would make faces at each other inside and roll their eyes heavenward at their parents' groan-worthy behavior.

But now he understood. He understood his dad's urge to hold the woman he loved in silent companionship. To sit quietly and enjoy whatever brought a smile to her lips. To hold on to a feeling that wasn't guaranteed to stay forever.

He understood Beauregard's lack of hesitation to hand over his wallet and all that was in it. He'd do the same for Mary Catherine. Hell, he'd give her as much as she needed, as much as she wanted. Everything she needed to pay off her loan and secure her parents' home he'd gladly hand over. More even.

His head tilted back, and he stared at the ceiling. *Okay, Mom, I get it now.*

She'd always told them, as his sister and he had moaned and laughed at her and his father's antics, that one day they'd understand. So she wouldn't bother to explain the why of it in the now.

Last night, when Mary Catherine had slipped into his bed, he'd experienced a peace and calm he hadn't known since the last time his mom had sat by his sickbed in his youth, running her fingers across his forehead and mumbling soft words of comfort. He'd experienced it as if in a dream. The grip of Mary Catherine's body as she took him in deep, the feel of her softness beneath his hands, the smell of her skin surrounding him. It had been euphoric and bittersweet at the same time. He'd gotten the sense they were saying hello for the first time, but they were also saying goodbye.

She'd said she hadn't made a choice between here and Ohio, but the non-decision seemed like a choice to him. Her commitment to Lawless remained unresolved. Her option to return home with Jeremiah left open in case she needed an out.

Leave it to Mary Cate to turn his world upside down again. He'd gone to bed hoping to be a better version of himself, a version that wouldn't take one last time with her just to fill himself up with a memory. Grabbing for himself something stronger than the grim reaper hauntings to keep him company alone on that ranch he'd wanted so badly but now didn't seem so all-fired important.

Standing, he walked over to the washstand and handled

his toilette. Once he'd dressed fully, he packed all his belongings and threw his saddlebags over his shoulder. He wouldn't be coming back here. At least not to this room. At some point, he'd relearn how to sit in this saloon and enjoy his favorite whiskey, maybe a card game or two. But he could never sleep under this roof again, not while Mary Catherine stayed in her rooms down the hall.

His fingers nabbed his Stetson by the crown. He settled it on his head with a long glance in the mirror. He didn't quite recognize himself. Whoever that was staring back at him wasn't the him who'd awoke under Lawless's golden sky yesterday.

Whoever that was had finally learned what it felt like to love a woman.

He'd also found out what it was like to lose her.

The violence he'd lived during his life didn't deserve to be paired with an angel like Mary Catherine Templeton. Even in retirement, he couldn't guarantee the ruthless actions he'd taken across the adjoining states and neighboring territories wouldn't follow him to Lawless. That comeuppance surely awaited somewhere around the corner. It was only a matter of time, and when that time came, he didn't want Mary Catherine anywhere near him or Lawless.

Hell, he'd seen her face in the aftermath of the shooting yesterday, and he hadn't even killed that man. He'd only wounded his hand. Probably wouldn't be the last time Blaaze had to use his gun in defense of self or others. What would she think of him then?

Murderer?

His gun hand flexed and fisted before he reached for the doorknob. The knob turned quietly, and he stepped into the hall. Hanging back from the railing, he spied his sister busy behind the bar with prep for the day. A few railroad workers were at a corner table eating and chatting in Spanish in contained voices.

He'd noticed more and more Mexican workers coming into town for provisions, which suggested Clanton had been right. The railroad was gearing up to lay more track. If the line ended right at the edge of Lawless as Clanton claimed, the town was about to explode. The land, the town accommodations and shops, even the farmers' crops were all about to triple or quadruple in value.

His head swiveled toward the kitchen door when he heard Mary Catherine's melodic voice. She was speaking to Jonas about the dinner menu. Abruptly, she stilled, and her attention swung his way before being pulled immediately toward the open front doors.

Mr. *The Third* strolled into the saloon like *he* was its owner and proprietor.

The man gave Addy an acknowledging nod and made his way over to Mary Catherine. He leaned in and kissed her on the cheek. Blaaze's grip tightened on his saddlebags.

This was something he didn't want to watch.

He headed for the back stairs and left.

~

Mary Catherine accepted Jeremiah's kiss to her cheek with her eyes on the upper landing. Her chest tightened when she saw Blaaze turn and walk away. She'd gotten the strange sense last night that he was making love to her so deeply, so passionately, as his way of saying goodbye.

As their bodies had moved together, she'd found she didn't care.

In the fresh dawn of morning, she found her heart cared an awful lot.

"I thought we could have breakfast together," Jeremiah said with a smile. His face held no trace of the tightness his expression had when he'd left yesterday.

Hopeful she hadn't ruined the friendship they'd always shared, she forced herself to return his smile and tried not to think about the brooding cowboy above. "That would be nice. Why don't you go wait in the parlor? I'll talk to Cook about preparing us something."

It was the first of many mornings with the two of them chatting about her business, what to do about her parents' home, whether she even needed that home since Jeremiah was intent on her making her home with him. They squabbled over her working in the saloon. He eventually let go of his concerns over her owning the establishment, but actually living above it and working within it was a situation Jeremiah thought beneath her status. No surprise that he found her subsidizing a brothel absolutely untenable.

Despite their squabbles and the polarities they faced over her lifestyle choices, Jeremiah refused to leave Lawless without her commitment to follow him back to Cleveland and set a date for a wedding. Mary Catherine found his dedication to her wellbeing endearing, even though she couldn't bring herself to assent to the nuptials he wanted. Her business wasn't her only concern. Her feelings for Blaaze rattled inside her in a confused tumult. She couldn't commit to one man when she had unresolved feelings for another.

Several days passed with Jeremiah and she at an impasse over their relationship. Blaaze made himself scarce around the saloon when Jeremiah was present. He didn't even do his usual skulking over a glass of whiskey at the back table.

He was probably getting his liquor from Tobias. On her excursions outside the saloon, she often spied glimpses of him down at the livery stable. She suspected he was staying close in case Clanton made good on his promise that his bid for the saloon wasn't over.

Blaaze always seemed to be walking away or turned so as to not see her. The first few times, she considered it a coincidence. When things continued that way, she reclassified the incidents to what Blaaze would call an "on-purpose" coincidence.

The thought made her sad. She missed him. She missed him something fierce, but she wasn't going to chase after him. She had too much going on to attempt to alter his perception that who she was didn't make sense for this town or for her being with him. If he was done with her, she'd live with it and focus on what had brought her to this town in the first place.

Luckily, business began to pick up, which helped keep her mind off Blaaze. Tobias sneaked deliveries periodically to the back door during the night. In an odd twist, her clientele seemed to love Tobias's moonshine even better than the whiskey she'd been serving. She wondered what Clanton would think if he knew he'd inadvertently handed her a ticket to profitability.

That weekend, she sat at the rolltop desk in her rooms late into the evening going over the saloon's ledgers. Her income had stabilized with the new, steady flow of customers and the presence of a bartender who wasn't helping herself to unauthorized extra pay. Still dressed, she'd gotten lost in the books of account. As she pondered her next priority, a shrill, female scream shattered the late-night stillness. Her gaze shot to the door at the sound, and her skin pebbled.

A different scream pierced the night right before a door

slammed open. Its loud bang against an adjoining wall made Mary Catherine jump from her chair and inadvertently knock Lila's journal off its spot on her desk. Grabbing it up, she rushed into the hallway.

Two steps out of her room, a mouse scampered over her foot, and she jumped with a screech. A glance over the landing rail showed mice pouring out of two bedrooms on the second level. Several men in various stages of undress attempted to stomp on the rodents, while two of the house ladies squealed and tittered, their hands and feet moving frantically.

A further glance below revealed a perplexed Addison standing behind the bar stoically eyeing two huge rats scurrying atop the scratched surface. The cowgirl grabbed a broom and swatted the pair toward the entrance. By the kitchen door, three more rats frantically gorged on what looked like remnants of one of Macey's pies.

People were rushing everywhere. Some men continued to attack the mini intruders. Other men rushed in horror toward the exit carrying any clothing they didn't need to be decently covered. Total bedlam ruled the saloon, but Mary Catherine managed to make her way downstairs.

Attracted by the shrieks and squeals, people began arriving from the street, including the mayor. Many entered the fray and did their best to contain or banish the infestation. Together, in time, the group managed to get the situation under control. By no means were they able to get all the critters that had mysteriously managed to infiltrate the place, but it was sufficient the saloon didn't have rodents crawling over every surface.

When the crowd finally cleared out, Mary Catherine dropped down on a bar stool and allowed her upper body to flop onto the counter.

Addison approached her, standing on the other side of the bar, and said to the top of her head. "You all right, boss?"

Moaning dramatically and shaking her head from side to side without lifting it, Mary Catherine said into the scuffed wood, "I give up. I absolutely give up." Her words got muffled between the countertop and the fabric of her sleeve. Slowly, she pushed herself to an upright position. "Hand me a bottle of whiskey."

With a skeptical look, Addison grabbed a half-full bottle of whiskey. Remembering her brother's reaction the other day when Mary Catherine had tried to pour herself a drink, the Blaaze lookalike deliberately sat the bottle before Mary Catherine but didn't offer her a glass to pour it in.

As if that was going to stop her, Mary Catherine thought. With a half-pout half-smirk at Lassiter Number Two, Mary Catherine grabbed the bottle with one hand and pulled the cork hard with the other. Her hand shot up wildly as the cork released with a huge pop.

"Ha!" She didn't need a glass. After the day—the week— she'd been through, Mary Catherine would get a drink any way she could.

Addison placed her hand over Mary Catherine's on the bottle. "I don't think this is a good idea."

An odd sense of déjà vu hit Mary Catherine. She'd been through this whole bottle tug-of-war with a Lassiter before. "You know, you're a lot like your brother."

With a choke, Addison released the bottle. "Whoa. You don't have to be mean about it. Go ahead. Have your drink."

Mary Catherine grinned at her reaction. Feeling victorious, she put the bottle to her lips and drank deep without caution. Fire exploded in her throat, and her eyes began to water. She coughed roughly, squeezing her eyes shut to fight the inferno attacking her insides.

Addison's eyebrows rose, and she tucked in her lips in a half-hearted attempt to hide her budding laughter. She dropped a glass of water on the bar and slid it toward Mary Catherine. "Here. Take a drink of this."

With big gulps, Mary Catherine downed the water and soothed her burning throat.

"I think maybe you're not quite ready for straight whiskey," the cowgirl said, making a second attempt to take the whiskey bottle from her.

Mary Catherine avoided the grab. "No, Addison. My place. My whiskey. My choice."

She rose and moved to the end of the bar farthest away from Addison and the door. She'd left Lila's journal tucked behind the bar there while she'd worked with everyone else to evict her unwanted tiny visitors. Continuing to drink from the bottle, she retrieved the journal and laid it on the counter in front of her.

Her first-ever drinking binge proceeded in silence.

Addison slanted a glance her way every once in a while, usually followed by a shake of the cowgirl's head.

Mary Catherine didn't care. She'd been through threats. She'd been through not enough money. She'd been through not enough alcohol. Now she'd been through vermin. *Ick!*

She was done. Enough was enough. A girl could only take so much.

Soon, her head started spinning, and she was finding it difficult to remain steady on her stool. Through blurred vision, the shape of two men materialized coming into the saloon. It kind of looked like Blaaze and Jeremiah.

Walking in together?

That couldn't be happening.

"Oh boy, I musta hav' too much," Mary Catherine slurred. "I'mma seeing things."

Addison walked over and pried the bottle out of Mary Catherine's hand. "Yeah, I bet."

Chapter 30

BLAAZE COULDN'T BELIEVE HIS eyes. Mary Catherine sat at the end of the bar, and she looked absolutely soused.

Jeremiah looked at the bottle Addy had taken from Mary Catherine. "How much was in there?"

"J-Jeremiah?" Mary Catherine stared at him incredulously.

He placed his hand on her back and rubbed. "Yes, Catie, I'm here."

Blaaze tried to remain stoic in the face of Jeremiah's familiarity with Mary Catherine, but his sister's speaking glance let him know he was doing a poor job of it.

"About half," Addy told Jeremiah.

"Half!" Blaaze boomed. "Addy, how could you let her drink half a bottle of whiskey?"

Mary Catherine grinned. "Oh, Blaaze. That is you. You're both here."

Blaaze gave her a curious look. Who else did she think he was? "Yes, Mary Cate, I'm here."

"Uh-oh." She pointed at him. "Mary Cate." Then at

Jeremiah. "Catie." She giggled, finding their battle of pet names entertaining.

His sister snickered, and Mary Catherine began to list sideways. Jeremiah stepped closer to her and used his body to keep the not-so-proper Miss Templeton from toppling over. The man glanced at Blaaze with a disbelieving look on his face. From his expression, neither of them had ever experienced this particular version of Mary Catherine.

"I didn't *let* her do anything, big brother. She was very adamant. This is her place, her whiskey, and her choice." Addy made a big show of wiping her hands against each other. "I serve drinks. I'm not the boss lady's keeper."

Blaaze lifted his hat and scratched his head with the same hand before replacing it. "I heard there was a big commotion. It led to this?" He motioned toward the leaning and noticeably drunk Mary Catherine.

"You missed all the FUN!" Mary Catherine told him with glee, putting growing emphasis on the last three words.

Despite her upbeat tone, Blaaze had to strain to understand her.

"Mice. No, rats. No, mice and rats. Lots of 'em." She giggled again. "It was awful," she added, trying to make a sad face, but she couldn't control her grin.

"Rats?" Jeremiah repeated.

"Yes! Loss and loss of razze."

Unable to understand what Mary Catherine was saying, Jeremiah looked at Addy.

She interpreted. "Lots and lots of rats. The place was swarming with them."

Taking a stool, Blaaze motioned for his sister to pour him a drink. "How did the place get infested with rats?"

"It was *all*-full."

"Yes, Mary Cate, you've said that," Blaaze assured her.

"I'm done for. The place is closed." Mary Catherine accented her last word with a hard slap of a hand against the bar. Her cheek immediately drifted down to the same spot, and a few tendrils of hair fell across her face. She adjusted her head so she could focus on Jeremiah through the waterfall of curls. "Can't have a saloon or a whorehouse when people don't want to stay here. They don't want to eat here." She hiccupped and continued with a sing-song slur. "And they *definitely* don't want to get naked here."

"That's okay, Catie. We'll settle your affairs and head home as soon as possible."

Blaaze exerted so much pressure on his glass he risked shattering it. The selfish man wasn't even going to try and talk her out of throwing away her inheritance, her route to independence. Of course, the best option for Mary Catherine's wherewithal was, in plumb fact, to leave town. Didn't mean Beauregard couldn't show some concern, even as a pretense, for how she'd feel about what she'd have to give up.

Mary Catherine reached for Jeremiah's hand on the bar beside her. "That's sweet of you, Jeremiah. But you don't want to get naked here either."

Jeremiah flustered. "Uh . . . what?"

"You know, that day at your parents' house. You didn't want me. Why didn't you want to get naked with me? Blaaze wanted to get naked with me. Didn't you, Blaaze?"

Blaaze coughed his drink out onto the bar. Wiping his mouth with the back of his hand, he sat impassively in the face of her fiancé's angry stare.

"This isn't the place for this conversation, Mary Catherine," Jeremiah said to her but kept his angry eyes on

Blaaze.

"It's not?" Her brow puckered.

"No." Jeremiah used two fingers to gently push the fall of hair away from her eyes and said softly, "And it's not that I didn't want you, sweetheart. I was trying to be a gentleman." His piercing gaze moved back to Blaaze. "Unlike some other people it would seem."

He took a step toward Blaaze but glanced at his gun belt and stopped.

"I can take it off," Blaaze drawled and stood up, reaching for the belt's buckle.

"*Boys*," Addy snapped. "Knock it off. She may be drunk, but you know she wouldn't tolerate you going at each other like two cocks fighting over a hen." She glared at Blaaze. "Sit *down*."

Addy waited for him to retake his seat then approached Mary Catherine.

"Okay, Miss Mary, I think you've said enough. Time for you to retire for the night." Addy pulled her off the stool before the roostered miss could say anything else incriminating.

Mary Catherine wobbled on her feet. Blinking at Addy, she said, "I can't stay here. We's didna get 'em all."

Blaaze didn't know whether Mary Catherine's blinking was to bring Addison into focus or because she was on the verge of passing out. Either way, she definitely needed to be put to bed somewhere. She was right; she couldn't stay here. He looked across the floor to where a large rat scampered for a corner.

Without a place of his own to offer her, the options were Miss Eileen's or Beulah's. Miss Eileen probably wouldn't take her now that Mary Catherine was connected to the saloon and brothel. And Blaaze didn't like the idea of her going with Jeremiah to Beulah's. Blaaze had no standing to object, however. The man was her fiancé or former fiancé or maybe just her next lover. Whatever he was, he now had the perfect opportunity to be alone with her . . . all night.

"Come on, Catie. I'll take you back to Beulah's with me," Jeremiah said.

He slipped his hand around Mary Catherine's waist, and she didn't resist. The easterner slid Blaaze a highbrow look of triumph before he led her outside. He helped her into the wagon he'd pulled up in at the same time Blaaze had arrived on Scout.

Blaaze turned away. When he heard the pair drive off, he grabbed his half-empty glass of whiskey off the bar and threw it against the back wall. It shattered into dozens of pieces and left a giant wet spot in its wake dripping rivulets of eighty-proof tears.

Ignoring the alcohol on his sleeve and the feel of his sister's watchful gaze, Blaaze walked out without saying a word. He mounted Scout and turned the stallion toward home. When he reached the edge of his land, he stared at the framed house easing into view.

The number of rooms framed out had increased from his original plan. He'd not consciously thought to build it with a woman in mind, but its larger than necessary floorplan for a single man stood like a mocking monument to a relationship he kept telling himself he didn't want and didn't need. Right now, the thought that he could exist with Mary Catherine living someplace other than under the same Kansas sky— under the same Kansas roof—pricked at him like the lie it was.

Not wanting to look at the symbol of his foolishness any

longer than he had to, he steered Scout into the barn without dismounting. He unsaddled and brushed down Scout before crawling onto the pallet he kept under the barn loft. He tossed one way then the other. His mind filled with images of Mary Catherine alone and naked with Jeremiah in his room at Beulah's. The thought of what they might be doing together haunted him.

In her inebriated condition, Mary Catherine was likely in no state to get romantic with the man. But Blaaze remembered the look in Jeremiah's eyes, the one that said he understood he'd made a mistake by letting his chance to be intimate with Mary Catherine pass. He'd been a gentleman, as he said.

Gentleman, my ass, Blaaze thought.

He was damn sure the man had no intention of being much of a gentleman tonight or, more likely, in the morning when Mary Catherine had sobered up. Jeremiah Dixon Beauregard *the third* had a clear path to remedy his prior blunder.

Unnerved, Blaaze dozed off with that thought stampeding through his mind. It wasn't long before the sound of the soft moans Mary Catherine made before she came rattled him awake. He could see her face beautifully contorted with pleasure.

Was she making that face now for Beauregard?

Was she making that face now for Beauregard but thinking 'bout him?

Flopping onto his stomach, he punched the blanket-covered straw beneath his head. The action did little to drown out her voice, or her face, or her naked body in his mind. All freely being given to Beauregard. Blaaze struck the pallet again. Then again. And again. He roared in frustration at the inadequate remedy for his waking nightmare.

He jerked upright with a howl so raw and anguished it made Scout rear in his stall.

He'd get no rest tonight without a little help. He stormed to the secret compartment beneath the floor in the back corner of the barn and removed one of the jars of Tobias's moonshine he kept stashed there. He could hear Tobias's voice warning him to take it easy, but he wasn't in an easygoing mood.

When he'd chugged nearly half the jar, he stalked out of the barn, moonshine still in hand, and grabbed up a hammer from the worktable that stayed outside. He kept moving until he stood before the wooden frame with gaping beams awaiting the promise of walls. He threw back another long swig of the jar juice then stomped up the front steps of his future house.

Putting all his frustrations in the swing of a hammer, he whacked the beam closest to him. Then he did it again. The feeling of fleeting satisfaction it gave was enough to pull him deeper into his destructive mood.

Alternating between drinking and bashing beams, he continued until he'd torn down the entire east side of the framing. When the moonshine ran out, he went for another jar. His actions became rote, and he lost all sense of time or thought. Mary Catherine's moans blissfully retreated, and somewhere amid the detritus of splintered wood, nails, and dust, he passed out.

~

Blaaze awoke the next morning to the feel of something nibbling on his boot. He squinted open his eyes but immediately shut them against the bright sun beating down through the roofless opening of a carpentry mess. He rolled his pounding head and glanced through the broken beams standing shadowy in the rising sun. His head throbbed, a gift from the jars of liquor he'd drowned his sorrows in last night.

The nibble at his boot came again along with an annoyed chuff. Tilting his head up, Blaaze saw Scout examining his footwear and pant cuffs as if to determine whether Blaaze were still a part of the living. Blaaze sat up and shook his foot to ward off the equine pest. He needed coffee—*strong* coffee—and a dip in the cold creek a few acres past where he planned to lay in a few crops.

After a bath and several cups of coffee, Blaaze leaned against the barn and stared at the mess that could have been his and Mary Catherine's house. He was on his fourth cup. His headache was receding, and as his whiskey haze cleared, he considered what an idiotic thing he'd done. And he wasn't only thinking about the house.

He'd let that man walk away with his woman. He'd basically given her away. He hadn't even put up a fight, hadn't bothered to tell her how he felt, and hadn't thought to tell her he'd been wrong and wanted her to stay.

He stood up straight.

He had time to fix that.

The realization made him toss the coffee remaining in his cup and saddle Scout. He needed to get to Beulah's before he was too late. He didn't care what might have happened between Beauregard and Mary Cate last night . . . or this morning. All that mattered was she give him a chance.

He rode hard to town. The closer he got, he noticed a mist of smoke rising in the distance beyond the livery stable. Men scurried to mounts and hastened toward whatever was on fire. Wasn't much out that way. It didn't look far enough out to be Clanton's spread.

As his brain made a terrifying connection, he heard someone shout, "Beulah's place is on fire!"

He urged Scout to go faster before a name completely formed in his thoughts. The name of the only person who mattered to him in this moment. *Mary Catherine!*

When he reached Beulah's, the place was almost completely engulfed in flames. The men had stopped trying to douse it with buckets of water. The boarding house couldn't be saved. Additional efforts would have meant nothing.

He swung down from his horse and found Addy in the crowd. "How'd this start?"

"No one knows." Addy looked over to where Beulah sat hugging herself, her face smudged with soot and her morning dress singed. "Poor Beulah."

Blaaze grabbed Addy's shoulders. "Mary Catherine?"

She gave him a sad look. "I haven't seen her."

Frantically, Blaaze began to look around. Charlotte stood wrapped in a singed shawl staring forlornly at the burning building. If she were in cahoots with Clanton, he doubted she would have been at Beulah's when the fire started. She would have been given a heads-up. Now, she'd need to find yet another place to ply her carnal wares.

Turning from Charlotte, he spied Beauregard hunched over his knees heaving in big gulps of air. Blaaze charged over to the man with Addy on his heels. "Beauregard, where's Mary Catherine?"

The man looked up with a stricken face. "I don't know."

"You don't . . . know?" Blaaze whipped his face toward the inferno. *No!* his brain screamed. He was moving before he consciously thought to make a step.

Beauregard's hand grabbed for him. "She's not in there, man."

Averting the man's grip, Blaaze started to run.

Addy charged after him and wrapped her arms around him. "Blaaze, stop. He said she's not in there."

He shook her off and ran for what was left of the boarding house. "I have to be sure."

"No! Stop!" Blaaze heard the panic in his sister's voice, but he couldn't stop.

Oomph. He hit the ground hard, tackled from behind. Pain seared his side, but he immediately rolled to struggle off the bull of a man who had rammed into him. The sneak attack gave the hombre an advantage, and he managed to sit on Blaaze's chest.

Looking up, he stared into the face of Jeremiah Beauregard.

The man pinned Blaaze's arms to the ground beside his head and yelled at him, "She's not in there, Lassiter. I checked. Everywhere. Everywhere she could possibly be."

Blaaze tried to buck him off. They were close to the same weight and size, so he only managed to shift the man's girth not free himself.

In frustration, Beauregard gave Blaaze's arms a quick upward yank and slam to the ground. "Think, man. Do you really believe I'd be out here if there was a chance Mary Catherine was still in there? Whatever you think of me, if there was any possibility at all that Catie was still inside those burning walls, I would be too."

The raw anguish in the man's voice got through to Blaaze. Beauregard's singed clothing and blackened hands attested to time spent searching through charred bric-a-brac. Blaaze went limp with momentary relief.

Waiting a second to make sure Blaaze wasn't about to renew his charge into the burning building, Beauregard eventually rolled off him into a seated position.

Blaaze sat up. "If she's not in there, then where is she?"

Beauregard shook his head. "I wish I knew."

Beulah appeared beside Blaaze. "This is Clanton's doing. I know it. I thought we had a deal to partner up, but he wanted it all. He got tired of me refusing to let him buy me out. So he decided to burn me out. The monster."

Rising, Blaaze gently gripped Beulah by the shoulders. "You sure, Beulah?"

"I'm sure. He's told me more than once I'd be sorry." She waved a hand towards the flames waning as the beams and cinders it fed on got completely consumed. A tear trickled down her cheek. "This is him making me sorry."

The town barber came over. "I did see them two boys who always do Clanton's dirty work riding the other way when we were heading toward the fire."

Blaaze watched another tear trail down Beulah's cheek before he released her and made a slow turn to observe the destruction around him. Beulah's boarders were in various stages of dress. Women cried over cherished belongings lost to the blaze. Couples hugged, simply glad they'd both made it out alive. If Clanton had done this and also taken Mary Catherine, he'd taken things a might too far.

With a determined step, Blaaze headed for his horse.

Beauregard jumped up and followed. "Where are you going?"

"If Clanton's taken Mary Catherine, I know where she is. I'm going after her." He rifled through his saddlebag, removed the small pouch he'd taken from his barn this morning, and pinned on the silver star it held.

The surprised look on Beauregard's face would have made Blaaze laugh if he wasn't so worried for Mary Catherine's safety.

"I'm going with you." Beauregard took another look at the silver star. "Marshal."

"No, you're not." Blaaze swung up onto his horse.

Beauregard grabbed hold of his reins. "I know how to use a gun, Lassiter."

"You know how to use a gun to solve problems the city way. We do things a little different out here."

"She means just as much to me," Beauregard insisted.

Blaaze stared down at him, pondering. "You pack quite a wallop for a businessman."

Scout turned his head towards Beauregard to check out the fella holding his reins.

Beauregard rubbed the stallion's snout and looked up at Blaaze with a dash of amusement behind eyes in an otherwise somber face. "I didn't start as a businessman. I started in my father's warehouse moving and loading tubes of rolled fabric and other materials. Every once in a while, I still help out in the warehouse. When you haul that kind of weight around most of your life, you tend to build up a little strength."

That explained a lot. The man didn't simply sit behind a desk and give orders. He wasn't afraid to get his hands dirty. Maybe he deserved more credit than Blaaze had given him. His money, high-end clothes, and family legacy didn't define the whole of who he was. But that didn't totally account for his behavior earlier.

Propping an arm on the saddle horn, Blaaze canted towards him. "Why'd you stop me from running into that fire, Beauregard?"

The man released Scout's reins and slipped his hands into the pockets of his dirty pants. "I understood the impulse, but I couldn't let you die trying to save a woman I knew wasn't in there." Holding Blaaze's gaze, he added, "Make no mistake, I still expect her to choose me when we find her. But I want her to choose me, not settle for me because you're not around. Allowing you to uselessly charge to your death served no purpose. I don't want to compete with the memory of a martyr."

Blaaze took up the reins and made Scout spin to face the opposite direction. "Me either," he replied pointedly. "When it comes to facing down outlaws and gunmen, this one you best leave to me."

A silent message passed between them before Beauregard said earnestly, "Bring her back."

"Only one thing will keep me from it." Blaaze kicked Scout into a gallop.

"Blaaze!" His sister lunged forward, understanding what he wasn't saying.

Tobias, having come from around the back of the smoldering building, grabbed her from behind securely around the arms and, lifting her off her feet, snatched her out of the path of Scout's hind hooves.

Intent on a mission he never thought he'd have to undertake again, Blaaze would start by trying to do this the honorable way. But if that didn't work, then he'd revert to his old ways. He'd go hunting. And this time, there was no bounty involved.

It didn't matter, though.

No amount of money would entice him to keep Clanton alive if any harm had come to Mary Catherine. Clanton and his men had been running roughshod over the townsfolks long enough. It was time to see what they'd do when they had to deal with someone who knew how to play just as dirty.

He had one stop to make before he headed to the hideout Clanton kept for his henchmen. He needed to retrieve a few items from Tobias's tack room.

His sister had said he'd used Tobias's abandoned spurs to make an entrance that day at the saloon.

He hadn't really thought about it that way at the time.

But this time, he did intend to make a statement with his entrance. And he wanted Clanton and his men to hear death coming.

CHAPTER 31

MARY CATHERINE SAT ON a pile of hay in a corner of the makeshift shanty that housed Jake Clanton's liquor still. For the most part they'd simply ignored her, leaving her to think up on her own all the horrible things they might do to her. She'd asked Clanton directly if he'd been responsible for Lila's and Clive's deaths. The arrogant fiend hadn't bothered to deny it.

She suspected the man intended to have her killed as well. He claimed he'd simply wanted to talk to her somewhere away from those he considered bad influences on her ability to be reasonable about his proposition. With his big plans for the town, which he intended to rename Clanton, Kansas, she didn't buy it. She'd already refused to sign over the deed to the saloon, and he hadn't bothered to push.

They were waiting for something. Something that had to do with her and, given some whispers she'd overheard, something to do with Blaaze. To keep her mind from wandering to morbid thoughts, she passed the time by rereading several entries in Lila's journal. Turning to the page she'd first read, she took in the words again, focusing particularly on the last paragraph.

> *If you find this journal one day, my Mary Catherine,*
> *know I love you, and I'm watching from above as you*
> *give Jake Clanton hell. He's gonna learn one way or the*
> *other that Templeton women are forces to be reckoned*
> *with.*

Mary Catherine wiped a stray tear from the corner of her eye.

You inspired me, too, Lila. And I tried. I really tried, she thought, hoping Lila could indeed hear her from above.

She closed the book and looked up when she heard shuffling outside. The two men keeping watch over her lifted their heads from their card game.

"You hear that?" one of them asked the other.

Mary Catherine strained to hear what he might have heard. Then a faint jangle sounded. *Spurs.*

She sprang to her feet. *Blaaze?*

Clanton's son ran in from outside and peeked back the way he'd come. "He's coming!" he said in an awed half whisper.

Jake Clanton appeared from somewhere around back, Charlie Wheaton at his side. When Charlie caught sight of Mary Catherine, he smirked at her. He'd been the one to lure her outside at Beulah's this morning, claiming he wanted to apologize and he had some information about Mr. Clanton.

She met his smirk with a steady glare. After a few minutes, his smirk faltered at the edges, and he purposely looked away from her.

"He's coming!" Clanton's son repeated. "I told you he'd come if we took her, Pa. I told you!"

Clanton motioned to the man whose hand Blaaze had shot to bring her along.

The man yanked her forward and stopped near the entry with the others.

They all stood inside watching a tall specter in the distance walk a slow, straight line toward them. Dust spiraled at his feet, and he was dressed much like he'd been the first time Mary Catherine had seen him, all dark. Dark denims, dark shirt, long dark duster, and dark Stetson pulled so low over his eyes his face was nothing but shadow.

His spurs jangled in an ominous, steady syncopation with each deliberate step he took. *Thud-clink. Thud-clink.*

A shiver rippled through the man holding her.

Thud-clink. Thud-clink.

If Satan were from Kansas, he'd look exactly like the lone figure bearing down on them with hands loose at his sides and an exposed gun holster taunting from the tucked back fall of a midnight duster.

Thud-clink. Thud-clink.

When he was a few feet from the entrance, Clanton yelled, "That's far enough, Lassiter. Stay right there."

For a few seconds, Blaaze stopped. Mary Catherine sensed his gaze sweep over her though she couldn't actually see his eyes. Finding or not finding whatever he was looking for, he resumed his slow approach. All the hired hands glanced nervously at Clanton. They all held guns and Clanton didn't, but he wielded the power in this clan.

Clanton motioned to her captor and said to his man, "Give him some incentive to listen to me."

Mary Catherine was yanked forward, and the press of a gun barrel wedged against her temple. Her pulse spiked and her unease mounted, but she refused to give these miscreants the satisfaction of hearing her cry out.

"Don't move, Lassiter, or I'll blow her head off," her captor yelled.

Blaaze stared at the gun pointed at her head and flexed the fingers next to his holster, but he continued to advance for several more steps before he stopped. "No. You won't. 'Cuz in the time it takes you to shoot her, I'll shoot you." His voice came out in a deep, unrushed rumble that rasped over them in an eerie chill. "So you'd both be dead. You sure it's worth it?"

The grit in Blaaze's voice made her captor shiver again. The idiot seemed to think about Blaaze's words then his gaze darted to Clanton for help.

"Don't worry about it none, Zeke. He's bluffing," Clanton assured him. "He likes that gal too much to risk any chance of her getting hurt." He laughed mockingly. "Or getting dead."

As immobile and imposing as the marble cast of Michelangelo's Hercules, Blaaze drawled, "What I'd like, Clanton, is to send you to hell."

Clanton walked toward him. "I'm sure you'd like to, but you won't. I see that glint of silver on your chest. I'd heard rumors you were a US deputy marshal. Huh! Seems the rumors are true." He stopped a safe distance from Blaaze's reach. "You can't just shoot me like you could if you were still a bounty hunter. Not a smart move on your part, Lassiter. Taking a lawman's oath. That star on your chest means you're honor bound to take me before a judge."

Blaaze's fingers flexed again. "That oath is the only reason y'all aren't already dead. I'm gonna act all marshal-like and give you boys the chance to throw down your weapons and surrender. I'll be nice and arrest you. Y'all do that, and I'll take you before a judge."

Zeke pulled Mary Catherine back a ways, bumping her temple with the weapon he had on her. She made a faint, unconscious sound of distress, which made Blaaze's head move a fraction.

Clanton recaptured his attention. "Since that's not going to happen, *marshal*, you might as well drop your gun right now."

"That's not going to happen either." Blaaze rested his hand on the butt of his gun.

"Ha!" Clanton scoffed. "It'll happen and more. I lured you out here to give you a chance to convince this gal to take my money and run on back east where she belongs. And to tell you to get right along with her. I've got plans for that saloon and this here town, Lassiter, and you've both been a fly in my ointment long enough."

Blaaze didn't respond. He stood his ground, quietly watching the posturing man.

"You hear me? Y'all need to *get*. You've stirred up enough trouble bringing that other marshal into things. Otherwise, I could have simply arranged another accident, and Miss Templeton would've been trouble no more." Clanton snapped his fingers. "But three of the saloon's owners coming to an accidental demise this close in time would have been too much of a coincidence for an out-of-town lawman. Even our accommodating sheriff couldn't have gotten around the questions that would've raised."

"You're gonna have to reevaluate those plans, Clanton. 'Cuz after I kill Zeke for his lack of manners, putting a gun to a lady's head and all, I'm gonna take care of the rest of you. One . . . by . . . one." His head shifted to look at Wheaton. "Hello, Charlie. You planning to die with these fools, or you going to be smart and surrender?"

Without responding, Charlie's gaze darted to Clanton. Clanton merely squinted at the boast. His other man and his son had Blaaze flanked on both sides, but Blaaze didn't show the least bit of concern. Charlie mistook Clanton's bravado as the upper hand and stepped slightly behind the man's left shoulder.

With a *tsk*, Blaaze said, "Wrong choice, Charlie. I think I'll shoot you first just for being plain stupid. Never mind being a thief."

Despite the gun to her head, Mary Catherine couldn't suppress the humored grunt that escaped her at Blaaze's words and Charlie's miffed expression upon being called stupid.

At the sound, Blaaze finally addressed her. "Mary Cate?"

"Yes," she said in a tight voice, trying to sound as composed as he looked.

"You all right, sugar?" He'd lowered his voice to that sultry purr he used only when they were alone together.

Her eyes closed momentarily, then she took a deep breath as she savored his presence. "Yes, I'm all right." She tugged against the grip of her captor, but his hand held firm. "Or at least, I am now that you're here."

She thought she saw Blaaze's lips twitch at her words.

"Glad to hear it, hon. Now, I need you to do something for me."

"Okay." Her gaze focused on the shadow that was his face.

"I need you to make a quick calculation. See, your friend there has made a mistake. The height's not in his favor."

Mary Catherine blinked twice in confusion. *Calculation?*

Her captor jerked her closer to his chest, keeping his gun

at her temple. "Stop with the secret messages, Lassiter. You try anything funny, and I swear I'll shoot her."

The gunman's chin bumped against the back of her head, and sudden understanding dawned. Her mouth dropped open, but she quickly shut it.

"You trust me?" Blaaze asked her.

Jake Clanton shot her a contemplative glance.

She ignored him, keeping her eyes trained solely on Blaaze. "Yes."

"Good. Then I need you to stand real still, sugar. No matter what gets said or done, I need you to stand perfectly still. Don't move an inch. Can you do that for me?"

She nodded her head, then remembered she wasn't supposed to move. So she held herself immobile and replied aloud, "I can." Nerves took hold, but she focused on her breathing, slowing it down to keep from making any anxious movements.

"Zeke," Blaaze said, "I don't understand why you let a lowly coward like Clanton make you do his dirty work. He's going to get you killed."

Zeke turned slightly to look at Clanton who had moved so he wasn't in the direct line of fire. Mary Catherine had no sooner felt the gun separate from her skin than a shot rang out and Zeke's head jerked backward before his limp body dropped to the ground. Three more rapid shots exploded and Zeke's card-playing buddy, Charlie, and Clanton's son were blown off their feet.

"No!" Clanton yelled as he watched his son's body hit the ground. He started to move, but Blaaze's gun aimed squarely at his chest made him stop short. He stared at his son's body for a second or two then straightened his shoulders.

Mary Catherine stared at Blaaze in amazement.

Everything had happened so quickly she hadn't seen his hand move for the first two shots. She felt wetness—what she suspected might be Zeke's blood—drip down her cheek. Tremors rippled through her, but she squeezed her fingers into tight fists and willed herself not to do anything that might distract Blaaze while he had his gun trained on Jake Clanton.

"You're not going to shoot me, Lassiter. Not with your lady friend looking on. What's she going to think about that, huh? She's already watched you gun down four men. Look at her. Zeke's blood fresh on her face. She's plumb scared. Now here I am, unarmed and hands up in surrender." He raised his hands and grinned at his cleverness. "You don't want her to see you gun down an unarmed man. A man you're obliged to arrest. Do you?"

Blaaze directed his gaze at Mary Catherine. His expression was unreadable. Outwardly, he appeared calm, but she could sense his concern over how she might be affected by what happened. Concern over what she might think of him after seeing him take four lives. But his concern was unwarranted. Clanton was wrong about how she felt.

She wasn't scared.

She was angry.

Walking over to where she'd dropped Lila's journal when Zeke had grabbed her to dangle as bait before Blaaze, she wiped her face with her sleeve.

Clanton had the nerve to address her. "Are you listening to what I said, Miss Templeton?"

She swiveled her head to look at the evilness that showed in his crooked grin.

"I know you're upset about your cousin and her beau, but as I told you, that weren't personal." He shrugged. "I didn't want to hurt Lila, things simply got out of hand. But none of that matters now. There's nothing you can do for your cousin. We are where we are. Try to understand. I may have lost this little skirmish, but I'll be back to claim what's mine. Clanton, Kansas ain't done for yet. Frontier justice don't always go as expected." He spread his arms and made a pitiful expression as if saddened by the unreliable state of the justice he'd just described.

"You're right, it doesn't." Blaaze yanked his star from his duster and tossed it on the ground in front of Clanton. "Unfortunately for you, today, I'm all the justice you've got." He raised his gun higher and pointed it at Clanton's forehead.

Clanton's smile faltered. "Now w-wait a minute there, Lassiter. R-remember who you are. Just because you threw that star in the dirt, don't mean you're not still a deputy marshal. You've got responsibilities."

Blaaze cocked the hammer of his pistol. Clanton swallowed noticeably, no longer as sure of himself.

Sensing he'd not be able to deter Blaaze on his own, he appealed to her. "You can't let him shoot an unarmed man. That's out and out murder. Don't matter that he's a lawman. He'll hang for it."

Mary Catherine looked down at Lila's retrieved journal and rubbed a thumb over its cover. "Murder?" She took stock of the dead men scattered around then considered the man whose greedy nature led him to believe he was entitled to do whatever he wanted to whomever he wanted to get everything he wanted. "I don't see any witnesses left to attest to murder."

Clanton snarled at her. "You haven't got the stomach to watch an unarmed man being killed in cold blood or to lie about it. I know it, and he knows it. Why do you think he's hesitated this long? Look at his face. It bothers him that you've seen him kill. Maybe you'll tell yourself Zeke and the others deserved it. But Lassiter's a cold-hearted killer that's what he is. That's what he'll always be. His only possible redemption today is to tie me up and take me in."

She rubbed her temple where the impression of a gun barrel lingered. "Before today, you might have been right about me, Mr. Clanton. But thanks to you, I've learned a few things about frontier life and frontier justice. So you're wrong. You're very wrong about me."

Summoning the will of steel Lila had admired her for, she adjusted to fully face Clanton. "This morning, you had me kidnapped and set fire to another woman's business in a vicious act of greed. You've tried to buy me out by putting me in a bind for money, to ruin my business by cutting off my liquor, and even admitted that you were responsible for trying to scare me out with a swarm of rodents." She shivered at the thought of that. "It almost worked. But I'm still here. I'm still here as the owner of a saloon I only have because you killed my cousin after you killed her husband."

"Her husband?" Clanton repeated in surprise.

Mary Catherine nodded. "Yes. They were legally married. They kept it a secret. And you see, there is something I can do about what happened to them."

Clanton scoffed. "What?"

She stepped over to the brewery owner and picked up Blaaze's badge. Then she walked closer to Blaaze so he could see her face clearly when she said her next words. "Look away."

Her head tilted a tiny, almost imperceptible amount, something Jake Clanton likely didn't notice, but Blaaze did. She could finally see his eyes, and he understood her message. The tension in his body, due to her presence in the face of what he truly needed to do, released.

Content with her choice, she headed for the exit, carrying Blaaze's silver star with her. A star he'd only put on because she'd needed him.

"Wait!" Clanton yelled after her. "You can't leave me with him."

Head held high, she left the barn with only a slight flinch at the sound of a single gunshot.

Chapter 32

BLAAZE HOLSTERED HIS GUN and left the still to find Mary Catherine. He found her standing next to Scout, her arm tucked under the stallion's neck and her face pressed against his shoulder. Blaaze pulled her away and wrapped her in his arms. She came willingly and clung to him.

"Are you all right?" he asked, his face buried in her hair.

She nodded against his chest.

Pressing her gently away from him so he could see her clearly, he raked his gaze over her to determine the truth of that for himself. "They didn't hurt you in any way?"

"No." She met his eyes. "Clanton wanted me to sign the saloon over to him. I wouldn't. I think he thought you'd persuade me to sign when you came and saw you were outnumbered."

He grunted dismissively. "It wouldn't have mattered if you'd signed Mary Cate. He would have killed you—us— anyway. You know that, don't you?"

"Yes. I suspected as much." She tucked her lower lip into her teeth and wrapped her arms around herself. "But people would have noticed when we didn't return."

"He'd have lied and told them we'd left town. The sheriff would have backed him up, and few people would have pressed the matter."

His sister would have asked questions and so would Tobias. But without the backing of the law, the two of them wouldn't have gotten very far.

He stared at Mary Catherine's concerned face, wondering how much of her unease resulted from what Clanton had put her through and how much resulted from watching him end the lives of five men. She'd told him she understood who he was. But understanding it and witnessing it were two different sides of a coin.

"Mary Cate, you understand that I had to—"

She stepped forward and placed two fingers against his lips. "It's over. What's done is done." She pulled his marshal's star out of her pocket and tucked it into one of the pockets of his duster. "We don't need to talk about it."

"But—"

Her fingers returned to his lips to cut him off. "*I* don't want to talk about it. Take me home. Please."

They stood with her fingers pressed against his lips until he conceded and nodded his assent to her request.

After lifting her onto the saddle, he swung up behind her. He adjusted her sideways across his lap, and they headed back to town. They didn't speak about what happened at Clanton's spread. They didn't speak at all during the ride. She wanted her silence, and he'd give it to her. She seemed resigned to the violence she'd witnessed, and so far, she hadn't shown any sign she was appalled by what Blaaze had done.

He'd talk with her later, after she had time to rest and shake off the effects of her ordeal. He slipped a hand around her waist and tipped her gently against him. Aware this might be the last time he got to hold her in his arms, he didn't want to take the moment for granted. She relaxed against him, and they rode on to the easy sway of Scout's steps and the soft clop of hooves against the trail.

When they reached town, Blaaze steered Scout to the saloon. Beauregard ran out immediately and reached up to assist the woman they both loved down.

"Mary Catherine," the man said with a sigh and hugged her to him. Pushing her out to arm's length, he looked her over. "You okay?"

She nodded at him, but he looked up at Blaaze for confirmation.

"She's fine," he said as he swung down.

"And the men who took her?"

"All dead," he assured him.

"Jake Clanton?"

"Clanton too." He stopped in front of Beauregard.

"Thank you," Beauregard said, offering him his hand.

The gesture surprised Blaaze. He stared at the man's proffered hand.

Hand still out, Beauregard added, "I know why you did it. Doesn't mean I can't be grateful."

Blaaze understand the sentiment. Clasping the other man's hand, he responded sincerely, "You're welcome."

"There she is!" Babs came rushing out of the saloon with arms spread wide. "We were so worried about you, Mary Catherine. What are you doing still out here? You've been through an ordeal."

Releasing Mary Catherine from the smothering hug she'd had her in, Babs shot him and Beauregard admonishing looks around Mary Catherine's head. "You gentlemen don't have no better sense than to have her standing out here instead of bringing her inside so she can rest?" With a harrumph, she led Mary Catherine indoors.

Neither Blaaze nor Beauregard were allowed to see Mary Catherine for the rest of the day. Babs and the rest of the ladies pampered her and kept her behind the closed doors to her rooms. While he'd been out looking for Mary Catherine, they'd done some earnest mouse trapping with the assistance of a few of the saloon regulars. Blaaze had also seen a couple of tomcats roaming free around the place.

It was two long days before he received word that Mary Catherine was ready for visitors. He'd stayed at the bunk room behind the stables during that time. He dared not leave the main part of town, too afraid Beauregard would convince Mary Catherine to take a train ride back east. She couldn't leave without knowing how he felt about her.

When he arrived at the saloon, Mary Catherine's trunks were stacked near the front door. He glanced around the saloon for her, but he didn't see her.

"She's not here," his sister let him know from behind the bar.

Blaaze walked over to her. "Where's she at?"

"She went to the train station with Mr. Beauregard."

"*Dammit.*" Blaaze jerked around and rushed for the door.

"Blaaze!" his sister called after him. "Wait a minute."

He didn't have time to wait. Mary Catherine had said the other night that she was done. She was closing the saloon. She'd been soused out of her mind, but alcohol told the truth. Even with Clanton dead, she'd been through an ordeal. The kidnapping must have pushed her to expedite her departure.

Dammit, he shouldn't have waited.

He'd tried to be respectful of her space. She'd needed time to recover from her kidnapping, watching men get gunned down around her, and probably feelings of complicity in Clanton's killing. Add all that to the news of her cousin's death by foul play and being held herself at gunpoint, her desire to put Lawless behind her real quick like shouldn't have been a surprise. Some part of him had thought she would at least say goodbye to him if she left. For her to hit the rails on the sly was a sneaky exit he wouldn't have expected of Mary Catherine.

That damn Jeremiah Dixon Beauregard *the third*. This was his doing. Blaaze wanted to throttle the man.

The man knew Blaaze wouldn't give Mary Catherine up without a fight. Maybe Blaaze didn't have wealth built over generations of free living or a fancy college education, but he had enough wealth stashed away to keep Mary Catherine in any style she wished. He also had a heart big as the Kansas plains full of love that could hold Mary Catherine through tough times till they were both old and gray.

Maybe she didn't belong in the rough frontier of Lawless, but she no more belonged in the stifling city of Cleveland, Ohio. The city where she couldn't be all she wanted to be, all she was meant to be, because she hadn't been born a man. Lawless was going to grow.

With the railroad set to get back under construction and a railroad stop planned to be brought right up to the edge of the town proper, they'd have many of the fine things a city like Cleveland offered soon enough. Until that time, Blaaze would spend the fortune he'd earned by his gun bringing to Lawless anything and everything Mary Catherine Templeton wanted from wherever in the world she needed it brung from.

They'd shared a lot in the short time she'd lived here, and he knew she had some affection for him. In time, he could get her to love him if he could just get her to stay. He wasn't above begging.

When he pulled Scout up at the station, Mary Catherine stood on the platform with Beauregard, his hand resting lightly against her cheek. She stared at him with a smile. She held something in her hand. Her ticket?

Mary Catherine looked up at the sound of Scout's hooves.

Blaaze dismounted before the stallion had fully stopped and rushed to her side. "Don't go with him, Mary Catherine. You have to stay."

Her brows puckered. "Blaaze? What are you talking about?"

Beauregard frowned at him. "Lassiter, this is a private moment between me and Catie"

"A private moment for you to convince her to give up all that she's built here to be your wife?"

"Yes," he said baldly.

Mary Catherine gave Beauregard a baffled look and started to say something, but Blaaze didn't give her a chance.

He took her cheeks between his palms. "Stay with me. *Please*. I don't care if you run a saloon or a brothel or work at a bank or all of them at the same time. Can he say that?"

Mary Catherine's eyes cut to Jeremiah.

The man's lips pressed into a thin line, and he looked as if he wanted to put those warehouse-honed muscles to use giving Blaaze a beating. Blaaze silently wished the man would try. He'd love nothing more than an excuse to sully those citified duds of his.

Beauregard might love Mary Catherine, but that love had limits. Mr. The Third tried to rein in his disapproval of her choice of living, her connection to a brothel, her desire to have a career outside her station as his future wife, but he hadn't completely managed it. This beautiful, courageous woman needed to become someone other than her true self to live with the easterner's love.

In this, Blaaze understood he had the advantage. His love was unconditional. Not something he thought he'd feel in his lifetime, but now that he had, he didn't intend to let it go without a fight. This one couldn't be fought with the gun on his hip. Not if he truly intended to come out victorious. He needed to fight this one with his words, with his heart, with his soul.

Blaaze pulled Mary Catherine's train ticket from her hand and handed it to Jeremiah. "You don't need that ticket."

Mary Catherine glanced at the ticket he'd handed Beauregard then at Beauregard, taking in his expression. He didn't speak. He stood stoically with one side of his mouth quirked, seemingly confident in his status with her.

Beauregard tilted his head. "Well, Mary Catherine?"

Mary Catherine eyed Blaaze quietly for a few seconds then shook her head in disbelief. "So it takes me leaving with another man for you to realize you want me to stay?"

"It's not like that." Blaaze lifted his Stetson and ran a hand over his hair. It was time for another haircut.

"You sure?" She snatched her ticket back from Jeremiah and stepped away so she stood off to the side of them.

Blaaze's heart sank.

~

Mary Catherine stared at the crestfallen look on Blaaze's face. She was confused as to what was going on. The man had been trying to convince her to leave town from the moment he'd learned she was the new owner of the saloon. A lot had happened between them since then, and he'd admitted that his reasons for wanting her gone had changed to simply a matter of her safety. But he'd never given any indication he'd changed his mind about her leaving.

Blaaze looked down at his boots then back at her. "I can't make you stay. I understand that, but whatever he can offer you back there, I can give you here. You don't have to go with him to save your family home. I'll buy it from the bank for you. I have plenty of money. I'll build you an exact replica here if you want. Just give me a chance."

She looked down at the paper in her hand. "This isn't a train ticket, Blaaze. You're right. I don't have to go back with Jeremiah to save my parents' home. This is a telegram verifying the purchase of my parents' house by—"

"I already bought it, Lassiter. I had my attorney make the purchase in the name of Mary Catherine Templeton." Jeremiah gave a nonchalant shrug. "As a wedding present."

Unbelievingly, Blaaze squinted at Jeremiah. "You bought her parents' house for her?"

"Yes." A self-satisfied grin spread across Jeremiah's face. "As a bribe?"

Jeremiah's grin widened. "No. But if it works in my favor." He shrugged again.

Blaaze looked as if he intended to knock the grin off Jeremiah's face with his fist. Meaning to avoid any fisticuffs between the two, she stepped in front of Jeremiah.

Blaaze glared at her. "So that's why you're leaving with him?"

Tired of this confusing roundabout, Mary Catherine had to end Blaaze's apparent misunderstanding. "I'm not going back to Cleveland today, Blaaze. I was simply seeing Jeremiah off. He was called back home to tend to some business."

"But I'll be back," Jeremiah offered.

"Jeremiah," she warned, giving him a chastising look. She didn't understand why he was baiting Blaaze.

"Not necessary," Blaaze said to him through gritted teeth.

Jeremiah pushed forward and placed his hands on her upper arms from behind. "That's not your choice."

"You're right. It's her choice." Blaaze looked at Jeremiah's hands then at her face. "Tell me this. Do you love him?"

"I-I . . . Jeremiah and I have known each other since we were children."

"That's nice." Blaaze took a step forward. "Do you love him?"

Mary Catherine looked over her head at Jeremiah. He gave her an encouraging smile. She really didn't want to have this conversation. "It doesn't matter," she said to Blaaze.

"Yes, it does," both men said in unison.

Mary Catherine sighed.

Of course, she loved Jeremiah. Not the way Blaaze meant. Not the way she loved Blaaze.

She and Jeremiah had already come to terms with that. She'd revealed her feelings for Blaaze to him this morning when he explained he needed to return to Cleveland to see to some business. He'd admitted he planned to come back for her. She couldn't let him leave with the continued hope that they had a future together, so she'd told him everything.

He'd been disappointed, but he'd understood. She'd felt a little foolish revealing her feelings for a cowboy who didn't think she even belonged in his town and would probably see her as no more than a convenient dalliance from time to time. But she couldn't explain that to Blaaze without revealing her true feelings for him.

"It's not that simple," she finally said.

"Seems pretty simple to me." Blaaze grabbed her hands and pulled her away from Jeremiah. "I love you. I was wrong. You do belong here. There's nothing Lawless can throw at you that you can't handle. Not the social judgment of the 'respectable' women folk, not the bawdy habits of sportin' women, not the rowdy antics of men who brawl in your saloon." A sheepish grin emerged over that last example.

"I . . ." She glanced behind her at a silent Jeremiah then looked back at Blaaze with disbelief. "What did you say?"

"You do belong here," he replied.

"Before that." She stepped closer.

He dropped her hands and rubbed a hand over his chin. "Um . . . I was wrong?"

She placed her hand on the center of his chest. "Yes, you were. But before that."

"Oh." He swallowed noticeably, but said softly, "I love you."

A smile she couldn't contain burst across her lips. "That's all I needed to hear."

"So you'll stay?"

She laughed. "I was never leaving, Blaaze. I'd already told Jeremiah that I couldn't marry him because I was in love with you."

"You did?" He glanced at Jeremiah's face.

"Yes," she and Jeremiah said in unison then both laughed.

Blaaze tilted his hat back and made a pensive expression. "But your trunks are packed and waiting at the saloon."

"Oh." She gave him a soft smile, beginning to understand this desperate confrontation. "I'm moving into Miss Eileen's. She wants to head to California to live with her daughters, so I bought her place. I'm giving my saloon apartment to Barbara Jean."

He grabbed her tightly and kissed her long and deep right there on the platform. When his head lifted, he had the purest, sexiest grin she'd ever seen. But then the grin faded.

Glaring at Jeremiah, he said, "Wait a minute. She'd already told you she was in love with me?"

Jeremiah smirked. "Yes."

"So what was with all this 'but I'll be back'? You intentionally let me believe she was planning to wait for you."

Jeremiah shrugged. "I thought you might need a little incentive to tell her what she needed to hear. She deserves that."

The call came that the train was boarding.

"I've got to go." Jeremiah grabbed Mary Catherine and hugged her. "You know where to find me, Catie." Releasing her, he assured her, "Should you ever need anything or change your mind, write to me and I *will* come back."

Blaaze stepped up behind her and wrapped an arm around her shoulders, pulling her against him with her back to his front. "She won't be changing her mind, Beauregard. Time for you to get on the train."

Jeremiah chuckled. "I'm going, Lassiter. But be sure you remember, if you step out of line . . . I'll be waiting."

Blaaze grunted, but then offered Jeremiah his hand. "Understood."

They shook. Jeremiah grabbed his valise and boarded the train. Blaaze and Mary Catherine watched until the train pulled off.

Once the train chugged out of sight, Mary Catherine turned in Blaaze's arms and asked, "When did you know you didn't hate me anymore?"

"I never hated you, Mary Catherine," he said, his voice low and soft. "I thought I made that clear the other night."

She stared at him skeptically. "I thought hardened bounty hunters tell the truth even when it might hurt."

His shoulders rose and fell on a deep sigh. "I might not have liked you much. You were bossy. And a nag. And a little too citified."

She couldn't help but smile at those words.

"But I never *ever* hated you," he said.

She wrapped her arms around his neck. "If I stay, I'm not giving up the saloon."

"I'd never ask you to."

"I'm not stopping my support of Barbara Jean and her ladies."

His hands found her waist. "Again, I'd never ask you to. I already told you I don't care about any of that."

"I wanted to make sure you weren't simply making empty promises in an attempt to change my mind." Feeling mischievous, she removed his hat and placed it on her own head.

He grinned and adjusted it to sit properly before replacing his hands on her waist. "Anything else you're not doing by staying?"

"Well . . ." She bit her bottom lip. "By staying, I'm not agreeing to marry you."

"Mary Catherine"—he gave her a peck on the lips—"you're mine. You're staying to be mine. Only mine. That means you become my wife."

"I am yours. Only yours. But we need to talk about how to make this work. I shouldn't have to give up everything I own to be with you."

"You wouldn't be giving up everything you own. I would never try to control your property or your money."

"But in the eyes of the law . . ."

"Ma'am," he drawled in an exaggerated baritone, "I am the law."

Her forehead fell to his chest, and she groaned. "Blaaze, you know what I mean. Stop being difficult. You don't make the written law. The written law says once I marry you, you can control everything I own."

"Kansas laws give women a bit more rights than a lot of the country. It wouldn't be as bad as all that. Besides, you're better with money than me. Maybe I need to give you control of all of mine." He pulled her closer until the whole of her rested against his front.

Frustrated, she pressed her hands against his chest to lift her head and narrowed her eyes at him.

Chuckling, he placed one hand at the small of her back and the other around the side of her neck so his thumb could play idly with her ear. "Fine. Then don't marry me. Live with me in sin for now. Or forever, if that's what you want. We can work it all out later. I don't much care, as long as you're with me."

A joyous, nonsensical sound squeezed from her, and she threw her arms back around his neck. "Deal!"

EPILOGUE

A FEW WEEKS LATER, Blaaze sat in a wood-backed rocking chair whittling delicate pieces off the carving he was working on. He'd had Miguel put his exceptional carpentry skills to work to make him two such rockers. He'd stashed the other one in the back of the barn beneath blankets and tack that Mary Catherine was unlikely to go near. The other one was for her, but for now, Blaaze liked that if she wanted to rock with him, she'd have to sit on his lap to do so.

He evaluated the carving in his hand. He'd started several pieces in the last few weeks and thought he was getting quite good at this whittling pastime. He turned the current piece back and forth a few times to get a sense of where he should focus next.

A large portion of the town had gathered on his land to help him finish framing up and raising the walls of his house. Today was Juneteenth, so they'd combined the work with a picnic celebration. The mayor's people and several other townsmen were originally from down Galveston way, and they liked to honor the traditions from their hometown. So

Lawless had started celebrating Emancipation Day in commemoration of June 19, 1865, the day the last of the enslaved in the Confederacy learned they were free by the terms of the final Emancipation Proclamation.

Blaaze had had to do some fast talking when Tobias first wondered what had happened to the framing they'd done before the fire at Beulah's. Tobias hadn't looked like he'd bought the explanation, but he went to work helping Blaaze rebuild anyway. The new work was mostly done, and now the ladies prepared for the picnic to come.

Mary Catherine, Babs, and the women from the saloon set out the desserts on a table a few feet away. Several townswomen had been asked to bring dishes. Surprisingly, quite a few of them showed up. Many were merchants or wives of the merchants Mary Catherine had been helping with their accounting. The pastor's wife and her group of women had opted out, not yet over Mary Catherine's threat to knock Alice's teeth down her throat.

The non-merchants who had come were fans of the work Mary Catherine and Babs, as the new sole owner of the brothel, were doing to improve the town. Business had been booming at the saloon. In their largess, the ladies committed to sharing their prosperity with the town. The fund set up by the brothel and Templeton's, as Mary Catherine had renamed the saloon, had sponsored the building of a new school for the town's children and created a Benevolent Society to support families in need.

Mary Catherine had been particularly adamant about the Benevolent Society. She wanted no woman in Lawless to ever have to revert to the sportin' life simply because she couldn't feed herself. She understood that some women chose the life, but she wanted options for those who didn't.

With the money she was pumping into the community, she was likely to own or have an interest in a large portion of the town soon. She always laughed when he said as much, but she hadn't been opposed to funding many of the women-led businesses Lawless's State Savings Bank wouldn't. The practice had become so common, Mary Catherine had begun the process to charter her own bank.

The local savings bank still wouldn't lend to women and forced them to bank only through their husbands. Mary Catherine figured she could offer the townswomen another banking solution. She'd sold the brothel business to Barbara Jean in a deal to be paid in installments, subsidized a loan for Macey to start her own bakery, and also loaned Beulah a portion of the money needed to rebuild on her land. The new Beulah's was intended to be a full-fledged hotel.

Blaaze loved that Mary Catherine would get to be a banker after all. She'd never anticipated that it would be at her own institution or that she'd have to move to the Kansas plains to do it. But life was unpredictable that way.

The smell of roasting pork tempted Blaaze's stomach. His gaze shifted to where Jonas stood over a large spit where he roasted the big pig Blaaze had bought from Mr. Johnson, Mary Catherine's farmer suitor. The man had asked an outrageous price, but Blaaze had paid it as a way to make up for having pulled a gun on the man during their little misunderstanding over Mary Catherine.

He watched her with the ladies. He still couldn't quite believe she was staying in town and she was his. His gaze was pulled away from his Mary Cate when he heard Tobias give a long, slow whistle.

Following Tobias's gaze, he noticed his sister putting her horse into the paddock with Scout. He gave his buddy a backward swat of a fist. "Lay off the whistling, you cad."

"I know she's your sister and all, but boy howdy. You sure I can't . . ."

"*No.* You can't," Blaaze barked. "So quit your asking, and while you're at it, quit your flirtin' with her."

"Man, you'd think you'd cut a friend some slack. She sure looks mighty fine in that getup. She know how to use those guns she's toting?"

Addison headed their way with a gun holstered on her hip and a rifle flung up on her right shoulder.

"Unfortunately, yes," Blaaze said dryly.

"Why unfortunately?" Tobias asked.

Blaaze gave him a baleful look. "You ever pissed off a woman who knows how to hit exactly what she's shooting at? Every time."

Tobias burst into laughter. "Can't say that I have, but she sure makes a fella want to give it a try."

"*To-bi-as,*" Blaaze warned.

The blacksmith threw up his hands in surrender, chuckling the whole time. "Okay. Okay."

Addy sauntered up and took the empty seat on the other side of Blaaze, laying her rifle across her lap.

"The womenfolk are over there," Blaaze said to her.

"Yep, I see them," was her unbothered reply.

"Don't you want to go chat with them, little sister?" He added the little sister part just to annoy her.

She didn't take the bait. She simply grinned at him. "Nope. Don't want to chat at all. I'm fine right where I am."

She and he always did have that in common. Neither needed an excessive amount of socializing. They were fine with their own company. Which often meant they were fine with each other's silent company.

Blaaze turned his attention back to his whittling. Marshal Bridger Malone was due any day now to oversee the search for a new sheriff. Blaaze had wired the marshal after his shootout at the Clanton spread. Since Sheriff Brennan had opted to resign and leave town after Blaaze suggested staying in Lawless might lessen his chance at a long life, the town was currently without an official lawman.

Not that it had been much of a problem so far. Word had gotten around about Blaaze's silver star. So everyone assumed he'd mete out justice if the need arose. He'd made a point, however, not to do anything to encourage that way of thinking. He didn't want Malone to get any ideas about Blaaze staying on as Lawless's law. That was *not* happening.

Mary Catherine came over and sat on his lap holding a slice of rum cake layered with drizzles of a creamy buttered spread made from the crumbs of her spiced cookies. Her cookie butter was his favorite confection. He didn't generally prefer sweets to meat, but when served by such a pretty temptress, he'd be happy to start with dessert. As she fed him a bite of the cookie butter rum cake, two riders pulled up.

Blaaze looked up to see Malone chatting with a new arrival to town.

Addy took one look at Malone's companion, closed her eyes briefly, and muttered "Fuck," before making a dash for the barn.

As she scurried off, Blaaze heard Babs croon under her breath, "Well, *hul*-lo, Daddy Lassiter."

Having never met his father, Blaaze wondered how the woman knew who he was. Macey, who was standing next to her, asked her as much.

"Honey," Babs replied, "any woman with eyes can see the apple didn't fall too far from that tree."

Mary Catherine glanced over Blaaze's features closely. He simply shrugged at her. Absent the salt-and-pepper temples and two decades of living, he supposed he was the spitting image of his father.

His father dismounted and immediately began scanning the crowd. He noticed Blaaze and nodded, but his gaze continued its search.

"Is he looking for Addison?" Mary Catherine asked quietly, trying to keep her eyes from wandering toward the barn to whence his sister had fled.

"Yep," Blaaze replied with a joyful pop of the *p*.

She shook her head at his understated glee. "How long, you think, before he figures out where she's hiding?"

Blaaze watched his father. "Um . . . about sixty seconds is my guess."

And sure enough, his pops took one look at Addy's horse in the paddock, double-checked the ladies at the food table, none of whom had Addy's height or bearing, and headed for the barn.

"Well, this is going to be fun," Blaaze said blandly. "Maybe I'll finally get rid of her."

Mary Catherine chuckled. "I guess I'd better get another piece of cake. The marshal will be wanting one."

Blaaze gripped her hips tighter to keep her from leaving him just yet and glanced over to watch Malone slowly walk his way with a slight limp. When the marshal took a seat beside him, Blaaze pointed at the leg he was favoring. "What happened to you?"

Malone looked at Mary Catherine before he said evasively, "It's a long story."

Handing the marshal the flask he'd stashed under his chair, Blaaze nodded in understanding. "Well, you'll have time to rest up while you're trying to find our new sheriff."

Malone gave him a sharp look. "You really gonna make me look? Why don't you—"

"*No.*" Blaaze didn't need to add any explanation. "And I'm not holding the position while you look, so you might want to settle on in at the sheriff's office."

"Dammit, Lassiter." He startled, realizing he'd sworn in the presence of a lady. "Sorry, Miss Templeton. No offense meant."

"None taken, marshal," she replied. "How about I get you a piece of cake?" She gestured with the plate in her hand. "Or perhaps a piece of apple pie? Sounds like you could use a large one."

He nodded in agreement. "A piece of pie sounds real good, Miss Templeton. Much obliged."

Mary Catherine rose from Blaaze's lap and looked down at the whittling project in his hand. "Wow. You're getting good at that. That one actually looks like a horse."

Tobias watched her walk away then looked at Blaaze's carving. "Finally got it right, huh?"

Blaaze waited until Mary Cate was out of earshot before he leaned toward his friend and whispered, "Actually, this time I was trying to make a dog."

Tobias burst into laughter.

Malone stared at them, unaware of what was so funny.

Unfazed, Blaaze leaned back in his chair and savored a long swig of whiskey from the flask he reclaimed from Malone. Uninvited family aside, all and all, it wasn't such a bad day.

Author's Note

Around the summer of 2014, I was at a conference and had the serendipity to sit at a high breakfast table with a gentleman who collected and sold classic and modern comic books featuring Black characters. When he learned I wrote romance novels, he asked if I ever wrote about real-life, historical people. At the time, I did not. So he decided to enthrall me with the story of US Deputy Marshal Bass Reeves, one of the first Black deputy marshals in US history.

The gentleman also indicated that he didn't understand why no one had yet done a movie about Bass Reeves. According to my storyteller, many who know the history of Reeves's career believe the marshal to be the inspiration behind the old 1950s television show *The Lone Ranger*. That show happened to be one of my childhood favorites (via syndication, of course), so the gentleman had me intrigued.

I became fascinated by the tale of Marshal Reeves. So when I returned home, I immediately ordered the book the gentleman had recommended, *Black Gun, Silver Star: The Life and Legend of Frontier Marshal Bass Reeves* by Art T. Burton. The more I learned, the more I, too, thought the marshal's story indeed deserved more theatrical attention.

By now, several films and at least one television series—*Lawmen: Bass Reeves* (2023)—have been inspired by or dedicated to the life of Reeves. The full significance and magic of this lawman, however, cannot be captured in a handful of works. I'm hopeful that he'll soon have as many screen oeuvres dedicated to his tale as the slew of bad guys along the lines of

Jesse James and Doc Holiday, or legendary lawmen like Wyatt Earp.

Though I was not yet writing historical romance when I first learned about Marshal Bass Reeves, the idea of doing a novel featuring a classic cowboy inspired by him planted itself firmly in my mind. One of the things I personally found really interesting about the story of Reeves is that he was said to "always get his man"—as they liked to say in old westerns—all except for one guy. This particular outlaw managed to get away simply because, according to legend, his horse was faster than Reeves's. Known to speak several native languages and move freely amongst many of the native nations, Reeves was also said to be a master of disguise. This, in particular, I considered great fodder for a historical romance hero.

It was quite a few years later (2020) before I had the opportunity to pitch to a publisher the concept of a historical Black cowboy who was a US deputy marshal and started drafting that book. However, the character that kept coming to the forefront of the story was not the marshal but his buddy, a bounty hunter he'd impressed into helping him catch a gang of bad guys. Before that book went into edits, however, I was given the opportunity to publish my first mass market paperback and my muse got diverted.

I had the choice of what type of story I wanted to release in mass market format. My publisher's data at the time indicated that historical cowboys were not trending in romance. So I opted to write a tale in a different historical subgenre that I also loved to read, Scottish historical romance, specifically Highlander romance. To quench a deep longing in me, I added a new perspective by making my Highlander hero Black. Thus, *Never Cross a Highlander* was born and pushed my western aside. At least, for a while.

When I returned to my romantic western, market forces for that subgenre hadn't improved and the project for which that story had been intended was no longer being supported. I let the manuscript languish for a bit but couldn't stop thinking about the bounty hunter Blaaze Lassiter. So with the encouragement of a few writer buddies, I decided to revamp the tale into what became *Untamed*.

Now, have no fear, I haven't completely abandoned my Bass-Reeves-inspired cowboy. In fact, he made an appearance in *Untamed*. Yep, you guessed it! Marshal Bridger Malone is actually the character I originally envisioned. I don't know why he chose to take a back seat in this introduction of Lawless, Kansas, but the muse does what the muse does.

The good news is this means my muse and I can revisit Lawless again. I've got lots of ideas after reading several other books covering the history of the American cowboy and cowgirl. If you're interested, you might check out one of these gems: *Black, Red, and Deadly* by Art T. Burton and *Black Cowboys of the Old West* by Tricia Martineau Wagner.

Another interesting tidbit I learned while doing research for this novel was the significant impact sportin' women had on taming the West. If you like old westerns like I do, you know there's always the madam with a heart of gold and/or the "house" ladies or sportin' women who serve as companions to powerful men in the town, both law-abiding and outlaws. While these women are frequently portrayed only as outcasts, fallen women, or immorals of little social worth, they were often some of the wealthiest people—yes, *people* not just women—in town.

Turns out brothels and their ladies were instrumental in the growth of the Old West. Not only did popular madams and sportin' women end up being wealthy, they regularly used their wealth to improve the communities in which they lived. They subsidized the construction of many important community and social buildings (like schools) plus funded entities known for benevolence, particularly towards women and children. Who knew?

I opted to sprinkle other interesting details about the progress of African Americans and women throughout the book. There's cameo homage to Nathan "Nearest" Green, the former enslaved man whose charcoal filtration distilling technique was used by Jack Daniels to create the distinctive taste of Jack Daniel's Tennessee Whiskey. There's a little tease of Kansas's history at the forefront of women's suffrage, with the reference to Susanna M. Salter, who truly was the first woman elected mayor in the United States (in 1887). And lots more.

It would take too much time to identify in this note all the little historical tidbits. However, I would love to share at some point more details about this history with others. So perhaps I'll develop additional content, maybe via blog posts or videos or other online resources, to expand upon some of the key events.

If you'd like to learn more, drop me a note and let me know you'd be interested. In the meantime, please look for the extended author's note (and possible additional resources) coming soon online. Be sure to join my newsletter (at lisarayane.com) to be the first to know when new materials and book releases drop.

Until next time,

Lisa Rayne

ACKNOWLEDGEMENTS

As always, tons of people deserve thanks for helping me take this book from idea to finished story. Most notably, massive thanks to Michelle McLean and Lexi Post, who wouldn't let me give up on this cowboy tale. Without their continued encouragement, Blaaze's story might still be trapped in my computer. Michelle particularly nagged me repeatedly—dare I say weekly?—to finish this book. She'd read the early chapters and told me she needed to know how it ended. Ha! So heart hands to you, Ms. Michelle.

I also, once again, must thank the incredible and giving soul that is Ms. Beverly Jenkins. During the Romance for Maui auction organized by Lucy Eden to benefit those affected by the summer 2023 wildfires in Maui, I bid on and won attendance to a world building class to be given by Ms. Bev. The top three bidders were granted a 15-minute, post-class Q&A session with the legendary writer. And, of course, I made sure I was one of the top three. During that Q&A, Ms. Bev patiently answered all our questions and shared her favorite resources for staying accurate with the early American history, lifestyle, and social details. I bought every single one of those resources, and the period-specific information I learned made this a better book.

To my editor, Jennifer Graybeal, and my proofreader, Kaitlyn Slowik, thank you for your expertise and polish that took this from a decent first draft to a cohesive and flowing story readers could love.

To all the readers who embraced my first historical romance (*Never Cross a Highlander*) and shared your fun takes on that story via reviews, social media posts, and TikTok videos, thank you for lifting me up at a time when other forces made me doubt the wisdom of publishing a romance featuring a Black Highlander. You showed me I wasn't the only one who needed this story or loved a badass hero who could turn the pain of his past into the power of protection.

This "Wow, you like me. You really like me!" moment goes out with double amazement to my new tribe of male readers who embraced Kallum MacNeill's story and waited impatiently for my next historical tale. Thanks, gentlemen, for helping me officially achieve a #RomanceForMen title and inspiring me to keep going. Little did I know that mixing my love of romance with my passion for action adventure movies would garner such cool readers of a different gender. And yeah, Zack Carleton and Mike the Accountant, you two specifically come to mind when I think of the key members of this group.

I truly do love communicating with readers. So if you like something about my books, don't hesitate to share that with me. You can find me on social media (@AuthorRayne) or contact me through my website (lisarayne.com/contact).

Finally, please consider letting other readers know what you think of *Untamed* by leaving a review (or just a star rating if you're pressed for time) on Goodreads, BookBub or StoryGraph and your book retailer of choice (like Amazon, B&N, or Kobo). Even if only a few sentences, good or bad, reviews help increase the visibility for a book and can help other readers decide whether to purchase it.

About the Author

 Lisa Rayne writes sexy, banter-laden historical and contemporary romance featuring badass characters across the span of time.

She's an EMMA Award winner, an Amazon bestseller, and her milestone historical romance centering Black protagonists, *Never Cross a Highlander*, garnered a Publishers Weekly starred review. The tale was lauded by Kirkus Reviews as "a flawless combination of modern-day issues and old-school romance."

When she's not writing, Lisa loves being an active track mom, binge-watching planner flip-throughs on YouTube, streaming action and superhero movies, and strategizing how to best attack her massive TBR list.

For all the latest news on Lisa's books, giveaways, and appearances, follow her on social media and sign up for her newsletter by visiting lisarayne.com.

@AuthorRayne

www.ingramcontent.com/pod-product-compliance
Lightning Source LLC
Chambersburg PA
CBHW032107310726
48972CB00001B/127